PRAISE FOR

# A BLAZE OF GLORY

"Faultless . . . [Jeff Shaara] gives depth to otherwise flat historical figures and incorporates the attitude and experience of low-ranking as well as high-ranking military personnel." —*Booklist*

"[An] exciting read . . . Shaara returns to the U.S. Civil War in this first book of a new trilogy. . . . This novel is meticulously researched and brings a vivid reality to the historical events depicted." —*Library Journal*

"Dynamic portrayals [of] Johnston, Grant and William Tecumseh Sherman." —*The Wall Street Journal*

"*A Blaze of Glory* is a stunning achievement by an outstanding writer. I recommend it to anyone interested in the Civil War. It's a vivid portrayal of the horrors of industrialized warfare, and it's not for the faint of heart, with its graphic descriptions of killing and wounding." —DAVID M. KINCHEN, HuntingtonNews.net

"Shaara is a brilliant historical novelist whose ability to transport the reader to the battlefield is unmatched. One can taste the gunpowder and blood in the air and, just like his characters, can be overwhelmed by the fear and horrors of war. Shaara pulls no punches, never romanticizing the conflict, and manages to create a wonderful, horrifying, human narrative of the battle. . . . *A Blaze of Glory* is a fine addition to Civil War literature." —*Deseret News*

"*A Blaze of Glory* is a riveting installment in Shaara's historical fiction catalog. Once more, the depth of his knowledge and research about the combat and its related soldiers is unparalleled." —Bookreporter

# A BLAZE OF GLORY

# A BLAZE OF GLORY

A NOVEL OF
**THE BATTLE OF SHILOH**

# JEFF SHAARA

BALLANTINE BOOKS TRADE PAPERBACKS

NEW YORK

2013 Ballantine Books Trade Paperback Edition

Published in the United States by Ballantine Books, an imprint of The Random House Publishing Group, a division of Random House, Inc., New York.

BALLANTINE and colophon are registered trademarks of Random House, Inc.

Originally published in hardcover in the United States by Ballantine Books, an imprint of The Random House Publishing Group, a division of Random House, Inc., in 2012.

This book contains an excerpt from the forthcoming title *A Chain of Thunder* by Jeff Shaara. This excerpt has been set for this edition only and may not reflect the final content of the forthcoming edition.

Maps by Robert Bull

Library of Congress Cataloging-in-Publication Data
Shaara, Jeff.
A blaze of glory: a novel of the Battle of Shiloh / Jeff Shaara.
p. cm.
ISBN 978-0-345-52736-3
eBook ISBN 978-0-345-52737-0
1. Shiloh, Battle of, Tenn., 1862—Fiction. 2. United States—History—Civil War, 1861–1865—Fiction. I. Title.
PS3569.H18B57    2012
813'.54—dc23        2012010107

Printed in the United States of America

www.ballantinebooks.com

4   6   8   9   7   5

Book design by Christopher M. Zucker

*For my friend Morris Miller*

*The horrible sights that I have witnessed on this field I can never describe. No blaze of glory, that flashes around the magnificent triumphs of war, can ever atone for the unwritten and unutterable horrors of the scene of carnage.*

BRIGADIER GENERAL JAMES A. GARFIELD,

U.S. ARMY OF THE OHIO

*(twentieth president of the United States)*

# TO THE READER

This is the first of a trilogy that explores the mostly overlooked stories of the Civil War that take place west of the Appalachian Mountains, what is usually referred to as the war in the "West." This trilogy will focus on three pivotal events: the Battle of Shiloh, the Siege of Vicksburg, and the final chapter of the war in Georgia and the Carolinas.

If you have read any of my books, you know that these stories are driven not by events, but by characters. For me, the points of view of the characters in this story are more appealing than the blow-by-blow facts and figures that are the necessary products of history textbooks. For that reason, I try to find those specific characters who pull me into the story, whose actions affect the history of the event, and whose own points of view will, I hope, bring that story to you in a way you find more intriguing and more personal than what you might have read in high school.

The primary voices in this book include historical figures unique to this story, and others who will remain significant throughout this entire trilogy. Some are well known: William T. Sherman, Albert Sidney Johnston, Nathan Bedford Forrest, Ulysses Grant, among a cast that will eventually include most of the major participants in the war that engulfs the South, from the Mississippi River to the Carolinas. Other characters you will not know at all. In the Civil War trilogy begun by my father with *The Killer Angels,* and through my own bookends to his classic work, *Gods and Generals* and *The Last Full Measure,* the voices came from the top: the generals. As my own work spread out to include World Wars I and II, I realized that generals do not always tell the best story, and certainly not the whole story. For that reason, this series will also focus on the points of view of those men we would now call "grunts." The search for voices can be challenging (and fun) and my choice of characters will be both obvious and questionable. I receive an enormous amount of email asking why some particular person is overlooked, or ignored altogether. I certainly mean no disrespect to anyone who played a pivotal role in any of these extraordinary chapters of our history. But my goal is not to offer a complete detailed history of the event. If that's what you seek, then by all means, read Shelby Foote or Jim McPherson.

This book has to be described as a novel because there is dialogue, and you are often inside the thoughts of these characters. But I recognize (and accept) the risk that you might not agree with my interpretations. That's as it should be. My research is painstaking (and voluminous), and I rely exclusively on original sources, in other words, the accounts of the people who were *there.* I make a strenuous effort to be historically accurate, to get the facts straight. I hope that when all is said and done, you will accept that what I am trying to offer you is a good story. Whether or not you are familiar with this history, I hope you will come to appreciate the diverse cast, whose points of view will carry you through one of the most important, dramatic, and horrific chapters of the Civil War: the Battle of Shiloh.

JEFF SHAARA

APRIL 2012

# CONTENTS

# LIST OF MAPS

# SOURCES AND ACKNOWLEDGMENTS

For the considerable assistance I have received in the telling of this story, I must offer my deepest gratitude for those who provided me with original source material, and those who offered their valuable time and resources. This list is not altogether complete, and so, for the following, and for those not mentioned: Thank you to you all!

Stacy Allen, chief ranger, National Park Service, Shiloh
   National Military Park
Sheila Amdur, West Hartford, Connecticut
Alan Doyle, Memphis, Tennessee
Roy Durrenberg, Milwaukee, Wisconsin
Patrick Falci, Rosedale, New York
Colonel Keith Gibson, Virginia Military Institute,
   Lexington, Virginia
Woody Harrell, superintendent, National Park Service,
   Shiloh National Military Park
Lee Millar, Collierville, Tennessee
Morris Miller, Tallahassee, Florida
Keith Shaver, Murfreesboro, Tennessee
Don Todd, Shiloh National Military Park
The staff of the National Park Service, Shiloh National
   Military Park

# INTRODUCTION

I n April 1861, the American Civil War erupts with the firing of artillery by rebellious officials from the city of Charleston, South Carolina, toward the Federal military installation called Fort Sumter, in Charleston Harbor. For decades, the disagreements and animosity between Northern and Southern states has been escalating, but when the cannons fire, those disagreements are replaced by mortal combat.

The first significant bloodshed occurs closest to the boundary lines separating North and South. In the East, Virginia sides with the South, while Pennsylvania goes North. Between them, Maryland remains steadfastly neutral. West of the Appalachians, the same situation becomes much more hotly contested. Between the Southern state of Tennessee and those states north of the Ohio River lies the large state of Kentucky. Much more so than Maryland, the political forces within Kentucky are angrily divided. The state legislature splits, and two separate state governments are formed, led by two governors. That competition divides the entire state, including the military. Regiments are formed that choose to fight for the North, while others go South.

As the two sides grasp the enormity of what this war might involve, the territories west of the mountains face logistical difficulties that do not apply in the East. One is the control of the enormously important Mississippi River. Small-scale battles break out in those areas crucial to both sides, key junctions and small shipping centers, increasing tensions in supposedly neutral Kentucky. Throughout 1861, the events in the

East, including the first major confrontation in Virginia, the Battle of Bull Run, are of little strategic significance to the armies struggling for control of the Mississippi River. North of the Kentucky–Tennessee border, the two armies maneuver and feel their way toward each other, uncertain generals and untested troops moving toward a conflict the magnitude of which none can truly predict. In the North, there are immediate concerns for protection of the river cities, including Cairo, Illinois, and Louisville, Kentucky. But the newly formed Southern army, under the command of Albert Sidney Johnston, pushes northward, very much aware that establishing positions in such towns as Columbus, Bowling Green, and Mill Spring, Kentucky, will provide a protective shield for the Southern states under his command, and will most certainly force a response from his Federal counterparts. Though Johnston's army continues to grow, fed by regiments from the states to the south, in Kentucky, there is as much outrage at the presence of the invading Southern troops as there is support for the Southern cause.

The Federal army is slow to mobilize, but they do not suffer the difficulties the Southerners face in equipping and supplying a fledgling army. The result is a somewhat clumsy standoff, as each side seeks to organize and train for the conflict that must certainly come. Adding to Johnston's woes, what has happened in western Virginia also occurs in eastern Tennessee. There sizable numbers of the population place their sympathies with the Union. There is little hope that the Southern cause will receive any support from the mountain regions, thus eliminating any convenient link with the Confederate forces east of the mountains. The Civil War becomes a war of separate theaters, divided by both rivers and mountains, linked together only by railroads. It is one more reason the Southern army cannot hope to hold off a strong Federal force that is organizing to drive them out of Kentucky.

Close to the Tennessee–Kentucky border, the Southern forces create an anchor that they hope will prevent the far superior Federal navy from driving straight into the heart of the western Confederacy, which could split Johnston's Kentucky defenses in two. Two forts are constructed at the mouth of each of the two major rivers that flow northward out of Tennessee, the Tennessee and the Cumberland. It is a geographical coincidence that at a point just south of the Kentucky line the two rivers curve toward each other, the gap between them no more than twenty miles. To Southern engineers, it is a logical place to build the forts, since either one can support the other, with either supplies or men.

The two forts are named Henry and Donelson, and great care is taken to design them primarily to defend against Federal gunboats. But Fort Henry, on the Tennessee River, and not yet completed, is constructed on low ground, prone to flooding, and offers no real barrier to an assault. On February 6, 1862, the fort is attacked. Federal general Ulysses Grant, with a force of fifteen thousand men, aided by a flotilla of gunboats commanded by Flag Officer Andrew Foote, confronts a Confederate defense that consists of seventeen guns, all of which are inferior to the heavy cannon on Foote's ironclad boats. After a brutally effective bombardment, the Confederate commander, Lloyd Tilghman, recognizes the futility of trying to hold the fort. Tilghman removes most of his troops to Fort Donelson, and surrenders Fort Henry and a handful of artillerymen to Grant. But Grant knows that Donelson is the greater prize. The navy gunboats make the short journey back to the mouth of the Tennessee River, steam up the Ohio to the Cumberland, and surge upstream once more. Expecting another easy victory, both Grant and Foote approach Donelson to find that this time the Confederate engineers have the benefit of much higher and much stronger ground. On February 12, 1862, Grant's infantry and Foote's gunboats make their assault. But Johnston understands the value of sealing off the Cumberland to Federal troops. The river flows directly out of the key supply depot and rail hub of Nashville, Tennessee, just forty miles to the south. Johnston reinforces the fort significantly. When Foote's gunboats begin their attack, they are surprised by the superior placement and accuracy of the Confederate artillery, which badly damages most of the fleet and gives Foote a serious wound. Forced to withdraw the boats, Grant's infantry is left on its own. Then Mother Nature turns against Grant as well, and a blizzard blows across the Federal troops, who have little protection from the elements. But Grant's superior numbers and the ability to maneuver give him the upper hand. With the fort virtually surrounded, the commanding general, John Floyd, after consulting with his two subordinates, Simon Bolivar Buckner and Gideon Pillow, decides to drive a hard thrust directly through and around Grant's position. But Floyd vacillates, allowing Grant the time he needs to strengthen his hold. The only sizable number of troops who make good their escape toward Nashville is the cavalry of Colonel Nathan Bedford Forrest. Forrest finds a clear path around the Federal flank and hundreds of his cavalrymen slip away through dense woods and a swampy morass without sighting a single enemy along the route, a route that Forrest knows could have afforded much of Floyd's army the same avenue of escape. Those few infantry who choose to follow Forrest's horsemen find the same clear path, making their way through the rugged countryside that eventually takes them to Nashville.

Though Generals Pillow and Floyd also slip away from the fort, most of their troops are left behind. On February 16, Buckner surrenders the fort to Grant, along with nearly eight thousand Confederate soldiers.

The fall of Forts Henry and Donelson opens a clear pathway for the Federal army, and at his headquarters in Bowling Green, Kentucky, Johnston knows he has no choice but to withdraw completely out of the state.

To the south, the city of Nashville receives a grotesquely premature message from Fort Donelson that Grant's army had been thoroughly defeated, the bluecoats driven back into the Cumberland River. The message sets off a wave of jubilation in the city. But on February 16, the messages change. The truth flows southward along with the retreat of Forrest's cavalry, and the celebration in Nashville turns to a flood of black despair. The citizens of Nashville realize they have been misled by their generals, who are nowhere to be seen and who have made their escape by abandoning their own men. Word follows that what began as a glorious fight had been decided not by strength and honor, but by surrender, that thousands of Confederate troops have simply been handed over to the victorious Yankees.

With Union troops now massing within forty miles of Nashville, the city is thrown into chaos. Already, refugees choke the roads southward, entire families on the move, salvaging anything they can carry, to avoid what nearly everyone believes will be the brutality and savagery of the Yankees. Those few soldiers who escape capture and those who occupy outposts south of Donelson quickly make their way to the great city, some seeking food and ammunition, some running from the ghosts in their own minds. The panic of the soldiers spreads panic to the city, and the army makes efforts to secure the vast mountains of supplies held in the storage depots. The first senior commander who arrives in Nash-

**CONFEDERATE DEFENSIVE LINE, JANUARY 1862**

ville is John Floyd, who attempts to take control of the city. But Floyd carries very little weight now since his inglorious surrender of so much of his army at Fort Donelson. Many of the civilians understand what the soldiers already know, that a man who scampers away from his own defeat, saving himself by sacrificing his army, is not a man who inspires respect at all. Floyd wisely leaves Nashville, continuing his journey southward to Murfreesboro, where General Albert Sidney Johnston now awaits, fresh from his own retreat out of Kentucky.

With the defeats at Forts Henry and Donelson, the broad defensive lines that Johnston had spread across southern Kentucky and into northeastern Tennessee can no longer be maintained. Both rivers that drive deeply into the Confederate center are now in Federal hands. Johnston knows that Nashville, sitting squarely on the Cumberland River, is simply indefensible. The single alternative to withdrawing from the city is to make a stand there, turning the capital of Tennessee into a bloody battlefield. It is not a viable alternative. Johnston's most urgent priority is to gather what remains of the Confederate troops throughout

Tennessee and Kentucky and to position those troops where they can best defend against the inevitable Federal invasion.

The last strong force of Confederate troops in Nashville belongs to Nathan Bedford Forrest, whose primary mission is to hold off the enemy for as long as he can, thus allowing the enormous supply depots and warehouses to be emptied, the arms, supplies, and food that the Confederate forces desperately need. Forrest knows to make use of the river, the rail lines, and any usable roadways to remove as much as he can from the city. But the outraged civilians will not accept that the fate of Nashville has already been decided and react violently by raiding the army's supply depots themselves. No matter Nashville's importance, Johnston's orders are clear and direct. His cavalry is to be pulled southward, and the civilian officials in Nashville and throughout central and northern Tennessee are informed that there will be no attempt to save their towns.

For victorious Federal forces west of the mountains, the stain of politics and ugly ambition begins to seep into what should be clear-cut military strategy. If the North is going to succeed in bringing down this rebellion, they must put into the field officers and soldiers who can focus on the job at hand, no matter what kind of wrangling clouds the air around them, no matter the quest for attention and a place in the history books. To confront them, the men chosen to lead the Southern armies must replace the glory and romance of the Cause with the stark reality of a bloody military campaign. If the Southern generals have any hope of defeating a far more numerous and far better equipped enemy, they will have to do it on their own soil, and make the Yankees fight on Johnston's terms.

PART ONE

# MANEUVER

## CHAPTER ONE

# SEELEY

NASHVILLE, TENNESSEE
FEBRUARY 22, 1862

"Keep those men out of there! They will not pass!"

Seeley's words were harsh, loud, the men around him doing all they could to obey. The shotguns hung by each man's side, and the lieutenant felt a shaking nervousness, was not ready to give the order that would point the long guns at these civilians. Like him, most of these troopers had never fired their weapons at anything but crude targets. Now the targets were men, surging toward him through the darkness, pushing their way toward the gaping doorways of the supply depot, a massive warehouse close to the river. Seeley had positioned his six horsemen in an even line, to block the way of the crowd, but the crowd was a mob, desperate and mindless, their goal the precious food and bundles of supplies that lay in the warehouse. A few cavalry meant nothing at all, and quickly the mob pushed into them, some slipping past, between the horses. He felt his own frustration rising, could feel the tinderbox explosiveness of the mob, and he shouted out again, could not help the higher pitch, his voice betraying the fear.

"You will stand away! These are government stores!"

Close between him and the next man, a civilian shoved hard, jostling his horse, punching it.

"Get out of my way! Damn you!"

Seeley steadied the horse, his outrage more of instinct, protective of the animal. He drew his saber, but the man ignored him, punched the horse again, and the saber rose high, came down hard against the man's shoulder, flat-sided, the man collapsing right below him. The civilian rolled over, crying out, shielding himself with one hand above his face. There was no blood, not yet, the lieutenant trying to get control, the horse calmer, the man crawling out through the horse's legs. The lieutenant felt relief, did not want blood. He raised the saber again, mostly for show, but most of the mob ignored him, ignored all the horsemen, still pushed into the warehouse, spreading out in the dark. Behind him a lantern was lit, the glow filling the vast building with soft light reflecting off the mounds of boxes and barrels, bundles of cloth.

More cavalrymen galloped close, and he looked that way, hoped to see wagons, the army's own efforts to gather up the supplies, to move them out of this vulnerable place. But there were only men, a sergeant leading six more, and so Seeley was the only officer, was still in command, the sole authority. The horse jostled beneath him again, men still slipping by him in a rush, and he felt the saber in his hand, could not just assault these people, could not add to what was fast becoming a riot. But still . . . there were the orders, the strict need to guard what was piled up behind him. He steadied the animal with the reins, shouted toward the other horsemen, "Formation here! Beside us! No one is to pass! We must protect the depot!"

The other cavalrymen had already seen the futility of that, were as uncertain as he was. He wanted to shout again, but the mob was growing, more people coming down the side streets, noisy and energetic, women alongside men, shoving their way past, seeking anything they could carry. Some came past him the other way, from inside, weighed down by loot, by the very goods he was supposed to protect. He fought for it in his own mind, how to control these people, how to obey the orders he had been given, the responsibility for this one depot.

"Stop them! They must not pass!"

Seeley's anger was ripening into full fury, the frustration complete, his orders useless, the crowd still swarming around the line of horsemen. Some of the mob was already disappearing into the streets, satisfied for now with what they had grabbed, bundles and boxes and barrels of anything. Out past the depot he could hear splashes in the darkness, away from the lantern light, something heavy tossed into the river. He turned his horse, rode out from the others, tried to see the river's edge, heard more splashes. Some of the civilians had made their way out the back side of the warehouse, were tossing their loot into the water. He could hear someone leading them, instructions barked out from a man he couldn't see. He knew it was one of them, a civilian, orders that carried far more weight than this lone lieutenant in a small column of cavalry. He spurred the horse, moved out around the corner of the building, was in darkness now, frightening, could see only a single speck of lantern light at the wharf. A few of the cavalrymen followed him, the sergeant, curious, their formation breaking down. From the streets out beyond the warehouse, a new crowd came at them, word spreading throughout this part of the city, fresh passion, hot enthusiasm for the treasure, no matter what it might be. The lieutenant turned the horse again to the lamplight, saw his men looking toward him, fear in their eyes, and he caught sight of their weapons, holstered at their saddles.

"Close up this line! Draw your shotguns! Prepare to fire!"

Seeley saw their hesitation, shouted it again, the men obeying, the long guns sliding out from the holsters, tense, nervous glances toward the civilians. Behind him two men rolled a heavy barrel out of the warehouse, and he pointed the saber at them.

"Leave that be! We have orders to fire! You will leave this place! By order of Lieutenant Colonel Forrest, these supplies are the property of the army! Return to your homes!"

One man stopped, close to the horses, shouted back at him, "You have no authority! We have seen your army! They ran through this city like a stampede of rats! Get out of our way!"

Another man moved out of the lamplight, held a bundle on his shoulder, pointed a finger at the lieutenant.

"We know you're going to burn our city! We heard all of that! Just to keep it from the Yankees! We'll not be driven out of our homes by a bunch of cowards! I have a family! We need to eat! You get on out of here!"

Others in the crowd slowed, some seeming to notice him for the first time, and he welcomed that, a glimpse of acknowledgment, a small glimmer of calm through the flood of panic. Others were turning toward him, and he wondered if the threat from the weapons had drawn their attention. He took a breath, shouted out, "No one will burn your city! The enemy is not close! But these supplies . . ."

"Bah! Your own men ran through here like they was chased by the devil himself! Them Yankees are monsters! And you ain't gonna do nothing to stop them! Well, we're not gonna be cut down like corn-stalks!"

A woman screamed toward him now, rage in her words, "We've got families . . . children! The Yankees are coming and you can't stop them!"

The moment of reason slipped away, and he could not respond, had no answers for the wild rumors, for their panic. The talk was past, and they resumed their movement, some back into the warehouse, more bundles and boxes hoisted up on shoulders, two men rolling another barrel out through the faint light, shoving it straight into the legs of his horse. Seeley held tight to the reins, gripped the saber hard, prepared again to strike, but something held him back, the civilians seeming to pull away, watching him, testing him. He shouted again, the high pitch of his voice rising above the anger from the mob.

"By order of Lieutenant Colonel Nathan Bedford Forrest . . ." He turned, looked down the row of horsemen, his face showing the final fear, the failure of his mission, no words strong enough to keep these panicked people from grabbing everything they could carry from the supply depot. "Raise your weapons! We have our orders!"

He watched as the shotguns rose, clamped against their shoulders, the beautifully brutal weapon they carried, the perfect tool for the close-range fighting of cavalry. The targets were many and close, and he closed his eyes, a cold shiver all through him. God, I cannot do this. Please . . . do not force me to do this.

The mob still paid no attention to the horsemen, and he glanced to one side, the soldier closest to him, the face of a boy, saw him cocking back the two hammers of the double barrels, felt his own stab of panic.

"Not yet! Wait for my orders!"

The mob had slowed around them, some of them staring up at the twin barrels of the shotguns, some of the civilians realizing what might happen now. One man stepped close to him, well dressed, his hat down in his hands.

"You would kill us like dogs? Is that what this army is? What will God say to that?"

The civilian spoke in a low, deep voice, and the lieutenant fought to respond, struggled through the tight shaking in his throat.

"I have my orders . . . to stop anyone from looting the government stores. I will stop you . . . any way I can. The army must have these supplies." He paused, more faces watching him. "Colonel Forrest is in command here. He has orders to protect the city as long as practicable. The enemy is moving this way, yes. But there is time. There is no need for panic!"

It was an explanation no one seemed to hear, the words more for his own horsemen than for the ugly fear of the civilians. There were more splashes at the river's edge, and he wanted to call out, to stop the foolishness of that, heard the young soldier next to him, one of the new volunteers, untested, a boy with a man's weapon.

"Sir . . . they're throwing everything away!"

Seeley looked out that way, but in the darkness there was nothing to see. At least here, in the lamplight, there was safety, some control over his own men. The crowd was thick in front of him, men still forcing their way into the warehouse, the darkness still filled with noise, meaningless shouts, more splashes. Another of the troopers spoke, the sergeant.

"What in blazes are they doin'?"

The lieutenant thought of what he had already seen, great mounds of smoked and salted meat, bundles stacked along the various wharves along the river.

"What they can't carry, they're floating off down the river. Food mostly. There's plenty of beef and bacon here."

"Ain't we supposed to stop 'em?"

The question infuriated him, a hard stab at his authority, the very job he was sent here to accomplish. The word rose in his brain, the only response he could think of. *How?*

The young private lowered his shotgun from his shoulder, spoke again.

"But . . . where's the stuff gonna float to? The river flows . . . *that* way."

Seeley stared out through the darkness, suddenly realized the man was right. The panic and chaos of these people had given way to utter stupidity. Yes, this damn river flows north. Straight toward the Yankees.

----

J ames Seeley had grown up in Memphis, the son of a banker, and like so many, had come to the cavalry responding to the call from Nathan Bedford Forrest, another businessman known well in the city. Forrest's cavalry force grew quickly, their number increasing by companies of horsemen who rode northward from their farms and villages in Alabama and Mississippi. Others came southward, from the hotly controversial counties in Kentucky, where *neutrality* meant different things to different people, the state still struggling under the divisive weight of politics.

As was happening throughout the newly organized Confederate armies, the horse soldiers brought little else to their new camps but their skill in the saddle, a skill that at least had set them apart from the eager young men who had settled into life in the infantry, or were quickly learning the art of firing a cannon. But even the men with their own horses had few weapons, and it had been Forrest himself who had secured arms for his own men, sabers and pistols, and then the double-barrel shotguns, weapons many of these men had never seen. The drill and the training had been rapid but the men had responded well, though few in the Confederate high command knew anything of Forrest. Like another cavalryman, John Hunt Morgan, Forrest began to be noticed by those who had reached the highest levels of the Confederate command, the men who were now generals, who labored under the weight of securing men and arms, and creating from scratch a fighting force that the Confederacy had to have if there was to be any hope of holding away the well-organized and well-equipped men in blue.

Before wearing the uniform Seeley knew nothing of fighting, and very little of weapons. But the men first chosen by Forrest to lead the training had seen something of a leader in this man of barely twenty-two, and with so many of the new troops eager but utterly unprepared for life in the army, Forrest and his company commanders recognized the urgent need for leadership. Within short weeks, Seeley had risen to the rank of lieutenant, an event followed by a stream of enthusiastic letters home to his young wife and parents, who urgently waited for any kind of news from their fledgling soldier. It was no different anyplace the war had already spread, families both North and South full of passionate certainty that their magnificent army would bless them with a quick and total victory. On both sides, the citizenry had shown pride and enthusiasm for the drums and parades of new recruits, so many believing that whatever this war would become, there would be celebration and glory for all the young men who made the long march.

Seeley's father had been among those, a man who knew nothing of the army. But the older man had still offered a lecture of caution that his son not shame the family, that the best measure of a man was his backbone for a stout brawl. Seeley's young wife, Katie, was less certain of that, and when the day came when Seeley marched off to join the grand parades, she had released his hand reluctantly, a short tearful kiss that tempered his lust for the Great Fight. There had been words, a final farewell from her that had settled into his heart with a nagging sadness. He would not accept that, not completely, that his wife did not want him to go at all, that this duty did not mean as much to her as it did to most everyone else. And so his letters home had begun immediately, and no matter how much joy he tried to communicate to them all, his promotion in particular, he could not hide from a frustrating uneasiness that she did not truly understand how important this was. Her message spread subtly through her letters, soft sadness, and he knew that all those things that mattered to the rest of the family did not truly matter to her. No matter how heroic he might become, what kinds of trophies of war he might bring them all, his absence had already taken something from her, left a wound he didn't really understand. They had, after all, been married for only four months.

In December 1861, Lieutenant Seeley had seen his first glimpse of the enemy whose very existence seemed to inspire so much hatred in the men around him, a hatred he tried to embrace, because it was the right thing to do. The fight had been at Sacramento, Kentucky, a brief affair that did little to turn the tide of the war. But there was more to the results than the handful of casualties shared by both sides. With three hundred horsemen, Forrest had surprised and attacked a force of nearly five hundred Federal cavalry. By using a double-flanking tactic, combined with an all-out frontal assault, the Confederates had won the day, the shaken Federals able to stand their ground for only a short while. Seeley's only direct confrontation with a bluecoat was a brief glimpse of the man's back, a horseman springing from a cluster of brush who did not fight, but instead spurred his horse away in a rapid retreat. Seeley had not been close enough to the man to fire his weapon, but in the primary assault Forrest and many of the others had traded a good deal of fire with the enemy, much of it manic and badly aimed. The aftermath was glorious. It was after all, a victory.

Seeley had been annoyed, knew that by dumb chance he had missed his first opportunity to cut down the hated Yankees. But that frustration had been tempered quickly by the sight of the first blood he had seen, a mortal wound that had brought down a Federal captain named Bacon. Seeley had not lingered close to the desperately wounded man, had watched some of the others, Forrest included, who had done all they could to make the man's final hours comfortable. He had been surprised at that, had expected the wounded Yankee to spit out viciousness toward his enemies, and them to do the same. When Bacon died, Seeley had thought of leading a cheer, but there was none of that from Forrest.

Whether or not the engagement at Sacramento produced much practical advantage for either side, higher up the chain of command, Forrest and his horsemen caught the attention of officers on both sides, and for the first time west of the Appalachian Mountains, Federal commanders began to take Confederate cavalry and their audacious commander seriously.

"Would you have me shoot them, sir? These are our own people. *My* people. Begging your pardon, sir, but to shoot them down for a barn full of goods . . . we could never come back here. We'd be no better than the Yankees."

"Do not explain the obvious, Lieutenant. You did all you could hope to do. I will not order anyone in my command to shed the blood of Southern citizens for no good reason. These are my people as well. Despite their panic, I do not believe the Yankees will do them such great harm. Not civilians."

"The civilians don't seem to agree with you, Colonel. I never saw such a thing. They were . . . well, they were crazed, sir. I admit that I feared for my men. If any one of those people had shown arms . . . had fired upon us . . . it would have been a disaster, sir."

Forrest stood, moved out from behind the desk of the makeshift headquarters. He was tall, wide shoulders, a taut-faced, handsome man. There would be no mistaking who was in command here. He moved to a window of the elegant room, stared into darkness.

"Put it out of your thoughts, Lieutenant. I have confronted a mob already, another of the storage depots, and I saw the same response. Thankfully, we used the horses as moving barricades, and drove the people back. But I heard the same as you. Somehow this absurd rumor has spread that we will burn this place, citizens be damned. You cannot cure that kind of madness from a people who embrace it with such fear. I know little of this General Grant. He is a West Point man, for certain. I saw no great brilliance in his capture of either Henry or Donelson. He had superior arms and used them with effectiveness. But . . . we spilled a great deal of their blood, and that will inspire some of them to revenge. You may depend on that. But no matter what other despicable faults our enemy may possess, no matter how they cling to a cause that no decent man can justify, I do not believe their professional officers are trained to be barbarians. No matter what anyone in Nashville believes, the Yankees are just men, not monsters."

"They come by their barbarism naturally, sir. I've heard the talk. They are using foreigners, savages. The Lincolnites have offered a bounty for the scalps of our soldiers."

Forrest looked at Seeley, a glare that silenced him.

"I will not entertain that kind of rumor in this headquarters. You wear the uniform of a professional soldier, Lieutenant. You will behave like one. Your men will behave like the gentlemen they claim to be. The Yankees have driven us to this war, and I have pledged to kill any one of those bluecoats who dares assault my country, who dares to raise his saber against my own people. That is as simple as it needs to be, Mr. Seeley. We have a duty to perform, and it is not made easier by encouraging childish nightmares among the people. You heard it yourself. The citizens of this fine city believe that it is *we* who are going to burn the place to ashes, correct?"

"Yes, sir."

"There you have it, Lieutenant. Panic is a disease. I admit, it can be a useful disease when rallying someone to your cause. But we do not re-

# 12 JEFF SHAARA

quire that here. What we need from these people is assistance. Yes, this city will be occupied by Yankees. There is no alternative to that, not right now. It is a catastrophe for this country, but from the army's point of view, it is simply a setback that we will one day correct. We are doing everything in our power to create an army with the power to dictate the terms of this war, but it is not an easy process, certainly not as easy as these citizens expect. We have done everything short of *begging* them to assist this army in a myriad of ways. When the war was elsewhere, they were very pleased to go about their own business and ignore every request we made of them. We insisted they blockade the river with obstructions that would hold away the Yankee gunboats, and the merchants cried out that we would hurt their pocketbooks. General Johnston beseeched them to dig earthworks, and they laughed at him. Their message was clear: Keep the war away, so that we may live in comfort, without inconvenience. Well, we have failed to do that, Lieutenant. So now they rise up like wild dogs and curse us for our failures. Until a man stands up against the enemy and faces the bayonet, he has no right to curse anything this army does. Richmond may judge our generals, and our generals may judge the troops in their command. But no civilian has the right to curse this army. These people refused to accept their responsibility to assist our cause, and now their city cannot be defended. That is a strategic decision made by General Johnston that has no alternative. But I refuse to feel pity for these people." He stopped, called out beyond the walls of the room. "Sergeant, have we heard anything of Mr. Stevenson?"

Seeley stood back from the door, saw the sergeant appear, an older man, hesitant.

"Uh, no, sir."

"So, every one of the railroad people and the commissary officers has vanished, is that correct?"

"Yes, sir, so it seems. Mr. Stevenson in particular was said to have left the city in his own railcar, well before we arrived."

"Wonderful. The president of the railroad company hears a thump of thunder from forty miles away, and scampers out of here like a mule with his tail afire. All of them . . . running from monsters that burst out of their own minds! What manner of men do we put in charge of such valuable posts?"

Forrest didn't wait for a response, moved to one side of the desk, pulled his hat from a small coatrack.

"Remain here, Sergeant. I need you here in the unlikely event someone brings any *good* news. Ride with me, Lieutenant. Our orders are to vacate this city as soon as the enemy appears, and General Johnston awaits me in Murfreesboro. I am to report to him there once our job is complete. I am doubtful we can salvage all the supplies and stores stockpiled here, but we will do all we can. Wagons, railcars, horseback, I don't care. What we cannot carry, we will burn. The people of this city have made their own beds, Lieutenant. We are not here to provide comfort for a few lions of Nashville society. This army must be fed and clothed and our men will have our blankets." He put the hat on, adjusted it, moved to the doorway, the sergeant standing aside. He turned again to Seeley, took a long breath, and the young man saw sadness, unexpected.

"Lieutenant, do you understand what we must do to win this war?"

Seeley felt weight behind the question, wasn't sure what Forrest was expecting from him.

"I think so, sir. We must kill Yankees."

"That is partially accurate. We must kill more of them than they can kill of us. But we must do much more. We must show more courage than the Yankees. We must show more spirit and more fire and more of everything that makes a soldier. There are far more of them, and they bring much more to the fight than we can put in their way, more artillery, more gunboats, more horses, more recruits. If we are to win this war, our leaders must be . . . well, *smart.* Or better than that, they must be *ingenious.* We cannot repeat the mistakes that occurred at Fort Donelson. We allowed the Yankees to get the better of our measure, Lieutenant. We must make better decisions, faster decisions, we must strike hard and often and in the most unexpected way. We must find the enemy's weaknesses and exploit them without hesitation." He paused and Seeley waited for more. Forrest said slowly, "As for you and me . . . we must have the will to face that man in the blue coat and we must drive our knife into his heart, and when the blood spills, we must not turn away."

Seeley felt Forrest's glare, nodded slowly.

"I understand, sir."

Forrest tilted his head slightly, still stared at him.

"No, son, you don't. Not yet."

On February 23, Forrest's scouts reported the arrival of the first column of Federal troops, just across the Cumberland River at the small town of Edgefield. Though great quantities of supplies still lay scattered throughout the depots and warehouses of Nashville, Forrest's men, and the others charged with shipping those supplies south, had no choice. What could not be hauled aboard wagons and the limited number of railcars had to be put to the torch. Then, with no fanfare, Forrest and his cavalry rode away from the city. Two days later, on February 25, the mayor of Nashville, who understood the perfect inevitability of his situation, surrendered the capital of Tennessee to the Federal forces, without a shot being fired.

## CHAPTER TWO

# JOHNSTON

MURFREESBORO, TENNESSEE
FEBRUARY 26, 1862

"We could do little else, sir. It was a most unglamorous affair."

Forrest was pacing, ignored the others in the room, and Johnston allowed the man's anger, would not insist on decorum. There was already too much anger in this army, and Forrest was one of the few who had earned the right to complain. Forrest kept up his pacing, filled the small office, avoided the others, who sat in opposite corners, away from Johnston's desk.

"I'm not sure how much of the stores were burned, General. We could not salvage as much as I had hoped . . . as much as I was ordered to, sir. This army will suffer for that." Forrest paused, and Johnston could see he had something more to say, something rehearsed.

"You have more, Colonel?"

"Sir, if you will allow, my men will return to Nashville . . . well, perhaps the southern perimeter of the city. We can strike hard at the enemy with discretion. No doubt the Yankees are feeling fat and lazy with their easy conquest, and their guard will be down. My men have become quite adept in the quick strike. I will assure you that our losses will be kept to a minimum."

Johnston shook his head.

"No. I believe the enemy is expecting us to stand tall, and he will be preparing for us. He knows what we sacrificed by abandoning Nashville, and he knows that our retreat was extremely unpopular. I am quite certain the citizens there are squalling every chance they get. I have great appreciation for the striking power of cavalry, Colonel, and your men have performed extremely well. But they have been in the saddle for too long, and you must not drive them to exhaustion. I am sending you south, to Huntsville. Camp your men there, and allow them rest. You cannot drive your men or their mounts without some respite."

Forrest stared sharply at Johnston, and Johnston felt the protest coming, held up his hand.

"No discussion on this, Colonel. Do not take this as an insult. I have approved your promotion to full colonel, and that is a high compliment. You should reflect on that. I know precisely what your men have accomplished, and you will continue to be a valuable service to this army. Many . . . *things* will take place in the next few weeks, changes perhaps, involving commanders or spheres of authority. Richmond is a noisy place right now, Colonel. There is a considerable lack of confidence in certain commands in this theater. We must all recognize where our best assets lie, whom we may trust and depend upon. Your good work is noted, and will be mentioned prominently to Richmond. But I need you to rest your men. Be prepared to return to action within two weeks."

To one side, the engineer, Gilmer, spoke up.

"I for one am pleased that we have at least one commander in the field who realizes what a war is."

Johnston knew that Gilmer was hot, had been as frustrated as anyone in Johnston's command by the failures at the two forts, and the astounding lack of cooperation offered the army by the civilians in Nashville. Johnston had heard this already, did not need another debate on failure.

"Let that be, Colonel. A discussion for another time. Colonel Forrest, you have your instructions. Offer your men my deepest respects and assure them they will be of great service to this army. But feed them, do what you can to replenish and refit their weapons, and see to your horses. I will call upon you when the time comes."

Forrest slumped.

"As you wish, sir. But the enemy is so close . . ."

"Right now, that is not your concern. Captain Morgan's cavalry are on the prowl between this headquarters and the enemy, and he reports success in damaging the bridges and rail lines that are in the enemy's hands. We are blessed with good cavalry."

Gilmer spoke up again, his arms clamped hard across his chest.

"And not much else."

Johnston did not need the engineer's contribution, not right now.

"Colonel Gilmer, your good work is noted as well. Please accompany Colonel Forrest outside, and see that my staff provides the horsemen with anything they require to begin their journey."

The instructions silenced both men, and Forrest offered a brisk salute, said, "I wish only to serve, sir."

Gilmer growled something Johnston couldn't hear, led Forrest out of the room. In a chair to one side, a fourth man sat back, observing, a smile on his face. The two men were alone now, and Johnston said, "What could possibly inspire your good cheer, Governor?"

"I do love *headquarters*. Generals can slice their way through the most thorny of situations just by their authority. That is never as simple for a politician. In my world, it is essential that we *dance* through our pronouncements, make sure that no one's feelings be injured."

"I do not seek to insult anyone. But I am in command, and until President Davis has a change of mind about that, I will not hesitate to tell my officers what I expect of them."

Harris laughed. He was a thin, balding man, his face adorned with a wide mustache. Officially, Isham Harris was the governor of Tennessee, but from Johnston's first days in command of the forces west of the Appalachians, Harris had been attached to the general's staff. It was an arrangement that seemed to work for both men, Harris appreciating Johnston's mannerisms, the habit Johnston had of choosing each word carefully. Johnston was soft-spoken, would never rail aloud at anyone in his command, no matter what he might be feeling. Some made the deadly mistake of assuming Johnston's slow speech to be slowness of brain, but Harris had always seen past that, had seen too many men in Nashville, and in the army, whose quick words did not always mean a quick mind. But Harris brought more than insight to Johnston's headquarters. As governor of what had become the most hotly contested state in the West, Harris was an effective bridge between the army and the civilian authorities. It was supposed to be a positive complement to the army's operations, that the civilians would heed their governor's call for labor and materials, as well as volunteers to fill the army's ranks. But to Johnston's dismay, and the dismay of most of the state governors, it seemed nearly impossible to convince the people that this was becoming a war in the most dangerous sense, that the bloody fights were sure to spread, that no one could expect to remain comfortable. Nashville had been the most infuriating example of a people who cherished the illusion that their gallant army would wipe the Yankee threat completely away.

Long before the Federal troops had moved toward the two rivers, Johnston had issued requests from Texas to Richmond that with the woeful condition of his army, the lack of effective weapons and training and supply lines, the only way the Confederates could hope to achieve a significant victory was for the Federal command to make a deadly stupid mistake. So far, the only mistake Henry Halleck seemed to make, and make repeatedly, was one of delay. Johnston had heard just enough about the backbiting and intrigue that had sifted through the Federal commands to appreciate that clashes among blue-coated generals might offer the Confederate army the time it desperately needed to prepare for any major conflict on a more equal footing. Even though Johnston had been able to maintain his ragged defensive line across southern Kentucky, the strengthening of his army had been woeful. And, finally, Halleck and his generals had found the will to send a powerful fist into Tennessee.

While Johnston was still headquartered in Kentucky, the Southern newspapers had of course demanded aggression, as though Johnston's army could simply rise up and march northward, threatening every city from Cincinnati to Chicago. Thankfully, Isham Harris seemed to be the one prominent politician who understood that even his own Tennessee could not be protected if the Confederacy did not equip and supply an army adequate to the task. It was the primary reason Johnston welcomed him to his staff. Harris was virtually the only politician west of the Appalachians who did not try to tell him how to run his command.

---

Harris absorbed Johnston's words, rubbed his chin, nodded.

"*You do not seek to insult*. Nicely phrased. I will remember that one. You really should consider politics, my friend. Once all of this military unpleasantness passes, I would heartily support you seeking some office. *Senator* Johnston, perhaps. Yes, that would be useful. We require a bit more respect in the Confederate government than some of the states seem willing to offer."

Johnston had heard this before, that by his many years wearing a uniform, he would somehow be entitled to govern.

"No, I'll leave government to those who enjoy that particular . . . game. You ever meet Sam Houston?"

"No, pretty sure I would remember that."

"I knew him well. Those who served under him in Texas came to understand that commanding and governing require different talents. He was the most unpopular man, with the greatest popularity of any man I ever knew."

Harris laughed again.

"You mean, he was respected and hated at the same time?"

Johnston paused, thought of Texas, fights and frustration, Indians and Mexicans and stubborn homesteaders.

"Sam Houston was . . . *obeyed*. Leave it at that. No other opinion is required. But I understand now how important that is. Here, I am *obeyed*. That would never be true if I was in a civilian suit in Richmond. Zachary Taylor understood that. Now, there was a man who was obeyed and loved, at the same time. But I must confess, when he ran for president, I was astonished. I knew he didn't want the job, but there were too many in this country who thought a general *should* be president. It's very easy for a man who has complete authority cast upon him . . . to become convinced he knows what's best for everyone else. And not just the army. I'll hold to my belief that soldiers don't necessarily make good presidents. Besides, I have no patience for politics. Another lesson I learned from Zachary Taylor: Give a politician the opportunity to intrude into the affairs of the army, and disaster will follow. Those who insist that their lofty offices give them special abilities . . . well, when men's lives are the price we pay for blunders, it is best to minimize blunders. Politicians seem to thrive on blunders. Taylor was a stubborn man, perhaps the most stubborn I have known. He wouldn't allow men of lofty position to assume command of anything, no matter how much pressure Washington put on him. Winfield Scott was the same way."

"Both were great generals, Sidney, but they both caught the *disease*. They failed to heed your philosophy, and so, when power called to them, they succumbed to it. Zachary Taylor won his election. Scott was more fortunate. He failed, and so his reputation as a soldier is secure."

Johnston was tiring of the conversation, had too many details gathered on his desk, too many disasters flowing through his army. He shook his head.

"Men of high influence want to influence everything around them. No way to run an army. I won't have it here. Men like Forrest . . . they earn their rank. This army is only beginning to discover how valuable that is."

Harris kept his smile.

"I am quite certain President Davis is discovering that even now. Or perhaps he is not."

"I appreciate your joviality, and I assume you are attempting to ease the strain I am under. But my capacity for humor is limited, Governor. We are in a crisis, and I'm not certain what we can do to erase that."

Harris stroked the mustache again, the smile gone.

"I fear for you, Sidney. Permit me to embarrass you, but you're the best we have, and this army's shortcomings might force Davis to make you the scapegoat. I am concerned. Too much stupidity out there, too little understanding of what you must deal with. If I were you, I wouldn't read a single word from these confounded newspapers. None of them. An empty drum makes the most noise, and there are a lot of drumbeats out there."

Johnston knew too well what Harris was referring to. It was too late to avoid the outbursts that were flowing all through the countryside, through the army as well.

"I don't care about newspapers. I have learned to ignore most of the caterwauling from civilians, all those officials who believe *wisdom* comes from any job that allows them to hold a pen. This army's problems go far beyond what some bugle-mouthed newspaperman complains about. We are suffering for reasons that go beyond anything I can control. We have made urgent requests for everything from men to arms to blankets to wagons to . . . well, everything else. And we are mostly ignored." He was growing angry, the feeling too familiar, too many frustrations. He reached for a pitcher of water on one corner of his desk, poured a glass half full, the water slightly cloudy. He drank, a bitter splash across his tongue. "Bah. Even the water is bad in this place." He looked at Harris again, felt grateful for the man's friendship, knew he could offer his feelings, no matter how indiscreet. He pointed to a letter on his desk, one of a thick pile. "Look at this one. Came in this morning. *'I fear your suggestion to send away our defense forces would place us in grave danger. The plague of a Yankee invasion force could manifest on our very streets.'* This comes from a mayor in southern Mississippi who is probably four hundred miles from the nearest Yankee. How is it that men who have never seen a Federal soldier, who have felt no threat from a gunboat or seen even a glimpse of cavalry, how is it that they insist with such passion that it is *their* town that is so important, that *their* farms and *their* courthouse must surely be the center of all we are fighting for? Ignorant souls stand guard in the square of their little village, believing that *they* are the most threatened, *their* town is the key to our very survival? I beg them to send us their militia, their men who have already volunteered to serve our cause. And this is the response. Without their own private army to stay close to home, they would be helpless in the face of certain destruction. Isham, it would require five million Federal troops and a thousand gunboats to conquer what the imaginations of a handful of our good mayors have already surrendered." He paused, studied Harris's unsmiling response. "With all due respect, Governor, Nashville may have been the most obnoxious place I have yet confronted. Just ask Colonel Gilmer. The man has a genius for engineering, for laying out the groundwork for a defensive position that would prove quite costly to the enemy. He begged, scolded, threatened, and shouted from the rooftops for anyone to offer this army the labor to complete the fortifications at Fort Henry. And no one came. He did the same for Donelson. And no one came. And then, in Nashville, they laughed at him. The blind arrogance of those people, insisting that no war would dare soil *their* fine city. Gilmer said it, and I did as well: If you believe this war is so far removed from your perfect tranquility, why not send some of your laborers, your materials where your army requires it, so that we may keep this ugly war away? The response? Oh my no, we cannot spare such things. So now Nashville is occupied by Federal troops. And the newspapers and everyone else cry out that they are such helpless victims, that the army has failed the innocent. When soldiers die . . . no one is innocent."

Harris was looking down, and Johnston knew the man understood as well as he did.

"Sorry, Isham. It is not appropriate for me to belittle those people we could not protect. They expected more from us, and we could not give it to them. If there is blame to be cast, it should be cast into this office. I am far more concerned with the morale of this army. The troops are also talking of our failures . . . of *my* failures. It is not from reading newspapers, it is from suffering a defeat when there should have been victory. At Donelson, good men were ordered to retreat from a position they knew was strong. These men came to this army with a willingness to fight. And they were ordered instead to retreat. I cannot walk among these men with great piles of paperwork . . . look here! Here is the problem! Just have patience! Maybe we will receive the muskets promised us, maybe Richmond will make good their shipments of artillery. Maybe ten more divisions will arrive next week from training facilities that do not exist!" He stopped, felt his hands shaking, looked self-consciously at Harris. "I apologize. It is unseemly for a man in my position to lose his deportment."

"Perhaps, Sidney, if you lost it with a bit more frequency . . ."

"No. You cannot command with bluster, with complaints. You cannot cast blame about like a handful of seed corn. I have communicated to Richmond my reports. Shouting out those reports to the countryside will do nothing to change what has happened." He paused. "Defeat can be a plague, and I know very well it has damaged us severely. We are fortunate to hold the men that remain in Murfreesboro. Today, we might have fifteen thousand men fit for duty, when north of us, the enemy has forty thousand. I know of the sick calls, I know we are losing men to desertion. We must find a way to restore their spirit." He paused again. "I'm not sure I am the man for that job."

"Oh, fine, General, so now you agree with those empty drums who write newspapers? Sidney, I have built my career by paying special attention to those newspapers, by using those men with the pens in their hands to reach the ignorant or the uncertain. I've been pretty good at it, too. But that isn't your job. Was there ever any expectation that you could attack the Federal cities north of Kentucky?"

Johnston shook his head, said, "No. We never had the strength to carry out an effective offensive campaign."

"And, what would have happened had you not withdrawn from Bowling Green? What would have happened had you chosen to make a fight for Nashville?"

"You know what would have happened. We would have been destroyed. The enemy was too strong, too numerous, and they control the rivers. I knew they were coming, and all I could do was anticipate where they might strike first. The rivers made perfect strategic sense. And we could not stop them."

"So, that sounds to me as though you made the right decision, the *only* decision. Yes, yes, my constituency does not agree with that. They think ten Confederates can whip a thousand Yankees, I've heard all that. Well, now their myth has been shattered. That's not a pleasant thing, you know. So they're screaming out their wrath toward this headquarters."

"That wrath goes far beyond Tennessee and Kentucky. There are some in Richmond who are already calling for my head."

"What of Davis?"

Johnston shrugged.

"So far, he continues to support my position. He is no doubt suffering for that."

"He suffers every day of his life. It comes with the job. It comes with yours, too." Harris paused, seemed to ponder his words. "Sidney . . . I have to admit . . . I had my own myth, cherished it, did not understand for many months how wrong I was. I truly believed that all the outrage against Lincoln could be contained, that this could be done peacefully. I thought that Tennessee could choose to secede from the Union, and join the other states in a demonstration . . . a *symbol* that would have a real impact on Washington, on Lincoln himself. It was a magnificent protest, a refusal to go along with policies that would ruin us, destroy everything that has allowed this nation to prosper. I knew that those fire-eaters in South Carolina were going too far, and that sure enough, they would pay the price, would bring down the wrath of the Federal army. I thought it was pure stupidity to shell a government installation, but shell it they did. Fine, what's done is done. But even then . . . I held out hope that perhaps . . . perhaps those cannons in Charleston would drive home our point, and that Lincoln would back down. I was utterly convinced that none of us would ever be called upon to put an army into the field, to fight a war. I did not expect the fire-eaters to prevail, and by God, they have prevailed everywhere. Where is the sanity? The Congress of the United States had every opportunity to stand up and take the hammer out of Lincoln's hands, and instead . . . they chose up sides, like boys in a school yard brawl. Well, now we have our brawl. And it's a bloody one. Now, there have to be men like you to make sure we spill more of their blood than they spill of ours. There can be no good from this, Sidney. No good at all." Harris looked down, shook his head. "I'm just a politician. I put great faith in *talk*. And so . . . I have become obsolete." He looked up at Johnston now, and Johnston saw red eyes. "This is *your* world now, General. God help you."


Though Johnston had military authority over a vast territory, and a vast number of soldiers, he was experiencing the dismay he had once felt in Texas and Mexico and California. Wars were started by politicians, and were fought by young men, and in between stood the generals. No matter the fire that had driven the Southern states to make their angry stand, the men put into positions of high authority by Jefferson Davis were often chosen for their political influence: governors, state legislators, local officials, who had at best done an effective job of assembling troops for this new army. The problem was not confined to the South, of course, and Johnston knew well what was going on in Washington. The cruelty of old age had sent Winfield Scott into retirement, the finest commander in either army now replaced by the ambitious George McClellan. The shelling of Fort Sumter had been nearly a year ago, and to the surprise of many, particularly in the North, the greater strength of the Union army had not squashed the Southern rebellion. If anyone on either side needed convincing that the fledgling Confederacy would fight and die to make their point, the battle at Manassas Junction had stood out like a beacon. There two clumsy armies had collided in a mishmash of disorganization, decided as much by confusion, panic, and dumb luck as by the wizardry of Confederate general Joe Johnston or this new light rising in the Southern command, the man the Virginians were calling "Stonewall." Since Manassas, the two armies had focused most of their efforts on maneuver and organization, building the lifelines for supplies and equipment, and searching for the men who might actually be able to lead. Already, the geography of the war had exceeded what anyone in Washington or Richmond had ever expected. It was not to be decided by some noisy clash of arms within earshot of either capital. The maps were expanding, potential battlegrounds opening up even beyond the Mississippi River, troops marching into far-flung towns and villages, while farmers and shopkeepers waved their flags with the manic joy of the ignorant.

With Johnston's forces in an untenable position in Tennessee, he knew that the protests coming to him from Nashville or Bowling Green were utterly irrelevant. There was no purpose to hand-wringing about what had gone wrong. He already knew. The army was too small, too ill-equipped and in several of the sharper fights, it had been badly led. The anxiety coming toward him out of Richmond was entirely expected, but Johnston's authority was still protected by Jefferson Davis, and as long as Davis believed in him, Johnston would focus on the most urgent priority in front of him. Tennessee had become an albatross, most of that state wide open to invasion by the Federal gunboats and the overwhelming strength of the Federal commands. Richmond had heard that message as well, and thankfully, had responded at least in part. Though many of the new generals were yet unproven on the battlefield, there were men in the Confederate command who brought genuine experience to the position, some who had cut their teeth in the Mexican War. One of those was Pierre Beauregard.

If Johnston had any reason to believe that his failure to hold the Kentucky–Tennessee line would cost him his job, those fears were sharpened by Beauregard's sudden arrival. But Beauregard paid his respects at Murfreesboro, did not carry any orders that put him above Johnston at all. Beauregard's professed point of view was that he had simply been sent to assist where the need was greatest. For now, that was all Johnston needed to hear.

To the civilian population impatient for heroes, Beauregard was already beloved by the Southern newspapers, and so by the people who read of his exploits. To Jefferson Davis, Beauregard's mantle of heroism was displayed with a little too much swagger. In Richmond, there was considerable grumbling that the *hero* had simply been in the right place at the right time. In April 1861, that place happened to be Charleston,

South Carolina. With great fanfare, Beauregard had ordered the shelling of Fort Sumter, and so had commanded the firing of the first shots of the war. Beauregard had also been one of the key players at Manassas, which of course fueled what seemed to be a lofty regard for his own abilities. But Jefferson Davis despised the man, a hostility that grew deeper when Beauregard attempted to insert himself directly into the operations of the entire army, operations that Davis held tightly in his own grasp. By rank, and presumably by ability, the senior commander in Virginia was Joseph Johnston, who could also claim major credit for the victory at Manassas. Joe Johnston had no need of a *partner* like Beauregard, and Davis knew he had to put distance between the two generals, whose personalities were already in conflict.

When Beauregard began to submit elaborate plans for strategy that stepped squarely on the toes of Davis himself, *grand plans* that Beauregard insisted were the only way the war could be won, Davis's patience ran out. Beauregard was ordered to the West, assigned to some vague position in a theater of operations that had already been assigned to others, Albert Sidney Johnston in particular. Johnston didn't have any particular hostility toward Beauregard, assumed that since the man was from Louisiana, he might assist in drawing troops out of those areas that had been reluctant to send their men off to fight in Tennessee. With the defeats at Henry and Donelson, and now, with the strategic need to pull the Confederate troops southward from Kentucky and central Tennessee, Beauregard's talent for organization seemed, to Johnston at least, to be an asset. If Beauregard was given any reason to believe he had been sent westward to replace Albert Sidney Johnston, Johnston had heard nothing of the sort. Johnston couldn't help wondering if the fiery and outspoken Creole was truly willing to accept a subordinate position in anyone else's command.

Beauregard quickly established his headquarters at Corinth, Mississippi, and for good reason. With most of Tennessee completely vulnerable to the far more numerous Federal forces, Corinth, situated just south of the Tennessee border, anchored the next most essential defensive line. The town had been created by the junction of two major rail lines, the north-south Mobile & Ohio line, and the east-west Memphis & Charleston line. The east-west line in particular was crucial for the South to maintain a supply and communication link from the Missis-

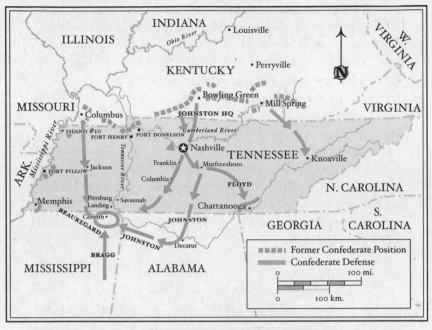

**JOHNSTON ABANDONS KENTUCKY;**

**THE CONFEDERATE ARMY WITHDRAWS SOUTHWARD TO CORINTH**

sippi River all the way to the Atlantic coast, and no one in the army, nor in the Confederate capital, faulted the strategy that called for a stout defense of the railroad. Corinth was even more valuable to the Federals, since the railroad could carry their own troops and supplies southward, from the Ohio Valley to the Gulf Coast.

Beauregard's arrival at Corinth had initiated even more calls for troops, urgent orders for any forces along the Gulf Coast not presently threatened to move rapidly to the rail center. Other troops were summoned from the west, troops who had been fortifying outposts closer to the Federal positions in Louisiana and Arkansas, that might be in danger of being cut off altogether. More troops were pulled in from the east, from various outposts in Alabama. While no one knew exactly what the Federal commanders were planning, it was certain that the coming of spring would mean movement, and Beauregard and Johnston agreed completely that the most likely targets would be Corinth or possibly Chattanooga. To throw misdirection at the Federal spies and cavalry patrols who might be observing Johnston's troop movements, General John Floyd had been given twenty-five hundred troops and ordered to march noisily from Murfreesboro to Chattanooga. In addition, Johnston himself had made indiscreet mention around his headquarters that his own movements, and the movement of his remaining troops at Murfreesboro, would be toward the south and east. The goal of the deceit was twofold. If the Federal command intended to target his army first, Johnston hoped to convince the Federals to charge off in the wrong direction, a lengthy jaunt toward Chattanooga. The delays that could cause in the Federal advance would allow Johnston time to improve the fortifications around Corinth. But, more likely, if Halleck intended to seize the rail center after all, it could be enormously helpful if the Federal generals were convinced that most of Johnston's troop strength had marched off elsewhere.

O n February 28, Johnston's columns began their march southward, evacuating Murfreesboro, filling the roadways that led first toward Shelbyville and Fayetteville, Tennessee, and down across the Alabama border toward Huntsville. Though the invectives still poured his way, harsh condemnation from civilian leaders in Tennessee and throughout the Confederacy, Johnston focused more on what it would take to assemble an army with sufficient size and strength to push back at the Federal troops that were already slicing Tennessee in two. No matter the validity of the criticism, or how vicious the wrath of the newspapers and politicians in Richmond, Johnston knew that ultimately, those words did not matter. There was one way to renew the spirit of the people, of the army, and of his own command: assemble an army strong enough to confront the enemy, and then destroy him.

## CHAPTER THREE

# SEELEY

NEAR THE DUCK RIVER,
CENTRAL TENNESSEE
MARCH 19, 1862

For long miles the roadways were nearly impassable, the travel miserably slow, rivers of mud deepening by the hour from the steady rain. There was no real alternative to the roads, the horses unable to maneuver at all through the dense thickets that lined most of the countryside. There were breaks in the thickets, open grassy fields, but there was risk there, the rain so intense that a short jaunt across a mile or more of roadless countryside might get them lost. Worse were the farmlands, not yet planted, so that the muddy fields were deep and soft, and could swallow the legs of their horses, a nasty potential for crippling injury to their mounts no cavalryman wanted to confront. Regardless of the weather, the farms themselves could be a threat of a different kind, and it had surprised Seeley to hear the colonel's briefing to beware the citizens, farmers, and shopkeepers. None of the horse soldiers expected to learn that even in Tennessee the civilians were not always friendly, did not necessarily support the army and their cause. Forrest had cautioned them that spies could be the most innocent to the eye, offering the friendly conversation, or the generosity of a pail of milk, a basket of eggs. The loyalty to their army was not guaranteed even from people whose homes the army claimed to protect, and more than once the cavalry had found a local man with maps in his pocket, showing troop movements, identifying regiments and their commanders. There was no good reason for any civilian to be carrying that kind of information, and the men who had been caught had almost always been traveling north, where the enemy waited for any information they could receive. It had infuriated him, all of them, to find that these good people whose homes lay firmly in Southern territory might not believe in the cause that the soldiers were willing to die for. And so, riding through the misery of the awful weather there could be no visits with civilians, no matter how tempted they were by the dry barn, the promise of temporary shelter. The mission was too critical and these men too few to be given up by a turncoat farmer who had some link to a Yankee spy with a fast horse.

The rain had been relentless, a long day made longer, and Seeley had guessed it to be after four o'clock when the captain had finally ordered them to stop. Captain McDonald had moved out from the column, taking Seeley with him. They were the only two officers in the troop, and McDonald had dismounted, leaned in close to what made for a dry place beneath a towering oak tree. There the captain had unrolled a map, had shown confidence that their objective, the Duck River, was close in front, but that meant that the road they were using was far too dangerous. The order to dismount had gone to the others, the horses led by their reins into the dense woods, what quickly became a swamp. In a small muddy clearing, one-fourth of the men had been designated to remain behind, to take hold of the horses, keep them in tight groups. It was always the precaution, that on a mission like this the men were too few to fight any kind of skirmish. The order had come the day before from Forrest: There would be no engagement at all, no matter what enemy they might find. The information McDonald's men were seeking was far more valuable than any results that could come from a firefight. With the men on foot, the shotguns had stayed behind as well; no need to carry the extra encumbrance. The men had grumbled about that, but in the swamp, slow going through deep muddy bog holes, the weapon was a liability and likely would be made useless by the mud that quickly engulfed them all. If there was comfort to be had from a weapon, they all carried the heavy knives at their belts.

The mud was deep and cold, the going too slow and too difficult for anyone to waste energy by complaining. They had already been soaked through their rain gear and whatever uniforms they might have, the exercise of crawling over and through the thickets at least helping to warm them up. As if to add to their misery, the wind grew stronger, the rain harder still, the sharp breeze driving the rain into eyes and ears.

They were spread out within close sight of one another, still moving forward, led by the compass of the captain. Seeley watched him, was suddenly grabbed, wrapped by a thorny vine, hung up by the ropelike strength. He tried to pull free, no strength in his legs, too much in the vine, and he reached for the knife at his belt, felt a hand on his arm, soft voice.

"No. Untangle it. Just step out of it. Knife won't cut this stuff."

He saw the face, muddy wetness beneath the eyes, Sergeant Gladstone, older man, something of the swamps that seemed to be a part of this man even in the best weather. His legs worked themselves free, Gladstone not waiting to be thanked. Seeley found the captain again, moved that way, mud still sucking at his boots, one man nearby stumbling, hands down in a soft pool, mud up to the man's chest. Hands helped him up, a curse echoing softly through the rain, but still they moved forward.

It seemed to be getting darker, but Seeley knew not to gaze upward, that eyes full of rain told you nothing. The downpour continued, the wind driving the rain through the trees like a flowing curtain. Fat streams and drops from the limbs above seemed always to find Seeley's collar, even the rubberized raincoat not keeping him dry. But no matter the weariness, Seeley kept that one sharp place in his mind, what kept the eyes focused, staring ahead. There was after all a purpose to this, that somewhere out there, an enemy might be waiting, and even if the Yankees were huddled blindly in this same misery, the men knew what Captain McDonald was trying to find, where this swamp must surely lead. Seeley did as they all did, felt and probed his way through the thickest places, the small openings usually holes of deep mud, and so the going was painfully slow. But the men who had groused loudest about leaving the shotguns behind were as calm and miserable as the rest, and even as they searched for some sign of an enemy, Seeley was utterly convinced that no other human had ever crushed their way through this swampy hell, wet or dry.

His boots were completely full of water, the mud growing thicker on his pants legs, like wax on a candle wick, heavier, denser with each step. He kept his eye on the captain, saw a change now, McDonald holding up a hand, dropping to his knees, peering through a thicket of low cedar trees. Seeley froze, fully alert, and the captain made another motion with his hand, pulling the others down low. Seeley crept forward, close beside McDonald, followed as the captain pushed slowly into the cedars. His heart was already pounding, exhaustion, but there was excitement now, and he had to see, ignored the hard chill of the water now pushing up above his waist. McDonald glanced back, another wave of his hand, holding the others in place, all of them on their knees, settling into the mud. If there were curses about that, Seeley heard nothing but the rain. He took a long breath of soggy air, watched the muddy faces, most of the men disguised completely by the filth that covered them. His eyes were filled by a gust of blowing rain, and he wiped by instinct, too quickly, his fingers too dirty to help. McDonald waved them forward, his hand giving the signal, *slowly*. Seeley watched them, no gripes now, respect for the captain, all of them knowing something dangerous might be very close. He looked again at McDonald, who turned away, satisfied his order was understood. When the captain began to crawl, the others did the same, pressing through the dense cedars, thick curtains of water on the tangle of branches. As they moved past the brush, they all saw what the captain saw. A few yards beyond the cedars was another low thicket of brush, and beyond that, the Duck River. Now they could all see why they had come, what this miserable mission was about. On the far side of the river was a great mass of blue.

McDonald turned his head slowly, scanned them all, nodded, another motion with his hand, the signal to stop, to lie flat. No one spoke, used only their eyes, the men gathering closer, in line behind the low cover of the brush. Seeley did his job, made sure they were spread out, glancing across the river with every breath. The rain was driving even harder now, a deep rumble of thunder somewhere above, and McDonald grabbed his shoulder, a hard hiss in his ear.

"We got lucky, Lieutenant. Right where they're supposed to be!"

Seeley guessed the river to be two hundred yards across, saw it was thick and muddy, noisy splatters by the rain, the current flowing by in a storm-fueled rush. Some fifty yards to one side were the remains of a railroad bridge, charred stubs of thick logs and stone, the bridge eliminated days before by the good work of other raiders. The Confederate cavalry had patrolled these roadways and river crossings for weeks now, doing as much damage as they could, most of them not having to fight weather as bad as this. The orders had come to all the cavalry units, that as the bulk of the army marched away from Murfreesboro, the bridges behind them were a priority, and so every effort had been made to cut any transportation lines that would allow the enemy to pursue.

McDonald looked toward his men, another signal, *sit tight,* and he peered up carefully through the brush. He turned toward Seeley, motioned him closer, and Seeley crawled that way, fought the wet goo thick in his pants, the stinging in his knees. McDonald pointed.

"Those two. Watch 'em."

Across the river, on a bluff a few feet above the water, two men rode close, high on horses, their uniforms disguised by black rain gear, but there was no mistaking their authority. Words were passed, arms waving, pointing, hot tempers, someone not afraid to show his anger. Behind them the uniforms were not disguised at all, dense rows of men in blue, spreading away into a clearing. Seeley saw it clearly now: An entire column of Federal troops had reached the place where the trail led to the remains of the railroad bridge, their officers no doubt discussing just what they were supposed to do next. Quickly, more men on horseback were gathering, a dozen now, some of them aides, limp flags hanging from crooked flagstaffs. Arms were pointing, and even through the rain Seeley caught a flicker of voice, a shout, obvious anger. Suddenly two foot soldiers waded out into the river, straight toward the crouching cavalrymen. Seeley felt a burst of heartbeats, put a hand on his knife, but the men waded out only a few yards from shore, were already waist-deep, struggling against the current, and just as quickly, they pulled themselves back to the others who watched from the bank.

McDonald reached out, patted Seeley on the shoulder, silent joy, and Seeley knew the meaning. Too deep to cross, too much current. The bluecoats would have to find another way. The Confederate cavalrymen that had come before them had done good work, and Seeley had been told already what the enemy commanders were learning themselves, that for miles in both directions, the Duck River was just as he saw it here. If the Yankees intended to cross anywhere near this part of the river, they would have to build their own bridges.

McDonald raised field glasses, studied, said, "Look for the flags. Try to see some detail. We need to know who these people are."

Seeley pulled his field glasses out of his coat, mud coating the lenses, and he smeared a finger frantically, cursed to himself, hoped McDonald didn't see. McDonald said, "Nothing they can do right now. They'll have engineers come up, probably supposed to be there already. Bet that's why that officer is so hot. He's probably in command, bet he's a damn general. And hot as a hornet. I'd love a chance to pick him off. Good musket would knock him right off'n his horse. Never know what hit him. Maybe I'll get you some other time, General Whoever You Are. Just wish I could see your damn flag, division, regiment, anything."

The captain paused, studied again with his field glasses, shook his head.

"Can't make out a single damn flag. Those bluebellies marched up here all full of piss, ready to grab General Johnston by the tail, and I bet that general over there was told the river might be shallow enough to ford. Not even generals can stop the rain. Looks like they're gonna have to just sit here, probably build a bridge. Otherwise, they're gonna have to wait for the water to drop. That could take a couple weeks."

The horsemen moved away from the river's edge, the limp flags following, the only one visible the long flowing Stars and Stripes. McDonald pounded a fist into his leg. "What's your hurry? Dammit! Who are you, anyway?" He glanced at Seeley now. "Keep looking... try to see..." He saw the mess that was Seeley's field glasses now, scowled at him. "*Reconnaissance* mission, Lieutenant. Keep those things clean and dry! What's the matter with you...?" McDonald stopped himself, and Seeley looked toward the others watching them, some laughing, the ridicule kept silent by the rain.

"Try to clean 'em up. Show these boys how you got that damn gold bar on your collar."

Seeley worked the lenses furiously, unbuttoned his shirt, his undershirt just as wet, but doing a better job at clearing the mud. He knew the others were watching him, knew the jokes would come later. He raised the glasses, could see smears of shapes, lowered them, saw more clearly with his eyes. Straight across the river was a wide trail that led out of the woods and open fields straight toward the wrecked bridge. In the middle of the trail he could see the raised hump of a railroad bed. But there were no tracks, more good work from someone else's patrol, John Hunt Morgan most likely. The blue troops were still coming forward, more columns spreading out both ways into the woods, some close to the river, some filling patches of open ground downstream, guided by more horsemen, the junior officers. He tried to count, gave up quickly, knew there were hundreds of them, probably many more behind them. His heart was pounding, jumping in his chest, and he ducked lower behind the brush. McDonald seemed to read him, said, "I don't want 'em to see us. But even if they do, not much they can do about it. They'll probably expect someone to be keeping an eye on 'em. Might even send a patrol over here, float across on a log, maybe somewhere over there somebody thought to bring a damn boat."

Seeley buttoned his shirt again, thought of the captain's wistful fantasy, one good rifled musket. Pick off those boys one at a time and they wouldn't have the first idea where it was coming from, not in this downpour. Of course, trying to shoot a musket in the driving rain was enough of a challenge as it was. Pretty hard to keep your powder dry. And a musket full of wet powder was a boil-on-a-backside to clean. He thought of McDonald's words, had no confusion about their mission. Be awful nice to know who you are, General. The whole bunch of you.

He blinked rainwater out of his eyes, felt a sneeze coming, did all he could to stifle it, bent low, held his nose, the sneeze exploding into his ears. McDonald said in a low voice, "They can't hear you from over there. Can you hear them? This rain makes a nice damn blanket over all of us. I'll get these boys back to the horses, make a camp. No fires. We need to eat something. You got any rations?"

"Yes, sir. Some hardtack, hunk of raw bacon."

"It'll have to do." McDonald looked around, pointed to the old sergeant, and another man, motioned them forward. "Sergeant, you and Hinkle stay with the lieutenant here, keep each other company. I want to make damn sure those bluebellies are staying the night. Look and listen, any signs of a camp, unbridled horses, wagons unloaded, all of that. Don't want them marching the hell out of here without us knowing about it. It gets too dark to see, you make your way back to us. Yankees are pretty scared of the dark, so once the sun goes down, they'll probably stay put." He pointed back away from the river. "The horses are three hundred yards straight that way. You get spotted, anybody hollers at you or shoots at you, crawl like blazes out of here, and make sure we hear you coming. I'm taking no casualties, and no one gets lost, not in my command. You get close to us, use a password . . . *Beauregard.* Call it out. Somebody'll answer you. For now, as long as there's daylight, try to see some of those damn flags. They're supposed to be proud of the damn things. I want to know who they are. That's the only damn reason we're here. I didn't join the cavalry to sit in slop."

The captain moved away, leading the others back from the river. Seeley watched him, waited for the last man to disappear into the darkening woods, thought, he sure cusses a lot. Probably not a church man. Don't hear too many officers in this army tempt fate with that kind of talk. Colonel Forrest, maybe a little. But if I had that much to be thinking about, I'd probably let down a little, too. Just don't let Katie hear that. Or Mama. Oh Lord, no, not Mama.

Beside him, the sergeant, Gladstone, growled, "Lookee there. See all that white? They're putting up their tents. That'll make the captain happy. Looks like they're planning on staying awhile."

Seeley saw wagons now, gathering on a hillside farther back from the river, supplies unloaded, men in motion everywhere.

"Tonight anyway. Good."

Gladstone pointed at Seeley's field glasses.

"Beggin' your pardon, sir, but you ought not be so mean to them things. Can be a man's best friend out here."

"I know. It was stupid. They slipped out the front of my coat."

The other man spoke, Hinkle, very young, one of the men from Kentucky.

"Can't see much of nothin' anyhoo. Gettin' dark fast. You see flags? This is dumb, if'n you ask me."

Gladstone punched the boy in the shoulder.

"The lieutenant didn't ask you; the captain neither. Dig the mud outta your ears and listen for bugles. Maybe they'll tell us something."

"Right. Hadn't thoughta that."

Gladstone moved to one side, toward a small crooked tree, stuffed himself against the trunk, a sliver of shelter. He dug into his own shirt, and Seeley was surprised to see a single-lens spyglass. Gladstone pulled it lengthwise, telegraphed it out nearly two feet long, held his hand out over the larger end, sheltering it from the rain, scanned the far side of the river for a long minute. He slid it closed again, looked at Seeley, a broad smile, missing many teeth.

"My pappy gave me this, sir. Navy man. Said he knew John Paul Jones. Well, said he knew a lot of things. Knew the damn rum bottle, that's for sure. But this here spyglass . . . a fine piece. You can see clear to the moon. Hmm. Maybe not tonight."

He seemed to hesitate, a glance at the muddy field glasses hanging uselessly around Seeley's neck. Seeley looked at the spyglass, and Gladstone huffed, said, "Well, all right. Give it a try, sir."

Seeley expanded the glass, impressed by the brass and leather, knew Gladstone was watching him carefully. He mimicked the sergeant, put a hand over the far end, shielding the lens, put the smaller end to his eye, was amazed at the detail. He scanned the far side of the river, could clearly see movement, even faces, the brass buttons, stacks of muskets, tents rising. Farther up the rise, more tents were going up, and he saw flags, but even the breeze didn't move them, revealed almost nothing.

"One looks like Ohio. Maybe. That doesn't mean a thing. Stars and Stripes . . . but I guess we knew that."

Gladstone said, "They got their big brass's headquarters back in those woods, I betcha. Under the big trees for *comfort*. They stuck the green lads at the river's edge. Flood rises up and grabs 'em, nobody'll care."

The sergeant laughed, and Seeley couldn't help a smile. He had already decided that if anything dangerous happened, Gladstone would be the man to follow, rank or not. Seeley could feel it, even in the swamp, knew that this man had never been lost in his life. Maybe, he thought, the captain knows that, too. That's why he left him here.

The thunder rumbled again, far away, and he glanced upward, the skies still heavy and dark, a hint of a setting sun. But the rain had slowed, the splatter on the river lighter, more sounds flowing across from the Federal camp. He looked again through the spyglass, thought, they got a pile of nice tents, that's for sure. I'd like to have one of those things. He shivered, the air cooler, another breeze whipping the misty rain in a swirl around him. And now Hinkle pointed, a chattering excitement in his squeaking voice.

"Sir! They're coming across!"

Near the railroad bridge, a half-dozen men had slid out into the water, were swimming furiously, reaching the first of the wrecked pilings, clambering up, their own island. On the shore behind them, a group of men had gathered, and now a rope was tossed out to one of the men perched up on the piling. He pulled what seemed to be a small raft, piled with some kind of black lump. Now another rope went out, caught by a second man, another raft floating out, pulled by the rope. Seeley watched with a hard burn of curiosity, saw four of the men swimming to the second of the five pilings, then the two towing the rafts. Hands reached out, pulling the men onto the second piling, the small rafts dragged close, then the process began again, the men moving toward the third piling, the largest, at the center of the river. On the far bank, an officer sat on his horse, watching, and Seeley thought, he's done this, sent them over. Probably picked his best swimmers. They're gonna be over here as skirmishers, lookouts.

Beside him, the sergeant said, "Those rafts . . . not big enough to be muskets. Pistols and cartridge boxes, I bet, wrapped in a raincoat. They can keep the powder dry till they reach this side. Then load up. Clever devils."

Seeley glanced back to the swamp, said, "We gotta get back, tell the captain."

"Easy there, Lieutenant. They're clever, but don't mean they're smart. Got me an *idee,* if you'll permit, sir."

Seeley felt a small surge of panic, looked at Gladstone, saw the same gap-toothed smile.

"What kind of idea?"

"Right now, they ain't armed."

"Neither are we."

"They don't know that. It's getting dark fast. We make enough ruckus, we can scare 'em to death."

"The captain said no engagement. No casualties. This is just . . . reconnaissance."

"I ain't for disobeyin' nothing, sir. But if'n we wanna know who those boys are, the easiest way might be to ask 'em. The captain wants information. Let's get him some." Gladstone pointed, the woods darkening even more. "The railroad bed is that way, and that's where they'll land. What you say, sir?"

Seeley heard a loud cry, looked out to the men in the river, one of them struggling, helping hands not helping enough. The man began to drift downriver, flailing, a high yelp. Men were shouting toward him, the men up on the piling staring helplessly as their friend was swept quickly away. Seeley felt sick, his heart racing, but the men on the piling stayed put, wouldn't do anything, and he looked across, to the officer on horseback, hard shouts, pointing to the crossing, pointing again, giving the order. Seeley could hear it all in his mind. No stopping. Nothing you can do for him, without losing maybe all of you. It's the only order the man could give. Seeley couldn't see the single Yankee now, too far, too dark, thought, maybe he'll find a snag, grab something. Maybe he's already gone. *Drowning*. God help him. Not a way I'd want to go. He looked at the other soldiers, the five men all perched up on the fourth piling, anger and agony in their movements. Gladstone was still beside him, had seen it all.

"That'll help. One less to worry about. And they'll be jittery."

The men didn't rest long, no time for grief, the darkness coming fast. Seeley watched as they slipped down in the water again, hands helping others, slowly, more careful. The two small rafts followed as they swam on toward the last piling, the last stop before they reached the near shore. Seeley felt the energy now, the sergeant's simple idea forming itself in his own mind, a deadly game, a game played by soldiers. He thought of the captain's harsh comment, the gold bar on his collar. Earn it, Jimmy. Earn it right now.

T hey had spread out, ten yards between them, Seeley closest to the railroad bed. The men were swimming straight toward him, splashes in a steady rhythm. It was too dark to see them, but out on the last piling, he could see two forms, men who seemed to stay put, and he thought, they're played out maybe. Too exhausted by the current. Or, the lost man's friends. They're not moving . . . no matter their orders. Figure their officer can't see 'em. So . . . now just three in the water. I hope.

The rain was nearly stopped, a thick wet fog settling over the river, and he slipped closer to the edge, the splashes a few yards offshore. Soon they'll stand up. It's time.

"You there! Yankees! Stop or we'll shoot!"

To both sides, the other two took his cue, more shouts.

"Yankees! Shoot 'em! Cut 'em down!"

"I got him . . . he's mine. Let me kill him!"

The men in the water began to cry out, responding, their helplessness carrying away any urge to fight.

"Give up! I give up!"

The first man stumbled up close to Seeley, still shouting, the man only feet from Seeley's face. Then he was down, the exhaustion sucking the energy from his legs, and he lay flat on the gravelly bank, said again, "I give up! Don't shoot!"

Seeley jumped on the man's back, dug a knee down hard, holding him firmly, but there was no strength in the man, just hard gasps, the man's breathing.

"Don't move, bluebelly! I'll put a ball in the back of your head!"

"Not moving! I give up!"

He looked up, foggy darkness, heard a manic explosion of splashes, listened hard, the swimmers moving away from shore. To one side, Gladstone called out, "They're running away! I wanted to kill me one up close! Damn you, bluebellies! Come back here so's I can run this here bayonet up your assbone!"

Seeley kept his weight down hard on the man beneath him, no struggle, a slight whimper from the man.

"Don't kill me, reb. I got babies at home."

"Then shut up! Don't move."

There was a rush through the bushes to one side, Gladstone running low, then down beside him. The sergeant shouted out, "Hinkle!"

The boy came at a gallop, stumbling out onto the railroad bed, breathing as heavily as the prisoner. Gladstone drew his knife, reached down, and made a short slice. Seeley jumped, thought, no! But he saw now, the sergeant had cut the rope that had been tied to the man's arm. He pulled it in quick draws, the small raft now sliding up the bank.

"See here, sir? We got us a bluebelly and a handful of hardware along with him. You like my idea now?"

Seeley said nothing, thought of the captain, the orders not to engage anyone.

"Let's just get him back to the others. We'll let the captain tell us if this was a good idea."

McDonald leaned close to the man's face, said, "He's stinkin', that's for sure. River water and piss. Who's got a match?"

"Here!"

Seeley stood close beside McDonald, a crowd of the others gathered close behind them, and now the match ignited, blinding, and Seeley saw the prisoner's face, clean-shaven, handsome man, and very scared.

"Please don't kill me. . . ."

"Oh, shut the hell up, boy. Only reason we'll kill you is if you don't answer my questions, that's all."

The match went out, and Seeley blinked hard, tried to see anything of the prisoner. The man was held down tightly on both sides by Gladstone and Hinkle, but there was nothing of escape in this man, the pure terror draining away any *soldiering* he might have brought to the uniform.

"Who . . . who are you? You a *secesh*?"

McDonald kept his voice hard, said, "Now that's your second mistake. I ask and then you answer. Your first mistake was swimming straight into a full regiment of the Confederate army's finest cavalry. What jackleg officer ordered you to do something that stupid? It was pretty stupid now, wasn't it, Private?"

Seeley thought, regiment? But he understood what McDonald was doing. No one needs to know there's two dozen of us, and a million damn Yankees across the river. The question was a trick as well, and the prisoner fell flat-faced into it.

"Captain Danforth's orders. Told us we needed to set up watch over on this side of the river, make sure nobody snuck up on us. The captain asked us if we could swim. I used to all the time . . . at home . . . all the time . . . Sandusky Bay. Corporal Boynton . . . said he could, but I knew he wasn't strong. He got swept away. You find him? He's always trying to be a hero, volunteering for everything. I knew he'd have trouble in that current. Tried to grab him . . . awful . . ."

"Oh for God's sake, son, I asked one simple question. This Captain Danforth, what company he command?"

"Company C, sir. Uh . . . maybe I ought not be telling you this. They told us . . ."

"Listen, son, you know what a Tennessee toothpick is?"

"N-n-no, sir."

"Somebody light another match."

The captain's order was obeyed, a flash of light bursting between them. McDonald was squatting within arm's length of the prisoner and Seeley could see that he had already drawn the long knife. The captain made a quick show, held it out, turning the blade to reflect the flicker of light. The match went dark, and McDonald said, "We all carry these, son. Sharp as the day I was born. They're real good for gutting a hog, or, even better, they'll split a Yankee from his chin to his soft privates. Sharp on both sides, so you can spin it around right inside a man's chest. Now, you can tell me what I want to know, or I'll show you just how sharp this blade is."

"Ohio, sir! Forty-ninth Ohio! Colonel Blackman! General McCook's Division! Please . . ."

"McCook?"

Seeley knew the name meant something to the captain, had to be important.

"How many more behind you?"

"Don't know, sir. Really! Don't know. Bunch of us, though. I heard the colonel talking. Said something about General Nelson . . . somebody else . . . oh Lord . . . I can't remember . . ."

The prisoner began to cry, hard sobs, and Seeley couldn't avoid feeling sorry for the man, a flash of thought, never be a prisoner. *Never.*

"Oh, wait . . . I heard the supply sergeant . . . said something about the river."

"The one you swam across?"

"No, sir! The Tennessee River! Some town, like in Georgia . . . I heard of it."

"Georgia? You're not making sense, son. You're in Tennessee."

"Savannah! That's it. Something about going to Savannah. The sergeant made a joke about it. Stupid generals gonna make us march all the way to the ocean. But somebody cussed him out for being stupid, said there was another one . . . another Savannah . . . in Tennessee!"

Seeley felt McDonald stand up tall beside him, and the captain said, "Lieutenant, get the men in the saddle. We can't wait. Bring this boy with us, until we can hand him off."

"How'll he ride, sir? No spare horses."

"You decide to let your sergeant run your command, Lieutenant?"

Seeley had waited for this, wondered if the value of the prisoner outweighed the risk they had taken. Of course, he thought. He knows I didn't make this plan myself.

"Sir, I saw an opportunity to grab a prisoner, get some information. Had to make a quick decision."

"Well, when you make decisions that go against my orders, you'll pay for it. Even good decisions. This boy'll ride with you. Hey, Yankee."

"S-s-sir?"

"You're gonna be tied up real snug to my lieutenant here. You ever ride a horse?"

"Not much, sir."

McDonald slapped Seeley on the shoulder.

"Enjoy your ride, Lieutenant."

Seeley waited for the prisoner to be pulled up to his feet, thought of the rope they would use, something stout to tie the prisoner against him. It was the only way in the dark, no chance for the man to fall off, slip away. He began to move, felt another hand on his arm, heard the familiar deep growl close to his ear, the voice of Gladstone.

"Nice of you to take the blame and all. But, beggin' your pardon, sir. For takin' the credit, you owe me a bottle."

# CHAPTER FOUR

## JOHNSTON

ROSE COTTAGE, CORINTH, MISSISSIPPI
MARCH 23, 1862

The newly assembled army around Corinth had been designated now the Army of the Mississippi, and though Beauregard had insisted the command belonged to Johnston, his actions suggested that Beauregard believed himself to be in the best position to manage the army's affairs. On the march from Murfreesboro, Johnston had to suffer through lengthy communications from Beauregard that could only have been interpreted as *orders*. The missives included a steady stream of requests and the requirements for Beauregard's own plans for troop movements, distribution of supplies and ordnance, and the proper construction of the defenses to protect the railroad. Beauregard's display of so much authority made Johnston wonder once again if Jefferson Davis had sent Beauregard west for this very purpose, but Davis's letters showed no sign of any lack of confidence in Johnston's command. Beauregard's behavior was simply . . . Beauregard.

To the Creole's credit, he was an efficient organizer, and his standing among the civilian population had produced significant results, new volunteers answering his call, the other commanders throughout the Mississippi Valley answering as well, supplies and troops continuing to march toward the crucial railway. Beauregard's success was an obvious contrast to Johnston's inability to produce the same kind of enthusiastic effort, one more example of the blame levied against Johnston for so much of the bad news that had come from the army's failures in Kentucky and Tennessee. Johnston was grateful as well that Beauregard had assumed control of an essential part of the army's change of positioning, since Johnston had to focus his attention on the rapid transport of the twelve thousand men he brought from Murfreesboro. That march also included the precious supplies gathered at Nashville, plus the urgent need to monitor any pursuit by the enemy, particularly the Federal cavalry. With Beauregard establishing his headquarters at Jackson, Mississippi, Johnston had allowed the Creole the authority to do whatever maneuvering was necessary to assemble as much strength as possible in Mississippi. On March 23, when Johnston arrived at Corinth, he could not avoid feeling seriously impressed by the success of Beauregard's efforts. Around Corinth, and throughout northern Mississippi, the Confederate forces numbered close to fifty thousand. Whether Beauregard expected to actually lead those troops in the field was an issue that Johnston knew he would have to confront.

Beauregard was a small, wiry man, handsome in the extreme, a trait that had made easy work for the newspapers in proclaiming him to be the South's most gallant hero, his French background offering easy grist for the public mill quick to proclaim him their own Napoleon. Johnston carried the annoying memory inside him still of a quote from a Richmond paper that declared with great emotion that the South's survival depended exclusively on *God and General Beauregard*. Johnston had wondered often, and he wondered now, if Beauregard believed that as well.

At the moment, in Johnston's new headquarters, he was more concerned with the man's appearance. Beauregard had been extremely ill for some weeks now, and it showed. The illness, something in the man's lungs, was draining his strength so severely he could barely stand. Beauregard's condition had not been helped at all by the journey from Jackson, where he was still quartered. But summoned by Johnston, he had gamely made the journey, and both men knew that very soon, Beauregard would make the move to Corinth.

Their meeting had been brief, but already his voice was giving out, Beauregard lying back on a couch in the living room of the private home that now served as Johnston's office.

"I am concerned for you, General. You did not have to make the journey here in such circumstances. This meeting could have waited. I apologize."

"For what? My duty requires me to be where you require me to be. I am pleased to report that your army continues to be assembled as we speak. I congratulate you on the swiftness with which your orders were carried out. No retreat is a joyous affair."

There was a hint of sarcasm in Beauregard's praise, and Johnston tried not to notice. After a silent moment, he said, "I have believed for a very long time . . . that hope is God's gift to the young. This army still believes in our cause, and I am certain that the men who made the march from Murfreesboro still have the spirit for the fight. It is not so easy to share their spirit when one views this war through tired eyes . . ." He stopped, suddenly realized Beauregard was appraising him, measuring every word, a test perhaps, maybe even something ordered by President Davis. Johnston cleared his throat, chose his words with more care.

"Despite the condemnation of this army's performance by those who . . . well, those who were not *there* . . . no matter our past difficulties, we must do what the country requires of us."

Beauregard coughed, harsh and liquid, a handkerchief to his mouth.

"I am not here to replace you. Surely you are confident of that."

"I am not confident of very much these days. There have been mistakes made, errors by some that were out of my control. In my position, losing control is an error itself. There is much yet to be learned by the men in this command who are not accustomed to the stench of war. If God has given me any of that *hope,* it lies in believing that failures will be corrected." He paused. "Pierre . . . if I may address you that way . . ."

"Address me any way you please, sir. I am in your service."

The arrogance was unmistakable, but Johnston took him at his word.

"Thank you. However, your *service* is something we should discuss. I do not have to explain to you the outcry against my command, the lack of faith from the people, from the politicians, from many in this army. I propose . . . with President Davis's approval of course . . . that my command of this army be placed in your hands. Your work here has been exceptional, and I am confident that will continue. Beyond that . . . you inspire a confidence from our soldiers that . . . for some time now . . . I have not. If you feel there is greater benefit to this army, that you command the campaigns we must surely confront here, I will not object."

Beauregard seemed surprised, the handkerchief dropping away from his mouth. He stared at Johnston for a long moment, the sickness apparent in the darkness of his eyes.

"A most generous gesture, sir. In different circumstances, I could see us shoulder to shoulder, inspiring this army to great victories. But this is your command. I serve as I am called upon to serve, and now that you are here . . . by rank, and by the confidence of the president, this is your army."

Now Johnston was surprised. Beauregard coughed again into the white cloth, lay back, the effort behind his magnanimity seeming to pull the last bit of fire from the man.

"Can I get you anything? Water? Something . . . stronger? I do not keep spirits in my headquarters, but surely Mrs. Inge has something in the house. She is a most gracious hostess."

Beauregard shook his head, and Johnston watched him, didn't know what else to do. He pondered the man's words . . . *different circumstances.* Yes, if he was well, this might be his stage after all. But even he knows a sick man cannot lead a fight. And . . . the president does not like him, not at all. That must play into this. But still . . . the army needs this kind of man, needs something to give them more *hope* than I have done. Johnston said, "Your loyalty to this command is noted and I must say . . . appreciated. As an alternative, I would recommend to the president, with your approval of course, that you be designated as my second in command, effective immediately."

Beauregard reacted only with a weak wave of his hand, a slow nod. The cloth stayed on his mouth, the sound of labored breathing making Johnston uneasy. Beauregard made no effort to sit upright, said in a soft voice, "That will be most acceptable. Great good will come of this, I am certain of that. There are good men commanding this army."

Johnston nodded.

"I suspect that very soon, they must demonstrate just how good they are."

After the Federal victories at Forts Henry and Donelson, the withdrawal of Johnston's army across the vast Kentucky–Tennessee line included outposts that stretched to the Mississippi River. But one key outpost was too important to abandon, the crucial river strong points at New Madrid, Missouri, and nearby Island Number Ten. Both had been well fortified with troops and heavy artillery, and they were a formidable barrier essential to preventing Federal gunboats from sweeping southward to Memphis. In early March, when Federal forces pressed their attacks toward those strongholds, General John McCown had seemed to lose confidence in his own command, and had withdrawn his forces from New Madrid with what Johnston considered to be careless haste. Though the position on Island Number Ten was continuing to hold out against a relentless siege by Union general John Pope, Johnston felt he had no choice but to relieve McCown, and so, he replaced him with his own chief adjutant, Colonel William Mackall. Whether Mackall could fare any better would be decided by the ingenuity and power that Pope's overwhelming forces brought to bear. But Johnston's confidence in Mackall had come from years of service with the man, who was as much a friend as an efficient staff officer.

Mackall had served Johnston as far back as California, well before the war. Then, both men wore blue, and Mackall had kept his loyalty to Johnston even as the War Department did not. As commander of the U.S. Army's California district, Johnston had widespread and absolute authority in a place very far from the eyes of Washington. It had been a difficult command, covering territory that blanketed thousands of square miles, from his headquarters at Benicia, near San Francisco, all the way to the newly established border with Mexico, below the San Diego Mission. Much of the population of California was Mexican, most of whom knew little of politics, and why, in 1848, their flag had suddenly changed to the Stars and Stripes. The American victory in the Mexican War put California and most of the Southwest into American hands, and with the sudden discovery of gold a year later, California took on enormous significance. A strong military presence was essential, and Johnston had been chosen without controversy as the man for the job. But the election of Abraham Lincoln changed the complacency of many of the residents, including the newly arriving Easterners.

The angry talk of secession from the Southern states encouraged something of a rebellion among many of the locals around San Francisco and the smaller town of Los Angeles. Noisy voices and angry calls from newspapers and other ambitious leaders began to suggest that a war that would divide the Union might create an opportunity for California, that the state should look first to its own interests. If California seceded, there would be very little that Washington could do to control such a problem so very far removed from the spreading violence east of the Mississippi. Johnston was suddenly confronted with a stirring cauldron of unrest, stoked by the fires from ambitious political forces who longed for California to become an independent nation. Johnston made every effort to strengthen the army's presence, quieting some of the voices, but when Johnston's adopted home state of Texas voted to secede, Johnston was faced with a far more personal problem, one of conscience. Like so many of the army's Southern officers, he knew he could not continue to serve a Federal army that might force him to wage war against his own home. His resignation sent deep shock waves through California, but unbeknownst to Johnston, those shock waves struck harder in Washington. His statement of loyalty to Texas, and thus, the Confederacy, produced an aggressive response from the War Department, who sent General Edwin "Bull" Sumner to relieve Johnston as quickly as Sumner could make the journey westward.

Sumner's arrival was a complete surprise to Johnston, and there was talk throughout the army that Johnston had actually been arrested, rumors running rampant that after his resignation, he had begun some kind of subversive activity against the army. Despite the suspicions in Washington, Bull Sumner seemed to know better, and rather than treat Johnston as a scoundrel, he had paid homage to Johnston's long service by allowing him to leave Benicia on his own terms, as long as he left quickly. Johnston obliged, and the loyal adjutant, Mackall, had gone with him.

Mackall had now served Johnston as his senior staff officer all through Johnston's command in the new Confederate army. But Johnston knew that his friend's abilities and experience qualified him for a command beyond Johnston's own headquarters. Whether or not the defense of Island Number Ten would be successful, Johnston had complete confidence that he had sent the best man available to do the job. But Johnston was losing a great deal of sleep over the fate of the army Mackall would command. Island Number Ten was now too far upriver from any serious reinforcement, and thus was too far removed from the more immediate concerns facing the army at Corinth. And from all reports, the Federal forces laying siege were far too strong for Mackall to resist for very long.

S
ince his arrival in Mississippi, Beauregard had witnessed first-hand the pitfalls of assembling a scattered and disorganized army. Those men who had retreated with Johnston from Mur-freesboro were for the most part a veteran group, and behaved like one. But around Corinth, the assembled masses were a ragged bunch, tossed together from outposts that ranged from Texas to Georgia, from the Florida Gulf Coast to Arkansas. Discipline was not only difficult, in many instances, it was nonexistent, which had immediately created a serious problem with the civilians in every place the army was building their camps. Depredations against the population, which included assaults and widespread theft, had to be confronted, and confronted with a firm hand. The one man who seemed suited to the task had already arrived at Corinth. General Braxton Bragg had responded to his superiors' desperate call for reinforcements by marching his forces northward from the coast near Mobile and Pensacola. Johnston and Beauregard both understood that Bragg's reputation for ruthless discipline made him a perfect choice to take on the task of whipping the army into shape, often literally. Bragg was roundly disliked by his subordinates, and it was his passionate love of the stick and his willingness to execute the most brutal offenders in his own command that gave him his reputation as a martinet. But right now, with a patchwork army in a desperate need to face up to an organized Federal threat, Bragg's ruthlessness was exactly what the army required. As a result, Bragg was appointed as Johnston's new chief of staff, with the authority to bring discipline and training to the gathering hordes any way he could. As a carrot for Bragg, Johnston assured him that when the inevitable fight came with the advancing Federals, Bragg would be assigned to command an entire corps in John-ston's army. Even Bragg's lack of popularity could not diminish the greater need the army had for experienced generals who could lead so many untested soldiers into a fight.

ROSE COTTAGE, CORINTH, MISSISSIPPI
MARCH 24, 1862

They came mostly alone, the staff officers staying back, taking the cue from Johnston himself. Bragg seemed willing to take over the proceedings, sat at the head of the dining room table, reacted to the gathering with the same kind of straight-backed, unsmiling discipline he applied to the troops. But the four men present were the most senior commanders of the newly assembled army, and of the four, Bragg held the lowest rank. Johnston sat in one corner, a position he preferred, would allow Bragg to assume a mantle of authority, at least until anyone else chose to take it away.

Beauregard's illness had put him on his back again, and Johnston still worried about the man, had begun to suspect that the other generals were wondering if the Creole might ever recover, a missing link this army did not need. With the disasters already inflicted on Johnston's command, the army in the West had challenges far beyond Corinth. From Arkansas had come word of a new disaster, a sharp fight at Elkhorn Tavern, a place known to the Federals as Pea Ridge. General Earl Van Dorn had already been ordered south by Beauregard, to add his forces to those around Corinth, but the fight in Arkansas had been unavoidable, and so, as badly as Van Dorn's troops were needed at Corinth, they were now reeling under the crushing blow from the Federals and likely wouldn't be moving south for weeks.

The third man Johnston had summoned to his new residence was more than a capable commander. He was one of Johnston's oldest friends.

Leonidas Polk had long been an ordained minister, had climbed through the hierarchy of the Episcopal Church to assume the respected position as bishop of Louisiana. But the war had brought Polk back to the roots that Johnston knew well. Polk had been at West Point with Johnston, and the two men had maintained a warm friendship for all the years since. Though some had criticized Bishop Polk for what seemed to be a contradictory reverence for both the Word and the musket, Johnston never doubted that Polk would serve the Cause. Tall and handsome, Polk was always a serious and thoughtful man, and Johnston

believed that he would become one of the army's brightest stars. Johnston knew his army needed all the stars it could get. Polk was also the
only man in the high command who had fought and defeated the Federal commander they were now expecting to confront: Ulysses Grant.
That fight had taken place the previous November, at Belmont, Missouri, and though neither side could trumpet a major strategic triumph,
Grant and his three-thousand-man force had been outmaneuvered and
beaten back with a considerable cost in casualties.

As they found their places in the dining room of the home that had
become Johnston's headquarters, Polk sat to one side of the table, seemed
to position himself where he could keep a watch on Beauregard, shared
Johnston's obvious concern. It was another trait of the man Johnston
had come to admire, and Johnston could never look at the man's eyes
without thinking of Polk's genuine grief over the death of Johnston's first
wife, Henrietta. It was a time in Johnston's life that could never quite be
stored away, and Polk seemed to know that, would never speak of those
days, unless Johnston brought it up.

At the large table, Bragg cast a quick scornful glance at the prostrate
Beauregard, one hand pounding the table in a light drumbeat of impatience. He turned, looked at Johnston, said, "So, General, are *you* well? Is
the army living up to your expectations?"

It was a clumsy attempt to draw praise, and Johnston thought of a
phrase, a scolding lesson he had once given his son. *Those who fish for
compliments catch only minnows.*

"I am well, Braxton. General Beauregard is not so fortunate. But we
are here to address our strategic situation, and there is some urgency."

Beauregard let out a faint high groan, sat up, said, "If I may be allowed, sir."

Bragg grunted, but knew better than to object.

"If you feel up to the task, sir."

Beauregard ignored the comment, said, "As you all know, we have
received definite intelligence that the enemy is encamped barely twenty
miles from this very spot. We also received some word from one cavalry
outpost that the Federals under General Grant were on the move,
driving southward directly toward our position, which caused considerable concern among the troops. Fortunately, those reports were proven
false. But the enemy is most definitely in place, is assembling consider-

able stores of supplies and armament, and when General Halleck feels the time is right, General Grant will be ordered to advance. As I have anticipated since my assignment here, it is more than apparent that Corinth will be his target. I am not confident that we are fully prepared to meet him." Bragg grunted, and Beauregard still ignored him, continued. "Anticipating that the Federals would strike the railroad junction here, it has been my goal to assemble an army with numbers sufficient to defend this place at great cost to the enemy. That, at least, has been accomplished. There are other concerns, however, that should be addressed. The lack of proper armament for our troops is chief among them."

There was a light rap on the doorjamb, and Johnston saw Wickliffe, one of his staff officers, now an aide to Bragg. Bragg huffed, "Yes, Captain. Speak up. Important matters here."

Wickliffe had served Johnston far longer than he had Bragg, seemed to share everyone else's hesitation about dealing with Bragg at all. He said to Johnston, "Sir, we have received a lengthy and urgent report from Colonel Forrest."

Bragg turned toward Wickliffe, seemed genuinely angry.

"Forrest? He's, what, a cavalry scout? Now why would you interrupt our meeting to tell us of some scout? We have just been discussing the grotesque inability of our outposts to scout anything with any accuracy. They spread rumor as efficiently as they spread their horse manure."

"Excuse me, Braxton. I should like to hear what Colonel Forrest has to say."

Bragg turned to Johnston, seemed to clamp down his objections, shrugged. Wickliffe seemed relieved, said to Johnston, "Sir, Colonel Forrest reports that a patrol under his command . . . Captain McDonald . . . observed an entire division of Federal troops encamped at the Duck River, not many miles from the town of Columbia, sir. Colonel Forrest reports the troops were General McCook's Division. They were halted on the far side of the river because of our destruction of the bridges in that area, but are working to make their way across. A prisoner was captured, sir, and revealed much." The captain paused, seemed to swallow hard, nervous. "According to Colonel Forrest, General McCook's Division is the vanguard of a much larger force, sir."

Bragg sniffed.

"McCook? Several of those *McCook* fellows in the blue coats. Ohio bunch, right? What in God's name is so damn important about a bunch of Ohio infantry at the Duck River? That's a pretty haul from here, if I recall."

Beauregard coughed, fought to control his voice, said softly, "General McCook commands a division in the Army of the Ohio."

Bragg didn't look at Beauregard.

"That's what I just said."

Beauregard ignored the slight, said, "*Buell's* Army of the Ohio. The latest we heard, they were camped around Nashville."

Wickliffe nodded furiously.

"Yes, sir. That's what Colonel Forrest said. But no longer, sir. The colonel says they're on the move. Colonel Forrest stresses in the strongest terms, sir, that this can only mean that General Buell's forces are intending—"

Beauregard interrupted.

"They are coming this way. Buell is marching his people to link up with Grant. That's why Grant is just . . . sitting where he is. He's not going anywhere until Buell joins him, reinforces him. General Halleck is no lion. This is a major operation for him, and he's not going into this fight with one claw. He wants them both."

Johnston had said nothing, absorbed the seriousness of the young man's report, thought of Forrest. This is not a mistake. Forrest knows better. And it makes absolute sense.

"Gentlemen, our priorities have changed. General Buell has changed them for us. Do we know Grant's strength at present?"

Beauregard nodded.

"Thirty to forty thousand, maybe more. Certainly not less. Buell most assuredly has that many."

Polk looked directly at Johnston, said, "If Buell brings his army alongside Grant . . . they will be too strong. We can never hope to stop them." Polk turned now, the staff officer still at rigid attention in the doorway. "Captain, did Colonel Forrest report if the enemy had yet succeeded in crossing the Duck River?"

"Sir, the colonel's report stated that the enemy was having some difficulty. Colonel Forrest insists with utmost urgency, sir, that the enemy is delayed . . . uh . . ." He brought a piece of paper from behind his back, glanced at it. "He . . . Colonel Forrest says that the enemy seems to be . . . *bogged down*. But it is certain that their engineers are working to move their forces across. It should be the same all along the river, sir. We have known for several days that we were successful in destroying every bridge that would be of use to the enemy, and the cavalry patrols are watching any location where the river could be forded. The poor weather has been most helpful to us, sir."

Polk nodded, a soft smile, looked again at Johnston.

"Then God has granted us a marvelous gift. With the rains, He has granted us time."

Bragg seemed confused, said, "There is never enough time. Have you seen my reports? The disciplinary measures have only been partially effective. As for weaponry, we have a dozen varieties of muskets and the proper ammunition for half that many. We were promised artillery that hasn't been manufactured yet! Mules that haven't been born!"

Johnston stood, the burst of cold energy rolling through him, stood above them all, saw the soft smile still on Polk's face, the sharp eyes watching him.

"I have faith in your abilities, General Bragg. We all do. But I also have faith in Bishop Polk. You see this as clearly as I do, correct, my friend?"

Polk spread his hands, silent, allowed Johnston to explain. Beauregard was upright now, seemed energized as well, Johnston grateful for that. Johnston spoke slowly, chose his words, careful, precise.

"In every fight, we have engaged the enemy in a cloud of confusion and chaos. It is the nature of war, and the nature of these two armies. When we fail, it is not because the soldiers fail. It is because our *decisions* are made by generals who suffer that same malady, confusion and chaos. But we have been blessed with a moment of clarity. I believe I understand exactly what we must do. General Grant has been ordered to wait. Therefore he sits, waiting. And so, we will *not*."

Polk said, "What is the distance to the enemy camps?"

Beauregard responded.

"Twenty miles, twenty-two. They are spread out on a high bluff, wooded ground, many fields. For reasons I do not understand, they have encamped on this side of the river, just upstream south of Savannah. The place is called Pittsburg Landing."

Johnston felt his own breathing in hard short bursts.

"It is one more gift. General Grant has placed his camps with his *back* to the river. Bishop Polk, is this not a message from God? An opportunity?" He didn't wait for Polk's response, the flow of words pouring through him. "We will make use of what God has provided us. Before General Buell can march his army to join General Grant, we will *join* him first. We will strike the enemy where he waits, where the *opportunity* waits. We shall mobilize this army as rapidly as is possible, and we shall march to Pittsburg Landing. We shall attack General Grant, and we shall destroy him." He looked at Polk, saw a reassuring nod. "God shall have mercy on them, Bishop. But we shall have none."

## CHAPTER FIVE

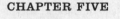

# SHERMAN

NEAR MONTEREY, TENNESSEE
MARCH 16, 1862

The rain seemed to come from the sky in great rivers, pouring over every surface with a rush of sound that reminded him of Florida. But the farther they moved from the river, the less he felt anything of the glorious days he had spent in the place where sunshine could cure the rainfall at a moment's notice. As they moved south upriver, the rain had been steady and driving, nothing to inspire the awe and wonder of a Florida thunderstorm. Those storms lasted mere minutes, blown past by their own violence, replaced by the blinding sun and crisp blue sky. Tennessee was nothing like Florida.

They had left the transports and one gunboat on the river, and Sherman led a column of infantry and horsemen inland, a probe several miles deep into the thickets and mud-coated roadways, places where even the rebels didn't want to be. There had been one sighting of gray cavalry, an encampment of men who were as surprised as the troops who stumbled upon them, and Sherman had given the sharp order for the men to get ready for a fight. But the rebels had scampered away, clambering aboard their mounts in a rapid retreat. The Federal skirmishers out front had reported back quickly that it was just a small cavalry detachment, and when the rest of Sherman's column eased forward to examine what had been the horsemen's camp, the Federal officers could see that all that was left behind were a few shelter halves, tin plates, a few bales of hay, and horse manure. The talk began, low chuckles from men who had nothing else to laugh about, that the rebels had been sent out here for punishment, some indiscretion that had earned them a campsite in the worst place on earth. Even Sherman allowed himself a brief laugh, had agreed that there was no other reason to put men so far away from any kind of comfort at all, camped in a sea of mud under ragged tents where no fire would burn, their horses tied to fence posts. The rebels had left one horse behind, a sickly sack of bones with an injured leg. Sherman had avoided studying the horse's misery and ordered it destroyed, a single bullet to the head, the only humane thing to do. To Sherman, the animals deserved more consideration than the rebels who rode them.

And yet the brief uneventful encounter had punished Sherman, the burst of fear he could not avoid. When the skirmishers reported the cavalry's hasty exit, Sherman had felt the familiar relief, that there had been no fight after all. But still the fear nagged at him, and he ordered the skirmishers to keep a sharp eye, that there might still be a mass of support waiting in ambush, the cavalry just a ruse. But they had seen no one else, and it infuriated him, drove him into a dark and brooding silence, a struggle against what felt like a quivering knife blade inside of him. In every ride into any place the enemy could be, the knife seemed to rise up and whirl through his brain, his own private torture. The cigars usually came then, giving him something to do with his hands, but out here, that wasn't even a possibility, the rain too engulfing. He gripped the reins hard with one hand, felt his fingernails digging into his palm, the other hand inside his raincoat, his fingers nervously twirling the brass buttons on his coat. The cigars were there, a bulge in his pocket, and he was tempted to try, but the rain was blowing straight into his face now, and he gave up the idea, took several deep breaths, saw the sergeant of the skirmish line again, another report, nothing out there, just mud and trees and the occasional farmhouse. And still, Sherman's fingers pulled at the buttons, couldn't avoid the hard relentless pounding in his chest.

"Sergeant!"

The man jumped toward Sherman's words, another quick salute.

"Sir!"

"Keep the men no more than a hundred yards to the front. You aren't doing us any good if you wander off. I want to know your men are doing their job, and that's your responsibility. Now move it! Keep them sharp. This is enemy country, and we know damn well we're being watched! I want no surprises!"

It was not the first angry burst the sergeant had heard, and Sherman regretted it, knew the man was a veteran, knew how to do his job. He wanted to apologize, held it in, not appropriate. The sergeant seemed reassuring, as though reading Sherman's odd fear.

"We're close up front, sir! They're good men! We'll be watching! With your permission . . ."

"Go on! Move!"

The sergeant scampered forward, his boots kicking up showers of mud. Close behind him, Sherman's staff officers said nothing. Like the sergeant, they had heard this before.

To the men who marched behind him, this mission was nothing more than an exercise in misery, ordered by some other general *back there*, whose boots were no doubt warmed by a delicious fire, a man whose primary duty was putting pen to paper, sending men out into some godforsaken place to make a glorious thrust into the enemy's land as though nothing bad might happen. But to Sherman, it was all bad. He followed the orders, of course, respected the man who issued them. General Charles Ferguson Smith now commanded this army, had been assigned to take over during the absurd melodrama that swirled around General Halleck's headquarters in St. Louis. After Grant's victory at Fort Donelson, what should have been a celebration had turned ugly. Instead of gratitude from his grateful commander, Grant had been relieved. Sherman only knew what floated through the army's headquarters, that Grant had been guilty of some indiscretion that possibly had its roots only in Halleck's mind, some fungus-like eruption of outrage that Halleck tossed toward his commanders for no reason anyone could explain. Sherman knew Halleck well, had known him since they were both green lieutenants fresh out of West Point. But that was too many years ago, even before the Mexican War, and now Halleck had been put in charge of the entire theater west of the mountains. If Halleck had some nasty little bone to pick with Grant, or took slight at something Grant had done, Sherman had nothing to say about it. He was only a division commander, one of five that had come upriver into southern Tennessee, who had little say in what happened back in St. Louis. At least, he thought, General Halleck had stayed up there. Marching himself into the field seems to be the last thing *this* commanding general wants to do.

General Smith, Grant's replacement, was one of the division commanders, had been chosen to replace Grant by both seniority and respect. He was an older man, had been an instructor and commandant of cadets at West Point, had taught many of the men who even now outranked him, Halleck and Grant included. Sherman held to one piece of optimism, that if Halleck was going to dole out commands to those who least offended him, Smith was at least a good choice for the job. But, to the men marching behind him, Smith was just another one of *them.* And so they marched through driving rain, across muddy roads, staring into the roaring violence of flooded streams miles from the river, using maps that said nothing of weather.

What his troops could not know was that Sherman was far more miserable and far more agitated by where they were, and why, than anything to do with the rain. Like much of Kentucky, Tennessee was enemy country, and out there, anywhere, to the flank, to the rear, those *other fellows* could be moving close, preparing the great assault, the trap. It was an infuriating panic he could not reveal to anyone, and if the staff knew what he was feeling, they dared not reveal that to him. As they rode deeper into the farmlands and dense thickets of black woods, his eyes focused into every opening, every ravine, every mud hole, anyplace someone could be waiting. No matter what the sergeant reported, no matter that the farmers had told them the enemy was miles away, his brain shouted out with perfect certainty that they would come, that his meager column would be swallowed by a screaming wave of enemy troops. He knew they weren't prepared for it, they had never been prepared, not in Kentucky, not in Virginia, and out here, the weather made them slovenly, slogging their way with minds focused on their own discomfort. It was one more log on the bonfire of his fury, that he couldn't grab every man, shout it into the faces, be ready! It wasn't the orders that drove Sherman's despair, nothing from General Smith. They were attempting to find a route that would take them close to one of the railroad bridges on the great east-west artery that led away from Corinth. So far, the farmers who had offered anything positive had said very little that would help, that the town closest to them, Monterey, was still too far from the railroad, and in fact, might take them right into rebel fortifications that spread out from Corinth. Sherman had let his staff talk to the civilians, the officers surprised that so many were willing to offer any information at all, only a few cursing these boys in blue for defiling their ground. But every moment when the staff and the civilians stood eye to eye, Sherman paid more attention to the land around them, the farmers' fields where the horsemen might still come.

I t had begun at Bull Run, a collapse of his own command that had certainly contributed to the collapse of the army. His unit had lost three hundred men, but it was more than the horror of death, of seeing the blood of men who followed you into the fight. For Sherman, that fight held many memories, none of them good, and his own collapse was the worst memory of all. Before the battle, as the army was organized and drilled, there had been all the boasting, the talk of the untested, men who thought of war as something far more fun than what they would find at Bull Run Creek. Along the march into Virginia, they were bolstered by the celebratory gathering of civilians, a vast parade of carriages, gaily dressed sightseers of grand old Washington, picnics and parasols and brass bands.

And then, they met the enemy.

On both sides there had been an utter lack of what General Smith would call *sophistication, disorder of the highest order.* There was very little to make a West Pointer proud, nothing that resembled the well-ordered display of soldiers, of *army.* To most of the generals, the battle had been fought by two great rabbles, driving into each other like hordes of savages. When the smoke and the noise began, the amazing eruption of artillery and musket fire, a great many of those men in blue who had marched to the battle with the proud air of soldiers had done what Sherman himself had done. There had been a fight, no doubt, but there had also been a collapse into panic and desperation.

It was the sounds that came first, and the smell of smoke, the sudden bursts of fire that ripped the air around them. And then came the worst surprise of all. The men who had been oh so proud of their uniforms were suddenly washed by the horror of splashing blood, the guts and brains of a friend, screams and dismembered corpses. As the battle joined in earnest, the horrors only grew worse, and those who found the will to fight stepped through smoke and stink and pieces of men, only to find that the men in the glorious blue uniforms had been driven away by the screaming hordes of rebels.

Sherman had been in command of a brigade, hundreds of men, but he could not lead them, had succumbed to the same panic and revulsion as the men who looked to him for . . . what? Rescue? Salvation? He carried that with him long after the fight, that when the enemy is there, death follows, and it is not clean. That horror had followed him to his command in Kentucky, when he replaced the hero of Fort Sumter, if anyone could deserve that title. But Robert Anderson had held out against Beauregard's artillery for three days, and so honor had been served, even if the fort was lost, the first great casualty of the war. But Anderson had lost some piece of himself in the effort, had become an aging shell of a man, and though he was assigned to command the increasingly dangerous theater west of the mountains, to Anderson's credit he knew he required the assistance of the younger, more able rising stars. Sherman's collapse at Bull Run was one of many collapses, and though Sherman condemned himself for his failures, the army, and Anderson, felt otherwise. Sherman was asked to join Anderson as his second in command, with headquarters in Louisville. But three months after Bull Run, Sherman's demons returned, and he began to believe that the rebel presence in Kentucky was a far greater threat than anyone above him could comprehend.

Calling for as many as three hundred thousand reinforcements, Sherman's panic became an unpleasant distraction, but when the newspapers latched on to the story, the distraction became Sherman himself. In the fall of 1861, he was granted a leave of absence by Henry Halleck, a generous move considering Sherman's loud and indiscreet claims of Southern military superiority. Though George McClellan was making much of the same show closer to Washington, Sherman's behavior was singled out by one newspaper in particular as a manifestation of insanity. Even with Halleck's supporting claims to the contrary, the story began to spread, and what could generously be described as Sherman's bouts with a deep moodiness, and a tendency to exaggerate the peril of his troops, now became far more dangerous to his career. But Halleck continued to support him, claiming that Sherman was more than fit for command of troops in the field, and Washington, so far removed from the increasing crises in the West, had no choice but to take Halleck's word for it. There was, after all, a desperate need for qualified commanders, West Pointers in particular, and so, after weeks of recuperation from the strain of his command, Sherman was put back into the field. But Halleck had learned his lesson. Sherman knew he would have to accept any command he was given, and Halleck put more distance between Sherman and those who sought his head. He was now subordinate to the more senior generals in the theater, Grant and Don Carlos Buell in particular. At the very least, Halleck assumed they could manage Sherman's talents while also keeping him under control. Sherman had learned his lesson as well, one in particular. He had acquired a healthy and vigorous hate for newspapermen.

On the journey southward, the broad, sweeping meanders of the Tennessee River had taken them past villages and outposts where people mostly stared out from the riverbank in silent boredom. At first glance, it seemed as though the people were oblivious of any war, as though the army in blue were just another casual visitor that passed along the waterways. But to Sherman there was nothing boring about the fat guns that pointed their black eyes toward the landscape of Tennessee, guns that Sherman often stood behind, as though guarding himself from some unknown weapon that might be pointed at *him*. The gunboats were necessary protection for the transports, which were heavy with soldiers who knew they were driving deeper into the heart of their enemy. So far that enemy hadn't shown the kind of fire that ran rampant through the hearts of their Southern speechmakers, the politicians and newspapers condemning these boys in blue to a fiery hell for their shameful invasion of sacred soil.

He rode with a slow bouncing rhythm, his fingers on the brass buttons, his brain aching for a cigar. There was nothing different about the countryside, or the dismal weather that soaked them all, and Sherman found solace in that, allowed his mind to wander. He thought now of Donelson, the final surrender, a very good day, and he remembered the prisoners, legions of filthy rebel troops marching away knowing of failure. It was the same kind of failure Sherman carried from the summer before, and he focused on that, thought, *we must know how to be leaders.* We give a man a musket and tell him to kill that boy over there, and if the man believes we are worth following, worth respect, incredibly enough, he'll do it. Damndest thing. The young . . . and they are so young . . . they'll do what a commander tells them to do, even if it's the wrong thing, even if they don't know that the commander is an idiot. If that officer panics and runs like hell, well, then it's over. It all collapses. The illusion of respect disappears. But you can't be surprised by that. That's what West Point is for, after all. Teach a man how to stand tall and give the order, and do it so those young boys will obey it. Not much more complicated than that.

No matter how many times you give the orders, you don't show them that you know damn well what's going to happen next. Doesn't matter if these boys are illiterate mudkickers or college boys. They'll still aim that musket and do their best to kill that scoundrel over there who might be trying to do the same thing back. And afterward, whoever took the better shot goes back to the camps, talks to the new recruits, tells them all about it, and so more illiterates and college boys pick up *their* muskets, and by damned, they get all excited, and can't wait to do the same thing. That's how a war gets fought. And by God, that's why you can't fall apart again. Making those boys pick up a musket and doing the job is a *good* thing, the *right* thing, no matter that a bunch of mamas back home think otherwise. Sorry, ma'am, but we need a big damn army right now, and there's no better way to make one than to gather up a bunch of boys and tell them how much fun they're going to have killing their enemy. Yep, that's how armies are made. We've got a good one, too. No doubt about that. The generals . . . well, that's a whole different thing. Damn shame. But by God, it won't be me. Not again. I can't . . . run. I can't.

He brought himself back to the rain, still the rhythm of the saddle, the horse's hooves slurping through mud a half foot deep. Beside him, the

engineer had come up close, McPherson, riding in sullen silence. They
had not expected the rains to continue, not for so many days, and Sherman knew that McPherson had something to say. Sherman waited,
thought, yep, I know just what he's going to tell me. No matter how good
our plan might be, out here, in this kind of mud, it doesn't much matter.
In this mess, even a good engineer's got nothing he can do.

Their mission had been sound, the orders definite, and Sherman
knew that General Smith had a pretty clear grasp of what was going on
around Corinth. Sherman's men had already made one attempt to shove
southward, up the river, several hundred troops on the transports, led by
Sherman's staff officer, Major Dan Sanger. That mission had been escorted by gunboats commanded by men who were eager to blast any
rebel target on the shoreline, but the targets were few and fleeting, ob-
servers and cavalry patrols mostly. The mission had been to drive into
Mississippi east of Corinth, hitting the railroad line at Eastport. They
knew there was a bridge, and if it could be taken down, Sherman's men
would slice a gaping hole in the Confederate supply line that the Federal
commanders knew was pouring rebel troops and equipment into their
growing strongholds around Corinth. It was similar to the tactic Grant
had used at Fort Donelson. It was one moment of glory that Sherman
embraced, knew that Grant embraced it as well. Days before, at Fort
Henry, the Federal naval gunners had earned perfect confidence that
they could destroy any kind of strong point the rebels placed along the
rivers. But Donelson was not Henry, and when the navy made their
grand attack, the results had been catastrophic for the same gunboats
that had been so successful at Fort Henry. It was Grant who had understood flexibility, and Sherman appreciated that, had seen that Grant
learned the lesson that had cost the navy so many casualties, and so
many good boats. Fine, Johnny Reb, you did good. Now try it again. You
point your cannon and your muskets at that big river, and wait for us to
do the same kind of attack. You might believe we're the stupidest enemy
in the world, and so we'll float up to your front door again, right where
you want us to be, and maybe we'll even stand up tall, hold the Stars and
Stripes high for you to see, give you another fleet of perfect targets.

Sherman had studied enough tactics to believe as Grant did, that the
best way to grab an enemy by the throat was to do it from the side, or
maybe even from behind. At Donelson, with a naval assault useless,

Grant had sent the troops overland, had hit the rebel works with a mass of infantry. It had worked, though Sherman knew what they all knew. The rebels at Donelson didn't just fold up, there was no mass panic, nothing of the inglorious retreat the boys in blue had shown at Bull Run. The rebel earthworks and fortifications had been planned with care, the wisdom that comes from a good engineer. He glanced at McPherson, wondered if he knew who the rebel engineers were, if there was a single man with good sense who had constructed Fort Donelson. Artillery-men, too, he thought. They had some big guns there, and some of their people knew how to use them, something the navy boys had learned the hard way. Sherman slapped at a whining insect that danced around his ear, thought, it was a tough damn fight, and they were killing our boys worse than we were killing theirs, but Grant knew he could bring in more, could keep at 'em, while the rebs had nobody else. It was good tactics and good work, but make no mistake. They handed Grant the fort because they had jackass generals. No shortage of those in either army, apparently.

Beside him, McPherson spoke for the first time in a half hour.

"General, with all respects, sir, this is as bad a mess as I've seen. Major Sanger couldn't get his people close enough to Eastport to do the job, and we won't do any better out here. Doesn't matter what route we take. Even if the men can swim across these flooded creeks, there's no way to take the heavy equipment, no way the guns or the wagons . . . well, you try to drag artillery across some of these overgrown ditches, you'll never see them again. Pardon me for saying so, sir."

Sherman had enormous respect for McPherson, knew the man had taught engineering at West Point. Every commander McPherson had served had allowed him to advance only with reluctance, no one want-ing to lose such a capable man. But advance he did, serving the Federal commanders in the West all the way to the top. The top now of course was Henry Halleck, but Sherman had been impressed that somehow Ulysses Grant had managed to convince Halleck that McPherson should leave those cozy offices at St. Louis, and come out here where the army was. Sherman had wondered why any good commander would think the best place for a crack engineer should be any other place but the field. He watched McPherson's gloom, thought, did Halleck ever think he might need a bridge built somewhere around his headquarters? All right, Sherman, no use trying to think like Halleck. *No one* thinks like Halleck, not in this part of the world, anyway.

"You saying this is a waste of time, Colonel?"

McPherson peered at him from under the dripping brim of his hat, his hand wiping water from his face.

"I am in your service, General. You want to ride further into these woods and wear out your men and horses in the mud, hoping we'll find some kind of magic passageway to someplace we can do some good . . ."

"That's enough, Colonel. You might be the expert, but I'm in command. Keep your sarcasm to yourself. I'd rather be anyplace else than wandering out in enemy territory on some nameless roadway. . . ." He stopped, kept the rest of the thought to himself. He turned now, held up his hand, the horsemen behind him knowing the signal, stopping abruptly. Sherman saw misery on a dozen faces, and behind the horsemen, the column of infantry, their brogans smothered by the soft roadway, their uniforms splattered with oozing mud. Sherman thought of General Smith, knew that their goal had been useful, important. But sarcasm or not, McPherson was right. He said nothing for a long minute, the faces starting to find him, no one showing a flicker of enthusiasm. Close by he saw Major Sanger, his aide, and said, "Major, we're not doing any better here than you did yesterday. Give the order. Turn these boys around and march them back to the river. Let's get on those damn boats and find a dry place to put our feet up. If General Smith wants that railroad busted up, he'll have to find another way."

SAVANNAH, TENNESSEE

MARCH 17, 1862

Sherman saw the festering wound on Smith's leg, the doctor wiping it with some kind of stinking ointment. The general was grimacing, said, "By damned, Treadwell, you might as well stick my leg in a keg of your Aunt Sally's corn liquor."

"Sir, I don't have—"

"Oh, shut up, Doctor. Just be done with it. It hurts like . . . it hurts. What more do you need to know?"

Smith looked up at Sherman.

"Someone's trying to do me in, Cump. I scrape my leg bone jumping onto the deck of a steamboat, and you'd think I'd been struck by lightning. Now it's all blown up and these doctors are flocking around me like pigeons on a parade ground." He paused, and Sherman saw a hint of fog in the clear, unsmiling eyes. "I do miss that, you know. Every minute of it. Lovely place, West Point. Lovely time. Young minds are the most fun. Nothing *closed,* no *conclusions* dropped into them like bricks in a flowerpot."

Sherman had heard this before, knew that Smith had been as respected and admired at West Point as any commandant in memory. It was something of a mystery why, now, he was outranked by a half dozen of the generals who had once been cadets in his classroom.

"I'm afraid, sir, I was more likely one of those bricks."

"Bah! I remember you. All of you. Worst thing that happened to *you* was that you missed out on Mexico. The whole lot of them learned something of soldiering there. Me too, I suppose. Scott and Taylor . . . good men, good generals. These young bucks learned from that, Cump. They learned about war, and they learned how to *win.*" He paused. "Get out, doctor. I promise, I'll summon again when we're through here." Smith waited for the doctor to leave the room, curled his nose at the smell from his leg that Sherman was trying desperately to ignore. "Got a message today from Halleck. Excuse me, *General* Halleck. He's had a change of heart. Or brain. Or his breakfast agreed with him. Whatever the reason, he's decided that General Grant is *not* an incompetent, lying, insubordinate fool after all. Didn't much matter that Halleck was the only one who believed that nonsense. But, the wire said, um, in different words of course, that Halleck has suddenly developed an unexpected dose of wisdom. He has reinstated General Grant to his command of this army. I am once again his subordinate."

Sherman absorbed the news, shook his head.

"Sorry, sir. You deserve better treatment."

"Nah. Don't give it a thought, Cump. Sam Grant is the man for this job. Donelson was his victory, big feather in his cap. That's what did him in with Halleck, you know. Our commanding general believes he can best fight our battles by sitting in a chair. Someone like Grant shows him, well, perhaps that isn't the best way. . . . Halleck takes umbrage, decides he better make it clear who's in charge. Grant's only mistake was not bowing down quite low enough. Maybe he should have wired Halleck a few more times, congratulating him on *Halleck's* glorious conquest." He stopped, cocked his head to one side. "You're friends with him, right? I don't wish to offend you, General Sherman."

Sherman thought of Halleck, shrugged.

"We spent a lot of time together . . . long time ago. Two lieutenants both too ignorant to know how ignorant we were. Fought like cats, feuded about half the time over something neither of us can remember. Best time we had together is the trip we took to Rio Janeiro, on our way to California. Marvelous place. We had some . . . uh . . . fun. I owe him a great deal. Might not be in the army at all if he hadn't put me back in command. I have made a few enemies."

"Yes, yes, I know all of that. He's your guardian angel, is that it? You spew out some amazingly stupid things to a newspaper reporter, and it's Halleck who keeps you from losing your career. I never really thought you were insane, by the way. Well, no more than the rest of us. Look where we are, for God's sake." Smith stared at Sherman's hand, fingers pinching and tugging at his short red whiskers. "You're a nervous man by nature. I've known that for years. But you don't know how to make good use of that. You get yourself all twisted into knots when you ought to be seeing the bright light of day. Halleck has confidence in you, I know that. Grant feels the same way. But . . . if I may say, Cump, you see too many demons in the shadows. This war is going to end soon, and this enemy out there is never going to stand up to our men, our officers, our guns. You have to believe that."

"You weren't at Bull Run."

"You're right. One fine mess. But it won't happen again. How many of you young bucks were in my classrooms? I know what kind of backbone you have, I know you'll learn from your mistakes. But the more mistakes you make, the more learning you have to do. Easy remedy for that. Stop making mistakes!"

Sherman didn't know what to say. He could see the pain in Smith's face, the leg shifting slowly, Smith unable to get comfortable.

"Perhaps you should lie down, sir."

"Yep, I'll do that. But you try to help me, and I'll kick you with the good leg."

Smith rose from the chair, shaky, his hands on the chair, keeping him upright, and for a moment he was motionless, his eyes closed.

"It hurts like blazes, Cump. Can't make it stop. They want to give me liquor, keep telling me it will dull the pain. A commander can't be in a fog, by God."

"Sir, you just said . . . Grant is in command. Take the liquor. Take anything. You're making *me* hurt."

Smith hopped on one leg to a narrow bed, lowered himself down with a groan.

"Ridiculous. I scraped my shin. This feels . . . you'd think I'd been hit with a grapeshot."

Sherman stayed back, watched as Smith struggled to lift the bad leg onto the bed. The leg was horizontal now, the effort past, and Smith seemed to relax, said, "Send the doctor back in here."

"Am I dismissed, sir?"

Smith seemed to come out of the fog, looked sharply at Sherman.

"No. Not yet. Forget the doctor. Your report . . . says we can't hit that railroad until the creeks go down."

"That's one alternative. In this weather we haven't been able to find a route suitable for putting enough of our people close enough to do anything useful."

"It's just rain. It'll pass. I've put Lew Wallace's Division at Crump's Landing, and sent Hurlbut's to Pittsburg Landing. The ground inland from the river there is pretty high. Hurlbut says there's a good bit of open ground, lots of creeks, but they're cut deep, so at least nobody's drowned yet. You encamp your division there as well. When Grant gets here, I'll make sure he knows why I chose the place, and from that point on, it's his decision what happens next. I'll recommend he put my division there as well. Plenty of room. Not sure I'll be able to go with the boys, but I'll try. I can't believe this . . . scrape my shinbone, and I'm a cripple, for God's sake." Smith laid his head back, stared at the ceiling. "Never thought I'd ever have any reason to end up in Tennessee. *Any* place in the South, for that matter. Oh yes, I remember, you actually like it down here. Forgive me for insulting your chosen piece of heaven. What is it you love so much? The swamps or the people who live in them?"

"I like Alexandria, Baton Rouge. Some good people there, good friends. I felt like I was doing some good with the military school. Used some of your lessons, by the way. Giving that up was . . . hard. But I couldn't stay."

"No, General, you couldn't stay. If you recall, those people decided to start a war against you. Likely your family wouldn't have been treated with much hospitality once you strapped on your sword."

Sherman knew Smith's mood was caused by the man's agony, didn't respond. There was no insult in the man's words. He admired Smith as much as any man in the army, and Sherman's eyes drifted to the bandage, a sickening bloom of red and yellow, the smell still filling the room, not all of it the medicine.

"I'll get the doctor, sir. Try to rest as much as you can. When Grant arrives, I'll tell him of your condition."

"I'll tell him myself. Go to your troops. Find them a dry place to pitch their tents. Keep your people out of the swamps. They've got some ridiculous creature, teeth and claws and whatnot. Eats people, I hear. You lose any men to that kind of nonsense, I don't want to hear about it. Alligators. Whoever heard of such a thing?"

"Yes, sir. I've seen them. You leave them alone, they usually do the same."

"If you say so. Now go on, get your men on the ground, set up your camps. We've got some time before anything happens. Halleck wants to make sure we gather up every soldier in a thousand miles of here before he'll be *comfortable* enough for us to attack."

Sherman looked out past the doorway, saw the doctor pacing, concern on the man's face. Sherman motioned to the man, a sharp wave of his hand, *here, now.*

Smith stared again at the ceiling.

"You're going to camp your men . . . where?"

Sherman felt a cold knot in his stomach, watched as Smith waved an arm, his mouth moving, no voice, a show of delirium. *Just a scrape on his leg.*

"You just rest, sir. My men will be at Pittsburg Landing."

## CHAPTER SIX

# BAUER

## THE TENNESSEE RIVER,
## NEAR SAVANNAH, TENNESSEE
## MARCH 20, 1862

"This thing's got hair on it. Still growing."

"Eat it anyway. There won't be another ration till we get into camp. That's what the captain says, anyway."

"Can't do it."

Bauer watched as Willis tossed the blob of white pork back into the pot. Willis had suffered already with the *camp gripes,* what every man in the company had endured at some point since their first introduction to the army's food. Across from Bauer, Patterson lurched forward, grabbed the meat, said, "Heck a mighty, Sammie, you gonna waste food, you toss it my way. Anything I stick in my gut's better than an empty hole. I hear the bellies of every one of you corn brains singing to me all night long. You gotta eat, keep 'em filled up."

Willis turned away, stared out to the shoreline.

"Can't keep anything *filled up.* I eat those damn crackers and they can't slide through me fast enough. All we've had to drink is the water out of this river. I can see things swimming in it. So half the regiment has been suffering . . . what they call it? Dysentery? Who thought that was a good idea?"

Bauer leaned back against the bulkhead, stared out with his friend, tried not to listen to Patterson chewing noisily on the lump of what was supposed to be sowbelly. Hair and all. Willis put his chin on the iron railing, and after a long silence, said to Bauer, "I gotta say, Dutchie, the wiry edge of excitement has done worn off. We been on this boat for four days, and ever since we left the Mississippi, this whole damn place is nothing but wilderness. A few darkies and trading posts. I'm still waiting to see something of this *rebellion* we're after. Startin' to wonder if the captain's lying to us, that the war's over and done. My pappy's last letter . . . he was hopping up and down about our *great victory* at Fort Donelson." Willis looked at him with sad, sick eyes. "I'm telling you, we missed it, Dutchie. The whole thing. They took so damn long to get us moving, all that drill and nonsense, too many days in St. Louis giving these pea heads time to find out how much fun liquor can be. I never knew there was that many taverns in the whole world. And those women."

Patterson interrupted through the half-eaten goop in his mouth.

"God's gift to the army, Sammie. Good for morale. Say what you want, but those ladies are happy to be showing off their patriotism. That's all it is. Devoted to the flag. Extra enthusiasm for these nice blue uniforms."

Willis looked back out to the shoreline, and Bauer said, "Just eat your sowbelly, Patterson. I'm not about to go dancing around with gals like I saw in St. Louis, or Cairo, either."

Patterson seemed to shudder, exaggerated it.

"Cairo . . . now I gotta say . . . you're right about those critters. The ugliest creatures on God's earth. Toothless wonders with black fingernails. And if that wasn't bad enough, every one of those gals had their daddy looking past 'em with a shotgun in his hand. They were friendly all right, but I met one . . . whooee, smelled worse than either of you two. But St. Louis . . . ah, now there's a place I'll remember. Not a daddy in sight. Might end up there permanent, when this is over."

Bauer turned away, saw Willis closing his eyes, ignoring Patterson's chatter, the turmoil in the man's gut too obvious. Bauer put a hand on Willis's shoulder.

"Maybe you oughta go down below. There's a two-holer right under us."

Willis shook his head.

"Nothing left to give. Just . . . knotted up. Hurts. It'll pass. Be nice if this loudmouth trollop hound would clam up." Willis turned toward Patterson now, who seemed oblivious, was scraping the metal pot for remnants of anything left to eat. Willis said, "How'd you get to be a damn soldier, anyway?"

Patterson looked up, licked his forefinger.

"Same as you." He put a hand on his heart, made an exaggerated gesture. "Told 'em I love my country. Love the flag. Hate secesh. Love Lincoln. Love darkies. And when I signed my papers the sergeant told me I'm gonna love fighting. He said we're off on the adventure of a lifetime. All we gotta do is carry a musket, and the army'll send us out on a grand journey to exotic lands."

"You three need to be below. We'll be pulling up to the landing soon. They're finally letting us off this tub."

Bauer looked up, saw the captain standing tall above them. Patterson said, "I even love the captain, pardon me for saying so, sir. And the colonel, too. With his permission, of course, sir."

The captain stared at Patterson, said, "Your mouth needs to be *closed* once in a while. Try it sometime. Now, get below."

Patterson snapped an unnecessary salute, still sat cross-legged, surrounding the round pot, thrust his fingers in for one more search. Bauer pulled himself up, one hand on the iron rail, Willis slower to move. The captain started toward the ladder that led to the lower decks, then stopped, his attention on the shoreline.

"You see that? Right out there. Makes my blood boil. That's why we're gonna win this war."

Bauer looked that way, a wide field of brown, fresh-plowed soil, and scattered across it, a dozen Negroes, most with hand tools, working the ground. Patterson said, "Told you, sir. I love the darkies. Come down here to set 'em free."

"Shut up. You see what they're doing?"

Bauer said, "Farming, sir. Guess they're getting ready to plant something."

The captain seemed annoyed, his point lost on all of them.

"They're *working*, you numskulls. And where are the white men? They make the slaves do the real work, while the *Southern gentlemen* court their ladies and drink their bourbon and fight their duels. All they know how to do. That's who we're fighting, that's the damn enemy. A bunch of coddled rich boys who don't know what a fight is. They're good at talking, good at rousing rabble. And those dirty devils think they can spit on our flag and tell the rest of us to go to hell. That's why we're here, and that's why we'll whip those devils before they know what happened."

Bauer had heard this kind of talk before. All throughout the training at the first camp, Randall, near Madison, there had been great bombastic speeches launched at them with much more flair and poetry than the captain's simple rage. It was the politicians who brought their flowery enthusiasm to the troops, men in fine suits who stood on cracker boxes and lauded the flag and the president and everything about the Union. Most of the troops had grown used to it, and after hearing so much of it for so many weeks, the more fiery the speeches, the more the soldiers ignored them. Some of the officers felt the same need, to encourage their men with ridiculous words. But Captain Saxe wasn't a speechmaker, the man mostly keeping to himself, doing the job, pushing hard for the company to learn its craft the army way. What Bauer liked about the captain had nothing to do with flowery words. There was an air of authority about Saxe, confidence that he was the right man to lead them. There had been talk from above, too, Bauer overhearing a conversation between two of the adjutants, that the regiment's commanding officer, Colonel Benjamin Allen, had already chosen Saxe to climb the chain of command as quickly as it could be arranged. As far as Bauer knew, the captain didn't seem the type to do the brown-nose campaigning for higher position, something too common in the growing army. Saxe had done nothing to show his men any more than hard-nosed discipline, was quick to punish the shirkers, and had little patience for the big-mouth louts like Patterson.

Bauer stared out at the dark-skinned men working the field, bare feet and strong backs, few of them paying attention to the long line of boats that passed them by. The captain was gone now, down the ladder, a last sharp command to get below, and Bauer started to move that way, made sure Willis was upright, could move at all. Willis suddenly lurched forward, vomited over the rail, and there was a curse from below, a brief chorus of laughter.

"Geez, Sammie, better get you down low. Maybe the doc oughta have a look at you."

Willis showed no acknowledgment, and Bauer knew immediately it was a useless suggestion. The doctor who accompanied them was the same man who had examined many of these men when they first volunteered. When their enlistment papers were signed, the first order the men received was to submit to a doctor's examination. Bauer had imagined all sorts of rigorous physical tests, coordination, strength. At the very least, the men would be examined for any illness that made them unsuitable for the long marches. Bauer knew he was healthy, had stood straight and marched into the medical tent prepared for anything they might ask him to do. He didn't expect to find the doctor most assuredly drunk, the man sitting shakily in a chair he never left. The doctor had told Bauer to stand in front of him and turn around once, then said, "Two arms. Two legs. You're a soldier."

Every man had been examined with the same result, and no one had been particularly enthusiastic when they found this same doctor assigned to accompany them south. When illness struck any of them, as it clearly had struck Willis, few of them even considered a visit to the medical tent.

Bauer kept the captain's words in his mind, had wondered often about the Southern soldiers, if the captain was right. If they're lazy, he thought, then this should be over already. Sammie might be right. They're not telling us anything at all. Maybe there's cleaning up to do, chasing down the secesh who are too stupid to surrender. Maybe we're heading for occupation duty, sitting tight in some city, keeping the citizens from causing any trouble. He waited for Willis, who began to follow behind him, one hand unsteadily on the rail. Bauer said, "I wonder if you're right. Maybe the big fights are over. There's sure a bunch of us, though. There's gotta be a hundred boats on this river. What you think we're gonna do?"

Behind them, the sergeant climbed up from the other side, gave the sick man a slight push.

"Move! The captain's ordered everyone down to the main deck. You boys thinking of hiding out up here, shirkin' off, you better think again! I'll bullwhip any man who doesn't show for formation. You hear me?"

Willis responded weakly, a sour frown on his face.

"I hear you, Sarge. We're going."

"Nobody in my unit on sick call, either! You puke again, I'll make you eat it!"

Bauer tried to avoid Sergeant Williams whenever possible, though of course, it was rarely possible. He reached the iron ladder, dropped down quickly, joined a packed crowd of men lining the deck, most seeking out their company commanders, falling into line, other sergeants doing most of the talking. Patterson was already there, and Bauer caught a glimpse of nervousness on the man's face, a glimmer of fear in his eyes. It surprised him, and Bauer was curious about that, if Patterson knew something. But there were no secrets on the transport boats, just rumors, a great many rumors. Bauer sniffed, thought, for all his talk, he's probably just a coward. I haven't seen a single thing we need to be scared of.

Willis was close beside him, pointed, and Bauer saw Captain Saxe, moved that way through the throng of men. The talk was low, urgent, a hum of expectation. Out to the right, another transport was moving up tightly against the bank, the black smoke rising in a thick column, drifting up into gray sky. Their own boat did the same, a grinding *thump* as the boat impacted the shoreline. Bauer fell into line, nodded to the man beside him, Graff, friendly, smiling back at him. Good, he thought. Graff's no coward. Just curious what happens next. Just like me. Graff said quietly, "This is really amazing, Dutchie. Look at us. Damn if we ain't an *army*."

B auer never needed to be reminded why he joined the army, and for the most part the rest of the boys in the 16th Wisconsin had joined for the same reasons. It was simple. What had happened in South Carolina, and then in Virginia, had roused considerable anger in places where politics had rarely been discussed. The emotions about the Southern rebellion made many of these men understand that their country was under attack, that what was coming out of Washington might be deadly serious. The threat to their country was becoming real and dangerous, and most of the men trusted President Lincoln. When the fights became bloody, and when Lincoln called for an army to stop the rebellion, the men who volunteered believed that joining up to fight for the Union was simply the right thing to do. Whether Captain Saxe was accurate in his description of the rebels really didn't matter. Bauer had never had any trouble accepting that the secesh, and the men who claimed to be their army, had to be stopped, even if it meant more of the bloody confrontations. Like most of the men in the regiment, Bauer had developed a healthy enthusiasm for doing his part, and so had suffered a nagging fear that whatever fight there might be, the 16th Wisconsin would get there too late to enjoy it.

Fritz Bauer had joined the army in his hometown of Milwaukee, the regiment assembled at Madison near the first of the year, finally mustered into official service as part of the Federal forces in late January, two months before. Like many in the state, Bauer was German, his father risking a great deal to escape the chaotic political turmoil that had spread through Germany in the 1840s. Fritz had been born on the sea voyage westward, and his parents had put every effort into educating their only child as an American. Unlike many of the Germans who now wore the blue uniforms, Bauer had virtually no accent at all, his parents adapting to their new country by learning and speaking only English, even in the privacy of their home.

His father was a sausage maker, had a small butcher shop in Milwaukee, the one throwback to the customs of the old country. On his first journey to the army camp, Bauer had been well stocked with a knapsack full of the kind of tasty provisions that had quickly disappeared. It was one of the first great lessons. No matter what treats they brought from home, they didn't last long, either stolen or bartered away. The packages came later, of course, caring families doing what they thought was proper to keep their boys fed, but many of those arrived empty, if they arrived at all. As infuriating as that was, the greater surprise was the food the army provided. The army believed in bulk and speed and the least expensive fare that could be obtained, and the men suffered for it. Bauer had his share of the gripes well before they left Wisconsin, and it fueled his sympathy for any of the others who suffered from the dysentery, the most common ailment they had yet to endure. His friend Sammie Willis had a double dose of agony, the boat rolling just enough to afflict him with the liquid misery from both ends of his body. There were others who suffered from seasickness, few having any experience with that at all. For the most part the rivers were calm, but to men who had never spent much time on a boat, any motion at all stirred up a surprising kind of trouble. Even worse than the rations, the fresh water supplies had lasted only a day, and the volume of traffic on the river meant slow going for the enormous fleet of transports, supply boats, and the gunboats that protected them. If they needed water, it would come straight from the river beneath them.

If the horror of the food and water was the first great shock, the second was the weaponry. The first muskets they were issued had been Austrian, a curiosity to Bauer. But during the few times they were allowed target practice, the adventure of that was instead a nightmare. The Austrian guns were heavy, unbalanced, and unreliable, and some of the most unfortunate found out they could even be dangerous. More than one finger and a number of teeth had been left in the soil of Camp Randall. But the frustrated officers could only placate the men by pointing out that other companies had been given a type of Belgian musket, which seemed to kill as many people behind the breech as it did anyone in front. But then came relief. Just before they were scheduled to leave the camp at St. Louis, the Dresden muskets had come, and for the first time the men understood that their colonel might actually have some real influence in this army. The reputation of the Dresden had spread long before the weapons themselves, and Bauer quickly learned why. The Dresden was comparatively lightweight, far easier to load than the Austrian pieces, and Bauer found he could actually hit a target without fear of the musket blowing apart in his face. Grateful sergeants passed along the praises of their men, a gratefulness that quickly rose up the ladder, Colonel Allen himself offering thanks to the ordnance department that someone in the army had finally shown some grasp of the obvious. If those rebels truly intended to fight a war, these blue-coated troops had best be equipped with a weapon that might actually accomplish something on the battlefield.

Though many of the new volunteers held on to their enthusiasm for a glorious rout of the first enemy they might see, Bauer and many of the others first had to absorb a dispiriting reality. Even with the far more reliable Dresden, the men learned what the veteran officers already knew, that passion for the cause had nothing to do with marksmanship. For the most part, their drills focused on maneuver, men shifting from column into line, responding to shouted instructions and bugle calls, and to Bauer's surprise, and the disgust of many, once they reached the army's vast camps at St. Louis, the men were rarely given much in the way of target practice. Most of the lessons with the Dresden involved teaching the men how to load them, as quickly and correctly as possible.

The officers understood, even if the men with the muskets did not, that there wasn't enough time to train these men how to hit a target. This was never going to be an army of sharpshooters. The tactics of the high command were based on numbers, that if enough of these boys were massed shoulder to shoulder in the face of the enemy, their sheer volume might have some good effect. It had been hoped, of course, that the rebel commanders didn't understand that principle as well. But that hope had dissolved, first at Bull Run, at Donelson, and just about everywhere else the two armies had collided. The rabble of this rebellion, those illiterate farm boys from cotton country who knew nothing of *soldiering*, had brought to the fight an alarming talent for shooting straight. It was the first lesson learned by the men who were now veterans, a kind of experience not yet a part of the 16th Wisconsin.

The regiment had gathered from every part of Wisconsin, many friends, brothers, old and young. Many were German, but many were not, and Bauer had made close friends with men from very different backgrounds. In the logic of those who knew little of European geography, Bauer was immediately tagged with the nickname Dutchie. It was common practice among the soldiers to devise the most creative and descriptive nicknames as they could. But the best Bauer could do with his friend Samuel Willis, was to stretch his first name to Sammie.

Bauer's father had been as supportive of Lincoln as many who had escaped Germany, and other lands where political chaos meant repression and a dispiriting lack of freedoms. The immigrants in particular held tight to a patriotic fervor, why this young nation's ideals had to survive intact. Bauer had no problem accepting the responsibility of joining the army and he shared that passion with most everyone around him. There were the shirkers, of course, the men who put on the uniform for reasons known only to them, reasons that had already resulted in the drumming out of the hard cases. There was supposed to be great disgrace in that, a ceremony that gathered the entire regiment as the man was forced to march past a gauntlet of drummers, sent on his way as a stark reminder that the army only wanted those who respected the uniform, or the job they had to do. But the officers had not expected there to be *so many* hard cases, many of them succumbing to temptations too easily available around the camps, mostly alcohol. It soon became apparent that if the army eliminated every man who failed to show some high standard of moral character, there wouldn't be enough men left for a fight. Though the most blatantly criminal were still eliminated, the drumming-out ceremony gradually faded away. Bauer knew, as did his ailing friend Willis, that the annoying Patterson might have been one of those who had barely slipped through.

"Line up! March off by platoon on my command!"

Bauer moved forward as quickly as the man in front of him, coughed through the clouds of black smoke, caught a single glimpse of Colonel Allen at the far side of the deck, waving the men forward. On the river alongside both sides of the boat, belching smokestacks poured out a dense cascade of stinking clouds, more boats than Bauer could count. He pushed forward in short steps, the sounds growing, not just voices, but machinery, the boats themselves. Out beyond their own vessel, the voices onshore were loud and official, and he saw the plank leading them down to the shoreline, a narrow strip of land squeezed tight against a tall embankment. Officers on horseback guided them to one side, a wide, sloping gap that rose up through the steep bank, a mass of men in some kind of order moving that way. He was part of a column, more horsemen pointing the way, and he began the climb, moved past clusters of officers, flags and aides gathered close behind them. He felt the jump in his stomach, not the agonizing sickness, but something else, excitement, could feel the strength, the great mass of blue troops driving up the hillside, like thick blue liquid pouring upward into a funnel. The bands were everywhere, close and faraway, a blend of discordant noise. He passed close to one now, a half-dozen drummers pounding away, a sergeant leading them in a rhythm that was no rhythm at all, and behind, men with fifes, squealing out something that had no resemblance to a song. But he was past them quickly, still climbing, marching alongside more lines of men, some from his own regiment, others, strangers, all moving in a dense mass up the sandy pathway.

At the top of the hill, the ground flattened out, and near the edge of the bluff he saw two log cabins, ragged and run-down, a meager sign of someone's efforts to make use of the high ground as a trading post. Beyond the cabins was a wide field, filled with unending rows of white tents. Up in front of the column, he saw the colors of the regiment, knew to move that way, saw familiar faces doing the same. The men on horseback were familiar, too, Captain Saxe, and now Colonel Allen, waving them out toward a wide roadway. The dense column began to divide, some men moving away in another direction, following their own flags on another road that divided the field where the tents had been pitched. Around the tents, men were sitting, small groups, campfires, some watching the new men coming ashore, others already used to it, men who had been there for days now. Bauer felt the power of that as well, the army even greater than he imagined it, more fields beyond, tents again, flags and blue uniforms, artillery and horses and wagons. The noise grew, more bands, and now shouts, different, not officers, but men in civilian clothes standing in front of open tents that were dingy and gray. Bauer had seen this in St. Louis, the sutlers, merchants who followed the army, who had some unknown ability to bring their wares and their equipment to places where every army would be. He saw leather goods, hanging on long poles, tin cups and plates, blankets and shirts and now, the food. The smells caught him by surprise, but it was no accident that some of the merchants were taking the time to fry meat, using their makeshift smokehouses, the astounding odors reaching men who for too many days had eaten nothing but army swill. Bauer felt his stomach rumbling, but the sergeant was there, the permanent anger, no one stepping out of line. Bauer saw an officer riding up close to one of the tents, his sword drawn, cursing the sutler, the argument growing. More officers joined the fray, but Bauer couldn't see any more than that, wondered if the man had the right to be there, or if the officers would just take what they wanted. In moments, none of that mattered, his focus on the men in front of him, the flag out beyond them. Saxe stared hard at the men in his command, the men marching away from the river, moving out into woods they had never seen, past ravines and creek beds, to find their own open fields and tree lines where they, too, would pitch their tents.

Behind them the empty boats were hauling up their planks, hoarse officers onshore directing the traffic, a continuing chorus of curses and commands, jumbles of orders for the boats to disembark, to clear the landing for the next in line. The men who came up the hill behind Bauer shared the same feelings, the enthusiasm, the excitement, so much anticipation for the *great adventure*. Some of the more curious turned to watch the boats, the flowing river nearly blanketed by the mass of vessels, moving in tight against one another, disgorging their men and supplies, horses and artillery. To the north, downriver, the procession was unending, so many columns of black smoke, drifting flat in a soft breeze, covering it all like a shroud.

## CHAPTER SEVEN

# SHERMAN

PITTSBURG LANDING,
ON THE TENNESSEE RIVER
MARCH 20, 1862

The ground was flat, dry, thick grass covering a wide field. To one side, the field fell away sharply into dense woods, and he saw men climbing up toward him, arms heavy with cut firewood. The camps of his division were almost complete, tents in long rows, most of them the large Sibley tents, capable of holding more than a dozen men. Already the fires were burning, thick smoke drifting with the wind, filling the treetops to the east. Nearly two miles that way, the river was still a massive logjam of boats, more men making the march inland. Most of them belonged to other divisions, spreading out in a pattern that seemed to make the best use of the geography. The open ground that spread west of the river was as General Smith had described it, high and mostly dry, sliced by ravines deep and shallow, some holding muddy water from the rains, some flowing away from small springs, clear clean water that the men found quickly. One of those was close to Sherman's camp, a choice location. Filthy water had plagued the men in every campaign, dysentery pulling too many men off the line, taxing the doctors, weakening the entire army. He had chosen his own camp near a small crude church, and there, among the patchwork of open fields, he had made his headquarters.

He sat high on the horse, felt the satisfaction of a job done well, the camp already organized, officers moving among their men on horseback, doing their own inspections. To the south, beyond a narrow thicket he could see flickers of movement, more wagons and white tents. It was another of his fields, another encampment, one of his brigades already marching out into formation, the drills under way. It was the one point he had stressed to his colonels, that the men must begin their drills immediately. It had nagged at him at first, that so many of his men were green, fresh troops who had never fired a shot at anyone. He had placed most of those men farthest inland, where the open ground allowed better room for maneuver. To the east, toward the river, many of the fields were still a chaotic mass of wagons and artillery, all the hardware of the army. Every division had its own contingent of cannon and cavalry, and so Sherman had ordered his own cavalry to probe out westward, searching for eyes hiding in the woods that might be taking stock of what this massive army had put in place. Sherman knew that the army's arrival at Pittsburg Landing had been no secret; there was never any chance that this much force could move through enemy territory without being observed. He knew as well that the rebel forces at Corinth, not more than twenty miles away, were increasing daily. It was the first report he had to make to General Grant.

THE CHERRY MANSION,
SAVANNAH, TENNESSEE
MARCH 20, 1862

"Any estimate of numbers?"

Sherman tugged at his beard, shook his head.

"We've been able to send cavalry patrols as far as the railroad, but they don't stay long. The rebels are out in force at every crossing, every bridge. What we know with certainty is that the rail lines are active. We've gotten that from the local citizens as well. There's a lot of bragging going on out there. Even the loyal Confederates want to crow about how badly we're going to be chewed up by their mighty army. One estimate said two hundred thousand troops had gathered at Corinth. One of the scouting parties, Major Pipkin, didn't give that any credence at all. We know who some of the commanders are, Johnston of course, and Beau-regard. Bragg is there, from the Gulf Coast, but Van Dorn is still a good ways away. The dirt farmers can crow all they want, but I doubt that any of those people, no matter how much they love their rebel flag, have any idea how many troops are down there."

Grant looked at Smith, who lay on his back, a heavy compress on the damaged leg. Grant lowered his voice, said, "You put much stock in this fellow Cherry? He reliable?"

Smith seemed highly medicated, the room still stinking of the com-press on his leg. He replied weakly, "Yes. He's a Union man. Questioned him myself for quite a while. Besides offering us his rather elaborate home for our use, he's sent a number of his servants out into the coun-tryside. They've been giving us pretty accurate reports of rebel move-ment, mostly cavalry patrols."

Grant looked around the room, scanned the furniture, glanced up-ward, seemed to appraise the ornate wainscoting high on the wall.

"Slaves, I assume."

Smith nodded.

"I assume so. Didn't really ask. He's wealthy for certain, one of the big landowners around here. Grows a lot of cotton. Well, I suppose they all do. But he's pretty upset by the war, and has no use at all for the rebel army."

Sherman said nothing, withdrew a cigar from his pocket, and Grant caught the motion, did the same. The smoke quickly swirled through the room, and Smith said, "More Union people around here than I would have estimated. The commander of the gunboat *Tyler,* Lieutenant Gwin . . ."

Grant nodded.

"I know him."

"He actually recruited some crewmen along the way. Seems there are more Union people in this part of Tennessee than we thought."

Sherman pointed the cigar at Smith.

"Not too sure about the wisdom of that. Spies can be a crafty lot. We need to question these people thoroughly before we let them that close."

Smith made a small laugh.

"Cump, the *Tyler* is sitting smack in the middle of the river. Unless those *spies* want to risk drowning, they're staying put. What kind of se-

crets are they going to reveal, anyway? We have boats and troops moving south? Every cider merchant in a hundred miles of here has already
set up shop somewhere between Savannah and Pittsburg. Tell you what,
you see somebody nosing around your headquarters, you do what you
want with him. I don't think we have much to worry about up here."
Smith looked at Grant, seemed suddenly to acknowledge Grant's authority. "If that meets with your approval, of course."

Grant waved a casual hand toward Smith, shook his head. He still
gazed at the décor in the room, fingered the cigar, kept his voice low.

"Impressive house. You'd think this is the kind of man who'd want us
out of his hair, let him raise his cotton and do what he will with his
slaves."

Smith shrugged.

"No answer for you, Sam. Two sides to every equation. Mr. Cherry
chose ours."

Grant glanced at Sherman, then again at Smith, rolled the cigar between his fingers.

"You think Pittsburg is the best place to mass the army? There are
other landings in both directions, plenty of room to maneuver."

Smith nodded groggily. Sherman had chewed on this for a while,
said, "I really don't think it's the best idea. If we spread out the five divisions . . . there are two more good landings to the south of Pittsburg . . .
Hamburg and Tyler. You've ordered Lew Wallace to hold his division at
Crump's. So why not do the same with the rest of us? With this infernal
weather muddying up every damn road, we ought to consider the advantage of using different routes toward Corinth, once we begin our operation. The roads do come together about halfway down to the rebel
position. We can unite the army on the march."

Grant shook his head.

"Thought about it. I want Lew Wallace where he is, in case we get
struck by a cavalry raid. We're vulnerable over that way, good roads that
could bring the enemy right up our backside. But the rest . . . Pittsburg
is a good place, and we should stay together." Grant moved toward the
closed door of the large room, opened it, called out, "Captain Rawlins!"

Sherman heard the response, closer than he expected, Grant's aide
obviously keeping close to his commander. Grant said, "You have that
map of the area south of here?"

The staff officer responded crisply, and Sherman saw him now, younger, thin features, a full dark beard beneath piercing eyes.

"Right here, sir. I would be pleased to show you the details. I've spent some time studying the terrain—"

"Not right now, Captain."

Sherman saw disappointment on the young man's face, a nervous tick to the man's hands, the same kind of habit Sherman had. Rawlins made a quick salute, which Grant returned, a gesture not necessary inside the house. Grant closed the door again, and Sherman caught the last glimpse of Rawlins's face, the eyes of a neglected puppy. Grant moved to a table, spread the map, and Sherman couldn't resist the question.

"Your staff officer been with you long?"

Grant stared at the wall for a second, seemed to weigh the question.

"Since August. But known him a great deal longer." Grant spoke more quietly. "He is no doubt aware of what we are speaking of here. I would not accuse him of planting his ear to the door . . . well, perhaps so. But I cannot fault him for his protectiveness. But he does . . . hover over me sometimes. Reminds me of my mother." Grant paused, was not smiling. "No, I cannot fault him. I need something, anything at all, he provides it. He provides things I didn't even know I needed. Right now, he provided me with his absence. Sometimes that can be useful as well."

Grant focused on the map, and Sherman finally saw the smile. Sherman said, "He sounds like the perfect chief adjutant. Sometimes, having our mothers in camp could be useful. Remind us we are not quite so . . . almighty."

Grant nodded, kept his eyes on the map.

"Try it sometime." Still focused on the map, he said, "If we may discuss matters at hand. You've seen this, I know. This whole area west of Pittsburg is protected by three major creeks, a natural defense, should we need one. Once we start the advance, we'll already be united, and Colonel McPherson tells me the roads are best out in that direction. Your reports said that the roads anywhere close to the river aren't suitable."

Sherman nodded, tugged hard at his own cigar, a cloud of thick smoke boiling upward.

"They're underwater, most of 'em. I gave up trying to put any force out toward the railroad. The only way we can make any progress that

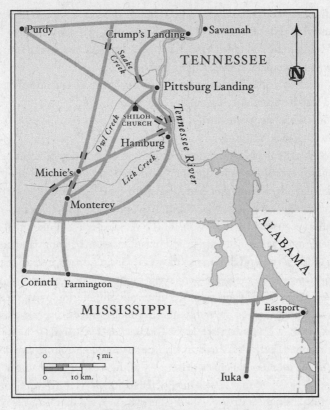

**CORINTH—SHILOH AND VICINITY**

way is with cavalry. We'll need more than horsemen to begin the assault. Artillery . . . well, Colonel McPherson will tell you, that's out of the question. What doesn't sink to its axles disappears altogether. This is the worst place for a campaign I've ever seen."

Grant rubbed his chin, studied the map, and Sherman tossed his spent cigar into a glass tray, brought out another one, stabbed it into his mouth. The smoke rolled through the room, and Smith seemed to perk up, said, "Cump, I've already told Sam, but you should know . . . I've recommended that William Wallace take over my division. My staff fought me on this. They won't accept that I can't just waltz out there and hop on a horse. Wallace is a good man. They'll listen to him."

Grant glanced at Sherman, and Sherman nodded his own approval.

Grant said, "Yep. Mexican War veteran. General Halleck had him promoted right after Donelson. I agreed with that. But, dammit, how long you going to be laid up? From what I hear, you stubbed your damn toe. How long you plan to sleep in this fine old mansion?"

There was a hint of seriousness in the tease from Grant, and Sherman felt a stab of discomfort, saw Grant hesitate now.

"Sorry. I know you're hurt."

Smith shook his head.

"No sorrier than I am, Sam. I'll be back on my horse as quick as I can."

Sherman could see affection for Smith on Grant's face, a slow, hopeful nod. Like Sherman, Grant had studied in Smith's classrooms at West Point, and Sherman knew that Smith had performed as well as any commander on the field at Donelson. At the very least, the ailment that had driven Smith to his bed was an inconvenience to the command structure of the army, and Sherman knew that Grant already had all the *inconvenience* he needed. He had every right to feel frustrated. Grant looked at the map again, and Sherman saw him staring away, seemed lost in thought for a long moment. Sherman wanted to speak, waited, allowed Grant his thoughts. Finally, Grant said, "I've wired General Halleck of my arrival. I've wired him of our troop disposition. I've wired him of my intention to attack the enemy at the earliest opportunity." He paused. "He wired me . . . wait for Buell. No attack . . . until we're *ready*."

Smith tried to sit up, struggled, Sherman moving that way, the older man scowling at him.

"Cump, I told you to stay the hell away from me. I can manage." He propped himself on his elbows, said, "I should advise you, Sam, that my orders from General Halleck were very explicit. I told him about Cump's excursion upriver, our efforts to wreck the rail bridge at Eastport. He approved that plan with one condition. He told us that we can make every effort to destroy any part of the railroad . . . *as long as we don't disturb the enemy.*" Smith's strength gave out, and he lay back on the white linens that draped over the narrow bed. "We succeeded at half the mission. No enemy was disturbed."

Sherman interrupted.

"Well, we did bump one cavalry unit out of their beds. . . ."

"Keep that to yourself, General. Halleck said . . . well, I just told you what Halleck said."

Grant let out a long breath.

"My orders are no different from yours. At last report, the bulk of Buell's troops are camped around Columbia, about eighty miles from here. He's on his way, but General Halleck isn't screaming too loudly at him to get here any faster than he's moving now." Grant sniffed, glanced at Sherman, as though cautious. "Took Buell two damn weeks to cross the Duck River. Not sure how long it will take him to reach us here. But General Halleck's orders are clear. We're not going anywhere until we're united."

Sherman caught the mention of rank, suddenly realized that every time Grant spoke of Halleck, he was formal about it. Well, he thought, he's being careful. Guess he's learned that lesson, too. Grant looked at him again, and Sherman suddenly felt he was being appraised. Grant took the cigar from his mouth, seemed to study it for a second, then looked at Sherman.

"Nothing I say leaves this room, you understand that?"

Sherman knew why the question was asked, stiffened, but he couldn't fault Grant for his caution.

"I have learned that talking out of turn is unwise. Nothing said here will be repeated."

Grant smiled, pulled hard on the cigar, smoke rising up in a hot cloud around him. Sherman was surprised by the reaction, and Grant said, "No matter what everyone else says, you're not insane. Just . . . stupid. I mean no insult by that, I assure you."

Even Smith laughed now, and Sherman absorbed Grant's words, still saw the smile. Sherman wasn't sure how to respond, wasn't accustomed to being the butt of a joke that hadn't turned out to be deadly serious. He tried to play along, forced a smile.

"I'm guilty of stupidity, but not every day. I promise you that."

Grant turned again to the map, the good humor fading. He used the cigar as a pointer, said, "Four divisions in place at Pittsburg. Good ground. Plenty of room to maneuver."

Sherman nodded, bent closer to the map.

"All good ground. Cut up with gullies and creeks, so there's plenty of good water. Open fields, plenty of room for drill. We're drilling every day now. So many new troops, worries me a little. But we'll get them in shape."

Grant stuck the cigar back in his mouth, Sherman doing the same, and Grant said, "You digging in?"

Sherman looked toward Smith, whose eyes were closed. Smith offered a weak flow of words.

"No. That was my order, and it came from Halleck. This is an offensive operation, and we're to regard it that way. I ordered no spades be issued the troops." He opened his eyes, fought for strength. "Begging your pardon, Sam, but Cump isn't the only division commander who's got a passel of new troops. Too many boys are nervous how they'll do, what the enemy is like, all of that. We hand them spades and pickaxes and tell them to protect themselves with dirt . . . well, morale will collapse. Not sure how much fear there is in this army, but if we show them *we're* scared what the rebels might do to us . . . it won't help. Like Halleck said, this is an offensive mission. Am I correct?"

Grant nodded, more smoke from the cigar.

"That is my understanding, once General Halleck decides we're . . . *prepared.*"

Sherman nodded, felt relieved by Grant's attitude.

"Exactly. I need my new men to learn more about fighting than digging a ditch. Right now, I've got every regiment on drill, every one of them, even the veterans. I just wish I had more veterans."

Grant turned from the map, stuffed the stub of his cigar into the glass ashtray, next to Sherman, who did the same with his second one. Grant noticed that, said, "Heard about you and cigars. Never seen a man suck one to a nub so fast. You ought to try enjoying the thing once in a while."

Sherman was surprised, had never paid attention to how fast the cigars disappeared. Grant said, "Never mind. That's your business. As long as you can keep a good supply of the things, doesn't much matter how many you smoke."

Behind him, Smith spoke up, still the weak voice.

"Does everything like that. Most nervous man I've ever seen. Heaven forbid he runs out of cigars. He'll tear every hair out of his head, pull every button off his coat. Just make sure when the fight starts, he doesn't spur his horse so hard he ends up a half mile in front of his men."

Grant smiled, but it faded quickly, and Sherman knew the talk that had spread through the army, the jokes losing their humor, especially to him. It was inevitable that the stain against him from the newspaper

stories would be slow to fade away, and if his reputation was to be res-
cued, no one could do that but him. He fought with his own demons
every day, and even now kept a scouting patrol in the woods out beyond
the camp of his division, one more precaution against any surprise
by the enemy. But the teasing, the ridicule was infuriating to him, far
more than it embarrassed him. Even now he wanted to protest, but he
knew that Smith respected him, and Sherman had sensed nothing from
Grant that felt any different. Grant had demons of his own, mainly the
one who sat in a plush office in St. Louis. Sherman could see the strain
on Grant's face, despite the glimpses of good humor, and Sherman
couldn't help but like the man. There was something to be admired in a
man who made every effort to stand tall while suffering under the thumb
of a martinet like Halleck, a man who believed in no one's abilities but
his own, whose jealousies toward anyone else's success had done nothing but create discord and confusion throughout his command.

Sherman had discovered to his dismay that he had one thing in common with Halleck. They both suffered from an unreasonable fear of the
enemy. Halleck's orders seemed to show clearly that he suffered that
agony even now, but Sherman had pushed himself to fight that, had
been helped considerably by the surprising thoroughness of the rebel
retreat. Johnston's withdrawal out of Kentucky and most of Tennessee
had offered a kind of comfort to Sherman that far outweighed the morale boost for the rest of the Union command. Since Grant's victory at
Donelson, that enemy had seemed to grow considerably more benign,
and now, their strengthening defenses at Corinth was a clear sign that
the rebels must surely believe what Sherman believed himself, that no
earthworks could hold back the kind of strength the Federal armies
were assembling. One more great fight could end the war. There was
nothing about that to drag Sherman back into the dark misery of his
own panic. For the first time since the war began, Sherman began to feel
comfortable with the spreading disdain the others felt toward these rebels, and he felt the same impatience he knew Grant carried, and Smith,
and maybe Don Carlos Buell. If Halleck would just give the order, the
operation would be spectacular, a victory that would secure Halleck's
reputation, and the rest of them as well. Why Halleck seemed so uncertain of that was a puzzle that Sherman had to ignore. He would, ultimately, do what he was told.

PART TWO

# IMPATIENCE

# CHAPTER EIGHT

# BAUER

FOUR MILES SOUTHWEST OF
PITTSBURG LANDING
MARCH 28, 1862

With so many fresh troops disembarking from the transports at Pittsburg Landing, Grant had to confront the challenge of just how to organize such a flood of new volunteers. Every division in his command had more than their fair share of these untried soldiers, a situation that any senior commander had to take seriously. None of the division commanders knew how these men would react the first time they confronted the enemy. With so many new volunteers arriving at the encampments, Grant made the decision to take some of that pressure away from the five existing divisions of his army. Those divisions, under Sherman, Lew Wallace, Stephen Hurlbut, John McClernand, and the injured Smith, whose troops were now under William Wallace, were to be supplemented by the addition of a new division altogether. On March 26, Grant received approval from Halleck to create a sixth division under his command, led by Benjamin Prentiss. Prentiss was not a West Pointer but had caught the eye of the army's high command during the Mexican War, serving primarily under Zachary Taylor. Months before, as the Confederates solidified their lines across Tennessee and Kentucky, Grant had placed Prentiss in command of the fortifications at Cairo, Illinois, at the crucial junction of the Mississippi and the Ohio rivers. Though the rebels had not made any serious move against Cairo, it was a vulnerable target, and Grant had never doubted that Prentiss was the man for the job.

Prentiss was a Virginian by birth, something no one in the high command seemed overly concerned about, even if some newspapers grumbled. But those papers had also grumbled about General George Thomas and the original general in chief, Winfield Scott, Virginians as well. None of those men had seemed as conflicted as many of the Confederates when it came to the passionate loyalty to their home states. Like Thomas, Scott, and several other Southern-born men of rank, Prentiss had never agonized over his oath as an officer in the Federal army. Prentiss's conflict had been eased considerably, since well before the war, he had relocated his own residence to Illinois. With competent commanders a critical need for the Federal army that had lost so many good men to the South, Grant had considered Prentiss to be one of the best men available to him.

The biggest concern Prentiss would have was the same concern shared by every one of Grant's division commanders. With so many new troops in the field, it was essential to impart as much discipline and training into these new men as they could. It was the one blessing of Halleck's frustrating delay in ordering the final advance against Corinth. At least with the camps now well established west of Pittsburg Landing, the men would have plenty of time to learn how to behave like an army. Whether they would behave as well under fire was something Grant would have to find out later.

They stood shoulder to shoulder in long rows, more rows close behind them. Out front, Bauer could see Colonel Allen, sitting upright on his horse, staring out with the stoic look of a man trying to show confidence in those men in the formation who were his own. Beside Allen, three other colonels, regimental commanders, sat silently on their own horses, each man seeming to sit more straight than the man beside him. After several minutes, Bauer saw movement through the trees, and another officer appeared, riding in a slow procession, trailed by a staff of a half-dozen men. Along the line, a few men were speaking, low voices mostly, the gathering of brass having the intended effect, keeping most of the troops orderly and, hopefully, atten-tive. The newly arrived staff officers moved to one side, clustered together with the staffs of the other regimental commanders, and now the new man rode forward, gave brief greetings to the four colonels, who kept their horses in rigid formation. Bauer had heard so many speeches that one more didn't inspire much more than vague curiosity. But this was the first time since they had left the Tennessee River that any senior of-ficer had taken the time to talk to them at all.

Bauer had noticed another difference from the usual assemblies. There were no civilians present, something others around him were noticing as well. Newspaper reporters seemed always to find their way to the camps, the senior officers paying them more gracious attention than they seemed to pay the men in the ranks. But no reporters were there. The newly arrived officer stepped his horse carefully toward the lines of troops, stopped a few feet from the front rank. Bauer could see his face, a good deal younger than Colonel Allen, who Bauer knew to be in his fifties. This man had a thick, compact beard on his chin, curled hair that flowed from his hat just down over his ears, and Bauer could see now that even on horseback, the man was huge, thick-waisted, even his horse larger. The youthfulness in his face didn't show any sign that he outranked any of the others, but clearly the man carried some authority that held the regimental commanders in their place. Behind the man, a single staff officer rode up close, shouted out, "Attention, Brigade!"

Beside Bauer, Willis said in a whisper, "When did we join a brigade?"

The men were mostly silent, and the staff officer spun his horse in a neat twirl, withdrew to merge in with the other aides. Bauer focused on the man close to him, could see the officer's shoulder straps, a silver eagle, felt disappointed.

"Not even a general. Thought they were gonna bring us Grant."

Willis shrugged, and they both waited, as the officer seemed to take a deep breath, preparing himself. Willis said, "Here comes the speech."

"Hush up."

"Gentlemen, I am Colonel Everett Peabody, until recently the com-mander of the 25th Missouri Regiment of Volunteers, those men down on the right flank of this formation." Peabody paused, waited for the inevitable cheer that rose up from that end of the line. The cheers faded quickly, and Peabody continued. "I am most honored to have been placed in command of the First Brigade of the newly organized Sixth Division of General Grant's Army of the Tennessee. That division, and all of you, are now under the command of Brigadier General Benjamin Prentiss. General Prentiss offers you his respects, and is now meeting with General Grant and the other division commanders, finalizing the organization of this army. The First Brigade standing before me now is composed of my own 25th Missouri, the 21st Missouri, the 12th Michigan, and the 16th Wisconsin. Many of you men have never served alongside . . . well . . . anyone. Certainly not men outside your own state. That will change. I have no doubt, and I share the confidence of General Prentiss, that you will make your mark on the reputation of this army, and of your country. Those of you who have stood tall against the enemy understand that the rebel is a man without dignity, without honor, a man who is fighting to destroy this grand nation, to soil our flag under the boot heel of an ungodly rebellion. With the blessing of Almighty God, we shall crush this rebellion, and reunite this nation under our beloved flag. If any man here is not confident of that, if any man here does not feel he is superior to the enemy he will face . . . there is no place for you in my command. For now, as we await our marching orders, your duty is here, in these fields. Your regimental commanders and their subordinates will be instructing you on the proper art of war. Learn those lessons well. We stand today on ground that the enemy claims solely as his own. We are said to be invaders of his sacred soil. He is only partially correct. This is sacred soil. It is American soil. And no man shall stand in our way as we raise the Stars and Stripes on every flagstaff in this land. Gentlemen, return to your camps. You are dismissed."

P atterson sat across the fire from Bauer, stabbed the low flames with the point of his bayonet, said, "Not much of a speech."

Bauer stuck a small log into the heat of the fire, watched as Patterson poked at the food on a tin plate, stuffed it into his mouth. Willis emerged out of the darkness, carried more firewood, others doing the same, the fires stretching across the field in a long row. Willis dropped the wood into a diminishing pile a few feet away from the fire, and Bauer looked at Patterson, said, "That speech was just fine. Short. Told us what we needed to know, what we already knew. That's what those speeches are for. Keeps us from forgetting why we're here."

Willis sat down heavily next to Bauer, held up his hands toward the fire.

"You're both pea brains. You're wearing a blue uniform. You have a musket and a bayonet. Somebody have to explain to you why you're here? Best part of the whole thing was watching the colonel sit out there trying to pretend he was proud of us."

Patterson sniffed, tested the hot point of the bayonet with the tip of his finger.

"They should have made me an officer. Told 'em I know how to do everything they needed. I can fix things, I can ride a horse, mule, anything else they'd need me to do. I know how to write, and I bet I can make a pretty good speech, too. Used to stand up in Sunday school and the whole lot would stare at me like they were in the presence of the angels."

Willis and Bauer stared at the man in silence, and after a long moment, Willis said, "Only angel that'll have anything to do with you is the one who's with your wife right now." He softened his voice, thick with sarcasm. "Watching over her, keeping her safe, all those long nights . . ." He spoke louder now, anger spilling into his words. ". . . when her big-mouth husband is off pretending to be a soldier."

Patterson never seemed to be affected by the harshness of Willis's jabs, ignored this one as well, a surprise to Bauer. Bauer could feel Willis's heat, knew there had been a letter the week before that Willis had taken badly, something from home he wouldn't share, not even with Bauer. As the days in camp grew more boring, Willis's anger seemed to leak out, squeezed from inside, often aimed at Patterson, or anyone else who deserved a hard knock. He had even spouted off to the sergeant, a thoroughly bad idea, the result a heavy blow from Williams's right hand that had given Willis a truly impressive black eye. But Willis didn't seem chastened. Bauer had rarely received a jab directed toward him, and when they had come, he tried to see the humor in it, realized that Willis was usually right about someone's jackass behavior, even if he spoke up about it too often. But the letter had changed him, made him more fiery, and more indiscreet, and Bauer continued to wait for the right time to talk about it, hoped that sooner or later Willis would confide in the best friend he had.

Bauer had always been the peacemaker, felt the need for that now.

"Look, they made officers out of people that got here first. Right? The bigwigs in every town who brought us all together. Besides, you can't have a whole army of officers. Somebody's gotta be out here to do the trigger pulling." He looked at Willis. "Sammie, I bet they make you a lieutenant before this is over. Then you can bless somebody out, and it'll be official. Like to see the sarge's face if they put a lieutenant's strap on your shoulder."

He laughed, Patterson ignoring him, Willis nodding, easing away from whatever bad place he had gone. Bauer continued.

"Besides, if somebody decides Patterson needs to ride an army mule . . . he'll smell worse than he does now."

Patterson continued to ignore him, oblivious, said, "I bet I could sit down with General Grant . . ."

Willis leaned back, his head settling in the grass.

"Oh, for God's sake. How did this mush brain get into the army?"

Willis rubbed his stomach, and Bauer said, "You doing better? You haven't been talking about it."

"My belly's calmed down. Ain't had to scramble my pants down all day."

Bauer had noticed that Willis seemed to feel better, the problems with the camp gripes easing off. There had been too many others who had succumbed to the sickness, and some of those had simply vanished, no word coming whether they were being tended to on the boats, or maybe just . . . gone. Bauer knew he had been lucky so far, tried to avoid drinking any water he couldn't see through.

"Glad to hear it, Sammie. You were giving me some worry."

Willis reached over, a quick slap on Bauer's shoulder.

"Don't worry about me, Dutchie. Just gotta get used to this grub they're feeding us."

Across the fire, Patterson stood, said, "I'm plenty used to it. Gonna get me some more. Pretty tasty. Whole lot better than what they gave us on the boat. I got one good idea, though. They oughta take these crackers, this hardtack, and stick it on those gunboats out there. Make the best armor, whole lot tougher than that iron they're using. See? Told you. General Grant could use somebody on his staff with good sense."

Bauer watched him leave, saw several others at the next fire doing their best to eat whatever had been ladled onto their tin plates. No one seemed to share Patterson's enthusiasm. Willis watched Patterson as well, said, "Quickest way I know of to lose this war: put that jack hole in charge of something. He actually likes this grub. The hog swill they gave us on the boats could have killed all of us, but this stuff . . . not sure it's that much *better*. Raw rice and raw beans? Every damn meal's the same. How much of this swill they expect us to eat? I bet the enemy's got it a whole lot better. They're close to home. Got their mamas making corn-pone or turnip stew, or whatever those secesh call food. Who can eat this stuff?"

Bauer had already forced down as much of the tasteless meal his stomach could take, said, "My mother used to make white bean soup. Best stuff you ever had, especially in winter. Warm you all the way down. She really knows how to cook. Miss that."

Willis seemed to mellow, sat up again, stared at the fire.

"I've had the best soup on this earth, same thing, white beans. My grandmother made it for us. Big pieces of ham, and thick soft bread. Soak it up like a pillow, stuff my gut so full I couldn't move for hours. My wife could cook pretty good, too. Probably still does." Willis choked off his words, sat in silence. Around them, the hum of the camp was quieting, another day of drill and marching passing under a darkening sky. Bauer stared out to the row of fires, a neat line in a wide corridor between the tents, reflections on a hundred faces, the tents stretching far across a flat field, great white cones in neat rows, more fires, more men. There was a curious beauty to that, and Bauer stared at the flames, the straight rows a testament to the precision drilled into them by the army. He looked over at Willis, who was staring down at his half-eaten meal, his tin plate sitting crookedly in the grass.

"This stuff is just plain raw. It can't be that hard to be a cook. Just boil the stuff for a while. Who can eat crunchy beans? Rice and raw beans ain't fit for anything but hogs. Maybe the artillery boys can use the stuff. Fire it at the enemy. Those beans'll do more damage than any canister. Maybe it *is* canister. I bet it'll blow a ragged hole in my guts before the morning."

To one side, Bauer saw Sergeant Williams scraping the last of his meal from his plate, saw the same scowling menace on the man's face he always saw. Bauer leaned closer to Willis, still wanted to lift the man's spirits, hoped he would talk about the letter, what kind of news he had gotten from home.

"You think anybody ever writes to the sarge? I can't believe any woman would have anything to do with him. Just a scoundrel."

Willis shrugged, didn't look that way.

"Leave him be. Maybe his wife's as mean as he is. Maybe meaner. Maybe she kicks him in the ass every chance she gets. Maybe right now she's off with some jack hole bank clerk, and he knows it. Probably why he hates us. Hates everything. Mail call ain't always what it's cracked up to be."

Bauer didn't have a response. To everyone but Willis, the mail call was the most revered custom they had, every man rushing to the wagons, canvas bags dumped out, a mad scramble for the sergeants to read out the names scrawled on the envelopes. Willis hadn't received a single letter in more than a week, but Bauer had a half-dozen, kept them in his coat. They came from both his father and mother, and with nothing in the newspapers of any confrontations anywhere near Bauer, the letters were light and newsy, full of gossip and good wishes, mostly encouragement from his father, stern scolding about obeying the officers, learning the drill, being the *right kind* of soldier. His mother kept her fears between the lines, and his letters to her had helped that, long pages written to her on the steamboats of the mundane voyage, the awful food. Now he wrote her of the camp, about Willis and Patterson, and some of the others, all of it positive. On every page, he made a point of telling her that there were no rebels, no threats, nothing but woods and water, miserable weather and bad food. He made jokes of it, and it seemed to work, the anxious fears in her letters tempered now, her writing more about gossip, more about *when he came home.* So far, he had been mostly honest with her, nothing yet in his army experience that had been anything but a mundane and curious adventure. No matter what might have happened anywhere else in this war, the men who commanded this regiment had seemed perfectly happy to make life as routine and miserably boring as they could. From Madison to St. Louis to the long voyage on the wide, muddy river, it was still a strange dream. Now, in camp once again, the dream had not changed, all these men in their blue uniforms sitting out in some open field in some strange place no one had ever been before. He had already accepted Willis's pessimism that the war would end without him ever actually seeing a rebel soldier.

To the side, at another fire, Sergeant Williams suddenly rose, stretched, still the nasty scowl, looked at the men around him as though seeking someone to torment. Willis dumped his plate into the fire, and Bauer whispered, "I bet that's why the sarge is so evil. He's eaten a whole lot more of this hog feed than we have. It's ruined his brain."

Willis rubbed his stomach, said, "Nah. He was just born evil. Even the officers are scared of him. Never heard anyone give him an order that didn't sound like it had a *please* attached to it."

Bauer laughed silently, the fire bringing on a comfortable sleepiness. He shed the coat, the thick wool hot from the fire, and now the sergeant was there, had seemed to creep up on them.

"You getting ready for bed, Private? You want me to help you with your nightshirt? Fluff up your pillow for you?"

Bauer felt the usual fear, closed his eyes for a brief second, didn't let Williams see that.

"No, Sarge. Just warm."

"Well, soldier, looks to me like you're grabbing too much of that good warm fire for yourself. So I tell you what. You need to clear out of the way, so the rest of these boys can get as *cozy* as you. The lieutenant from B Company has ordered a guard detail to move out in those woods. He's already chosen a dozen men to form a picket line. But I'm gonna offer him one more. So grab your musket and get moving. You fall asleep out there and I'll have you bullwhipped."

Bauer slumped, slid the coat back around his shoulders.

"Right away, Sergeant."

"Hold on, jackleg. The password out there is *pisspot*. In the dark, you forget that, and somebody'll shoot you. Or maybe that's not the password. Maybe I got it wrong. Well, that's not really my problem. I'm gonna be sound asleep and I'm gonna use your bedroll. That way, I ain't gotta go outside to use the latrine."

Bauer stood, had heard that kind of crude threat before.

"Yes, Sergeant."

There was nothing else to say, and Bauer knew it always went like this, that no matter the duty, Williams would make it as miserable as he could. It was just the man's way of having *fun*. He went to the stacked

muskets, pulled his away carefully, saw several men moving out into the
darkness, the others assigned to the picket line. He followed, knew the
musket wasn't loaded yet, but the other men were already at the tree line,
dropping down into total darkness, and it was no place for a man to get
lost. He hurried his steps, thought, I'll load it when I get there. There's
gotta be somebody in charge who'll tell us where we're supposed to set
up. There hasn't been a speck of noise from any of the pickets since we
been here, so no point in getting all twisted up about it.

The ground sloped downward, and he felt his way past the first of the
trees, heard men in front of him, low murmurs, the footsteps mostly silent on the rain-soaked ground. The night was cool, getting cooler,
heavy wet clouds, no stars, no moon. He glanced up, caught faint
glimpses of the skeletons of the tree limbs, and he was startled by a harsh
whisper.

"This way! Move it! You're late!"

He couldn't see the man, heard others moving by, coming back toward
him, grumbles and curses from men who had been out here for . . . how
long? Bauer didn't know, hadn't thought to ask the sergeant how long the
duty would last. One man bumped him, unavoidable collision, and the
man cursed, then said, "Out of the way! There better be some grub. I'll
shoot the cook if he's gone to sleep."

The man was past him now, more grumbles, and another man moved
close, startled him with a shout.

"Hey! You keep an eye out! There's ghosts in these woods! Big ones!
Nasty critters. Don't get scared! Big ole snakes, too! As fat as your leg!"

The man chuckled, was gone, and Bauer suddenly slowed his steps.
He had heard this kind of talk already, knew the one piece of truth in the
man's teasing was the presence of snakes. He closed his eyes, took a
breath, opened them again, no difference, nothing to see. To one side, a
voice, low and harsh.

"Line up here. Stick close to this creek, but stay on this side of it. Form
a line, keep ten paces apart. Make a sound, let the next man know where
you are!"

He could hear the creek, a low gurgle a few feet in front of him, the
ground soft and wet. He stepped back, felt for a tree, his hand pushing
through vines, a tree trunk more narrow than he was. He eased himself

down, the vines cushioning him, and he shifted himself, tried to get comfortable. To his left, a hard whisper.

"Here! You there?"

Bauer assumed the man was speaking to him, responded.

"Here! Against a tree. Creek in front of me!"

The man didn't respond, but behind them both, the harsh voice came again, the sound of a man in command.

"Everybody know the password?"

Farther down to the right, one man called out, too loud.

*"Ulysses?"*

"Shut up! You wanna let the secesh know? Somebody rams a bayonet in your gut . . ."

"Sorry, sir."

"Anybody comes through here, anybody tried to cross the creek, you ask for the password! He doesn't answer, or he says the wrong thing, you put a hole in him! I'll be back here about fifty yards, and I'll gather you up at dawn." Bauer began to recognize the voice, thought of the lieutenant from Company B, older man, tough, somebody worth following. The questions were answered now, how long they would be sitting in these woods. But the final question had the answer he had suspected. Williams had given him the wrong password. *Just for fun.*

He blinked hard, convinced he was awake, felt something crawling on his pants leg, slapped at it in a panic, some kind of insect, nothing larger. He didn't like the thought of snakes, had seen only a few when he was a boy, hunting trips with his father. There were always the teases about *rattlers,* every small snake they ran across resulting in a mock scare, his father exaggerating the danger. He had no idea what an actual rattler looked like, doubted he had ever seen one. But the soldiers here were talking of them daily, the boggy ravines said to be full of them, or any other kind of terrifying creature the soldiers could dream up.

Even as a child, he hadn't really been scared of the dark. And then he went deer hunting with his father, and made the marvelous discovery that animals could actually see in the dark, no matter how blind you

might be. To the curious boy, it made the dawn a time of enormous curiosity, the most tense time of the day, your eyes trying to figure out
what that motion was, if that shadow in front of you had really moved.
He had been convinced of that one time, when he was no more than
twelve, barely able to hoist the old flintlock, and had taken careful aim at
what certainly had to be a huge deer. The shot had knocked him backward off a stump, and when his father rushed to him, they discovered he
had shot a bush. The teasing was unending after that, his father offering
to take him hunting for *haints*. At first the boy had thought it to be some
kind of animal, redemption for his foolish and embarrassing imagination. But then his father told the others, neighbors, that his son was a
master at killing *haints. Hain't a damn thing*. After that, the boy learned
that when things moved in the dark, it was best to wait for daylight before shooting at it.

He smiled, remembering the trips with his father, bitter cold, snow
waist deep. He pulled his coat tighter, the night cooler now, nothing like
Wisconsin of course, but the dampness of the ground beneath him had
seeped up through his clothes. To one side, he heard snoring, was immediately annoyed, one man not doing the job. Bauer sat up straight,
stared into the dark, thought of making a noise, something to warn the
man, thought of his own sergeant's threat. Yep, he's good with a bullwhip. But I don't see him out here. Never seen him do much of anything,
really, except cuss and show off his meanness. From farther that way, he
heard a sharp hiss.

"Hey!"

The snoring stopped, and Bauer heard a rustling, the man pulling
himself awake. Good, he thought. This is too important to be that stupid. Bauer had never objected to guard duty, actually liked it, appreciated that the picket line was the eyes that would see anyone who didn't
need to be there. He knew of the grumbling, men marching out in a
sulk, as though the duty was punishment, the picket line sent out as
sacrificial lambs, the first men who might be killed. To Bauer, that just
made the job more significant. He embellished the duty, even now,
smiled at the thought that he *was the first line of defense* for the whole
country, standing vigilant against the enemy. Well, he thought, sitting
anyway. Standing gets pretty tiresome after a few hours. At least these
vines are soft. He stared again, scanned hard into nothing. They all knew

that the rebels were no more than twenty miles away, and rumors flew through the camps every day. Word had been passed that rebel cavalry had been sighted, and some of the pickets had actually fired at what they claimed were enemy troops. But no one had produced a body, or even a prisoner, and so the officers tried to keep that kind of talk quiet. He remembered the scolding phrase Captain Saxe had used. *A camp is no place for facts.* But still, he thought, they're out there, and we're here, and somebody must have figured out what's gonna happen next. He wondered about that, too. It was something he kept out of his letters home, the nagging fear what he might do if a musket ball flew past his ear . . . or worse. Some of the men teased the others about running away, that those who talked so much about sticking a bayonet through a secesh were most likely the ones who wouldn't stand up to them at all. But running away . . . that was the worst offense you could commit. They say they'll shoot a man for that. For trying not to get shot. I guess that makes sense. Depends I guess on how good a runner you are. But . . . no, stop that. You ain't running. You could never go home if you did that. Never look your father in the eye. Oh God, no, you could never admit to being that kind of man. Nope, no running away.

He realized suddenly that he could see, a dark gray mist swirling past him, shapes forming, mostly tall and thin. Trees. He sat up straight again, worked through the painful stiffness, felt one leg numb, the harsh tingling now rolling through it. He flexed it, rubbed with his hand, the tingling worse, a thousand bees crawling on his skin. He sat back against the tree again, stared ahead, could see the curve of the creek bed, very narrow, a long step across. He thought of water, his canteen empty, wondered if this creek flowed close to a camp, or maybe from somewhere out beyond the troops, from woods that might be clean. His thirst grew, no fighting it, and he flexed the stiffness in his legs, crawled forward, toward the swirling rush of the water, and out in front of him, beyond the creek, he heard a loud snort. He knew the sound. It was a horse.

He froze, could hear the steps now, more than one, and the mist began to clear, daylight easing into the trees, and the shapes were there, a half dozen, and on every horse, a man.

And he remembered now. His gun was not loaded.

To one side a voice called out, startling him.

"You! Password!"

The horses seemed to lurch, and a flash from a musket burst out, blinding. But there was light enough to see, his vision clearing, and the horses began moving quickly, a hard shout, another musket firing down the picket line. He felt the helpless panic, reached his hand for his cartridge box, fumbled, cartridges dropping, his fingers useless, cold and stiff. More muskets fired, bursts of sound from all along the line, but the woods were empty, no sign of the horses, and now a new voice, the lieutenant.

"Stop firing! What did you see!"

"Cavalry!"

"Cavalry, sir!"

The man was there now, fast steps through the soft mud, and Bauer saw him, an officer's hat, staring ahead, a pistol in his hand.

"You sure?"

"Yes, sir! Six, maybe eight of 'em!"

"You sure they were rebs?"

"Yes, sir!"

Bauer stared into the gray light, trees and brush, nothing else, thought, well, not sure about that. But they didn't answer the password. Didn't have time.

"You all see 'em?"

"Yes, sir!"

"Sure did, sir."

Bauer responded as well.

"Yes, sir! Looked like six or more!"

The officer stepped forward, made a small jump over the creek bed, kept his pistol out, pointed it forward.

"Anybody fall? You tell if you hit somebody?"

No one responded, and the lieutenant holstered his pistol, stepped forward.

"Move up here. Search around. One of you might have gotten lucky. I gotta report this, and if you boys were shooting at damn ghosts, it'll be my ass that gets chewed."

"No, sir! They were there."

"I saw 'em for sure, sir!"

The officer kept moving forward, slow, deliberate steps, and Bauer saw others doing the same, following, keeping their distance on each side, the men crossing the creek. Bauer followed, pulled his feet through the deep mud, tried to jump the water, one foot landing square in the center. He slogged ahead, keeping up, and now the officer stopped, bent low.

"I'll be damned. Hoofprints. They were here. Sure like to know who they were."

"Had to be secesh, sir!"

"Yes, sir. Had to be!"

The officer stood, stared out into the woods, motionless for a long minute, seemed to ponder his next move. Bauer could see the treetops easily now, felt wet mist on his face, watched the officer turn toward him, the face familiar. The lieutenant moved back to the creek, stepped across, said, "Let's go. We're due to be relieved. I'll make my report to the captain. He might ask you what you saw, any details. Don't make up some fool story. Just tell him the truth. It was probably one of the patrols we've been told about. There's said to be rebels crawling all over the countryside, trying to figure out who we are."

The others flowed back through the woods, and Bauer moved with them, felt the wet misery in one shoe, stepped more carefully over the creek. They began to walk up the long slope, through the trees, the wide field finally opening up in front of them. Men were waiting for them, their relief, but more, men with muskets who had heard the commotion. Bauer felt suddenly important, part of something big, fought a shiver, thought, I saw them. The enemy. Coulda shot one. *Shoulda* shot one. Stupid pea brain! Load your damn musket! Not making that mistake again.

He saw a horseman now, the man riding close, Captain Fox, commander of B Company.

Bauer waited while the lieutenant made his report, some of the others adding their own flair. The captain listened impatiently, said something about Colonel Allen, rode quickly away. The lieutenant dismissed the men, seemed not to notice that Bauer wasn't one of his, and Bauer walked out into the great open field, the long rows of tents, men stoking the exhausted fires, the clank of tin plates. The army was coming alive, another day in this strange empty place. The routine tried to plant itself in his brain, more bad food, more dirty water, more formations and bugles, and more of the senseless danger from Sergeant Williams. Bauer moved toward his own camp, those thoughts rippling through him, but he thought of Willis now, could feel the excitement, knew he had to tell him everything, that finally there was something more interesting than marching in the incessant drills. He savored the memory, the delicious image of the horsemen, riding so close to him, ghostly and dangerous. Cavalry . . . the *enemy*. He knew with perfect certainty, this was already his best day as a soldier. He felt wonderful.

## CHAPTER NINE

# JOHNSTON

NEAR ROSE COTTAGE, CORINTH, MISSISSIPPI
MARCH 30, 1862

He had attended the services at the Baptist church for two reasons, going primarily as the guest of Mrs. Inge, and as well on the advice of his staff, that the town needed reassurance that their army walked with God. Even Johnston sensed that the citizens he saw were an uncertain lot, that behind whatever indignation that showed toward the Yankees, they held back their enthusiasm, as though hoping for some kind of sign that it was all going to turn out all right. He understood their fear, had seen it before, in Kentucky and Tennessee. In every place where massive gatherings of troops spread all across their lands, there was the inevitability of some unknown horror that seemed to overwhelm the civilians. On this Sunday morning, the preacher had been respectful of his audience, so many gray uniforms, and Johnston had not been surprised by the man's rousing sermon that emphasized a call for fiery damnation toward the great invasion of the infidels from the North. If the citizens drew inspiration from that, more the good, but Johnston could not avoid a certain emptiness to the call for a Heavenly butchering of the enemy. There had been various examples of butchering already, and God had not yet shown a preference for one side or the other. But still he offered his thanks to the preacher, along with a strong suggestion to his staff that the offering plate be filled. After all, if this one

Baptist preacher could somehow summon God's aid, Johnston would not object.

The service had been surprisingly brief, barely an hour, the preacher seeming to understand that his audience had *business* to attend to. As he exited the church, officers were waiting with papers, reports of the ongoing entrenchments, the good work of engineers and men with shovels. But it was not the time, and he insisted they come to his headquarters, that for now, in the brisk chill of a cloudy morning, he would make the short walk down the hill to Mrs. Inge's home without the business of the army dogging his every step.

Most of the troops had been organized in strengthening fortifications north of the town, the most logical place for the Federal troops to assault, though even before Johnston had arrived, Beauregard had seen to extensive defensive preparations far out along the railroad both east and west. Johnston and his commanders had discussed whether they should advise the civilians to vacate the town, that the inevitable assault could do far more than frighten them. But the reality was that most of them had nowhere else to go, and from all he had been told, by his staff, by Mrs. Inge herself, few were inclined to leave. Instead, many presented their fears and suggestions directly to his headquarters, were met by guards and his staff, who politely listened to the passionate concerns for the safety of their families, or what the Yankees might do to their homes. Kind and encouraging words were all the army could offer them, along with the never-ending plea that the people help supply the army with food and clean water. But Johnston had told his staff to pay close attention to the particular complaints or fears of the civilians, and what he heard was encouraging. Johnston realized that the people of Corinth were fully expecting the Yankees to come south, to attack the town. That meant that his own plan, the strike against Grant's army that was so consuming his generals and their staffs, had not been spread out all across the countryside, either as rumor or fact.

Once the army lurched into motion, of course, any hope of secrecy would vanish, at least in the town. Whether the enemy could be approached without making their own defensive preparations was, to his generals, a point of severe disagreement. But doubts about the enemy's actions were not Johnston's biggest concern. First things first. The plans had been put on paper, the maps checked and copied, distributed to the generals who would lead four corps of Confederate troops northward. Every general had been schooled on what his role would be, and what was expected of his command. Johnston knew there were doubts about whether the plan could be carried out, but there was no time now for debate. The orders had been given, the order of march understood by the men who would lead it.

The four corps would be commanded by Hardee, Polk, Bragg, and Breckinridge. John Breckinridge was to some a surprise choice, having come to the Confederate army only during the past autumn, well after the war had begun. Breckinridge had served as vice president under James Buchanan, and had made his own run for president against Abraham Lincoln. Though his commitment to the Southern Cause had been somewhat late in coming, no one doubted it now. Johnston knew that Breckinridge had been a good soldier in Mexico, and would be one now, and his leadership skills were unquestioned. He had been assigned to Johnston's army to replace General George Crittenden, a man who had seemed destined for high rank. But Crittenden suffered from a lapse in personal behavior and so had crossed swords with Braxton Bragg. During his hard-nosed reorganization of the forces around Corinth, Bragg had discovered that Crittenden was known often to be *in liquor*. Bragg's intolerance for any officer imbibing in spirits was sufficient cause that neither Beauregard nor Johnston could argue with Bragg's insistence that Crittenden be replaced. Breckinridge had no such stain on his own reputation.

William Hardee was the final link in the chain of organization that Johnston now controlled at Corinth. Of all the commanders Johnston had at his disposal, Hardee was likely the most capable man they had, and his selection to command a corps had met with no objection at all, not even from Bragg. Like many, Hardee was a West Pointer, had already served with some distinction, including a term as the military academy's commandant of cadets. Besides admirable service in the field in both Florida and Mexico, Hardee had authored what was considered the last word on infantry drill and training. His work, most often called simply *Hardee's Tactics*, had been widely used in the Federal army since its publication in the mid-1850s. It was a source of pride to an army whose officers had been trained primarily in the textbooks of Napoleon, that one of their own would become a most respected authority on the drill and maneuver of troops in the field. But like so many in the old army whose loyalty was determined by geography, Hardee was a Georgian, and had caused considerable dismay in the North when he pledged his loyalties to the Southern cause.

For more than a week prior, the order of march had been discussed and argued over, but there was no real controversy that Johnston had to confront. By the time Johnston had reached Corinth, Beauregard had already done much to put a plan of attack on paper, and so Johnston conceded most of the planning to Beauregard and his capable staff, most notably Colonel Thomas Jordan. Jordan was regarded by Beauregard with the same level of respect that Johnston felt for his own adjutant, William Mackall. With Mackall now in command of the crisis at Island Number Ten, there had to be someone to fill the position closer to Johnston himself. It was unusual in the Confederate army to have an official chief of staff, and though that was now Bragg's title, once the campaign was under way and Bragg returned to the field, Johnston would need a staff officer capable of taking the reins in nearly any situation.

Beauregard had insisted that the man for that job was Jordan, and in a surprisingly generous gesture, Beauregard had offered Jordan to serve in the role that Mackall had once filled. Knowing that the ailing Beauregard had relied on Jordan for much of the detailed planning that had already taken place, Johnston had every reason to share Beauregard's faith in Jordan's ability. Jordan was another of the West Point graduates, who had served in Florida against the Seminole Indians, as well as making a notable performance in Mexico. There was one other piece of lore about Jordan's history that Johnston couldn't ignore. At West Point, Jordan had been the roommate of William T. Sherman. Though Beauregard hadn't given great notice of that delicious irony, Jordan clearly did. There was a fire to the man that demonstrated to Johnston that he had something to prove, if not to his own superiors, then perhaps to the redheaded adversary who waited quietly at Pittsburg Landing. Immediately Jordan began to tackle the detailed drudgery that ensured the Confederate forces were organized properly, fed and equipped as well as the commissary officers could deliver. Very soon, Johnston was impressed.

With April now right upon them, Johnston knew that if there was to be an effective attack on Grant's army, the time had come. No matter what might be on paper, routes of march, and the geography that lay between the two armies, no one could put any kind of plan into action until the weather allowed it. Throughout March, the gathering armies had been separated by what amounted to twenty miles of paralyzing mud. With the army now as prepared as Johnston could hope, the frustration of that was maddening. Every day he had scanned the skies, his spirits raised by the occasional glimpses of blue. But those glorious days had been too few. As he stepped slowly out of the church, surrounded by well-wishers and his own officers, Johnston had glanced upward again. If anyone noticed at all, they might have thought he was offering a prayer. And they were right. While others had used the somber gathering in the church to seek hope and protection for home and family, to pray for those who were far away, or those who had passed on, Johnston's prayer was far more direct. All he had requested was a break in the wild inconsistency of the weather, enough to allow the roads to dry, to harden the mud that kept his army penned up in sullen misery.

They moved down the hill in a slow, somber procession, the other generals taking differing routes to their own headquarters. Beside him, Mrs. Inge held her arms close across her, gloved hands wrapped with a shawl of colorful wool. As they moved out into the street, wagons began to move, but Mrs. Inge had insisted they walk, the stroll to the church not long enough to require the preparation of a carriage. On the walk up the hill to the church, the stinging numbness in Johnston's toes had already made him question that decision. Silently, of course.

She walked close beside him, and he watched as she waved to a neighbor, a carriage that rolled noisily away down a side street. Johnston pulled his coat more tightly around him, but still the chill found him, a relentless wind that rolled up the hill toward him. He caught a silent shiver from her, and he thought of offering his arm, had a brief argument with himself, his gallantry winning out, the thought taking hold that there was nothing inappropriate about the gesture. She was, after all, his hostess.

"Madam, if you don't object, please take my arm. This breeze is harsh enough, and there is no need for both of us to suffer. My coat is far more of a shelter than your wrap, certainly."

She smiled without looking at him, eased closer, hooked her gloved hand through his arm, settling closer to him, though not so close to cause the officers and civilians behind them to gossip. He thought of looking back, knew his staff would allow him several yards of distance, close enough for a summons to any one of them if need be, but far enough not to overhear whatever conversation he might have with the woman who had done so much to provide her home for all of them.

Johnston had entertained no unconscionable thoughts about the woman at all, had never strayed from absolute loyalty to his own wife. There had been talk, of course, the kind of talk that surrounds every army, some of the people in Corinth offering their basest suspicions. But his staff put that to rest at every opportunity. If there were scoundrels in this army, the men targeted so viciously by the whip of Braxton Bragg, no one had to be concerned that the commanding general was among them.

Johnston knew only a little of Mrs. Inge's husband, that he held the rank of colonel, was off somewhere that neither of them was certain of. It was the way so often now, scattered units scrambling to come together into any kind of organized resistance, strengthening so many vulnerable places where the Yankees might confront them, confrontations that could come quickly once the weather improved.

After a moment, she said, "My cook, Gloria, has been instructed to prepare a warm dinner for us, General. Your staff is most certainly invited. A day like this calls for something to warm the insides of body *and* soul. She does prepare a wonderful potato stew, which I hope your men will find appealing."

Johnston gave her arm a slight squeeze with his own.

"You are more generous than we deserve, Mrs. Inge. My staff will be grateful, and I assure you, it will come from the heart."

The words tumbled out awkwardly, and he stopped himself, didn't want any hint of affection to seep into their conversation. His mind rolled over the words. *From the heart.* What's the matter with you? She has been nothing but kind, and her graciousness comes from loyalty,

nothing more. He struggled to respond, to do away with the awkwardness that seemed to infect him in every social setting.

"My wife is not especially skilled at making soup. In Texas, there are
potatoes, of course."

"I did not know that, General."

He stopped again, more frustration. But the mention of his home
touched a place he had tried to keep hidden, a crack opening in that part
of him that held so many memories.

"China Grove. That's the name of my plantation. Beautiful place.
Well, it's more of a ranch, I suppose. We do grow cotton there. Sugarcane
as well. I have a truly magnificent orchard, fruit and nut trees of all types.
And I grow vegetables of all sorts. I truly enjoy that, digging the soil. It
is one of those quiet joys that takes a man away from everything else. My
wife Eliza understands that." He paused. "I do wish to return there very
soon." He could not help thinking of his home, knew the fruit trees were
beginning to blossom, realized with a sudden sharp sadness that he
would miss the opportunities for the slow strolls with Eliza, both of
them admiring the fragrance of the flowers, what she spoke of with quiet
reverence, the trees slowly birthing their bounty, a gift from God they
should never take for granted.

"Is it near the gulf, General?"

"China Grove?" He was surprised by the question, wondered if she
was simply being polite to ask. "A dozen miles perhaps. Brazoria County,
near Galveston. Have you been there?" He scolded himself again,
thought, of course she hasn't been there. No one has been there but Texans. She laughed softly, her voice holding a musical gentility he had
heard from so many of the people of the town.

"Oh my, no, General. We have never traveled west of the Mississippi
River. The colonel prefers to stay close to home." She paused, and he
understood why. She continued, a colder tone in her voice. "Of course,
in these times, he must do his duty."

He had become more curious about her husband, knew he was widely
respected in Corinth, but served in a unit Johnston knew nothing about.

"Have you received any letters from him recently?"

He immediately regretted the question, far too personal, was even
more annoyed with his social clumsiness. Again, she seemed not to no-

tice, said, "Last week. He was somewhere to the east, in Alabama. He could not say with detail."

"No, I suppose he could not. It is not proper for an officer to reveal his whereabouts, with the enemy so close. Messages can be intercepted, and enemy cavalry does precisely what we do, patrolling the countryside, seeking such information. It is all a part of the game we must play. Probing, seeking information, keeping a close watch on each other's movements, positions. Your husband certainly understands that."

She said nothing, and he was grateful for that, had never been comfortable in casual conversation with anyone, certainly not the wife of one of his officers. He stared down the hill toward her home, thought of the warmth that was awaiting them, a pang of anticipation in his stomach for the meal he knew her servants would prepare. He thought of Eliza now, could never completely avoid his homesickness.

"My wife writes when she can, but she is so very busy with China Grove. So many details, so much work to do. I regret leaving her, but, of course, it can be no other way. As you understand, madam, it is difficult being absent from family. My son is in Richmond, serving on the staff of the president."

She turned toward him.

"I am surprised by that, General. I have heard that many of our senior officers have their progeny serving close. Is it not your privilege to do the same?"

"That's precisely why I do not, madam. My son William is a capable officer, but there are challenges enough in this command without anyone suggesting that I make a place for my own son. Actually, my staff is smaller than most. Some fault me for that, but I find it to be an advantage. Less complaining, less bickering. I have always felt a large staff is too much tail for the kite. There are those in this army who do not agree. That is, I suppose, their right. Unless it interferes in the job we must do." He shut off the words, the voice inside of him angry. Stop this mindless jabbering! She does not care about the business of the army. "My apologies, madam. It is not necessary for you to suffer the goings-on of a soldier with too much on his mind."

"Nonsense, General. If I may offer, though, I would suggest you find the opportunity to write your wife as often as you are able. It must be terribly difficult for her to be so far away from both her husband and her son."

His steps slowed, her words striking him in a very cold place. She seemed to notice the change, looked at him, said, "I'm sorry, is that not appropriate?"

"William's mother is not alive, madam. Eliza is my second wife."

She pulled her arm away, put her white gloves to her face, genuinely upset.

"Oh dear me. I am so very sorry. Please forgive my indiscretion. I should not be delving into such personal matters."

He glanced back behind him, saw his staff stopping, held by the firm hand of Governor Harris, keeping their distance, reacting to the halt in his steps. Johnston nodded slightly to Harris, knew the governor would be watching him carefully, sensitive to protocol, quick to respond to anything Johnston might suddenly need. He was suddenly grateful for that, the man's friendship, something of *home* in that, a good friend, not merely a subordinate who follows orders. He looked again at Mrs. Inge, saw the deep concern lingering in her eyes.

"Please do not be concerned, madam. That tragedy was a very long time ago. And it is not a matter for avoiding. I have come to accept it as the Way."

He looked down briefly, knew that Harris would know that to be a lie.

A sharp breeze swirled suddenly around them, leaves in the air, a harsh whisper through the bare tree limbs above them. He saw her shiver, her face very red, and she closed her eyes for a brief moment, fighting the cold. He extended his arm again, which she seemed grateful to take. She gripped him more tightly, but he knew his coat could not warm both of them, was barely enough to warm him. He looked down, measured his steps, not wanting to rush her. But the chill was growing painful now, a miserable stinging in his ears, and he looked down the street toward her home, very close now. Rose Cottage had been two long blocks from the church, and he glanced at the other homes nearby, some, like hers, framed by the gray skeletons of oak and pecan trees. Some of those homes were even more grand than the Inge house, and he knew that nearly all of them were occupied by his other senior commanders. It was a show of graciousness from the citizens of a town who seemed to understand with perfect certainty that, no matter the optimistic words of their ministers, no matter the heavy crowds that filled the churches on this cold Sunday morning, it was their army that might be their only salvation.

He continued the slow pace down the hill, the wind louder now, details creeping into his mind, the papers he had been shown, reports, intelligence, all those things he would now attend to. As they reached the front walkway to her home, he could not help staring down at the blowing dust, the mud finally hardening along the roadway.

# CHAPTER TEN

# JOHNSTON

Soldiers of the Army of the Mississippi: I have put you in motion to offer battle to the invaders of your country. With the resolution and discipline and valor becoming men fighting, as you are, for all worth living or dying for, you can but march to a decisive victory over the agrarian mercenaries sent to subjugate you and despoil you of your liberties, your property, and your honor. Remember the precious stake involved; remember the dependence of your mothers, your wives, your sisters and your children, on the result; remember the fair, broad, abounding land, and the happy homes that would be desolated by your defeat.

The eyes and hopes of eight millions of people rest upon you; you are expected to show yourselves worthy of your lineage, worthy of the women of the South, whose noble devotion in this war has never been exceeded in any time. With such incentives to brave deeds, and with the trust that God is with us, your generals will lead you confidently to the combat—assured of success.

The order was read to every regiment by every low-level commander, passed down to each by the four corps commanders who would lead the march. Johnston had written most of the words himself, but it was Colonel Jordan, Beauregard, even Bishop Polk, who helped craft the words. It was natural for him to ask. He knew he was not good with speeches, and if this army was to perform in the field, the men must be given some spark of inspiration from the man who claimed to lead them.

They were to march out of their earthworks at six in the morning on April 3, a quick and orderly surge of power that would flow northward on the network of roadways that spread out in parallel courses through the rolling countryside. The orders had been plain and direct, each one of the four corps commanders knowing precisely where Johnston was to be, when his troops were to march, and which route they would take. The orders spelled out the timetables, the rendezvous points, the eventual position of the battle lines and the precise moment when the attack on Grant's army would begin. The original plan of attack called for the three corps under Hardee, Polk, and Bragg to make their rendezvous within a few miles of the Federal position, with Breckinridge and the reserves close behind. There the troops would be spread into an enormous arc, the corps side by side, to burst forward as one great mass into Grant's encamped troops, striking hard into whatever configuration Grant's divisions had arranged themselves. With efficient coordination between the three primary corps and Breckinridge's reserves, the attack would commence precisely at dawn on Saturday, April 5. The arrangement of Grant's camps meant very little to Johnston. Every scouting report continued to insist that Grant's army was completely immobile, and was in no way organized to receive any kind of assault. Johnston felt confident that as long as the Federal forces continued to be utterly oblivious of Johnston's advance, there would be little that Grant could do to stop the enormous wave that was rolling toward him.

The plan had been tooled and refigured for several days, and Colonel Jordan had been tireless in traveling from headquarters to headquarters, delivering the communications directly to each of the commanders, placing maps in their hands, giving carefully worded instructions as to the logistics of the plan. With so much of the maneuver and the planning spelled out in such detail by Beauregard and Jordan, Johnston had to believe that *finally* the right people had been put in the right places. Unlike Donelson, this time capable men were in command, and with Jordan's amazing efficiency, Johnston began to feel a sense of destiny, as though this victory were preordained. To begin the campaign, to put the troops into the roadways and direct them northward to accomplish the great victory he could already see in his mind, the overwhelming de-

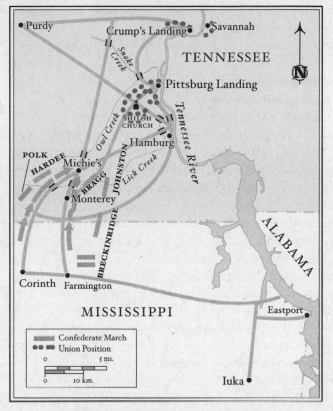

**CONFEDERATE ADVANCE OUT OF CORINTH**

struction of the Federal army, Johnston's only immediate task would be to give the order that began the march.

On April 2, he did.

### ROSE COTTAGE, CORINTH, MISSISSIPPI
### APRIL 3, 1862

"No, sir. They are not at the intersection. General Hardee's troops were somewhat . . . ah . . . tardy in their movements. That delay forced General Polk to halt his men until the roads to his front were clear."

"Well, Colonel, are they *clear*?"

Jordan looked down, and Johnston could see the same frustration he was feeling himself.

"No, sir. General Polk's wagon trains are still close to the town."

Johnston felt the burn in his brain, paced the room with surging anger, something he rarely did.

"Why was Hardee delayed?"

Jordan glanced at Beauregard, who sat in his usual perch on the couch. Beauregard said nothing, stared at the floor with grim resignation. Johnston ignored him, was beginning to understand that, with Beauregard's illness, it was Jordan who was filling the void and was probably responsible for many of their decisions. Jordan responded in a quiet, measured voice.

"General Hardee insisted that his order to march be put into writing. The original order had been given him this morning, but he would not accept it . . . verbally."

"So? Did you comply with his wishes? Did you write out the order?"

Jordan took a deep breath, his careful responses digging into Johnston's fury.

"Yes, sir. But . . . in the confusion of all the activity at headquarters . . . the order was not delivered until this afternoon."

Beauregard spoke now, his voice still raspy, the struggle to speak through the nagging illness.

"The roads are not as we had hoped. General Bragg is not pleased that his route of march is very difficult. He has been unable to reach the first rendezvous point. There is still too much mud. The horses cannot pull the wagons with any hope of speed. Artillery is mired. General Bragg's report was somewhat . . . profane."

Johnston absorbed the news as he had absorbed it all day. Besides the brain-piercing frustration was a heightening sense of alarm.

"If we do not assemble our forces at the desired point, we will be unable to effect the attack. We will be forced to delay. Every moment we delay is a moment the enemy could determine our strategy."

Beauregard nodded, as though this had been expected all along. Beauregard rubbed a hand on his throat, made a low cough.

"I have always believed that an uncertain offensive was unwise. Perhaps we should have waited for the enemy to emerge from his camps, and make his strategies known to us. We could have struck him on the march, when he was strung out, in no position to make a defense. The mud would have been *his* enemy and not our own."

Johnston stared at the ailing man, moved to his usual chair, sat slowly, never took his eyes from Beauregard.

"This plan of attack . . . was *yours*. Now you are telling me this is not the correct plan? You wait until our army is in motion . . ."

The words choked away, and Johnston forced himself to keep the anger tightly inside, was never a man to launch violent words at anyone. Beauregard seemed not to notice Johnston's mood, said, "I merely point out that it is always good strategy to strike an enemy while he is unprepared."

"Do you have some evidence that General Grant is *prepared* now?"

Beauregard seemed to run out of energy, and Jordan read his commander, spoke up.

"No, sir. Not at all. But there is risk, as you say, that if we delay, the enemy will become aware of our intentions. If we allow him the time, he could prepare a firm defensive posture."

Johnston was beginning to despise Jordan, a silky smoothness to the man's speech.

"I understand risk, Colonel. I have lived with risk my entire career. Without risk there is no hope of achieving anything positive. Is that concept alien to you? The enemy is perched in his camps with orders, apparently, to sit idle until he is reinforced. I know of no situation that could benefit us more, that could lessen our *risk* any more than the opportunity General Grant has presented us. *Opportunity*, Colonel. Consider the word, if you please. We must seek the means to drive an entire army from our soil. From all we can gather, that means lies before us with perfect clarity. The weather has improved and yet I hear excuses that miserable roads are grinding our advance to a standstill. I did not expect any such complaint. Neither did you." Johnston calmed himself as much as possible, a desperate effort to hold to some kind of decorum.

"If I am not mistaken, you labored over these plans for weeks, even before I reached Corinth. You both have shown nothing but confidence that this would be successful. Now . . . you tell me that we should rely instead on the fantastic notion that General Grant is so magnificently stupid, he would spread his army all over the countryside, even more so than he already has. He would march his people in such a way as to invite attack when he is most vulnerable. He knows we are observing him, does he not? Our cavalry is not invisible. He has picket lines and guard posts and none of those people are blind." He fought to keep his voice low, heard boots in the outer rooms, conversations, did not want any of those men to hear the discussion that was burrowing a deep hole into his sanity. He moved to the curtained window, drew back the soft cloth, saw a hitching post lined with horses lathered with sweat, dripping with mud. He had seen the same all day.

"Someone has arrived. There will be more reports, Colonel. See to them. Keep me informed of our movements."

Jordan nodded, backed away, said nothing more. He pulled open the door behind his back, and Johnston said, "Leave the door ajar. This council has concluded." He looked at Beauregard now. "Unless you have something to add."

Beauregard shook his head weakly.

"I have nothing to add. It is in God's hands now."

Johnston tried to avoid the thought, but it flooded through his mind. *God did not design this attack.* He kept his silence, moved out into the larger room of the elegant home. He had always enjoyed Mrs. Inge's décor, the portraits of her relatives, glassware crowding the mantel, set there as a precaution, out of the way, the careful hostess aware that her sitting room and sunporches had been converted into a place for soldiers. But still there were touches of family, of civilians, small paintings, tapestries, soft lace on colorful chairs. But he would see none of that now, felt suddenly as though the house were a maddening prison, smelling of mud and sweat and dirty wool. In several of the rooms, staff officers and aides had left a trail, the unavoidable dirt of the roadways smeared onto wooden floors. Johnston heard the chorus of voices throughout the headquarters, the chatter of their reports unable to disguise anger and frustration. They noticed him now, men suddenly standing back, some at attention, acknowledging him, and he stared at them, scanned the papers in their hands, could see his own anger on their faces.

He said nothing, heard movement behind him, from the smaller office, caught the ugly smell of medicine, a sickly odor as Beauregard slid out past him. The Creole moved with slow purpose, made every effort to keep himself steady, a good show for the staffs. Johnston said nothing to him, watched the man move outside, his own aides gathering around their commander. He will return to his quarters, Johnston thought. Best place for him to be. Johnston had a sudden burst of cold concern, had not really considered: What if he does not survive this? How ill is he, after all? No one seems to know, and he never seems to get better. What will we lose if he passes on? Johnston looked at the others, some moving again, papers, low conversation. His question had no answer, his mind too filled with the chaos of his army.

Out on one of the sunporches, he saw Governor Harris sitting with two of the staff, clean uniforms, the men who stayed close to the headquarters. A third man stood before Harris, the miserably wet figure of Lieutenant Baylor, one of Johnston's aides. Baylor was obviously exhausted from a long ride, and Johnston wanted to know more, but he held back, saw mud-smeared paper on Harris's small table. It will come in time, he thought. I do not have to hear every piece of bad news. To one side, Thomas Reynolds was occupied in low, intense conversation with another aide Johnston did not know. Reynolds had been governor of Missouri, was another of the government men whose positions had been swept away by Federal forces. Like so many of the others, Reynolds sought out the military command, seeking any means possible to help the Cause. Reynolds nodded toward Johnston, who returned the gesture, but Johnston was absorbing all he could of the scene, and he saw more of the familiar faces, and those not known to him, those aides who served others, doing their work, the good work that should have been carrying this army forward. He stepped past them, saw heads following him, self-conscious glances, moved out into gray daylight, felt cool mist in the air, held out his hand. No rain, he thought. But . . . no sun. Is this some kind of punishment? Are we to be afflicted with even more miserable weather so that we keep to our shelters, and await our fate? He shook his head, knew better than that. No, it is just . . . spring.

"Would you care for company, General? Or am I interfering?"

Johnston knew the voice of Isham Harris, suddenly welcomed the presence of a *friend*.

"If you don't mind muddying your shoes."

Harris was beside him now, was waiting for Johnston to lead the way. Out in the road, all through the streets, Johnston could see men in motion, wagons and horses, and among them, clusters of men just standing, motionless, as though they had nowhere else to be. There were officers as well, horsemen, a few flags, but in every direction, he could feel the sluggishness, the complete lack of urgency. An officer rode past, trailed by a young aide, the man saluting Johnston without a word. Johnston returned the gesture with his own, the officer's reflex, could not avoid an angry thought. Where are *you* supposed to be? What orders are you . . . ignoring? But the words stayed inside him, the man only a lieutenant, no authority to change anything that was happening. Or to make anything happen more quickly.

They walked slowly, the mist heavier now, and Johnston realized he had forgotten his hat.

"This is not a good idea. But still . . . there was a need to get away from . . . all of that."

"I am at your service, General."

It was unnecessary formality, but Johnston understood that Harris was opening the door, would discreetly listen to anything Johnston wished to say. Johnston avoided a mound of horse manure, tried to keep his boots out of the deepest mud, fresh now, the drying of the ground changed by a new storm the night before. He tried not to see that, his mind taking him to other places, the memories he could share with a friend.

"I fought a duel once."

Harris stopped, clearly surprised, but Johnston kept moving, Harris quick to catch up, regaining his composure.

"Well, General, I did not know that."

"Few around here do. Texas. My word, it's been . . . twenty-five years. Felix Huston was his name. Officer. He was *offended* that I was promoted to a command that he felt was rightly his. He may have been right. Or not. Didn't matter. His pride inspired him to challenge me, and my pride forced me to accept."

"Well, clearly, you were the victor."

"No, actually, I was severely wounded. But the victor . . . well, you never saw so much contrition. Everyone thought the wound he had inflicted was mortal, and that I would be gone any hour, so Huston obliges me by suddenly bowing to my every wish. He accepts my authority, follows my orders, even as I'm lying on what everyone assumed to be my deathbed. Worst thing I did to him was survive." Johnston paused. "Not sure where he ended up. He's not in the army, for certain. I think dueling took his stomach away. Perhaps I am the *victor* after all."

Harris laughed.

"You do surprise me, Sidney. I never took you for one of those brash types, big mouths and fists to match."

"I was much younger. Youth makes allowances for stupidity." He paused again. "Not sure how to explain that when it applies to generals." He stopped walking, Harris looking at him, knowing there was so much more to say. "There is confusion in every quarter. You saw the reports, more than I have, most likely. The maps are so perfectly detailed, the crossroads, the rendezvous points. Every general in my command knows his duty today. And yet . . . we are like blind children, running into each other, stumbling on our own feet and crying about it. Yet I cannot condemn them. These are good men, capable, efficient soldiers. Bragg . . . Hardee. We put Breckinridge in the rear because he was the least experienced in the field . . . and Breckinridge reports that he cannot move to his appointed location because everyone else is in the way."

He began to walk again, and Harris followed, and after a silent moment, Harris said, "You are certainly familiar with Shakespeare. One of his plays is titled *A Comedy of Errors*. That seems to describe what is taking place today."

Johnston stopped again, saw a smile on Harris's face, did not share the joke.

"There is no comedy here, Isham. A great many men could die in the next few days, and if we fail to launch this assault in a timely way, it could be a great many more. If the enemy realizes what we are attempting to do, he will prepare to meet us. From all we have observed, we are very likely matching the enemy in numbers. Two foes of equal force . . . that always favors the defender. We have been blessed with time, and despite our problems with the roads, I am blessed with good men, officers who created the best plan of attack, to take full advantage of our situation. We need this victory, Isham. The people . . . everywhere . . . *need* this victory. The Federal army is a plague that must be destroyed. There can be no other way."

Harris looked at him, hung on his words, seemed surprised now.

"I have not heard you speak that way, Sidney. You know those people well, you were schooled with many of them. You have fought alongside many of them. You have always told me that these two armies are alike, good men, led by good officers, fighting for different causes. I curse Abraham Lincoln every day, and I may curse his generals. But I do not know those men the way you do. You have usually shown respect for them. God forgive me, but I cannot. Politicians negotiate and bargain and draw up maps and boundaries and sign our documents and treaties . . . that is our world. I don't know if President Davis has my appreciation for Shakespeare, but he surely understands that we are but single actors in a much larger play. That play is thus far a tragedy of horrifying proportions, and not just for your army." Harris stopped, seemed to hold to his emotions, shook his head. "My people are enduring torment, Sidney. I understand why the newspapers have blamed you for abandoning Tennessee. But the fault is not yours. I am here in your headquarters, out of danger, while the Federal troops occupy my city, most of my state."

"Stop it, Governor. You have done what is necessary, as have I. You lectured me once against giving credence to the great volume of wind that comes from newspapermen. I took your advice. But this war surrounds us. In time it may engulf us."

"All right, Sidney. I understand the pressures put upon you, upon all of you. I know that a victory against General Grant will soothe our people a great deal. I know how frustrated your officers are for . . . forgive me . . . their *meager* performance today. I know that your army—our army is not performing to your expectations. But I cannot ever escape the duty I have that goes far beyond this army." Harris paused again, and Johnston could feel the man's energy, a passion for the moment that Johnston respected. Harris seemed to search for words, glanced around, as though expecting eavesdroppers.

"You may speak openly, Isham. I assure you, there are no newspapermen to record your words."

After a quiet moment, Harris said, "I have seen what I expected to see in the people here, in Mrs. Inge, so many others. When I entered politics, I believed we were one nation, all of us, America, one people brought together for a single ideal. But I was wrong. The South is one nation. We share so much, our beliefs, our culture, and we are willing to wage war for the right to hold to that, to preserve everything we are. The North . . . they are mixed breeds, a mongrel dog beside a purebred hound. They share nothing that we share, no identity, no culture. They farm in Illinois and they run factories in Boston. If I go to Charleston or Atlanta, I know what I will find, how the people will regard me. I am the same as the men I see. But if a man in Minnesota travels to New York or Boston, he is in another world, isolated. What cause do they share? It is not possible they have a common bond. And now, because they out-number us, they elect a president who does not represent anything of the South, and instead of reaching out and finding common ground . . . instead of being a leader, he orders his generals to bring their soldiers to our towns, to force us to become . . . *them.*" He looked hard at Johnston. "You are quite correct. They bring a plague, and it is our duty to elimi-nate it."

Johnston absorbed the man's intensity, nodded slowly, said, "I have not heard you so . . . passionate about our Cause. But I must disagree with you on one point. Look at this army. It is just as I saw in Texas. These men . . . they are men of every station, rich and poor, merchants and farmers. But more than that, this army is . . . every *kind* of man. Old and young, decent men, men with an evil streak, the generous, the greedy, the honorable and the profane. I fight the Federal army because they have invaded us with guns, because they march to our homes and insult us with their false authority. But I have no doubt that the man in the blue uniform carries a musket and is willing to die because he is committed to his cause, as we are committed to ours. If that was not true, the muskets would not be out there. He would not be dangerous. Make no mistake. The Yankee is very dangerous. I believe we have better commanders, and despite the difficulties we face today, our generals will prevail over his. Most of the generals in this command are men who broke their oath as officers in the United States Army. I know of no man here who does not reflect on that. The soldiers will fight because they respect the men who lead them. That is true in both armies. Those peo-ple in their blue uniforms might be a mongrel mix, but then . . . so are we all."

Harris shook his head.

"Then we will disagree, Sidney. Your orders to the troops said it better than I could. We are a better people. We are fighting for everyone in the South, the women and children, homes and land and our very existence.

I pray every night that our generals and our soldiers are superior to theirs. Every Southern man holds to that faith. God *must* support our cause and our efforts."

Johnston felt a stab of discomfort, had heard too many around the army and in the newspapers claim that God was most certainly on *their* side. It was a phrase that had been included in his own message to the soldiers, and he still pondered that, if he should have tried to inspire the men by ordering them to trust that a victory would be given them by the hand of God. He had thought of it when the words were written, and he thought it again now. Can anyone truly know? And what of the Yankees, the devout among them who pray as we do? What must God think of them? Johnston pushed the thoughts away, said, "I must do my duty, Governor. God will decide in His own way what is best." Johnston looked up, the sky darkening, the dull gray of the daylight fading. "We should return to Rose Cottage. I have much to learn yet about our progress today, our positions. You should take the time to prepare your trunk. We will be leaving in the morning. As we march northward, I must move my headquarters. Keep to your prayers, Isham. My own involve matters closer to my command. I only ask that we be allowed to move. . . ."

His words trailed off, and he looked out through the fading light, saw wagons in motion, more officers, their staffs and their flags trailing behind. He watched them in silence, had no idea who they might be, what regiment, which commander bore the responsibility for their particular delay. He watched them move up the hill toward the Baptist church, toward the roadways that would lead them out northward, one more piece of his army plodding along the muddy roads with sickening sluggishness. He glanced up, the mist still wetting his face, and he saw flickers of lamplight, the windows of the homes close by, the headquarters of the men who were out there somewhere, leading his army. He turned, began the muddy slog back toward his own headquarters, knew there would be more reports, more reasons why the plan had crumbled, excuses and blame. He saw the lights in Mrs. Inge's windows, moved that way, the town darkening around him.

## CHAPTER ELEVEN

# JOHNSTON

## ROSE COTTAGE, CORINTH, MISSISSIPPI
### APRIL 4, 1862

He did not expect tears.

"Please, madam, you are embarrassing me."

Mrs. Inge wiped a small white handkerchief discreetly across her eyes, smiled at him, made a short curtsey.

"Then I will offer you only a simple farewell, sir. Your visit here has been an inspiration. The entire town will miss your presence. As most certainly will I."

Johnston was still embarrassed, looked around self-consciously, civilians gathering in the streets, many offering gifts, most giving a heavy handshake to the men who had made temporary homes in their town. Johnston saw his aide, holding the reins to his horse, the big bay he called Fire-Eater.

"It is time, madam. Your hospitality has been most appreciated. We shall perhaps return very soon to celebrate a great victory."

"We will pray for you, General. Oh!" She seemed to recall something, a momentary fluster. "Gloria has prepared something for your ride. Sandwiches and some cake. I almost forgot. Let me fetch them for you."

Johnston looked again at the horse, knew from a dozen glances at his watch that it was already past ten o'clock. He saw the black servant now, Gloria coming out onto the porch, a small cloth bundle in her hand.

Mrs. Inge took it, swirled around and with the soft smile he had seen so often, she unraveled it, produced smaller bundles wrapped in cloth.

"Here you are, General."

"No . . . thank you, madam. A soldier travels light. We have adequate rations. I cannot take such bounty from one who has already been so generous. The town must conserve what it has. You have given so much to this army."

He could see the disappointment in her eyes, but the smile remained, enough to hold his guilt away for denying her gift. His staff had already mounted their horses, lining up with the color bearer in the muddy street. He felt the hard itch of urgency, his mind focused on what lay ahead, what he still had to do, took the reins from his aide, prepared to climb up on the horse. She was there now, surprising him, said, "May you have safe travels, General, and a triumph over our enemies."

She leaned close, a brief, uncomfortable hug, then stepped back, made a curtsey, lowering her head. He did not hesitate, climbed the horse, raised his hat to her, said, "If we return here, madam, it will be in triumph."

She backed away, stood beside the Negro servant on the steps of her house, more of the townspeople drawing close, appreciating the moment, the meaning of this journey. He sat silently on the horse, stared away, a tumble of details in his mind, thought, what is there yet to do? Nothing that can be accomplished here. He knew how much talk there would be, knew that each of his generals would have their own report, that bickering and accusations would fly, the pride of men clouding the reality that they had not moved this army with the speed required of them. He could not focus on that now, said in a low voice, to no one in particular, "I have overlooked nothing. It is time."

He pulled the horse into the street, a gentle nudge with his spurs, and without looking back, he led his staff up the hill.

The roads were still muddy, the hooves of the horses soaked in thick gray goo. There had been yet another storm during the night, but the sky above them now was a blaze of perfect blue, the warmth from the sunshine bringing sweat inside his coat. He marveled at that, could not help thinking that this was a sign, some hint of a magnificent Gift yet to come. But the sun had not yet cured what ailed the roadways, and so, after a short few hours' ride, they were already passing pieces of his army, wagons and guns mostly, supply trains that could not move as men moved. Officers were scrambling as he passed, cursing at the men who cursed at the mud they struggled against. Wagons were swallowed to their axles, some tilting precariously, swarms of filthy soldiers and teamsters doing all they could to move their equipment forward.

Beside him and slightly back rode one of his adjutants, Colonel Brewster, and close beside Brewster, Isham Harris. There was no chatter, no idle conversation, and Johnston could feel the tension in them, and inside himself. He looked down repeatedly, measured the depth of the soft road, thought, a day or more and the sun should dry this out. But . . . we must be in our positions before that. We should have been there by now.

The young lieutenant, Baylor, rode up to the head of the small column, said, "Sir, beyond that far curve is the village of Monterey. All three of the corps commanders are in this vicinity. I have spoken previously to the proprietor of the general store there, who was most hospitable. It could be a good location for a council, should you desire, sir."

Johnston stared up the road, more wagons to one side, saw an artillery piece missing a wheel, its crew doing what they could to repair it. There were a few shouts directed toward him, but not many, not what he had heard before. He tried not to think on that, didn't really know what it meant. They are frustrated, he thought, as frustrated as I am, as we all are. And they are tired. This march is short but tedious in the extreme. But I must know they have the spirit. I must know they are ready to make this fight. Yes, a council is called for.

"Very well, Lieutenant. We shall stop ahead."

He turned in the saddle, the faces of his staff showing their alertness, waiting for any order.

"Major Munford, accompany the lieutenant to the village ahead, see to the facilities. We shall halt there for now. Send word to the corps commanders who can be located that I wish to see them as quickly as possible."

Munford saluted, Baylor as well, and Munford looked back, motioned to the couriers, the men who would ride fast, who knew how to ask the questions along the way, to find anyone Johnston needed to find. The men gathered in the road in front of him, and he nodded to Munford, the command given, the small piece of his staff riding away in a muddy gallop.

Johnston turned to the others, said, "Do we know where General Beauregard is?"

Major Hayden spoke up, another of the volunteer aides.

"I was with him briefly this morning, sir. Colonel Jordan advised me that General Beauregard was feeling well enough to ride, and would most certainly join us on the journey."

Johnston felt some relief from that, nodded his silent appreciation to Hayden. He saw Harris looking at him, unsmiling, the governor measuring it all, learning as he observed, trying to understand the flaws of the army, and what anyone could do about repairing them. Johnston seemed to read the question in Harris's face, said to them all, "Well, then, I suppose we shall sit in this place for a while and see if General Beauregard can locate us. I do not intend to be difficult to find."

The cavalry patrols had continued to spread out everywhere the Federals were thought to be moving, and in nearly every report, the horsemen had insisted that around the camps of the enemy, nothing at all was happening. *Nothing.*

There had been one exception, but rumors infected even the men who saw the enemy firsthand. Johnston knew that Lew Wallace's Federal Division had been positioned at Crump's Landing, several miles north and west of the main body of Grant's army. The cavalry scouts up that way had observed what seemed to be Wallace's entire force suddenly moving west, away from the river, driving out toward the town of Purdy, which would be the most logical place to stage a raid against the north-south rail line farther west at Bethel Station. Despite the urgent call to intercept the Federal forces from several of the cavalry commanders, Wallace's force turned out to be a minor shove, a probe that was stopped by Wallace himself, which resulted in no significant engagement, and no real threat to the railroad.

But the cavalry's initial panic had seemed to infect Beauregard as well, who suddenly latched on to the belief that the Federal forces were intending to capture that part of the railroad, and possibly drive farther west toward Jackson, Tennessee. The edge of panic in Beauregard's reaction had disturbed Johnston, and once the Federal troops in that area were clearly identified, and their intentions understood as little more than an exploratory probe out from Wallace's headquarters at Crump's Landing, Beauregard's attention had thankfully returned to the original plan. Johnston had no doubts at all that Grant was still at Pittsburg Landing, still waiting to be reinforced by Don Carlos Buell, and once the two armies joined, they would drive hard toward Corinth. The plans hashed out for a hard strike against Grant were, to Johnston, the only plan that had any chance of a major success. It was the kind of common sense that Johnston had observed in every theater of combat he had experienced: When the enemy sat motionless in front of you, and you had any possibility of surprising him with a hard-charging assault, the advantages were all yours.

MONTEREY, TENNESSEE
APRIL 4, 1862, 3:00 P.M.

Beauregard had arrived barely an hour after Johnston, his staff trailing behind him in a formation that seemed to Johnston to be a longer tail than any kite required. But Beauregard's work had been essential to this campaign, and Johnston would not criticize the man's efforts, and the necessity of a large staff, even if, now, those plans were becoming distressingly unraveled.

Johnston had ordered his aides to erect the headquarters tent, the work done as efficiently as usual. He stared at the dingy canvas now, already missed the comforts of Rose Cottage. He tried to push that from his mind, knew that out here, with the army driving closer to the enemy, hospitality was not something he should be thinking about. The headquarters tent held one other meaning, which he absorbed with growing frustration. He had not expected to spend this night so far from what he had hoped would be the point of attack. Monterey was barely halfway between Corinth and Pittsburg Landing, and still miles below the army's primary point of rendezvous, the intersection that brought the two primary roads together at a place called Pebble Hill, occupied by a house that the maps showed as *Michie's*.

The only corps commander to the front who had appeared at Monterey was Braxton Bragg, whose troops had marched out of Corinth along the same route Johnston and his staff had followed. The road was not nearly as well traveled as the parallel course to the west, where Hardee's and Polk's troops were designated to march. All three corps were to converge on the intersection at Michie's, where they would diverge again, Bragg moving more to the east on another parallel route, while Hardee and Polk continued to move to the north. According to Colonel Jordan's original plan of march, this would put Bragg on the right flank of the army, with Polk and Hardee to his left, once the entire force reached their stopping point, close to the enemy camps. To Johnston's enormous dismay, Bragg's troops had made no such progress, and even now, some were blocking the route where Polk was to be passing through, with various regiments from both corps spread out in several disconnected locations along the entire route. It was becoming clear to Johnston that the intersection that held so much value for the advance of the army had instead become a bottleneck of the worst kind.

"We should have hit them a week ago . . . maybe before then! Now I am mired in a sea of mud. This is unacceptable!"

Bragg was pacing, his energy draining everyone else. Beauregard showed the effects of the ride, sat on a small camp chair, leaning slightly, his back against a small oak tree. He straightened up, an obvious struggle, said, "Braxton, there was never any chance of mounting an organized assault until this army was in place. We had to gather every available unit, and the commanders to go with them. Surely you understand that. You were a great part of the accomplishment. I for one am grateful for all you have done."

Bragg didn't seem calmed by Beauregard's compliment, still fumed, stared down as he paced in the wet grass, a furious frown.

"The weather. The cursed weather. Have you seen the roads? Well of course you have. Rivers of mud a half foot deep! We could have avoided all of this. Driven northward on the railroad and come at the enemy from the west."

Johnston said nothing, sat in his usual position in the opening of the tent, a small field desk to one side. He had no energy for Bragg's ranting, hoped Beauregard would point out the obvious. The Creole obliged, said, "General, we could never have moved this entire army up the railroad in a short amount of time. The enemy would have detected that and destroyed us in detail. With all respect, the plan now in effect is a good one. The cavalry reports—"

"Bah! Cavalry! The glorious horsemen who ride in great parades with the sole priority of inflicting a blush on the pretty cheeks of the local females. The information they bring us is either too obvious to be of any use, or is simply wrong!"

Beauregard rubbed a tightly clenched fist across his chest, and Johnston could see he was too weary for this, would certainly have no patience for Bragg's absurd objections to a plan that was already in motion. Beauregard made another effort to straighten himself, coughed loudly, said, "That is hardly accurate. Without the cavalry, we would know nothing at all, and our plans depend on the complete knowledge of the enemy's position and his movements. You know that. The latest report tells us that the vanguard of General Buell's forces are no more than forty miles from Crump's Landing. The opportunity, our advantage, if there is one, is diminishing."

Johnston knew those reports, and he spoke now, the first time since Bragg had launched his verbal tantrum.

"There is still time. The Federals are encamped and show no sign of movement. We have cavalry patrols far to the north and east, and they continue to do all they can to slow General Buell's march. We must recognize the usefulness of that. I have received reports that General Grant's communications to General Buell have not displayed any sense of urgency."

Bragg spun around, faced him, lowered the tone of his voice just enough to demonstrate some awareness that Johnston was in command.

"May I be allowed to tell you about *urgency*, sir?"

Johnston nodded.

"We are ordered to begin our assault on the enemy at dawn tomorrow, is that not correct?"

"It is."

"We will not be prepared. I have units I still cannot locate. I have no doubt that General Polk is hopping mad at the delays he is facing. His troops had to halt their march while we were trying to clear our way through that infernal Michie's place. We should not have made contact with General Polk at all! We sent people up to the intersection and continued the march as ordered, moving out to the east. But there were gaps in my lines, and before I could reach that place, General Polk had arrived, and sent his wagons through to the north. But not all of them! The intersection was jammed solid, like a rat in a drainpipe. And so, my corps is scattered, General Polk's Corps is scattered. And we are supposed to sort all of this out by nightfall, so that we may continue our proper placement, according to orders, to make our attack at first light! With all respect to both of you, until I can gather my forces into a command that I can actually organize, it is unlikely there will be an attack at all. To order men in such a state to move forward . . . well, sirs, it is folly."

Johnston felt an increasing gloom spreading through him, had always believed that Bragg's fury was most useful directed toward the enemy. He looked at Beauregard, who had slumped again against the tree, with apparently nothing to add. He heard hoofbeats now, a shout from his staff, saw a rider coming up the muddy road. There were aides trailing the man, but not many, someone's efficient journey, the only sign of urgency Johnston had seen all day. The men dismounted now, and Johnston saw the familiar flag. It was John Breckinridge.

Johnston stood, was surprised, moved away from the tent, Bragg close behind him.

"General, I did not expect to see you so quickly. Are your troops closing up?"

Breckinridge saluted him, and Johnston saw the clear blue eyes, the sharp mustache shading a frown. Breckinridge said, "I regret, sir, the reserve corps is having some difficulty making progress. Many of my men are still near their camps near Farmington. The wagon train is the worst problem. Most are buried hard in the mud. We are working as energetically as we can, but the going is slow. I report this, sir, with sincere regret."

Breckinridge had always shown the talents of the politician, and unlike Isham Harris, Breckinridge's sins against the North were magnified in the Northern papers as the worst kind of black deed, a traitorous abandonment of the U.S. Senate, and a direct slap at the sanctity of the high office he had once held. If anyone in Johnston's army had reason to agonize over the decision to join the Southern Cause it would be the former vice president. But Breckinridge was here now, in command of the invaluable reserve corps, and obviously, any conflicts he had were neatly cast away.

Johnston absorbed his report like a spreading disease.

"Do you believe you can have your people in their designated position by tonight?"

"I will make every effort, sir. I will toss aside my horse, and march them on foot, if it inspires them to quickness."

"That would not be prudent, General. But please make every effort to march your men forward. I do not have to tell you the importance of your reserves to this campaign."

"Certainly not, sir."

Johnston felt a sharp breeze, looked up now, the blue skies erased by a thickening gray haze. He stared, others following his gaze, and now the first drops came, slapping the ground with small patters that drooped his shoulders, that settled into his brain like one more sickening failure.

"Gentlemen, it appears the rain has returned."

## CHAPTER TWELVE

# SHERMAN

NEAR SHILOH CHURCH
APRIL 4, 1862, 3:00 P.M.

With the good weather that morning, the sounds had carried easily through the expanse of woods, and the Federal picket lines, and even the camps themselves had begun to hear noises that could only come from a gathering of men. From out of the west, shouts were heard, laughter, the clank and squeal of wagon wheels. Rumors had begun, spreading along the picket lines with mindless energy, the rebel cavalry pushing closer, more aggressively, some insisting that the sounds were just echoes from other Federal camps. But there were more inspiring rumors, that the noises had to come from something much larger, that in the distant fields and roadways, surely there was danger from the approach of the enemy.

The most untested soldiers were the first to feel the edge of panic, and even their officers could not hide their fears, some of them reporting with nervous certainty that they would likely be attacked. But higher up the chain, where experienced men had faced the enemy before, orders were issued that took the sting from the rumors, comforting words that cavalry patrols were a nuisance but little more. So many of those patrols had already been observed by the pickets, some by Federal cavalry, making their own forays into the enemy's land. There had been clashes, most of them minor, but the rebels seemed intent on avoiding any real confrontation, their patrols mostly glimpsed from great distances, a fleeting burst of activity across a wide field, the enemy horsemen quick to withdraw. When the horsemen had met, it was usually a surprise to both sides, hoofbeats disguising the same sounds coming toward them from down the curving road. Often the two columns of horsemen were suddenly facing each other with no choice for the surprised officers but to give the order to attack. The firefights were usually quick affairs, but there were casualties, the unlucky, men struck by musket balls, or the chance firing of a recklessly aimed carbine. Few among the Federal cavalry commanders were inspired to push out seeking greater confrontations. There was no surge of revenge for fallen comrades, or even for saving face. Rather, the Federals probed the woods and trails with more caution, and it seemed that the rebels were doing the same. The primary mission for the blue-coated horsemen was to prevent the rebel patrols from drawing too close to the camps, no careless loss of prisoners, no intelligence that someone far away in rebel headquarters would find useful. The Confederates seemed willing only to harass, to test the willingness of the Federals to make any kind of fight at all. This day had begun no differently, cavalry probes, observation, sometimes with a casual wave from great distance, men watching their counterparts with amusement, contests with marksmanship, the company's best shot trying to knock down someone *over there.*

In the camps of the infantry, the sounds of any confrontation rolled back to them as hollow echoes, dull thumps, scattered and distant. But there were officers who were not comfortable sitting blind, and so some of the regimental and brigade commanders had ordered more patrols, men on foot, to follow the trails, pushing beyond the static picket lines, to see more of what the cavalry saw, to test the bravado of whoever might be testing them.

But then the rains had returned, and the sounds and the enthusiasm were erased by the steady hiss from the downpour through the tall trees. The men from the 70th Ohio were like so many others, the order simple and direct, to move out westward, probing, scouting what might lie farther out in front of the pickets. One squad moved in familiar misery, the unlucky half dozen who were chosen to leave behind the comfort of their tents, their fires, a mission most thought was an enormous waste of time and dry clothes. They kept their slow march on a wide trail, a wagon road, thick mud that soaked their shoes, the wet slime soaking their pants legs. The rain hid any noise, but still they pressed forward, following their lieutenant, a man as miserable as the men he led. The mud had deepened to the point of absurdity, and the frustrated lieutenant dragged his men off the trail, pushed them through the woods, wet leaves slapping the men's faces, heavy drips of rainwater rolling into coat collars and cartridge boxes. They moved mostly in blindness, their greatest concern that the lieutenant would get them lost. The woods had been a curse, vines and low branches, and they welcomed a patch of open ground, moving more quickly, a hint of tension, competing with the sense of futility, every man thinking more of dry socks and coffee than any glimpse of the enemy. Like so many of the open fields, this one was punctuated by a small farmhouse, and whether its occupants were there or not, the lieutenant made a beeline for the marvelous sanctuary of a dry space.

When the rebel cavalry came, they came knowing that the Federals liked their shelter, and so the horses moved with stealth. Their officer had seen this before, Federal troops too comfortable, and so the horsemen kept as silent as possible, approached the house from behind, or what might be a blind spot, finally emerging from the closest stand of dense trees. In a few seconds the farmhouse was surrounded by horsemen now on foot, and though there was musket fire, the rebels had every advantage. The success was complete, the Federal troops facing the muzzles of two dozen of the enemy, their lieutenant understanding his fate, that he and his six men had no choice but to surrender.

"**W**ho?"

"A squad of pickets from the 70th Ohio, sir. They're just . . . gone. We have to assume they were taken by the enemy."

Sherman crushed the cigar in his teeth, tried to pull smoke through it, useless now, tossed it out into the rain, grabbed another from his pocket.

"Captured by *who*, Captain?"

"Unknown, sir. We assume it was one of the rebel cavalry patrols.

They seem to be everywhere. Our own cavalry continues to report frequent confrontations."

Sherman paced the small space inside the meetinghouse, what the locals had told him was their church. The building was rough-hewn timbers, barely large enough for his staff.

He had heard too many of these reports, some of them caused by the panic of the untrained, some by officers who seemed anxious to build their own reputation by being so much more vigilant than the next man down the line. One of those had been Colonel Thomas Worthington, who commanded the 46th Ohio, and who had made himself such a thorn in Sherman's side that he was banned from Sherman's headquarters. Worthington was a much older man, had brought his regiment to Pittsburg Landing nearly three weeks prior, and demonstrated a wholly inappropriate eagerness for taking command of the entire operation. Once in camp, Worthington had plagued Sherman with his predictions of certain disaster, had insisted his men be supplied with near a hundred axes, to throw an abatis into place, defying the orders that came from Grant, which of course had come from Halleck. Worthington had even bypassed the chain of command, had gone straight to General Smith, had asserted his own supposed expertise on just what the army should be preparing for. After several such visits, even the patient Smith had tossed Worthington from his floating headquarters.

"Are you certain of this, Captain? By any chance is this report coming to you from Colonel Worthington?"

The captain smiled, then corrected himself, shook his head.

"No, sir. Colonel Buckland spoke to me himself, sir."

"By damned, I am sick of the enemy's little games. Has Buckland done anything to investigate this?"

"Yes, sir. The colonel reports he has ordered his picket lines strengthened and has ordered a full company forward, in effort to pursue whatever enemy is responsible."

"I thought you said it was cavalry, Captain. Does Buckland think his foot soldiers can catch a cavalry patrol?"

The young man glanced downward.

"I cannot answer that, sir."

"Well, I have my own answer. The 5th Ohio Cavalry is camped just out to the northwest of here. Order Major Ricker to lead a hundred of those men out west of Buckland's camp. Have Ricker investigate the placement of Buckland's picket line and determine what the hell is happening out there. Send a courier to Buckland so he'll know I'm not going to tolerate this kind of nuisance anymore. I've been listening to that chatter all day long, musket fire and whatever else is going on. Half the time it sounds like a damn barn dance, complete with banjos and fiddles, and squalling house cats. If there are rebel cavalry who think they can dance their way close enough to spit on us, I want them driven out of here. Tell Major Ricker if he finds them to kill every damn one of them. These men might be green, but they are capable of following orders and keeping some kind of military discipline. I'm more convinced that all that racket we're hearing out there is coming from our own people. This isn't a damn hunting party. I'm sick of hearing all this talk, all this blasted panic caused by a few enemy cavalry. You have your orders, Captain."

The man saluted, moved out quickly into the rain. Sherman struggled with shaking hands to light a new cigar, felt the soggy tobacco limp in his hands, the spray of rain infesting even his most simple pleasure. To one side, two of his staff officers sat in the church's only remaining chairs, and he saw them studying papers, assumed they were pretending not to hear him. More of his aides were gathered inside one of the headquarters tents, and he called out to them, his tone of voice unmistakable. He waited, tapped his foot noisily on the plank floors of the small church, glanced at the soggy cigar again, tossed it angrily out into the rain. Men were coming toward him quickly, and they stopped short, stood at attention, seeming not to mind the rain. He shook his head.

"Get in here. I don't need anyone on my staff drowning. Ridiculous damn weather."

The staff crowded into the church, water flowing down and across every surface, the musty smell of stinking uniforms curling his nose. Sherman stood back, waited for them to get completely inside. "Damn. You boys need to take a hike back to the river, douse those clothes in some clean water. Maybe douse you, too." He stood with his hands on his hips, couldn't prevent his annoyance with what seemed to be the chaos of his own front lines. "You got the water out of your ears? Good. Now listen. Send my order to every regiment that I want the picket lines to be strengthened across our entire position. Have the commanders put some fresh men out there. I don't know how much longer we're going to be holed up in this godforsaken swamp, but I'm through having my brigades panicked by ghosts. If I have to order a full-scale drill formation I will. We've got some boys out there who seem to have forgotten why we're here. Tell every company commander I want the miscreants sent to the river. I'll not have the unruly affecting the rest of this command."

His orderly had kept to one corner of the small church, the man expectant, ready for anything Sherman needed of him. Sherman turned to him now, said, "Mr. Holliday, will you please locate some dry cigars. There is a box in my trunk, at the foot of my bed. The ones in my coat have been made useless by this damnable weather. Locate some matches as well. I never should have tossed away that flint box."

Holliday moved quickly, disappeared back out into the rain, splashing his way to one of the nearby headquarters tents.

"The rest of you . . . Captain Hammond, send an inquiry to General Prentiss. See if he is experiencing the same kind of supposed harassment from the rebels, or are his men hearing ghosts as well. If he's got rebels to his front, kindly suggest he drive those damn mosquitoes away. Major Sanger, stay close to me. If Ricker's cavalry doesn't do the job, I want you to be ready to lead somebody out there yourself. Or find somebody who can. How blessedly difficult can it be to clear these woods of a few damn rebels?"

SHILOH CHURCH
APRIL 4, 1862, 6:00 P.M.

Ricker was dripping wet, a pool of brown water forming at his feet, a smear of dirt across his face. Sherman could see he was obviously pleased with himself.

"It was a brisk affair, sir. We took their measure, and gave back plenty."

"How brisk?"

"I must admit, sir, that the infantry had beaten us somewhat to the chase. When Colonel Buckland learned his men had been captured, he ordered forward a full regiment. Begging your pardon, sir, but I thought that to be somewhat excessive. But we reached the correct field by following the sounds of a fight. With all credit due Colonel Buckland, his infantry had been successful in locating the rebel horsemen. It is possible, of course, that it was the other way around. The rebel cavalry could very well have set an ambush, in case any of us took umbrage at their capture of Colonel Buckland's squad. But there was a scrap, sir, and we determined quite quickly that Colonel Buckland's men were in something of a pickle. The reb cavalry were giving it to them pretty hard, but our arrival took care of the problem. Those rebs weren't looking for a fair fight, and it was apparent that when we drove toward them, we put the fear of God in them. They fled the field. I have not heard if Colonel Buckland recaptured his lost squad, sir, but I am pleased to report that we were able to grab a few of those rebels in return. They're outside."

"How many?"

"Ten are here, sir. We left wounded in the field. They're being cared for."

Sherman had a burst of curiosity, moved to the doorway of the small church, peered through the thickening darkness, could see the rebels sitting in a mass under a fat oak tree.

"Bring me one. Pick the one who looks the most scared."

Ricker motioned to one of his men, and Sherman kept his stare outside, the rain light and misty now. Ricker's cavalrymen spread out down one of the trails that led away from the church, a loose column of weary troopers, those who saw him sitting straight in the saddle, a clear sign that they knew the day was theirs. He nodded toward one of the officers, thought, yes, good. We need more of you out there. Ricker's right. They're not looking for a fair fight. Just . . . bullying us, picking at us like fleas on a dog. Well, enough of that.

He felt a gust of wind, a light spray on his face. The rain had nearly stopped, but the trees near the church were giving up the wetness in their leaves, and he cursed to himself, backed away from the door. Across the open yard, one of the rebels was pulled toward him, no sign of a uniform, a thick patch of greasy hair matted across his forehead. The man was escorted by two of Ricker's men, and Ricker followed, stood behind the prisoner, said, "Get inside, secesh. You get to meet a real general."

Sherman tried to look imposing, glanced around, the chairs in the church too small, undignified. All right, I should stand anyway, stare at him eye to eye. He crossed his arms, tried to ignore the aching need for a cigar.

The prisoner climbed the short steps into the church, was in front of him now, held tightly in the grip of two of Ricker's horsemen. Sherman studied the man, very young, a wisp of a beard on his chin, his homespun clothes stained with days of mud. He didn't seem frightened at all.

"So, boy, what's your name?"

The prisoner puffed out his chest, made a good show of defiance.

"That would be Micah Goolsby."

To one side, one of his escorts jerked him hard.

"You say *sir* to the general!"

"Reckon not. You done caught me. That means I ain't a soldier no more."

Sherman was fascinated more by the man's deep drawl than by his attitude. He had rarely heard such a pronounced accent since Louisiana.

"You're right, boy. Your war is over. So, you've got no more secrets to hide. Where are you from, Mr. Goolsby?"

"Brooksville. That's Mississippi. Down south of here."

"Don't know the place. I doubt you'll be seeing it for a while. So, who was it sent you out here in this infernal weather, just so you could take potshots at my boys?"

The young man weighed the question, seemed to debate whether to respond, but after a long moment the debate was settled.

"Reckon you'll find out soon enough. Colonel Clanton. He rode us up here mad as a hornet. Seems we lost a couple of our men to one of your picket posts down toward the river a ways. The colonel don't take kindly to Yankees stealing his men. We decided to get a little of that for ourselves. Did, too. But . . . well, it weren't my lucky day. We was about to round up a whole passel of Yankee infantry when your horsemen showed up."

Sherman glanced at his staff officer, Major Sanger, who nodded, said, "Heard of Clanton. Not sure who commands him."

"And you ain't gonna know nothin' more about that, neither. Not till he rides right in here and grabs the whole lot of you!"

Sherman admired the man's spark, said, "Well, now, we'll be certain to give our regards to your Colonel Clanton."

"Oh, you'll be doin' more than that, *General sir*. There's gonna be a full out beatin', right here. When it's over, you'll be tossed in the river, or driven to hell. Either way, you fellas is gonna learn that we ain't takin' none of this from you Yankees. You best git back on those steamboats right now."

Sherman said nothing, thought, so, if he knows about the boats, he's been close enough to the river to see or hear them. They might have been watching the landing ever since we got here. Crafty bastards.

He had heard all the man's boasting he needed, said to Sanger, "Major, I'm returning to my tent. There's a box of cigars in the bottom of my trunk, and one of them requires my attention."

Ricker said, "What do we do with these prisoners, sir?"

Sherman thought a moment, looked around the small church.

"Stick 'em in here. I'm not wasting time or men to haul them back to the river. They can sleep dry for tonight, and they'll be easier to guard." He looked at the boy in front of him, still defiant, but there was a small crack in the boy's bravado, a hint of a tear in his eyes. Sherman smiled to himself, thought, that's more like it. Now you understand. Take a good look around you, Mr. Goolsby. This is the United States Army you're playing with.

"Thank you for speaking with me, Mr. Goolsby. You get a good night's sleep. Then, tomorrow, we'll send you back to where we keep the cannibals. They do like Southern meat."

He didn't wait for a reaction, clamped his hat hard on his head, moved out into the rain, turned toward the larger tent, the urgent need for a cigar all he could think about.

# CHAPTER THIRTEEN

# SEELEY

SOUTHEAST OF SHILOH CHURCH
APRIL 4, 1862, 9:00 P.M.

They pushed through the dark muddy trails, kept the horses as quiet as they could, no one speaking, no orders shouted out. He was one of nearly two hundred horsemen, a snaking line that kept back far enough from the Federal camps so they would not be detected. He knew that some of the other cavalry had pushed too hard, were more aggressive than they were supposed to be. The result had been a scattering of engagements, brief and manic fights with a few casualties, but Captain McDonald's company had not yet fired a shot. There had been Yankees, and throughout the day, Seeley and the others had caught their brief glimpses of blue-coated horsemen. Most were across a ravine, or far up ahead on the same road. But so far, those men wanted no part of a fight, and Seeley took some pride in that, was beginning to accept what Colonel Forrest had drilled into all of them. They were better men, better at the job, and even if the Yankees had better weapons, talk of repeating rifles, or carbines that required little time to load, it was the spirit of Forrest's men that Seeley believed gave them every advantage. That no Federal seemed interested in standing up to them now was just more evidence.

Their mission had been to screen the advance of the infantry, primarily Bragg's Corps, the men who were to spread their combat formation out toward the river. But the bulk of Bragg's infantry had not come up, just a scattering of advance units, men who called themselves lucky, who had made most of their march before the new rains had come. For most of the afternoon, orders had come to McDonald, and they expressed what had to be the entire command's aggravated frustration, that no one had kept to their schedule. Their mission had been unchanged, move discreetly, stealthily, continue to serve as a screen to prevent Federal cavalry from gaining any real intelligence about just what Johnston's army was trying to do. But so far, Johnston's army had accomplished very little, no great lines of foot soldiers hunkering down in vast formations, preparing for the great assault that would come at dawn. And if there was any need for a screen at all, the Yankees showed no sign of testing it. Patrols were seen, and the crackle of the fights had echoed through the fields and woodlands, but it was obvious to McDonald, to every cavalry commander, that the Yankees weren't really seeking much in the way of intelligence at all. With the darkness, the rains had nearly stopped, and even from a mile away, Seeley could see the glow of the campfires, the Yankees going about their routine as though no cavalry were in these woods at all.

M cDonald halted them, a harsh whisper spread back along the column, the only way to communicate in a darkness that was dense and oppressive. Seeley kept his position in line, had passed along the order to the sergeant behind him, that man doing the same. The night was growing thick with sounds, insects mostly, frogs and crickets that Seeley had heard all his life. But there were other sounds as well, voices, and the halt in the column had come so that McDonald could estimate the distance. Seeley stared into dense trees, knew they had passed this way in the daylight, a steady march that covered a very specific piece of what was supposed to be Bragg's front lines. But the voices they were hearing now were not Confederate, and Seeley made his own judgment, guessed the men to be no more than two hundred yards away. A horse sidled up close to him, and he heard the growling whisper of Sergeant Gladstone.

"Bluebellies having a party, eh? Like a camping trip with my young'uns. They'll be building fires out here, next thing you know."

Seeley had no idea Gladstone had children, tried to visualize that in his mind, what kind of father this crusty and crude man would be. The voices were mostly from one place, a hilltop beyond the black trees, and suddenly there was the crack of a musket, a loud whoop, more laughter. The words were disguised, but the mood certainly was not, and now there was commotion in the brush, pushing out toward the road, away from the Yankees. Seeley felt his heart jump, but Gladstone said, "Deer. Dumb bluebellies are huntin' deer. Well, shootin' anyway. Bet they been shootin' rabbits, too. Not a care in the world. Guess that'll make the colonel happy."

Gladstone eased his horse away, and the column kept still, Seeley staring toward the voices, the laughter quieting. They have no idea we're here, he thought. And even if they do, they don't seem to care much one way or the other.

He heard a rustle of horses, a rider coming back toward him, knew from the man's gait it was McDonald. The captain whispered, "Officers!"

Seeley spurred the horse lightly, moved to one side, away from the others, and McDonald was there now, others coming up from the rear of the column. There were four lieutenants, and Seeley looked around, saw them all gathering close.

"Listen here! We need to backtrack to that creek we passed a mile or so behind us. Good water, and we can hold tight there until dawn. I've gotten no orders since sundown, and our job hasn't changed. We're to screen the advance of General Bragg's right flank, and that's what we're gonna do. I have no idea where that flank is right now, but it sure ain't where I was told. But I'm not taking any chances of stumbling into a bunch of General Bragg's worn-out soldiers who're nervous about what they're supposed to do next. We'll dismount, put up shelter halves, and wait for dawn. If the attack happens when it's supposed to, we'll be ready to help. That's all I know, and that's all we can do tonight. Turn your squads around, march back to that old bridge. We'll spread out in those woods, on the west side of the road . . . the right. I'll send a courier back to the south, try to locate someone in charge, let 'em know where we are. Let's go."

The order passed along the column, the men turning their mounts, the column beginning to move. Seeley was more toward the rear now, eased his horse forward in the sloppy mud. He thought of the shelter half, a piece of canvas he hated, what was supposed to be protection from rain. But so far, the storms that had blown past the cavalrymen had swirled rain right through any kind of protection, the chilling weather soaking through the wool coats, boots, anything else a man hoped to keep dry. It had gone on for so long now that when the daylight had broken that morning, with dry blue skies, the men had stood for long moments, staring up in perfect fascination. With the men quickly in motion, the sunlight had sliced through the soggy woods in a glorious display that drained the men of their misery. But the clear weather had brought Yankees, and the skirmishes had come, and Seeley knew that the joy of dry weather had put both sides into motion. By mid-afternoon, when the skies darkened yet again, word had reached them of the delays, and Seeley had already seen the mud on the roads that had so plagued the foot soldiers, and worse, had sucked down the wagons and limbers of the teamsters and artillerymen. But the cavalrymen kept their enthusiasm for the job at hand, no one expecting that delays on the march would change anything, that by tomorrow morning, the great assault, what might be the final assault, would drive the Yankees straight back into the river.

They pitched their individual shelters, some using the canvas beneath them, keeping the wet ground away. No one had complained, no one protesting the order that would keep them out here, so close to the enemy, so deep into the constant misery of the weather.

Seeley found a stout tree, piled wet leaves into a soft mattress. He moved out from his shelter, checked on his men, on Gladstone, everyone doing what he had done. The men were spread all along the road, set into place by the captain to be in the best position to ambush anyone who happened to stumble past. Seeley had wondered about that, McDonald's certainty that they would know the enemy from their own men, but the captain had perfect confidence that his patrol was the only one designated in this stretch of roadway. Seeley had to accept that McDonald knew what he was talking about. If horsemen came, they would be Yankees.

He slipped into his shelter now, the whining of mosquitoes immediate, joined by the background of chirping crickets, croaking frogs. The Yankees had quieted, for now, or else had gone into shelters of their own. Even the enemy needs sleep, he thought. They're not devils or godless beasts. Just poor dumb volunteers, sent down here to conquer people who won't be conquered. Simple as that. Just as simple what we're gonna do to them.

He pulled his coat up around his face, tried to escape the mosquitoes, the only remedy there was. The sounds were muffled now, and he tried to calm his heartbeat, to find some way to sleep. He felt the cold turn in his chest, thought of the Yankees he had seen that day, scattered bursts of musket fire, but nothing like he had hoped. He let out a breath, stuffed his hands into his wet coat pockets, lay motionless, the softness of the leaves not nearly soft enough. It would have been wonderful, he thought, a hard charge right into those bluebellies, scattering them to the hills. He had practiced waving his sword high over his head, alone of course, making the piercing scream they had repeated in their drills. The mock fury had come, too, but he knew it would never be like that, that when it was time to face those bluebellies, when the sword went up, it was serious and deadly, and a man had to prove himself better than his enemy. I *am* better, he thought. We are all better. They won't even stand up to us when we're right in front of them. They take their potshots and scamper away. Scared rabbits. Not what I expected. Not a bit. He thought often of the man he had captured back at the Duck River, the terrified Yankee whose only mistake was that he was a good swimmer. Wonder where he is now? They send him home with a parole? Not an officer, so maybe he's in one of the prisons. Not me. Nobody's gonna catch me. I got a good horse . . . good commanders. He stopped himself, didn't want to think on that, on what it would mean if he had to *escape.* Nope, I don't plan on running away from anybody. I'm going home a hero. Maybe we all are.

He knew there would be no sleep, his thoughts roaring through his head, fantasies of what would happen tomorrow, what kind of confrontation they would find. It didn't happen today, he thought. Maybe not my time yet. But the Almighty has a plan, no doubt about that. All I ask, Lord, is you let me at 'em. Let Katie and everyone else back home know that when I come riding down the street in Memphis, people will stop and wave and say, now by God, there goes a soldier.

## CHAPTER FOURTEEN

# JOHNSTON

NEAR MONTEREY, TENNESSEE
APRIL 5, 1862,
MID-MORNING

Before midnight, a new storm had blown up, a blustery violence that brought down tree limbs and flattened tents. By dawn, when the attack was scheduled to begin, the rains had ceased, the sun rising to a clean, misty sky. Even in the worst of the downpour, Johnston had continued to move, and if there had been any sleep at all, it had come in the saddle. As the sun rose through the trees, Johnston had stared often at his pocket watch, the 8 A.M. timetable crawling toward him like the onset of a miserable sickness. He had ridden across most of the places his troops were supposed to be, had found what his generals already knew, that there were great gaps in the lines that were supposed to have been a solid force. By the scheduled time of the attack, Johnston knew it could not happen. The army was not yet ready, and no matter the forcefulness of his orders, or the energetic efforts of his generals to reclaim control of their disorganized troops, the army would be forced to wait. Throughout the morning, as hour passed hour, the bright sun rose above flowering treetops, the air crisp and breezy, the roads starting to dry. But still the army lagged, some troops finding their place in line only to discover they were isolated, their commanding generals

far back, still pushing forward their men and their artillery, all the crucial pieces of the army that for two days now had floundered in the mud.

Along what was to have been the assault lines, Hardee's Corps was
mostly intact, the one bright spot in the maneuvering that had gone
close to schedule. But Hardee knew he was not strong enough to start
anything with the Yankees to his front, whether they expected him to be
there or not. As Bragg's troops advanced, even his furious efficiency
could not push the right people into place, and Johnston did what Bragg
was doing, kept moving, staff officers in tow, messengers scrambling to
find the regimental commanders. Johnston himself had found units
who were lost, or just confused, some of their leaders inexplicably stopping for the night, their men kept motionless in distant fields, like lost
children waiting for the rescue from a parent.

By noon, most of the army had sorted itself out, but the attack formation was far from complete. Far behind the lines, troops and artillery
continued to slog their way through the country roads and farm lanes.
By early afternoon, some troops were still far away, some still jumbled
together with other units, too many men and too many wagons vying
for the same miserable roadways. Other units seemed to be nowhere at
all, even their corps commanders having no idea what had happened to
entire regiments, and in Braxton Bragg's case, one entire division.

As the hours ticked forward, Johnston's frustration swelled into fury,
and when he stumbled across the wayward colonel or the brigadier who
was no place he was supposed to be, Johnston did all he could to hold his
temper, to give the appropriate order, explaining in tightly wound words
the expectations, the directions. As he left each location, the anger he
fought so hard to control began to chew at him, sickening his stomach,
sweat in his shirt. When the sun passed its zenith, Johnston finally had to
accept the fact that with barely half his army in the place they were supposed to be, there was no way to salvage the day. On this Saturday there
would be no attack. Johnston had no idea how many miles he had ridden,
how many troops he had seen, how many officers shared his frustration
that on this gloriously beautiful day, the opportunity for a fight was slipping away. As he made his way back toward his temporary headquarters
at Monterey, he knew his horse was exhausted, as much as its rider, and
Johnston had finally to concede that he could not just drive the animal to

death. With the village a half mile to his front, he had stopped, ordered his staff to remain behind, spurred the horse into a small clearing where no one could see. He dismounted the horse, led it to the edge of a patch of deep grass, sat, the horse standing obediently still, the one witness to the struggle he endured to hold back the emotions. The tears were brief; not even in solitude would he grant himself the favor of letting go of his control. It had been like this before, the death of his first wife, and then, years later, the death of his young daughter, the girl gone now a dozen years. There would be no great display of sorrow, his loss kept silent, locked away. As he sat alone in the grassy field, he held it back still, would fight the frustration as he always fought it, one more piece of God's test, that no matter the tragedies or the failures, he would stand firm, he would accept what role he was to play. The loss of his daughter had thundered through him as the greatest test of all, and he had expressed his sadness to his friends through letters, releasing his emotions in words on paper. That pain had eased now, replaced by the agonizing absence from his beloved China Grove, and the woman who would pray for him to return.

The horse waited patiently for him, and Johnston leaned down, plucked a tuft of grass from the soggy soil, could smell the mustiness of so much rain, one more reminder of his love of the earth, of all he had missed by joining this new army. The decision had been so difficult for so many, including men who served him now, but it had never been difficult for him. No matter his love of the land, his love of the army could never be denied. He had to believe that Eliza understood that. But her letters came often, soft hints that she pained for his return. He found no fault with that. It was a pain he shared. He had thought the relief from that might come before now, that the angry talk about his poor performance in Kentucky might have ended his career. But President Davis believed in him, perhaps more than Johnston believed in himself. No doubt his reputation was damaged, and despite all Johnston had said to Harris, he felt the sting of his critics, had hoped in some quiet place that this campaign could give him vindication. That is selfish, he thought. But to retire to the land with the honor of a duty well done . . . that does mean something, no matter what I tell anyone else. Eliza knows that, certainly. I could never go home and plant my vegetables and pretend I am happy if I left my duty undone, if my honor has been squandered by failure. He smiled, shook his head. I cannot admit that to Governor Harris. I must pretend that the newspapers mean nothing, that my reputation beyond this army means nothing. He stared up at the blue above him, a strange thought curling through his mind. I do not love this. The army, yes. But not this war. I believe in what we do, but it brings me no joy to watch this nation pulled apart. He glanced around, self-conscious. No, that is not a conversation I can have with anyone. I am not reluctant, after all. There can be no hesitation. Even now, with so much of this campaign planned by others, men who are supposed to answer to me . . . I do not object to that.

He couldn't help thinking of Beauregard, and the annoying Colonel Jordan. As the march out of Corinth began, and the astounding difficulties with the logistics were quickly apparent, the plan of attack the two men had so carefully designed had been changed completely. Beauregard had insisted that instead of the great arc, with the three primary corps strung end to end, the army could best strike the enemy in parallel lines, each corps lined up behind the other. The focus would center on the small church the locals called Shiloh, above the crossroads at Michie's. Beauregard's strategy now called for a sharp hammer blow that would strike the enemy in waves. Beauregard had announced the change to Johnston with a matter-of-fact smoothness, bolstered by the oily assurances of Colonel Jordan that with so many difficulties putting the army into position, this would be a far more practical alternative. Johnston had found it difficult to object, had to accept that these men had drawn up their strategy after weeks of study, and if they believed this was the best way, then he would not order otherwise. I have to trust them, he thought. I have to trust in every officer in this command, or I am no leader. I cannot lead by decree, by forcing myself into every decision.

He did not look at his watch, glanced up at the sun, knew it was growing late, already mid-afternoon, a final confirmation that no attack could be launched at all. He climbed up on the horse and moved back out of the field, could see the staff was waiting for him, obedient, loyal, good men, men he had grown to respect, men who understood more of his moods than he wanted. He rode close to them in silence, the emotions drained now, no one questioning where he had been, or why. He rode back toward Monterey with a calm sadness, saw more aides waiting for him, saw anxiousness, men waving frantically. He glanced back at the officers close behind him, saw shrugs, surprise. He spurred the horse, led them forward at a trot, said, "Well, let's find out what's happening."

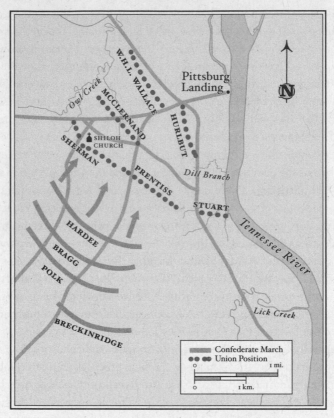

**COLONEL JORDAN'S "NEW PLAN" OF ATTACK**

NORTH OF MONTEREY, TENNESSEE
APRIL 5, 1862, 4:00 P.M.

He saw them in a cluster, standing in the middle of the road. As he rode
closer, the faces turned toward him, and he saw the hard looks of men
who had nothing pleasant to say. The staffs of the generals were off in the
distance, each in a gathering to themselves, the message clear. This was
not a meeting for everyone to share. Johnston looked back, said,
"Remain at a distance. Obviously, there is some debate taking place."

He rode closer, the men in the road watching him, various looks of
disgust on their faces. It was the first time he had seen Beauregard, Polk,
Bragg, and Breckinridge in one place since Corinth. The missing com-

mander was Hardee, who he knew was up with his troops on the front lines. The only other officer there was Gilmer, the engineer, who Johnston knew had come from Hardee. Gilmer was the only one who saluted him, which Johnston returned, and Johnston thought, well, at least if they talk about Hardee behind his back, Gilmer will be a reliable witness. The men were arranged in something of a semicircle around Beauregard, no surprise there at all. Johnston dismounted, saw crisp nods in his direction, no one else saluting. Beauregard turned away from Johnston, as though his arrival were a mere inconvenience, but Polk spoke up, looking directly at Johnston.

"I will not be blamed for this. My troops made every effort to march according to orders, and we made as much progress as conditions allowed. To suggest that my men are the cause of the delay is an outrage."

Johnston did not speak, moved up beside the group, stood away to one side, would not be the center of their attention. Beauregard glanced at him, seemed satisfied that Johnston was showing what to Beauregard must have seemed like appropriate deference. Beauregard said, "There is more to our difficulties than the delay in reaching our designated positions. The men are as undisciplined as I have ever seen them. We have issued the strictest orders that silence be maintained, especially as we approached earshot of the enemy. That order has been widely ignored, and is being ignored as we speak. Stand here in silence, and hear it for yourself! There is scattered musket fire in every part of our position, the pickets going about their usual routine of clearing their muskets, as though no enemy is within miles of our position. I have observed men playing games, pursuing rabbits and squirrels as though this is some kind of social outing! Men are calling out to one another, and some are in communication with enemy pickets, shouting curses and threats, giving perfect warning to the very men we are hoping to surprise! This entire plan is crumbling about us, the rotten timbers of a rotten house. It is the worst possible result of a strategy that is no longer under my control. I have entrusted this campaign to you, and you have responded by tossing our advantages to the four winds!" Beauregard struggled with his voice, was drawn, pale, the anger taking away what energy he had been able to muster. But Johnston could see more coming, the others still silent. "I rode with General Hardee along his lines, at his invitation. I rode to offer inspiration to the men, to offer them a silent message that all was well. They responded by cheering me! In full hearing of the enemy positions! Hardee's officers had to scramble about like madmen to quiet them. It was as ridiculous a demonstration as I have seen."

Bragg spoke up now, carried the frown that Johnston was accustomed to.

"Why in God's name would you ride out in front of troops who were sitting in line of battle? We put those people there prepared to engage in a full-scale attack. Their blood is up! That's what we train them for! Of course they cheer you. Your presence is certainly an inspiration, but your choice of timing was . . . ill-advised."

Beauregard sniffed, but he did not respond to Bragg's logic, seemed exhausted, obviously hoping someone else would speak out. The first was Breckinridge.

"There is one other unfortunate problem. My men have consumed nearly all of their rations. We issued them five full days, but the march weakened them, and most did not take such careful accounting as the commissary officers."

Polk responded.

"That is not unusual for men going into combat. I have often seen stockpiles of rations designated to provide for a week's time devoured in two days or less. Men who believe they are facing death don't pay much attention to instructions from the commissary."

Bragg waved his arm.

"That is of minor concern. We will have the wagons move up as quickly as these roads are cleared. Rations will be provided. My own commissary has ample supply. I will see that rations are distributed as rapidly as practicable."

Beauregard clenched his fists, seemed to squeeze strength into his body, removed his hat, slapped it hard on his pants leg.

"Enough talk of rations! This has gone beyond foolishness and frustration. We are facing the greatest danger imaginable, and there is only one solution, one salvation for this army. This plan has been destroyed in its entirety. To attack the enemy from such a situation as we have now is not only madness . . . it is murder. The most critical ingredient of this plan was surprise. That has now been violated, eliminated completely. The enemy must certainly be aware of our presence, and must surely be making preparations for our advance. We have put thirty thousand men in his front, and not one of them has obeyed the instruction to behave with secrecy. It is as though we are designing this attack with the greatest possible tragedy in mind! We have one alternative. We must withdraw this army back to Corinth, and man our defenses. We must strengthen our works there in anticipation that the enemy will launch his own strike. General Grant most definitely outnumbers us in every way, and he must surely know every detail of this disaster. He will not sit back and allow us time to prepare yet another plan!"

Johnston felt a bolt of lightning cut through him, could feel the surprise of the others, every man seeming to step closer to Beauregard, who once again slumped in weakness. Polk turned to Johnston now, said, "I have heard nothing to indicate that the enemy is entrenching. We have heard no shovels or axes, no felling of trees."

Bragg was louder still.

"Nothing of the sort! No scout, no picket has reported that the enemy is doing any more than he has done for the past two weeks! I admit to being furious at the stupidity of the men in our command who have jeopardized the element of surprise. But there is no indication that the enemy is doing anything to prepare for an attack. If I am not mistaken, this very spot is no more than two miles from that country church, which I have been told is the headquarters of General Sherman's Division. If they were digging trenches there, we would know of it with perfect certainty. And you would have us withdraw?"

Beauregard nodded, seemed utterly defeated.

"We have no alternative. For the sake of this army . . . for the sake of this cause."

Polk looked at Johnston, the question hard in his eyes.

"If we order this army to withdraw . . . we will destroy what morale we have given them. Sidney, you have said it yourself, we have all said it. This army needs a victory. To concede a defeat before the first volley . . ."

Beauregard looked at Johnston as well, as though measuring him, a test of just who was in command. They all looked at him now, and Johnston lowered his head. He felt his heart racing, could not avoid the sudden gravity of the moment. He turned, motioned to his staff officers to advance, felt the sudden need for someone he could trust to hear his words. There was Polk, of course, and he looked at the bishop now, saw hope in the man's face, the optimism that Johnston would make the proper decision. He watched as Harris and Munford and Colonel Preston drew closer, saw the rabid curiosity on their faces, but his staff would ask nothing, would know only that he wanted them close. He looked at them all, one by one, saw the same optimism from Colonel Gilmer, saw Bragg's glare at Beauregard, a look of utter disgust. In the distance he saw Colonel Jordan, the man straining to hear all that was said, and Johnston could not help thinking of the old phrase *the power behind the throne.* Is this what you have counseled Beauregard? Or is this from his own heart? Is this Beauregard's way of protecting his reputation, so that if this plan fails, he can claim it was not his idea after all? What kind of absurdity drives this man, drives both of them? It cannot be. It can never be.

"We have been forced to a delay, but this army is prepared for a fight. This army is positioned for a fight. If we require additional rations, there is most certainly an adequate supply close by in the enemy camps. Gentlemen, we will attack at daylight tomorrow."

He turned, did not wait for a response, would not hear any more of Beauregard's outrageous backtracking. He moved toward his own staff, put a hand on the horse, saw Polk staring at him with a slight smile, a respectful nod of the head. The others were moving away from Beauregard now, the sickly man still standing in the middle of the road, silent, seeming to stare at nothing. Johnston climbed the horse, his officers close, waiting for the next order. To one side, Colonel Preston eased close, said in a low voice, "Is General Beauregard correct . . . that we are greatly outnumbered?"

Johnston realized, of course, they had heard it all, every word. Good.

"Colonel, it does not matter. I would fight them if they were a million."

## CHAPTER FIFTEEN

# SHERMAN

SHILOH CHURCH
APRIL 5, 1862, 3:00 P.M.

He had sent his report to Grant, then amended it, sent another, offering nothing in the way of alarm. The reports coming in from his front lines were growing in number, and in every case, Sherman was infuriated by the men who were in command, and felt no need to cause any more excitement at Grant's headquarters at Savannah than the ridiculous rumors warranted. Sherman was beginning to understand that this was the price he was paying by having too many untested officers commanding too many inexperienced troops. The anxiety had spread among many of the regimental commanders, had affected even his brigade commanders, who often were less experienced than the officers beneath them. Two of those, John McDowell and Jesse Hildebrand, were much older men, with virtually no military experience at all. Colonel McDowell had the good fortune to be the elder brother of General Irvin McDowell, who had led the Federal troops at the Battle of Bull Run. But John was still learning the most basic of command decisions, not helped at all by the fact that one of his own regimental commanders was the astonishingly annoying Colonel Worthington.

In Sherman's Third Brigade, Colonel Hildebrand insisted on managing his command without the assistance of a real staff, no officers to spread around the various tasks required of any commander. As well, Hildebrand held tightly to the command of his own regiment, the 77th Ohio, even though his sphere of control included three other Ohio regiments. Sherman understood the flaws in this organization, but Sherman was still trying to familiarize himself with the personalities above him, the chain of command that had passed through both General Smith and General Grant, all of them suffering under the twitching thumb of Henry Halleck.

The apparent nervousness of his senior officers was inspired by an increasing number of confrontations with bands of rebels. Sherman was perfectly comfortable with the Confederate cavalry patrols that were doing all they could to watch his movements. It was their job, after all, and one he would have expected from horsemen in any army. As the picket lines strengthened across Sherman's front, more and more of those sightings were confirmed, bands of gray-coated horsemen gathering in distant fields, often fully in view, some of those seeking some opportunity to sweep in for a rapid capture of the unprepared platoons of Sherman's men, those who were careless, or just unfortunate. But the more capable of Sherman's officers had refused to allow the rebels the perfect freedom to conduct any kind of harassing operation. Colonel Ralph Buckland commanded Sherman's Fourth Brigade, and Buckland had little patience for watching his men plucked right out of their picket posts. Even after the incident that resulted in the capture of the rebel prisoners, Buckland had kept a strong force out in front of his camps, and the resulting confrontations had grown stiffer, the aim and the maneuver more efficient. As his infantry shoved out toward the Confederate cavalry, Buckland's men began to trade fire with more vigor than most of the Confederates seemed willing to share. It was only then that Buckland's men received a surprise that halted them in their tracks. As the rebel horsemen retreated, the jubilant Federal pursuit was suddenly met with fire from rebel artillery. Buckland's infantry responded appropriately. They retreated back to their picket lines.

Sherman had heard the artillery, had stood outside his tent near the crude church and tried to measure the distance, a task made difficult by the undulating ground and the great patches of woods. It had surprised him as well, but his mind worked through that, and he justified it by the simple explanation that any sizable body of cavalry would most likely have field artillery in tow. The rumble from the rebel guns had been a positive sign that Buckland's men had done the job, and the rebels were falling back, more frightened now than the men they had targeted.

### SHILOH CHURCH
### APRIL 5, 1862, 5:00 P.M.

I have caused injury to my leg. A nasty spill on my horse in the torrent of last evening. I trust my presence is not required in your vicinity today, as the ride would cause me considerable discomfort. The doctors advise me to rest, and insist that by the morrow, I will be more mobile.

Sherman put down the note from Grant, thought, yes, one more casualty. Hope he heals well. Halleck doesn't need any more excuses to shove Grant out of the way. He's a good horseman, too, not like some of these city boys out here who claim to be soldiers. I wonder how many of my officers have more experience stepping in horse manure than they do sitting in the saddle? He scolded himself. No, don't dwell on that now. You have to put the best appearances on this you can. They are a nervous and agitated bunch, and I have to be the one who shows them some decorum. He glanced into a small dressing mirror hanging on the tent pole beside him, said aloud, "And that's not your best talent, Sherman."

He heard a crack, too familiar, a musket shot from far out in the woods west of his camp. There were others, a chorus of firing, the sounds flowing toward him from a half mile away. He stood, moved to the opening of the tent, thought of riding out. No, you've done that already. It's just more of the same damn thing. Buckland's taking care of things in his front, for now. But what is it with these damn rebels that causes them to be such a nuisance? They've even cost us casualties, though not as many as we've taken from them. Not sure about that, actually, but damn it all, I have to assume I can trust my officers to tell me the truth.

After a minute or more the musket fire grew silent, and he waited for more, saw others across the headquarters clearing staring that way, all of them doing the same as he was. No, he thought, just one more *episode*, one more report somebody will send back so I know the world is about to end. He moved back to his small camp chair, thought, they even have you jumping up and down like a grasshopper. This can't be good for the morale of the men anywhere out here. Prentiss is probably going through the same thing, but I have more new recruits than he does. We should drill them again, keep it up, especially with the weather improving. Until General Buell gets here, we're not moving at all, so if the sun decides to shine, we should make good use of that.

He stood again, retrieved a cigar from his pocket, lit it with a dry match, something he no longer took for granted. He moved again to the opening in the tent, looked toward the church close by, thought of the rebel prisoners the night before. They were gone now, escorted back to the river by men who volunteered for the job with a little too much enthusiasm, men who seemed anxious to be somewhere other than rebel countryside. That had bothered him, and again he blamed the officers. Jumpy, too damn jumpy. Can't have that. Maybe I need a council, bring every damn colonel back here and sit them down. He imagined that scene in his mind, the gray-haired old men who had never seen combat. Worthington, Hildebrand, and McDowell were all older than the generals who outranked them, and Sherman wasn't certain that any of them might be older than Charles Smith. At least some of the younger ones are West Pointers, he thought. But not enough. It's all up to a bunch of new recruits, might as well be a mob. They gather in their hometown, elect the richest, mouthiest bastard among them to be their colonel, and he puts on his cap, clamps his legs around a horse, and rides out here like he's gonna whip the rebs all by himself. Before he even gets here, he's already made every damn one of his soldiers mad at him for one thing or another. There must be some manual somewhere, something that teaches these jackasses that the best way to lead their men is to figure out how to be hated by one and all. Yep, that's good leadership. Hell of a way to build an army.

The cigar warmed him, the delicious smoke rolling around his face, a soft breeze blowing into the tent. He lowered the cigar, took a long breath, thought, God grant me simple pleasures. Maybe some that aren't so simple. Like finding me better officers. He glanced up, blue sky and sunshine, thought, guess I oughta thank You for *this*. The weather stays this nice, I'll order this whole damn division out on maneuvers. Maybe

send the whole lot of them on *patrol*. I can convince Grant it's just . . .
drill. Drive through these woods and clear out every damn reb, like a net
through a fishpond. Then parade those gray-backed devils through here
so every damn one of my boys can get a close look at just how ferocious
these creatures are who're giving us the jumps. The colonels will be first
in line to see that. Worthington in front.

He looked toward the church again, knew some of his staff was inside,
doing the good work, supply mostly, trying to negotiate for the food and
forage the division required. The forage was becoming a new problem.
For reasons no one had adequately explained to Sherman, the cavalry
was being reorganized, the units that had been attached to each division
being shifted, the commands changing. Has to be Halleck, he thought.
That's how he keeps control. Make changes so nobody understands what
the hell is going on without asking him.

The transferring of the horsemen had come as recently as the night
before, and Sherman had to grit his teeth as he watched his 5th Ohio
Cavalry riding to their new post, to report wherever the paperwork de-
creed to be their new home. To replace them, Sherman was expecting
the 4th Illinois to arrive at any time, those men who would be his new
*eyes*. Colonel Dickey, he thought. Don't know the man. Hope he's decent
at his job. All I can ask.

He pulled smoke from the cigar again, saw it was already shortened
by half, thought of Grant. Hell, I like the things. Shouldn't be anybody's
business if I smoke 'em faster than he does. He stared at the church, saw
an officer emerge, moving to a horse, a quick climb, a sharp shout at the
mount, the horse turning, carrying the man quickly away. Sherman
shook his head. Hell of a hurry to go nowhere. Now Major Sanger
emerged, stood in the narrow entranceway to the old building, raised
his arms in a leisurely stretch. He saw Sherman now, was suddenly
self-conscious, pulled himself together, and Sherman waved toward
him, no, don't worry. No scolding for enjoying a blessedly warm day.
Sanger stepped down, moved toward him, but even now there was no
urgency in the man, and Sherman appreciated that.

"Nice to see you aren't in a panic, Major. Sets you apart from everyone else in this command."

"Oh, uh, no, sir. Just went through all the requests for supply, and I was surprised to see an urgent request from General Hurlbut, asking if we could supply some of his men with ammunition. Seems one of the Michigan regiments was sent out from the river with no cartridges at all. With your permission, sir, I'll have the ordnance officer send over some of our supply. We have plenty, as best I can figure."

"Bull. Tell Hurlbut to get some from the supply boats. We hauled all that weight out here, he can do the same."

Sanger didn't seem surprised at the order.

"Of course, sir. I'll have a messenger relay that . . . in polite terms, of course, sir."

"Unless Hurlbut is sober, manners won't make a damn." Sherman regretted the words, knew that Hurlbut's reputation as a hard drinker was hearsay. "Don't repeat that, Major."

"Certainly not, sir." Sanger glanced around, changed the subject.

"Those prisoners, sir, last night . . . they were a motley group. Never heard so much big talk from so few useless men. I guess, when you're captured, you can make all the claims you want. They kept telling anybody who would listen that the greatest horde of graybacks you ever saw was going to come sweeping through here. Wouldn't shut up about it. When we got them ready to march to the river, I had to weed out a couple of the guards. Replaced them with some of our hard cases. I hope that isn't a problem, sir."

Sherman pondered that, said, "Why'd you have to change the guards?"

"Their sergeant told me that some of his boys were taking the rebel talk too seriously. Sergeant Lassiter it was, sir. He said it could be bad to let these men spout off all that rebel nonsense, might spook some of the people at the river. You know how rumors get started, sir. So I authorized the sergeant to take along a few of our disciplinary problems instead. I did receive a courier this morning that the prisoners were received by the provost, none the worse for the trip. But I would imagine that if they kept up all that chatter, one of the boys Lassiter picked might have decided to loosen a few rebel teeth."

Sherman cocked his head to one side, the cigar clamped in his teeth.

"What kind of hard cases? Liquor?"

"Yes, sir. We had to stockade a few of the Illinois boys. Seems some hard cider got in through the provosts. Made for a problem over in the far field. They mixed it up with some of the Iowa boys. All this sitting

still, got some of these boys too nervous for their own good. That musket fire, all the talk of cavalry . . ."

"Yes, I know all that. But not sure it was a good idea putting hard-case
troublemakers alongside a bunch of rebels. You sure they got to the river
without any trouble?"

Sanger seemed to hesitate.

"They got to the river intact, sir. That's what the courier said."

"Don't do that again, Major. I don't want any vigilantes in this army.
Those rebs were just talking, and our boys are probably doing the same
thing out there somewhere. *Yep, now you're gonna get it, Johnny Reb.*
Hardly ever heard of a prisoner who can keep his mouth shut, no matter
how hard we train 'em to do it." He paused, lit another cigar. "Maybe the
rebs have the same problem we do. All these men come running to join
up to the cause, and nobody's got the time to train them to be an army."

Sanger glanced away self-consciously, looked toward the church, but
no one was moving, still nothing that required him to be anywhere else.
He looked at Sherman again, seemed to inflate slightly, said, "I've been
thinking about this, sir. There's a good deal of talk, and I'm thinking it's
true. We've got nothing much to be concerned about when it comes to
the rebs. Begging your pardon, sir, but you know they're dug in tight at
Corinth. Smartest place for them to be, according to all I've heard.
They're not an army fit to make an offense, so if I was their commander,
I'd build me one strong defense, and settle in right there. Troubles me
though that a good many of our boys might shed blood trying to drive
them out of that place. We're giving 'em too much time to dig in. I've
heard that Corinth is a fortress."

Sherman had heard this kind of talk from most of his colonels, didn't
want to hear it from his own staff officer. But Sanger seemed oblivious,
stared out toward the soft whisper from the trees, then went on.

"Colonel McDowell said to me yesterday . . . said that the reb soldier
is too vulgar to stand up tall. Says we'll drive them out of Corinth just by
the gleam on our bayonets."

"Clamp that down, Major."

Sanger seemed surprised, his breezy mood halted.

"Yes, sir. Sorry, sir."

"I was at Bull Run, Major. I saw what the rebel soldier can do, and I
saw what it was like to stand up to bayonets. Try it sometime."

Sanger made a short bow, said again, "Sorry, sir. I meant—"

"You meant what you said. You're wrong, that's all. The rebel *cause* is a vulgarity. But the soldiers are not that different than what we've got here. And their generals are good men, most of 'em, anyway. I know a good many of those men down there. Schooled with them, served with them. In Louisiana, I dined with some of them. Can't say I like them all that much, but you can bet that when it comes time to stick your bayonet into their hearts, you better be ready for them to do the same to you. You ever find yourself raising your sword, you can bet the man you're facing is raising his. What makes us better than him is training, and right now, I'm not all that comfortable. I brought these new men out here in these fields so we can whip them into fighting condition. By the time General Halleck orders us out on these roads, these men better be tougher than they are right now. You can wager your pay, Major, that even if Corinth is a fortress, Johnston, Hardee, Bragg, the rest of them . . . they're doing everything they can to build an army out of those farm boys."

Sanger looked past Sherman, his attention caught, and Sherman heard the hoofbeats now, turned. The rider was familiar, and Sanger said, "That's Lieutenant Fulton, the quartermaster—"

"From Colonel Appler's regiment. Yes, I know."

The rider jumped down in a stumbling heap, righted himself, and Sherman saw sweat on the young man's face, panic in his eyes.

"What's wrong with you, Lieutenant?"

The man tried to gather himself, and Sherman saw others approaching on foot, more of his staff drawn by the commotion.

"I said, what's wrong?"

"Sir . . ."

The lieutenant was clearly nervous, glanced at the gathering officers, then back to Sherman.

"Sir, Colonel Appler reports that he observed a battalion of secesh cavalry, and ordered several companies to pursue them. We heard considerable musket fire, sir, and Colonel Appler was most concerned. Our men did return in haste, and told . . . they reported to Colonel Appler that the secesh cavalry withdrew behind a line of butternut infantry. The colonel has ordered the entire regiment into battle lines, sir!"

The words had come out in a single breath, and the man sagged, breathing heavily. Sherman was more than annoyed, the feeling too familiar.

"Lieutenant, I have heard these same reports now for two days, or longer. Tell me. Did you sustain heavy casualties?"

The man seemed confused at the question, realized his response would be the right one.

"No, sir! A couple of men were wounded, but I didn't see them."

"Is the field littered with the bodies of the enemy, Lieutenant?"

"Not that Colonel Appler indicated, sir."

Sherman pulled the last draw of smoke through the dying cigar, tossed it aside with a disgusted stab of his hand.

"Your 53rd Ohio is in . . . that direction, correct?"

The young man followed the point of Sherman's finger, nodded slowly.

"I believe so, sir."

"What I believe is that this army is under specific orders, issued by General Halleck, through General Grant, and through me, not to engage the enemy. If Colonel Appler has disobeyed that order, then at this moment, we would hear the sounds of a general engagement. Do you hear the sounds of a general engagement?"

The lieutenant stared out in that direction, the only sounds the wind in the leaves of the tall trees.

"I do not, sir."

"No, you do not!"

Sherman reached into his jacket, withdrew another cigar, felt his hands shaking, focused his anger on the young man, who seemed to quiver under his stare. Sherman wanted to shout at the man, the voice in his brain. Damn you! Damn all of you! What kind of army is this? Sherman struggled to light the cigar, the match unsteady in his hand, tossed it aside, drew another. Sanger stepped closer, a match in his hand, and Sherman stared at him as well, withering, furious. Sanger backed away, already knew of Sherman's anger, and Sherman leaned closer to the lieutenant, his words flowing out in a low hiss.

"Here's what you do, Lieutenant. You return to Colonel Appler. You tell him to take his damn regiment back to Ohio. There is no enemy closer to this army than Corinth!"

## SHILOH CHURCH
### APRIL 5, 1862, 8:00 P.M.

He was becoming convinced that the message he had sent back to Colonel Appler might be wrong. The newly assigned 4th Illinois Cavalry had finally arrived to his front and their commander, Colonel Lyle Dickey, showed none of the mindless panic Sherman had seen too often from the others. Dickey had reported what others were saying as well, that within a short mile or two of the westernmost picket lines, Confederate cavalry had again taken up position, and for the moment, seemed intent on staying put. The same reports came from the easily agitated Hildebrand, and from Buckland as well, more of Sherman's regiments reporting direct contact with rebel horsemen who were becoming less inclined to scamper away. With darkness now over the field, Sherman had gone to see Hildebrand himself, had suffered the rant of an old man who knew almost nothing of tactics and maneuver. But through the panicky agitation was real observation, specific numbers, and a few more rebel prisoners who boasted with the same vigor as the ones Sherman had already seen. Hildebrand's regimental commanders were repeating what the cavalryman Dickey had said, that beyond the woods to their immediate front, the rebels were no longer sending out harassment parties, and that quite possibly, the cavalry was backed up by artillery and even infantry.

As he left Hildebrand's camp, he rode back toward the old church in silence, a handful of his staff officers in tow. He thought of Halleck, the absurdity of the order that nothing should be done to *disturb the enemy*. We cannot find out what the enemy is doing if we cannot *disturb* them. We sit idly by and wait for General Buell to arrive, and in the meantime, the enemy's out there dancing around the countryside close enough for us to watch. Buell should have been here ten days ago. Five days ago. What does it matter? Buell is not here, and until he arrives . . . there's not a damn thing we can do but sit here. Stupid. Amazingly stupid.

He reached into his coat pocket, empty, realized now he had smoked a half-dozen cigars on the way to his brigade commander's camp. Now all he could do was clamp his knees hard against the flanks of the horse, stare into the darkness, broken by flickers of his own campfires. The night was cool, but he felt a clammy wetness in his shirt. He closed his eyes, fought it, but the old twist was returning to his brain, the cold black hole opening up, and he gripped the reins in his hands with a fierce anger, struggled against the panic, fought the swirling anguish that forced him into perfect certainty that in the darkness around him were red hollow eyes that watched his every move.

## CHAPTER SIXTEEN

# BAUER

The Sibley tent had been as packed with men as could fit inside, sixteen, in a space designed for fewer. In every space was some piece of a man, a foot, arm, a feeble resting place for a head, usually on a crushed hat, or any other piece of clothing they could find. The milder temperatures had helped, of course, but still the nights brought a stinging chill, keeping them under their thin wool blankets. The disappearance of the rain had been the grandest blessing of all, the muddy avenues through the camp drying, the misery of wet socks one less torment.

For several nights now the noisy activity in the woods out to the west had caused sleepless nights for some, Bauer among them. The most vocal of the men insisted the noises came from hordes of unseen rebels, their evidence the occasional discharge of a musket, a drumbeat, men cheering, calling out in the distance. But the men who kept their calm dismissed that kind of talk, and Bauer had tried to absorb that it would make little sense for an enemy close by to just gather secretly, only to reveal themselves with careless racket. Every man knew that when the pickets returned from their duty, each of those men fired his musket into the ground, clearing it, so that the powder didn't become a damp clogging mass buried deep in the barrel, requiring a major effort to clean. Even the most nervous had to admit that the lay of the land could cause voices to bounce through the gullies and hillsides in unpredictable ways, the breeze working with the geography to blot out the sounds, or deflect them in another direction.

Inside the Sibley tents, the worst sounds came from the men who actually found sleep, whose snoring drilled into the brain of any man who felt the nagging fear that the enemy might actually be closer than the officers were telling them. To those men, a night's sleep was a rare luxury, and Bauer had lain awake staring up into the dull white above him, wondering just what might be happening out in those woods, the dark streambeds and ravines where he had seen the rebel horsemen. Despite the various miseries caused by the rain, there was comfort there at night, the steady hiss and rattle and shiver on the canvas soothing in its own way. But tonight, there was none of that, the only sounds the grunts and whines of the men too close to him for Bauer to escape.

The rumors of the rebel patrols had galloped through the camps like a runaway horse, tales of their own men hauled away in the night, some from the very tents where the men now tried to find some sleep. Even those who knew more of the facts exaggerated the numbers, though no one could actually name any of those missing. The officers had done their best to calm jittery nerves wherever they found them, and Bauer had heard enough of the ridiculous claims to convince him that he wasn't the only one who suffered through anxious nights. But Bauer would not admit any of that, not even to Willis, though he knew that his friend was alongside him in the tent, silent, staring up, as he was, sleepless for reasons that had nothing to do with rebels. Willis showed no fear at all, dismissed any talk of enemy patrols, and Bauer had no reason to believe Willis was afraid of anything, not the sergeant, not the sounds of the muskets that rattled through the trees. Bauer stayed close to him on purpose, as he had always done, hoped some of that steel courage would become his own.

Willis had been silent all night, but Bauer could feel that his friend was awake, that once again, Willis's lack of sleep was more likely from something far beyond what might lie out in these woods. Willis had betrayed his stoicism with a moment of sadness, Bauer catching a quick glimpse of Willis rereading the single letter he carried in his pocket. Bauer would not ask him, had made up his mind that whatever was in the letter was Willis's own business, that a friend should not pry. If Willis wanted to talk about it, Bauer would be there with a sympathetic ear. He knew there would be little sympathy from the others who shared the tent, certainly not the loudmouthed Patterson, who seemed to take nothing seriously.

Patterson had perfected the knack of slipping out undetected from the tent, only to return before the dawn's first bugle call always stinking of liquor and cheap perfume, his jabbering at reveille annoying everyone with his amazing tales of that night's particular adventure. Almost always there were women involved, the camp followers who had taken up their illicit posts closer to the river. Patterson's tune had not changed since St. Louis, as though the man had made the discovery all by himself, that there were women who followed the army everywhere they marched, and that for a gift of liquor or a little silver, the women were obliging in ways that Bauer found appalling. That kind of talk came from others, of course, but Bauer had heard more from Patterson than he wanted to know about the mysterious tents pitched just beyond the guard posts, out in deep woods or downstream just far enough to be invisible to the patrolling provosts. Several of the others had succumbed to the temptation Patterson laid before them, and a few had been successful at his trick of slipping away, partaking in what the man called his own special *morale booster,* the perfect cure for the utter boredom of life in the camps. But others were far too clumsy, hauled by the provosts or their own officers back to the tents, sometimes to the stockade.

Bauer had no sympathy for any of those men, had done all he could to avoid the adventurous tales of bawdy damsels, stories more graphic than anything Bauer really believed. But there was an unavoidable agony in Patterson's ribald behavior, and Bauer suffered through that as well, the curse that came from loneliness, that *thing* that Patterson seemed to find so easily among women. Before joining the army, Bauer had been smitten more than once by the discreet flirtatiousness from some of the young ladies who dared look his way, usually in church, or at some social function. But his nerve had nearly always failed him, and he had seen the disappointment in the faces of the ladies, that this kind young man with the innocent smile was too shy to make any advances at all. His hesitation only made his longing worse, angry frustration at the easy talent for conversation that poured out in abundance from some of the other boys. He had thought the uniform would help him, that a soldier would have no such fear, and the ladies had responded to that as many always did. But still, Bauer's shyness had given him no relief. Instead he had marched off to this war with the fantasy planted deeply inside him, that one day he would take a girl by the hand and sit her down in the soft grass by the lakeshore, enjoying a picnic, and the giggling talk of lovers, talk he could only imagine, talk made vulgar by the men like Patterson.

It was too dark for a pocket watch, and his had stopped working days before. But he had a knack for measuring the length of his sleeplessness, was convinced it was well after midnight, hours before the jolt of reveille, which always came just before dawn. Around him in the tent, some men were coughing, adding more noisy torment to the other sounds, and Bauer knew he had been lucky not to have been stricken by all the sicknesses that were spreading through every camp. The doctors seemed to be no help at all, the field hospitals overstuffed with men who were forced to sleep on the ground. If there were remedies at all, most said they were worse than whatever illness they carried, and Bauer heard talk that it was the curse of insect bites, these Southern woods home to creatures Northern boys would exaggerate, just as they had exaggerated the great hordes of rebels who waited just over the next hill.

B auer turned to one side, looked toward Willis, the man's hat over his face, meager shelter from the rumbling and trainlike snoring that rolled around inside the canvas tomb. He listened, watched, saw movement from Willis, the hat coming down, Willis sitting up slightly, propped on his elbows.

"You awake, Dutchie?"

"Yep. O'course."

"Belly killing me. Gotta get to the hole."

Bauer rose as well, was suddenly grateful for any opportunity to escape the tent. Willis pulled his knees in, paused, seemed to curl over, a soft groan. Now Bauer was up as well, avoided kicking the man on the other side of him. He knew that was Reiner, a small, wiry man Bauer had known since the camp at Madison, since the beginning of the regiment's formation. Reiner was one of the sleepers, seemed not to mind anyone else's torment, and seemed somehow to avoid the ritual trampling from the maniacal act of Sergeant Williams's personal brand of reveille. Bauer glanced at him, heard nothing, then turned, leaned close to Willis, made a soft whisper, "I'll go with you."

"You crazy?"

"Gotta get out of this place. I'll just wait for you. Keep the rebs away."

Willis planted the hat on his head, said nothing more, and Bauer could sense the man was too sick to object to anything. Both men stood now, ducking low, avoiding the canvas above them, and no one else seemed to pay any attention. Willis slipped quickly out through the tent flaps, and Bauer stepped carefully, hesitated, stared at the opening, thought of Williams, wondered if the sergeant was there, somewhere in the darkness, waiting for just this moment to inflict some new kind of punishment. Bauer took a last step, miscalculated, felt the foot of one of the men beneath his own, heard a yelp, a curse. He moved quickly now, escaping outside, heard voices from behind him, anger, more of the men awake than he had guessed. He looked off to one side, knew the route to the straddle hole, Willis already gone, and Bauer slipped out that way, silent, moved into the wide avenue between the long rows of tents. The grass there had been trampled away, but the ground was harder, no mud this time. He felt the chill, had left behind the tent's one advantage, the combined warmth of the men who occupied it. Straining to see through the darkness, he eased between two tents, wouldn't stand out, nothing to cause an overzealous guard to challenge him. He was suddenly grateful that there was no sign of Sergeant Williams.

There was movement through the open areas of the camp, flickers of motion caught by specks of firelight from dying campfires. Most of them were guards, and he could hear the soft sounds, low talk. He realized suddenly that the sky was filled with stars, and he stared up for a long minute, tried to recall the last clear night he had seen. His eyes wandered, driven by curiosity. Bauer knew very little about astronomy, had heard talk of telescopes, the magic of curved glass, bringing the stars closer to the eye, could recall scary tales of the man in the moon, older boys using the night sky as an excuse to tease the very young. But there was no moon now, and he pulled his coat tighter around him, was surprised to see a quick streaking dart from a meteor, watched it disappear into nothing, wondered if he had seen it at all. He thought suddenly of his father, yep, maybe you saw a *haint,* smiled, but then there was another streak, longer, brighter this time. He was intensely curious, thought, where did it go? What was it, anyway?

Across the avenue came the shuffling of footsteps, and he looked that way, knew it was Willis, the man bent over slightly, gripping his own stomach. Bauer stepped back out into the avenue, let Willis see him, wanted to ask if he was all right, but he could see Willis moving in place, a slow dance of a man whose guts were tied in knots. Willis seemed to wait for him to move closer, then said, "Geez. It's dark as Egypt out here. Had to follow the smell to find the place. Feel a little better though. Let's get back in the tent."

The thought of that had no appeal to Bauer, and he said, "Go on. I'm gonna stay out here. Reveille can't be that far away. Kinda nice."

He couldn't see the look on Willis's face, knew if his friend was feeling better there would be a joke about that, some jab at him for standing alone in the cold, dark morning. But Willis said nothing more, headed for the tent, and now Bauer was alone.

From far out in the woods more sounds came, not human, the call of an owl, soon answered by another. Bauer stared out through the rows of tents, a sleeping army, mostly anyway, and he looked toward the east, no hint of dawn, the horizon visible only by the boundary where the stars disappeared. If the weather stays like this, he thought, we're in for drill, that's for certain. They'll line us up and march us back and forth all the livelong day. Unless someone comes riding through here with new orders . . . and what would that be? You boys move on out of this field, find you another one. Or maybe . . . change position with those boys from Iowa over there. Change of scenery. Yep, that'll give the generals something to do. One giant game of checkers. He looked up at the stars again, felt suddenly sleepy, inspiring the blossoming nonsense in his brain. He needed to sit, moved toward the fire pit, knew there was a chopping block, and he found it, sat down, felt cold coming up, ignored it. He stared at the stars again, hopeful, wanted to see another of those streaks, stared until his eyes danced and watered. But the heavens wouldn't cooperate, and instead the weariness in his brain took him home. He saw the face of his mother, could remember the delicious smells coming from the heavy cast iron pan that would be filled with his father's perfect sausage. Bauer had been very young and the fire very hot, and he had foolishly grabbed the handle, the sudden eruption of pain from the burn one of those lessons every young boy has to learn. But his mother seemed to suffer along with him, and he would never forget her crying as she pressed his hand into a crock of soft butter. Bauer didn't remember if that had done anything to help, only that his father had cursed him for ruining a perfectly fine mess of butter. But the one memory stayed with him, that she seemed to share the pain of his awful burn. It was a piece of her that came to him even now, in her letters. *Be safe.* Yes, Mama, I will be safe, and I will come home.

He felt the homesickness rising, scenes he couldn't avoid. We could churn some butter, he thought, or boil some syrup, help Papa with the hogs. He had hated the chores, but now it was very different, an attractiveness that probably wouldn't last, once he was home again. He yawned, knew that all the images were just dreams. It's just . . . home. God, I miss them. I miss it all.

The bugle surprised him, a sharp knife slicing through the calm of the starlight. From the tents, the men rolled out with the usual curses, but this morning was different, Bauer noticing as well as the others. It was far too early for reveille. He sat alone in the cold darkness, lost in thoughts and a haze of sleepiness, but outside had still been a more pleasant place than the tent. The growling of the men filled the darkness, and he stood, reluctantly, moved out into the wide avenue that ran past the tents. There were men on horseback, directing the sergeants who directed their troops, a line starting to form, weary men stumbling into one another, enduring the grumbling shouts of the lieutenants, the shoves in the back from the sergeants.

Bauer moved toward his own tent, heard the order coming from the closest man on a horse, knew the voice of Captain Saxe.

"Muskets! Grab your musket! We're not here for an inspection!"

The men seemed to stagger again, moving in and out of their tents, the clatter rolling all along the avenue, and Bauer realized other men were up as well, beyond his own company. He tried to see more detail, could feel the men moving about, one man bumping him, hard, no words, Bauer feeling the steel of the man's musket against his arm. He fought to see, the darkness suddenly split by a sharp light, a lantern, someone's piece of wisdom. He blinked, fought the brightness, saw another of the sergeants, Champlin, checking the muskets as the men fell into line. Champlin was one of the good ones, nothing like the barbaric Williams, and Bauer moved that way, toward the gathering lines of men. He walked out into the wide avenue, saw the speckles of light spread all over the field, more lanterns, another column of men forming beyond the next row of tents. More horses came past, a kind of urgency that brought them dangerously close to men, still not fully awake, others already seeking some place to sit, out of the line of sight of the sergeants. Fires began, the routine of the men who made the coffee, but he heard orders, sharp anger from sergeants he didn't know, the next avenue filling with more men than were around him now. Questions came from the men around him, from his own brain. What's happening? Why are we up so early? This is a heck of a time for a formation drill. Another horse rode up close, the officer dismounting, and Captain Saxe responded, did the same. There were others, still on horseback, and Bauer could see the hint of a flag, thought, Colonel Allen . . . or someone who knows something. He felt the shared excitement, most of the bellyaching growing quieter, the men increasingly curious. The lantern came close to the officers now, and Bauer saw faces, Allen, Saxe, Captain Fox, the men who would answer the questions. Colonel Allen went for his horse, climbed up, and just that quickly, was gone. Now Saxe climbed his horse, shouted for quiet, the order enforced by the hard grip of the sergeants, the harsh whisper of the lieutenants. Bauer stood in line, felt himself shivering, excitement more than cold. Saxe moved the horse across the road, shouted out, "Fill your cartridge boxes! Forty per man." He paused. "Take a hundred if you can carry them!"

Bauer heard the wagon now, rolling up the avenue toward them, orders echoing all around, the one that mattered coming from Saxe.

"Line up by platoon! Plenty of cartridges! Let's move! No time to waste!"

Bauer felt the men around him pushing that way, felt for his own cartridge box, always on his belt, empty or not. He saw the men up on the wagon, boxes opened, grabbed a handful of the dense paper, stuffed his cartridge box full. A hundred? He grabbed more, dropped some into his shirt pockets, the pocket of his pants, thought, that'll wreck 'em, for certain. But . . . he's the captain.

The men drifted back into line, Saxe moving on his horse in tight steps, and Bauer could feel the man's tension, still no answers. The men formed their line again, still the grumbling, and close beside him, a man was shoved forward, a hard punch from behind, the voice of Sergeant Williams.

"Where's your musket! You been out of pocket? I'll nail your ass to a tree. You play dumb with me and I'll have your teeth!"

Bauer looked away, hoped Williams wouldn't notice him, but the hand was on his shoulder, the familiar clawing grip.

"You run away, and I'll cut you to little pieces!"

But Williams wasn't focused just on Bauer, moved down, repeated another absurd threat to another of the men. Saxe turned the horse close by, no sign he paid any attention to the curses and threats from any of the sergeants. Down the roadway, the men seemed to be in place now, and Saxe shouted, "Extinguish those lanterns!" He didn't wait for the order to be obeyed, continued. "Company A . . . muskets in hand, all of you!"

Down the line, one of the lieutenants shouted out, "In hand, sir! Cartridges, too!"

"Good! You should know that Colonel Peabody has ordered us to picket duty. We're to move out right now alongside some Missouri boys who are already out that way. Colonel Allen has instructed three companies of this regiment to the duty. The rest will remain here. You boys are the lucky ones. You get to have a walk in the woods. Let's move out on this road. No stragglers. Follow me!"

Bauer waited for the column to move, the lantern light gone now, his eyes trying to adjust. Beside him, he caught a glimpse of the small, wiry man, thought, Reiner, I think. Where's Sammie? He looked around, still too dark to see faces, thought, God I hope he isn't too sick. Maybe he's still in the tent. Williams will kill him for that.

The column was in full march now, men focused on keeping their balance in the darkness, no one speaking except the sergeants, more of the murderous threats from Williams, from others farther down the line. Bauer looked out to the side, across the open field, no daylight yet, those lanterns beside the next rows of tents gone as well. I guess they're moving out, too, he thought. Who? Company B? Maybe C? We're not all going, he thought. Why? We have to help . . . who? Missouri boys? Why? What'd they do?

The sounds around him were like so many others he had heard, the tramp of feet, the harsh yells of the sergeants, hoofbeats from more men riding past. It was just like the drills, just like so many formations and so many miles of marching, but the tension was very different, and he could feel the weight of the cartridges at his belt, thought, why a hundred? The musket was up on his shoulder, and he felt the bulge at his pants leg, the extra cartridges. Use those first, I guess. They'll just fall to pieces if I keep 'em there too long. Might get wet, too. No other place to put them. He stumbled, looked down, took careful steps, the hardening roadway cut by ruts and wagon tracks. The pace was quick, and he stayed close behind the man in front of him, glanced at the man beside him, knew by the man's nervous gait it had to be Reiner. He tried to see any faces, thought he saw Willis a few rows in front of him, wanted to get close to him, but the column was in full march now, and he had done this too often, knew to stay in line, knew that Williams would find him if he didn't. He glanced up, still the stars, darkness and noises, and a cascade of questions.

T hey had settled into thick woods, a wide field to the front, but still the darkness covered everything, the stars flickering down through the treetops. Bauer didn't know which way was east, but he scanned what little horizon he could see, and he thought, gotta be close to dawn. Gotta be. No clouds, no rain, at least not yet. Where the heck are we?

The men had settled down in line, each man close to the next, more men behind, a formation of pickets far more dense than he had seen before. There was talk, inevitable, men asking the same questions he did. For now there was nothing anyone could do but wait for daylight, for some sign or signal why this march had been so important.

He adjusted himself into soft dirt, thick leaves all around him. There was a snore, to one side, always someone falling asleep, and he tried to ignore that, wished now he had stayed in the tent. The bleariness of his eyes was playing the usual tricks, shadows in motion, shapes suddenly appearing where none had been before. After what seemed like a long hour, the woods began to grow lighter, and he realized they weren't really in deep woods at all, not like before. Beyond a thin row of trees was an open field, deep rolling grass, surrounded by trees, more of the dense woods. He sat up straighter, heard men still talking around him, but gradually they began to grow silent, and he saw stares, out to the front, realized now there was a strange hum, coming from far across the field, from the woods beyond. There was nothing distinct about the sound, the chilly air of the dawn blanketing the noises. He focused, tried to hear more, glanced up again, the stars still faintly visible, and now new sounds, birds, close by, chirps and calls, the woods coming alive. But the hum seemed to grow, uneven now, breaking into small pieces. It was very far away, no kind of sound he had heard before, and he thought of bees, or chattering birds, but there was nothing to see, no answers to this mystery, either. Some of the men began their talk again, but others stood, one of the sergeants close by, Champlin, staring hard across the field. The lieutenants were rising as well, stepping out into the grass, arms crossed, hands resting on the scabbards of their swords, staring away in silence. To one side, behind, he heard horses, a rumble of hoof-beats, and now a sharp voice. He turned that way, saw the company commanders, flags and couriers and the large figure of Colonel Peabody.

Across the wide field there seemed to be smoke, a low, soft cloud, gray fog, clinging to the trees, no other movement at all. The strange hum was closer now, louder, the buzzing of bees giving way to a broken chatter, his brain clearing for a sharp instant, the sounds more familiar. The horses behind him galloped off, the officers scattering, moving out in front of their men, the captains making their way to the front of each company. Bauer could hear it now, the sounds growing clear and dis-tinct, a cold stirring inside him, a thick line of men preparing to move out into a field, toward the sound of muskets.


APRIL 6, 1862, 6:10 A.M.


They had crossed the field, the musket fire still to the front. The thick grass ended at a stand of woods, and there was wispy smoke, drifting through the treetops, the thick odor of sulfur dropping down on the

men as they moved. Bauer was breathing heavily, his legs keeping him
close, but the excitement of it all was draining him. To one side, a line of
men stood in a small field, holding muskets, and he saw a wound, a
filthy white cloth wrapped around one man's leg. Another column of
troops came through the woods, were held in place by an officer on
horseback, the man shouting, the soldiers staring hard at Bauer and the
Wisconsin men as they moved past. The officer was close to Bauer now,
and the order was clear, distinct.

"Move out behind this column. Keep in column of fours!"

The voices of the men grew around him, expectant, nervous, the rustle of deep grass as they moved once more into a field. In front of them,
the sounds of muskets had slowed, coming in single pops, some farther
away, off to the right. Bauer saw horsemen moving past him, a rapid gallop, the sound of a bugle in the distance, then another. Now musket fire
came again, closer, off to the left, through a stand of trees, someplace
Bauer couldn't see. The field was wide, woods on all sides, and he followed the men in front of him, saw a lieutenant holding his sword high,
waving them on. The grass was knee-deep, brush in dense thickets, and
the men had to slow, pushing through thorns and briar bushes, impatient officers on horseback keeping to the front of them, shouting them
forward. For a long moment, they moved in silence, the urgency suddenly gone, and Bauer saw officers gathering, low talk, one man pointing to the far side of the field. Bauer's heart was pounding, and he heard
a single musket fire, diagonally across the field. He stared that way, ignored the chatter from the men around him, saw a thin line of men in
blue rise up, standing with muskets at their shoulders, a burst of smoke,
the sound of the volley reaching him quickly, the men firing away, in the
other direction. Bauer watched as they dropped down, hidden by underbrush, and there were more muskets, farther away. More smoke was
drifting off to the left, a thin haze in the trees, and he felt a hard hand on
his shoulder, knew already it was Williams, the sergeant shouting close
to his ear.

"You run, and I'll shoot you! Any of you!"

One of the officers broke from the cluster of horsemen, rode straight
toward Bauer, reined up a few yards in front, and Bauer saw it was Captain Saxe.

"On my command, battle formation toward that picket line! Our boys need some help! Rebs out in the next field. Stay together, no gaps, no stragglers." He raised his sword now, and behind Bauer the bugler went to work, the command they knew well, the call to battle lines. Saxe waited for a long minute, the men performing the task as they had so many times on the parade ground, on the fields a mile east of where they stood now. Saxe raised his sword above his head, waved it in a sweeping circle, shouted, "Forward, march!"

Williams shoved Bauer in the back, unnecessary, the men all moving together, one more piece of the training imbedded in all of them. Bauer pushed his feet through the thick grass, saw a lump of blue straight in front of him, down in the grass, saw it was a body, the man curled up, seeming to sleep. Bauer stepped around him, another shout from Williams, close behind him.

"Stay in line!"

Down the row, a major stepped out in front, leading the way, a colonel riding to one side at the same pace, a sword still in his hand. Down to the right, another officer moved ahead on horseback, familiar, one of the other unit officers. Bauer tried to keep his stare straight ahead, saw the thin line of blue rise up again, firing again, muskets pointing out toward an unseen enemy. Bauer saw now that the field was narrowing into a corner, and beyond there was another field, just as wide, grassy, and open. The blue picket line was up again, began to leave their cover, were moving back toward the mass of their own men. There were no more than two dozen of them, and Bauer saw fury and panic in their faces, most not stopping, moving right through the advancing column, their officer shouting orders.

"Pull back! Re-form behind these men! Fall in line!"

Bauer watched one of the men come straight toward him, dirt on his face, wild eyes, the man suddenly smiling at him.

"Johnny Reb's out there! We gave it to 'em! They's runnin' away!"

The man pushed past him, obeying his lieutenant, and Bauer didn't look back, could feel more men stepping up close behind him, the battle line thickening. The man's words stayed in his brain, repeating, Johnny Reb . . . *Johnny Reb* . . . Yes! This is it! Now we'll do something! They can't run away . . . not yet! I wanna see them!

In front of them, Captain Saxe kept his position, turned his head toward them, still waved his sword, another order, another bugle calling out behind them. Bauer knew the order, reacted with instinct, the musket butt down on the ground, the cartridge quickly in his teeth, tearing the paper, pouring powder down the barrel. The ball went in now, his hand pulling the ramrod from its slot along the stock of the musket, the thin steel pushed down the barrel, seating the musket ball in place hard against the powder. All along the line, men did as he did, the battle line now ready and he watched the captain turn away, facing out across the next wide field, his sword high. To one side, along the edge of the woods, there was a sudden volley, a battle line of Federal troops Bauer hadn't seen, and he looked that way, smoke spreading out in a thick cloud. Return fire came from far out in the field, from a fence line, men in brown and tan shirts rising up. But they did not stay, and Bauer saw one of them waving frantically, pulling those men out of their cover, the fence thick with brush, a swarm of men now scampering away. Bauer watched them, thought of the picket he had seen, the man's words. Yes! They're running away! We have to go after them! His brain watched the scene, counting them, a dozen, two dozen . . .

Beside him, a few men down the line, he heard a strange cry, a cheer, loud and grotesque, a whooping yell. It came from Patterson, and Bauer looked that way, saw Willis close by, staring straight ahead. Bauer felt relief, wanted to move that way, to stand beside his friend, but there was no time, the captain shouting out another order, and behind Bauer the bugler began his call again, *advance*. Immediately the lines responded, Saxe again pushing his horse out into the field, all of the men in Saxe's company clear of the brush and trees. Bauer looked to the side, saw the other battle line, flags, horsemen, more men in blue, marching out with them. He couldn't avoid a yell of his own, no words, just a yelp, the pure joy of the moment. He glanced around, tried to see everything, watched as Williams punched another man in the back, meaningless curses. All around him the shouts were unceasing, raw fury toward the enemy and threats from the sergeants to men who needed none.

Bauer looked ahead toward the captain again, could see past him, the end of the second field, saw the scampering rebels, a few turning to fire, small pops and puffs of white smoke. But still he marched, one part of the great strength, and he felt it, his breathing coming hard, the pride, the perfect scene, marching after a ragged band of fugitives. Around him other men were shouting, all of them caught up in the energy of the moment, the men watching their enemy fleeing in a desperate run. The captain stayed out front, leading the men with the same calmness, the steady rhythm, other horsemen down the way doing the same, all pressing the fleeing rebels. Saxe suddenly halted his horse, seemed to stare straight ahead, a better vantage point than the men he led. Bauer's line was drawing up closer behind Saxe, a few yards, the officer perched on a slight rise in the field. The noises still rolled forward from the men, a steady chorus of shouts and cheers, Bauer joining in, even Patterson just one part of the whole, the men sensing their first delicious taste of victory. Saxe spurred the horse again, did not look back, and Bauer saw the sword hanging in his hand, the captain staring ahead into the far trees toward another gap at the end of the field.

The line still pressed forward, and Bauer could hear musket fire far to the left, a new fight opening up somewhere beyond the woods, but the firing was scattered, distant, and he climbed the gentle slope of the field, moving closer to Saxe, who was motionless again. Bauer was suddenly curious, thought, do we stop? The captain seemed to stare straight ahead, studying something in the distance, and Bauer wanted to see, made a quick glance to both sides, the battle line complete, energized, his own men, the men of Company A. Now the captain turned slightly, shouted out something Bauer couldn't hear, something about Wisconsin, about courage. Then Saxe turned, spurred the horse again, moved out past the rise, leading them again, and Bauer crested the rise. On the far end of the field was another fence line, ragged split rails gripped by dense underbrush, and he saw movement, half a hundred men rising up, the volley blowing toward them. The whistle and zip of the musket balls ripped past him and Bauer flinched at the sound, a wild cry in his brain. They're shooting at us! The line kept moving forward, closer, and he held his musket in a tight grip, heard the orders, the lieutenants, Sergeant Williams, the words in a harsh blend with a new burst of fire to their front, another volley from the half-hidden rebels.

Bauer kept his eyes on them, was very close now, some men in the line beside him firing on their own, ignoring the yelling from the sergeants. Bauer saw Saxe stop again, the sword high, and he seemed to jerk, his body rippling in a single shiver, Saxe falling backward, toppling from the horse, landing in a loose heap in the grass. Bauer stared in horror, saw the horse turn, nose down, as though prodding its rider, and

Bauer felt the sickening shock punching into him, stepped forward with automatic steps, closer to Saxe, the horse, Bauer's eyes fixed on the captain's face, a spurt of blood coming from the man's neck, blood spreading out on his white shirt, the handsome face, empty eyes staring up, at nothing. Bauer wanted to stop, took a quick step that way, shouted, uncontrollably, "He needs help! They hurt him! Get help!"

But the hard fist had him, Williams, yanking him away, harsh, filthy words, more men on horses moving out, leading them, the lieutenants still marching in front of them. The fence line seemed empty now, no sign of anyone, but just as quickly they were there again, rising up, a thick line of butternut and gray, another volley bursting out, smoke and screaming whistles, and now there was a new sound, a hard crack, and the grip on his shoulder gave way, the sergeant falling forward with a hard cry, curling up, rolling, squirming on the ground. Bauer stared down, stopped, but the men behind him pushed on, a hand on his back, prodding him forward. Around him others had fallen, collapsing in dead heaps, some twisted, screaming, and Bauer saw it all, couldn't help the odd fantasy skipping through his mind, children at play, *I shot you . . . you're dead.* But the roar of sounds was growing, clearing his brain, another volley from the rebels, and now the shock began to release him, and he heard the burst of fire from the men around him, more shouts from the lieutenants, one of them falling, the blue coat disappearing into the tall grass. Around Bauer, some men began to run, falling back, more sharp cries, screaming from a man close to him, and he turned, saw Patterson, on his knees, the man's mouth open, surprise in his eyes, then tilting backward, gone. Bauer felt the surge of panic, more men running back, the line breaking up. But there were others, Willis, another sergeant, Champlin, still the yells from the lieutenants, pulling the men forward.

He stared ahead at the rebels along the fence, not hidden now, the line of blue very close. He raised his musket, felt helpless, weak, tried to aim, to see anything, caught a glimpse of motion, fired wildly, the musket kicking his shoulder. He stopped, the lessons swept from his mind, the thought forced into him, the instinct shaken, but the words were there. Reload! He dropped the musket, the routine repeated so many times, fought through shaking hands, hard breaths, a thundering beat in his chest. His thoughts were scattered, shock and chaos, and he thought of the captain, wanted to look back, see if he was up, if he was just wounded, now the image of the sergeant, Williams, terrifying man . . . nowhere . . . not a man at all. The thought echoed through him, childlike, he won't be able to yell at me. And now there was movement in front of him, the rebels rising up from the fence, but they weren't firing, they were running away, the word planting itself in his mind . . . *retreating*. Men around him kept up their shouts, and he saw one of the lieutenants running hard toward the fence, far out in front of the men, climbing up and over, charging the withdrawal of the rebels, firing a pistol, urging his men to follow. More men were running forward now, the line scattered, disorganized, their fire wild and scattered. But the chase was on, the animal after the prey.

Bauer tried to run with them, to keep up, the unloaded musket dragging beside him, and he reached the fence, forced himself over, one step at a time, swung his leg clear, dropped down into the thicket, shoved through the thorny brush. He searched frantically for the lieutenant, saw him now, waving the sword, waiting for the men to move up with him, and the officer turned, kept moving forward, but only a few steps. Bauer saw the officer suddenly halt, as if ordered, the man standing completely still. But the lieutenant wasn't hit, didn't fall, just stood in one place for a long moment, then turned, looked back at his own men. Bauer ignored him now, wanted to see more, had to see the rebels running away, the men who had shot down the captain . . . and Patterson . . . and now other men were climbing into the underbrush beside him, pushing through, the ground rolling up into another short rise. Some of the others were halting as well, as though frozen, staring out. Bauer cursed the musket, fumbled again at his cartridge box, pushed his way out of the underbrush, moved close to a man, realized it was Willis. He let out a cheer, pure joy at seeing his friend, wanted to say something, anything, but Willis ignored him, was staring straight ahead, motionless. There was an odd breath of silence, a pause in the chaos, and Bauer tried not to hear that, began to load the musket, ready for the next shot, ready for the pursuit to begin again. Willis was looking at him now, and Bauer saw a deadly stare, strange, and Willis pointed to the front, no words. Bauer looked out toward the next field, saw a single rebel moving away, dragging a wounded leg, the man disappearing into another thicket. But he could see now, the thicket was not brush and under-growth. It was men.

In the clearing out beyond the field, the first sunlight was collected in a dense mass of reflections, and Bauer felt a cold stab in his chest, real-ized now why the lieutenant, why the rest of them had stopped. As far out as he could see, the field was lined with men, and just above the mass, the glimmer of a thousand bayonets, and behind them, another thousand, and a thousand more. It was the rebel army.

PART THREE

FURY

## CHAPTER SEVENTEEN

# JOHNSTON

He had slept in an ambulance, a minor luxury he did not take for granted, since he knew that his army had slept on the ground, with their muskets close at hand. For much of the early evening, he had ridden with Bragg, seeing to the feeding of the men, finding some way to move ration wagons forward, the drier weather an enormous help. But after midnight, Johnston had been alone, if only for a short few hours, much-needed rest, sleep coming to him even on the thin padding in the ambulance. Well before dawn, the sleep had ended, too much in his brain, too many details, too much anticipation of just what would happen, a day that would be very different and very special.

At the campfire, he had enjoyed the wonderful heat of the thick, sugary coffee, another luxury he allowed himself as often as the staff could provide it. It had been a vice since his earliest days in the army, when coffee had been his personal choice over alcohol. The destruction that affected so many of the officers was too vivid an image, and even now, he knew that there were generals who might not be fit at the critical moment. It was something Bragg had preached against, had issued punishment for, but Johnston knew that if a man intended to destroy himself, there was little that the army's discipline could do to stop it. There were other vices as well, and he knew it came from the weakness of man, that his army would be no different than those other boys, no matter how ruthless Braxton Bragg's punishment could be.

With the comfort of the coffee cup in his hand, he had been tempted by the sandwich in his pocket, though the orderlies had provided a more military breakfast of cold biscuits and the remnants of a slab of bacon. The gift from Mrs. Inge had not been discovered until he was well on his way from Corinth, and it brought a broad smile he did not explain to his staff. It remained in his pocket, and he knew that very likely the bread was stale, that mold would come very soon. But he also knew that the gift would inspire talk, even from his own staff, the kind of chatter that could lead to rumors of some impropriety between the general and the hostess. He had no patience for that. For now the sandwich remained where she had put it, wrapped in cloth, a slight tug of weight in his coat. At the very least, it would remind him that his hostess was one of many who had put their faith in him, and in his army. Today he would justify that faith.

His quiet enjoyment of the coffee and the campfire had been interrupted unexpectedly by a council of war that he did not summon. To his annoyance, it was to be a continuation of the meeting that had taken place the afternoon before, a meeting that he thought had been firmly settled. Johnston could not fathom that anyone would be confused about his orders for this morning's attack, and he knew that those orders had been passed down the chain of command to every regimental commander. Johnston was fully confident that every officer in his command knew where he was supposed to be, and what would be expected of his men. But the energy for the predawn meeting had come from Beauregard, and once again there had been heated discussion, all of it inspired by Beauregard's incredible lack of confidence in his own plan, his insistence *still* that the attack be postponed, or called off altogether.

Johnston had endured the gathering not just by listening, but by carefully watching the faces of the others, Polk and Bragg and Breckinridge, all of them as resolute as before, responding to Beauregard's hesitation with formidable displays of heat. The arguments were as stiff and one-sided as they had been the day before, every corps commander making plain that the army was in position, knew its duty, that the plan was sound, and that any suggestion of retreat would be a disaster for everyone involved. But Beauregard had not wavered, had heated up as well, and Johnston began to realize that his second in command was not making his argument because of strategy, that what they were hearing from Beauregard was not just a dwindling commitment to his own plan. Johnston could see it on the faces of the others, Bragg especially, no surprise there. Bragg had stopped short of a major breach in subordination and Johnston knew that what was left unsaid made little difference. The senior field commanders of this army had to accept that, for reasons that no one truly understood, Beauregard had lost his nerve.

Johnston had accepted the validity of one part of Beauregard's argument, the astounding inability of the army to maintain any kind of silence. Throughout the woodlands and fields where Hardee's men had made their temporary camps, the officers knew that they were barely a mile from the enemy's pickets. And yet the men had behaved as if there were no enemy at all, their discipline virtually nonexistent. Though orders had been explicit against campfires, the exasperated staff had reported to Johnston that fires were everywhere. Though muskets were ordered to be left unloaded, muskets were fired, a cluster of men offering potshots at any woodland creature they could find. The necessity of silence had been expressed with perfect clarity to every company commander, and through the night, those orders had proven to be incredibly useless. Every commander had been taught the value of surprise, that this attack would succeed primarily because Grant's army was apparently not prepared to defend itself. As he rose from the brief rest, Johnston fully expected a staff officer to be waiting for him with the one report he hoped never to hear: that the enemy was responding as they should be responding, by digging in, that the sounds of axes and shovels would be widespread across the entire front. As he emerged from the ambulance, all that met him was the small campfire, his wonderful pot of coffee, and close at hand, his staff officers awaiting the specific instructions for the new day.

Incredibly, there were no reports about enemy activity at all. The infuriating delays that had plagued the army seemed not to have caused any crisis at all, except perhaps the one in Beauregard's mind. Johnston had stood to one side during the predawn debate, and as was his custom, he allowed his men to blow off their steam and make their points. But the final word was his, and this time his solution seemed to satisfy all of them. Beauregard was ordered to maintain the army's primary field headquarters to the rear of the advance, what would be a well-positioned, and possibly stationary landmark, so that any courier could find it, a place where reports could be delivered without fail. By keeping to the rear, Beauregard could keep a broad hand on the general disposition of the attack, and so his talent for organization and logistics would be made useful. Johnston would do exactly the opposite. He would ride out with the army, keeping touch with the attack as it happened, relying on Beauregard to inform him of weakness or failure, so that Johnston could react quickly by moving to every point on the field where he might be needed, where indecision or uncertainty might require a definitive order.

As though Beauregard needed a punctuation mark to Johnston's order, the meeting had concluded with the first sounds of a growing battle, a chorus of musket fire drifting back across the two miles that separated Johnston's camp from the front lines of Hardee's men. Johnston had noted the time, ordering Major Munford to write down the precise minute when the firing began. It had been 5:14 in the morning. The musket fire and the clear thump of artillery had launched each of the generals to his horse, and Johnston had felt their energy, had seen the camaraderie, each man encouraging the others, which had given Johnston the greatest encouragement of all. The time for talk, for argument, for hesitation had been erased by the one task the generals had passed on to the men who carried the musket. As they rode away into the dim light of dawn, each of his corps commanders had heartily agreed with Johnston's parting pledge, that by noon they would water their horses in the Tennessee River.

If Beauregard had been the exception to the raw optimism for the coming fight, Johnston had watched him ride away with one thought drilling into his brain. Today will be costly, will be momentous to our cause, and if we are fortunate, it will be glorious. Perhaps it is best if General Beauregard commands the paperwork.

APRIL 6, 1862, 6:20 A.M.

The debate was forgotten completely, the coffee a memory. He rode hard, making his way along the lines of Hardee's men first, had to see it for himself, that the movement was forward, that the lines were solid, that the first burst of fire had not caused any problems.

He had not yet seen Hardee, but the men who moved through the thickets and across the rolling ground had responded to him with gratifying cheers. He rode now along a narrow lane, his men driving off to one side, eastward, into the first rays of sunlight. To his front he saw men on horseback, motioned with his hand to his staff to follow, moved that way. The faces were familiar, which surprised him, and he reined the horse, saw the young face of John Marmaduke, who welcomed him with a crisp salute.

"Colonel Marmaduke, are we performing to your expectations this day?"

Marmaduke was not yet thirty, was a West Pointer whom Johnston had commanded in the Utah expedition and since. He was a lean, tall man, who sat straight-backed in the saddle, gave every appearance of an officer to be respected.

"Sir, my regiment has the honor of holding the center of this entire line. We will not break. We will never break."

Johnston smiled, couldn't help a surge of affection for the young man, reached out, their horses close, put a hand on the man's shoulder.

"My boy, today we must conquer or perish."

Marmaduke seemed to sag slightly from Johnston's touch, but it was not weakness, the young man looking at him with emotion in his eyes.

"Sir, we shall make you proud."

Johnston pulled his hand back, realized he had gone to a place that he rarely revealed. Johnston turned the horse, his attention caught by a burst of musket fire. He wanted to ride that way, but it was not the place for him to be, the first sounds of a fight that needed only the guiding hand of a lieutenant, the drive of the man with the bayonet. He was startled by the hard thump of artillery erupting from the woods across a deep ravine. He couldn't see the guns, but the thunder of the cannons drove into him, shaking him, and he stood in the saddle, tried to see, but there was only smoke, and inside of him, a surge of pride and the joyful feeling of power and certain victory that he had already seen in every officer and every soldier on the line. He made a quick glance toward his staff, who were lined out in the narrow roadway behind him.

"We should keep moving. Colonel Marmaduke does not require this command to prod him to his duty."

He looked toward the young man again, saw the same crisp salute, responded to it, and Johnston knew there was nothing more to say. He spurred the horse, the troops in line close by pushing out into the woods, down into the ravine, making their advance, but not before responding to Johnston's presence with one more rousing cheer.

# CHAPTER EIGHTEEN

# SHERMAN

NEAR SHILOH CHURCH
APRIL 6, 1862, 7:00 A.M.

The sounds that brought him out of his tent had been curious at first, a scattering of musket fire that annoyed him as much now as it had for the past several days. But with the hint of daylight came far more, many skirmishes in many places, the fights growing more intense.

With the sun almost into the trees to the east, he lit the cigar, his first of the day, moved slowly toward the horse. His orderly, Holliday, was waiting with the reins.

"Private, this should not be. It just should not be. We have pickets in force across the entire front. There would be word from someone out there if there was trouble, if all that commotion was something . . . different. There should be, at any rate. I am not at all pleased with the abilities of my senior officers."

He turned, saw a pair of staff officers emerging from his tent. He had left them behind to complete a report for General Grant, one more note to reassure the army's headquarters that in these camps farthest from the river, there had been signs of a *saucy* enemy, but that Sherman had no concerns the army was under any kind of serious threat.

He looked toward Captain Hammond, saw the paper in his hand, said, "Have you completed the message?"

"Yes, sir. Should I order a courier to deliver this—"

The young man stopped, seemed to notice the growing volume of sounds that spilled toward them, said, "Sir . . . forgive me, but that does not sound like a skirmish. There . . . that's artillery, sir."

Sherman still looked at the paper in Captain Hammond's hands, thought of Grant. He is injured, and I don't know how badly. That is not helpful, not right now. By damned, I wish he could ride out here, hear this for himself. Sherman was truly annoyed now, clamped the cigar hard in his teeth.

"Dammit, I'm going out there. Mount up, both of you. Color bearer, too. These men are so damn agitated, I don't want anyone mistaking me for the enemy. Bring at least three couriers with us." He paused, turned toward the loudest sounds he could hear. "That artillery is coming from Hildebrand's Brigade. I want to know whose cannons are raising so much hell, and why."

Hammond and Major Sanger moved to their horses, taking the reins from another of the aides. Both were up now, Sanger motioning for the color bearer to move close, the man already unfurling the Stars and Stripes. Hammond focused on the woods, and Sherman could see nervousness in the young man's face. After a moment, Hammond said, "General, the firing is coming from down that way as well . . . toward General Prentiss."

Sherman looked to the left of the church building, could see nothing but a glimpse of the next open field, the rows of white tents. Now he heard drums, steady, the *long roll,* a commander's signal to bring his regiment into a battle-ready formation.

"Who the hell is doing that?"

The question went unanswered, another chorus of drums rising up through the woods, and now more artillery, hard thumps not more than a quarter mile from the church.

Sherman took the reins from Holliday, said, "Mount up, Private. Let's go find out who's doing all this confounded firing. If those damn rebels are driving in our pickets, I want to make sure we respond with enough force to drive them all the way to Corinth. I don't trust Hildebrand or McDowell to know what order to give."

He turned again to the officers, saw the expectant face of Lieutenant Taylor, one of his youngest aides. Taylor was a competent staff officer but had made a nuisance of himself by pressing Sherman for permission to ride forward too often, especially when word came from the brigade commanders of any kind of skirmish. But Sherman appreciated the young man's enthusiasm, knew that Taylor only wanted to see something of the rebels that an aide-de-camp might never observe, a kind of adventure that the young man seemed afraid he would miss completely.

"Well, Lieutenant, I suppose you intend to accompany us?"

"With your permission, sir."

"Fine, perhaps this morning you will finally get a good look at those rebels who are making you so impatient. If you were a little less useful around here, I'd send you out there for good, let you serve this army as a field officer."

Taylor spurred the horse up alongside Major Sanger, beamed a smile.

"Thank you, sir."

There was a new burst of firing to the northwest, out toward Sherman's right flank, the right flank of the entire army, which had been anchored along the marshy swamp that ran along Owl Creek.

"Now what?"

Again there were no answers, and Sherman climbed up on the horse, spit out the spent cigar. He glanced toward the color bearer, ever present, the couriers scrambling into line, but still his attention was drawn to the musket fire that rolled toward him all across the front lines, interrupted only by the drums, the long roll now coming from camps farther to the left, toward Prentiss's Division. Well, hell, he thought. Do any of those people intend to tell me what's happening?

"Let's ride, gentlemen. We'll head straight for the Third Brigade. I want Colonel Hildebrand to tell me firsthand why we're using up so much ammunition."

T he closer Sherman rode to Hildebrand's camps, the louder the firing in what seemed to be clusters, as though the skirmishes were taking place in every isolated hole where the pickets had kept their positions. But along the roadway, Sherman was dismayed to see ambulances moving back toward him, a clatter of wheels and rattling boards, driven by men who had no interest in stopping. But they could not help seeing the flag, and every teamster knew him, knew that if

Sherman ordered a halt, he had best halt. Sherman watched three move past, dust rising around him, and he was growing more angry, still had received no direct word from any of his commanders. Down the narrow road, another ambulance clattered forward, and he lurched the horse directly into the path, held up his hand, his other on the pistol in his belt. The teamster understood perfectly, yanked hard on the reins, the horses jolted to a halt. Sherman moved to the rear, looked inside, saw three men, lying flat, close beside one another, one of them awake, staring back at him, blood on the man's legs. There was a sharp moan from one of the others, and Sherman saw an arm shattered, wrapped in dirty cloth, a ripped, blood-soaked shirt. He looked at the third man, saw foam spreading on the man's chest, and he caught the sweet damp smell he had tried to forget. He pulled the horse away, said to the driver, "Who are these men? Who ordered you to the rear?"

The man stared at him, silent, intimidated, and Sanger was beside Sherman, said, "You will answer the general!"

Sherman didn't need the assistance, leaned closer to the driver, a hard stare into the man's wide eyes.

"I said—"

"Captain Yancey, sir. These men are hurt bad. He said to haul them to the river."

"Who are they?"

"Soldiers, sir. Ohio soldiers."

Sherman felt the helplessness of a man shouting at a rock.

"Go! Don't stop until you find a hospital. Captain Yancey is right. They're hurt bad."

The man seemed happy to leave, slapped the reins on the horse, the ambulance rattling away. Sherman fought through the dust, said to Sanger, "I'm not familiar with this Yancey."

"Fifty-third Ohio, sir. Company commander. Not sure which one."

"Doesn't matter. That's Appler's regiment, and if we can't find Hildebrand, we'll find Appler."

They rode hard, a cloud of dust of their own, the roar of musketry steady to the front, more erupting out to the left. The road turned into a wide field, and he knew the place, solid rows of tents, the camps of Hildebrand's Brigade. They didn't stop, Sherman driving past the tents, only a few men there, some hurrying to get dressed, to join what was blossoming into a hard skirmish not more than a few hundred yards away. Sherman ignored them, pushed closer to the most intense sounds, heard artillery firing in a tight rhythm, six quick shots, an entire battery, and he moved that way, followed the rising smoke. They climbed a rise and Sherman halted the horse, could see the guns in the cluster of trees, their crews scrambling around them, the good order of men who knew their jobs. He saw faces look his way, but no one came toward him, and Sherman ignored that, knew those men were taking orders to fire from someone who might actually know what they were firing at. The staff halted in line behind him, and he scanned the trees, smoke in every direction. He searched for horses, flags, someone in command, his hand probing the pocket of his coat, the instinctive search for the cigar. No, dammit, not now. To one side was another clearing, more tents, and he turned, saw Captain Hammond watching him, waiting for the question.

"Whose camp is that . . . over there?"

"That's the 53rd Ohio, sir. Colonel Appler."

Sherman scowled, kept up his horse's hard pace, thought, Appler. Useless. Sees a flock of cavalry and sends his entire regiment chasing after them. He's probably the one who ordered these guns to join the festivities.

"Let's see if we can find Colonel Appler."

He spurred the horse hard, led them into Appler's camp, the sounds of the fights not far to the west. Around the tents, men were in quick motion, some half dressed, stacks of muskets knocked to the ground, coffeepots spilled beside campfires. The men seemed to be scrambling in every direction, a handful of officers on horseback galloping through the tent rows, rousing what seemed to be stragglers from their tents. Sherman watched the scene, cold fury inside, thought, this is just *marvelous*. Perfect discipline. I'll find Appler and wring his damn neck.

"Over there! That way!"

He pushed on, the woods past Appler's camp giving way to a wide field. The smoke was drifting everywhere now, and he caught the sulfur stink, looked out across a field a quarter mile wide, heard a chorus of musket fire down toward the left, near a thick tree line. There were men in motion there, and Sherman could see a mass of blue moving out of the trees, some in a full run, an obvious retreat. He cursed to himself, raised his field glasses, stared that way, tried to see details through the smoke. There were officers on horseback, more than one color bearer, all of them falling back out of the wood line. He fought the urge to ride that way, a small voice inside him keeping him in place, one tiny flicker of panic, the infectiousness of watching men running from a fight. He shouted aloud now, deflected the voice outward, toward the men on horseback, the men who were supposed to be in control.

"Stop them, damn you. Do your job!"

He kept his glasses on the scene, the woods seeming to belch hordes of blue troops, the officers retreating with as much energy as their men, no one making an attempt to rally the men at all. Sherman felt the horse buck slightly, realized he was pulling hard on the reins, the horse's head up, protesting. The urge to ride into the smoke was growing, the need to grab the man in command, any officer he could find, toss the man out of the saddle.

"Damn them! What are they doing? I want one of you to find Appler, then find Hildebrand! This is idiocy!" He held the glasses with one hand, tight to his eyes, shouted again, "Turn them, damn you! What in hell are you running from?"

He forced himself to calm, to observe all he could, knew there would be a remedy to this, that he was too strong, and that close by, the other camps could help whatever crisis had erupted in front of Appler. He kept the field glasses at his eyes, one hand pulling a cigar from his pocket, reflex, and he stuffed it into his mouth. Immediately the young Holliday was there with a match, the orderly always efficient. Sherman ignored him, but the cigar was lit, the smoke calming him, and Sherman kept his focus on the far end of the field, some men forming a line, firing a volley into the woods. He still wanted to ride there, to see what he could not from the knoll, the smoke filling every open space. He was surprised to hear Hammond, close behind him.

"Sir! Colonel Appler is said to be in these woods to our right!"

Sherman still watched the fight, more of his men returning to the line of fire, absorbing the retreat like a thin blue sponge, thickening, holding their ground.

"Good . . . good. Now drive them back! Whoever they are, whatever they are. Cavalry, I hope. Chase those scoundrels to hell!"

"Sir . . ."

It was Sanger, and Sherman ignored him, thought of Appler, the

woods . . . *that way.* The wrong way. You should be out there with your
men, damn you! He held the glasses locked to his eyes, chewed the cigar
with a manic anger, Sanger again, "Sir . . . an officer . . ."

To the right, a man ran close, shouting, and Sherman heard the words,
the panic in the man's voice.

"General . . . look to your right!"

Sherman lowered the glasses, saw the man pointing, looked out
toward the woods that way. The trees were fifty yards away, and through
the gaps emerged a line of men, muskets high, bayonets, none of the
men wearing blue. He stared at them for a long second, the soldiers
seeming to absorb the scene as he was. Now they responded, the muskets coming up, and Sherman raised his hand, instinctive gesture. The
burst of fire blew past him, and he heard the sickening crack, Holliday
falling close beside him with a sharp grunt. Sherman felt a sting in his
hand, looked at it, a bloody puncture in his palm, the blood flowing in a
stream onto his pants, onto the horse. He looked down, saw his young
orderly on the ground, motionless, the young man's horse dancing to the
side. Sherman looked again at the gray troops, his brain surging into
focus, and he made a fist with the wounded hand, clamped down on the
blood, said, "My God . . . they are attacking *us!*"

"Sir . . . this is no place—"

Sherman didn't need the words of caution, wheeled his horse in a
tight arc, a loud order to his staff, "Move!"

He spurred the horse hard in the flanks, the animal responding,
the men following at a gallop. There was another volley from the rebels,
but the shots were wild, their opportunity missed. He searched the
trees, guided the horse through narrow openings, saw a cluster of officers, some directing blue troops into line, sending them toward the
fields, saw now it was Appler. Sherman jerked the reins, wheeled the
horse that way and Appler stared toward him with eyes that showed a
man desperately afraid. Sherman's mind was already in motion, far beyond the single moment, the single line of rebel troops.

"Colonel, hold your position! No retreat here! Do you understand?"

Appler seemed dumb with shock, did not respond. Sherman was already moving past him, knew there was no time for this, to soothe one
man's panic.

"I will send assistance! Hold here! Do not retreat!"

Sherman slowed the horse, a manic surge of thought, the face of Hildebrand, old man, useless. Where the hell is he? The others . . . Buckland, good man, Buckland should be here. He will hold any line. Appler still watched him, said nothing, and beside Appler, a man was pointing, a hard shout.

"The men are pulling back! It's the rebels!"

Sherman turned, halted the horse, and he saw now the woods filling with Appler's men, a hundred or more, others flowing back farther to the right. Sherman felt a cold sickness, the scene too familiar, a stab of memories from Bull Run. The musket fire drew closer, the men running past him now, unstoppable, and behind them, out in the broad field, the slow and steady pursuit, a vast, dense line of gray.

## CHAPTER NINETEEN

# BAUER

SOUTHEAST OF SHILOH CHURCH
APRIL 6, 1862, 8:00 A.M.

He ran, stumbled, his feet slurping through mud, tried to push through the deepest part of the gulley. Around him, the others were moving past, some staggering through the dense woods, wrestling through tangles of vines and small trees. He fought past the mud, began to climb, the trees giving way, more open ground. He stopped, gasping, stared at the rows of tents, so familiar, realized they had made it back to their own camp. Others kept coming up from the ravine, pausing to catch their breath, others not stopping at all. One man ran straight into the side of a tent, seemed swallowed by the white canvas, punched his way through, screaming, terrified. Bauer wanted to stop the man, but his legs were heavy, frozen in place, his lungs burning with the remnants of smoke. He turned away from the crazed man, suddenly didn't care, stared instead at where he had come from, the tree line that fell away. More of the Wisconsin men were climbing up, some without muskets, some with small wounds, one man holding his arm, crying as he ran past Bauer. The name came to him, Billy Walbridge, another of the men from Company A, and Bauer shouted to him, the man slowing, recognizing him, a single word through the sobs.

"Dutchie!"

"Stop running! This is our camp! Safe here!"

The man looked back to the trees, seemed to calm, looked now to his own wound, blood seeping through his fingers, a hard grip on his forearm.

"I'm shot, Dutchie! I'm gonna die!"

"No, you're not! Just your arm. There's a lot worse. The docs'll fix you up for certain!"

Walbridge seemed to believe him, and Bauer tried to be reassuring, took the man's arm, looked toward the tents, some place there might be bandages.

"Come on, we'll find something to wrap that."

"I'm gonna lose it, Dutchie! They'll cut it off!"

"No they won't. It's just a small wound."

He pulled Walbridge with him, pushed into the closest tent, searched frantically for anything to tie around the man's arm. Walbridge yanked away from him, the man's panic returning.

"We gotta keep moving, Dutchie! The *secesh* were right behind us! Can't stay here!"

Bauer released the man's arm, bent low to pull a shirt from a pile of clothes, and immediately, Walbridge was gone, out of the tent. Bauer felt a wave of despair, held up the shirt, useless gesture.

"This'll work."

He stepped out of the tent, more men running past, but there were officers now, a man on horseback, the sword high, and Bauer saw the red face, the hard shouts of Colonel Allen.

"Line up here! Form a line right here! Wisconsin men! Fight for your homes! For your families!"

Allen spun the horse, tried to head off some of the running men, others obeying him, the panic seeming to pass for some. There was a lieutenant, Smith, another man from the company, and he took up the colonel's call, ran hard, grabbing men, turning them around. Some escaped him, but others stopped, seemed to regain something, as though they only needed someone to tell them what to do, someone in command. Bauer moved that way, close to Allen, who watched him briefly, pointed to him, shouted out, "Yes! Move up here! Form a line alongside this man!"

Bauer realized the colonel was talking about him, and he felt the weight of that, stood with the musket across his chest, others falling in beside him, the line growing. Men still surged up from the woods, most of them exhausted, more wounds, but there were muskets, and they responded to Allen, the man motioning with his sword, pulling his regiment together.

Bauer looked at the musket in his hand, suddenly had no idea if it was loaded. He had fired a half-dozen rounds, mostly wild, targets too far away, or no targets at all. Many had done the same, the massed line of rebel soldiers pressing into them in a wave far more powerful than anything Colonel Peabody could put in their way. Bauer looked at Allen, thought of Peabody, riding with a mad rush along the lines, doing all he could to form up some kind of stand against the rebel attack. They were too many, he thought. How could we do that? Just . . . stand there?

He had watched them come with stunned amazement, neat lines, the orderly march forward, flags and horsemen and drummers. The order had been passed down the line, one organized volley, but that had just made them blind, the smoke hiding the rebel advance. Some of the men had reloaded, one of the lieutenants, the same man he saw now, Smith, ordering them to fire at will. When the smoke began to clear, the rebels were that much closer, relentless, a volley of their own blowing through the thin lines of the men from Wisconsin and Missouri and Michigan. Some of the men close to him had returned fire, but the strength of the enemy was overwhelming, pushing closer step by step, another volley, vast sheets of flame and smoke and the sounds of musket balls whistling by, the sound of cracking bone. The line could not stand for long, and Bauer had tried to reload one more time, saw the faces of the enemy, ragged, filthy men, no uniforms but for the men on the horses. It was the faces that took away the last bit of courage, and he had turned with most of the men around him, every soldier sharing the sudden desperate need to run.

And now, he thought, we're here. Like it never happened. He glanced back, his mind not quite believing that they had reached their own camp, strange, bizarre chance. He was convinced now, the musket was not loaded, no time, the last shot into smoke, blind and foolish and desperate. He pulled out a cartridge, the routine, the paper in his teeth, poured the powder down the barrel, realized that others were doing the same, following his lead. In front of him, more men came up from the woods, one dragging a bloody leg, helped by another man with a bloody face. Others came wearing unfamiliar insignia on their hats, and Bauer knew what that meant, that a great many men had separated from their units, the woods too thick for any kind of order. The colonel kept up his shouts, guided them into the thickening line, more lieutenants down the way, no one calling to their companies, no one concerned with who was in charge of what men.

The line stretched most of the way across the camp, some men down on one knee, trying to breathe, to gain control. The sergeants were taking position, following the calls of the officers, spreading out behind the men. But there were not many of either, and Bauer thought suddenly of Sergeant Williams, a very bad man, a dangerous man. Gone. He could not avoid the image of Captain Saxe, tumbling back from the horse, a horrible flash of memory he would never forget. His brain held to the sight of the horse, turning, as though surprised, his head down, poking the body of his master. Tears came now, Bauer trying to keep it away, the loss, the grief . . . even for the horse. What happened to him? Dead probably. And Patterson. The look of surprise there, too, wide eyes. This was *fun* to him. Maybe to some, it still is. He looked down the line, searched for Willis, had not seen him since they had run. He scanned the line, some men doing the same, staring back at him, searching faces, men calling out to one another. Allen kept up his shouts as well, hoarseness in the man's voice, moving back and forth along the tree line, still pulling his men out of their panic. Now another horseman rode clear of the trees, one of the captains, Pease, Company D, and he moved up close to Allen, a brief, harsh conversation, Pease moving away quickly, to the far end of the line.

Bauer felt his breathing slow, the pounding in his chest not as frantic. He realized for the first time that the sounds had not stopped, that the steady roar of musket fire was still there, mostly to the right, the thunder of the artillery coming in rumbles, like the hard sounds of a storm. With the calm in the men around him, they all seemed to hear it, men looking that way, some asking aloud who that was, one lieutenant saying something about General Sherman. Allen rode past again, the line steady, prepared, and Bauer saw the blue soldiers still coming back through the woods, saw grim faces and hatred, the panic not so pronounced now. He knew, some instinctive voice inside him, that these men were different. He watched the faces, staring back at the line, and there was disgust and outrage, the men who stood together moving slowly toward this new line, Colonel Allen's line with a look that put the words into Bauer's mind. They didn't run. They stayed out there and fought . . . and now they had to pull back . . . because we didn't stand with them.

He saw another horseman, another of the commanders, his men following him up from the ravine in a column. *Orderly retreat.* Bauer said the words to himself, felt suddenly sick, dropped his head. What did you do, Fritz? You ran like a damn rabbit. He looked at those men, who filled in behind Allen's line, adding strength, no one speaking but the men in charge. And now he saw Willis.

The small, thick man moved out of the trees holding another man under the arm, came toward the line with slow steady steps, moved toward Bauer, didn't seem to see him, kept walking, through the line. Bauer turned, wanted to say something, to call out to him, watched as Willis laid the man down beside one of the tents. Then Willis stood, seemed to appraise the line, a glance at Colonel Allen, and then a glance at Bauer. His expression never changed, barely a hint of recognition, and Willis came toward him with slow steps, falling into line just behind Bauer. Bauer nodded to him, but there were no smiles, and Bauer was suddenly consumed by shame, knowing without asking him that Willis had stayed *out there,* had stood facing the enemy as long as anyone could. And Willis would know that Bauer did not.

He watched as Willis loaded his musket, then turned again to the front, saw Colonel Allen holding the horse steady in front of his men, and Allen said aloud, "Hold this line! This is your camp. In these tents are your belongings, your letters, everything you brought to this field. No one shall get through here! You men from Missouri, Michigan. You stand now with Wisconsin men. We welcome you, welcome your courage. We will get you back to your proper place in time. For now, we need you here. Until I am ordered to march you elsewhere, this is where we shall stand. The enemy could come at us from those trees . . . or from either end of this field. Be ready. Check your cartridge boxes. And keep your aim low!"

Allen turned suddenly in the saddle, drawn by something in the trees. Bauer felt his heart leap, heard a steady hum, but different, not musket fire. Just . . . men.

Allen spurred the horse, moved down to the far end of the line, seemed to know exactly what was happening. Bauer stared at the trees, nothing to see, but the noises were more distinct, and from close beside him, a voice, low words.

"Drums."

Bauer felt a shiver, checked the percussion cap on his musket, glanced down the line at the lieutenant closest to him, saw the man drawing his pistol, turning toward the line, a quick shout, "Be ready, men!"

There was a nervous rumble from the men, anticipation, the drums still seeming to be far away, no kind of threat. But Bauer had already learned about sounds on this ground, that the woods and the hills masked and distorted everything. His breathing came in short, hard surges, his heart beating heavily, and he felt sweat on his face, stinging his eyes, had not paid any attention to the skies, not since the stars had gone away. He glanced up now, blue and beautiful, the sun on his back, and climbing higher above the distant trees at the far side of the camp. His brain made a note of that, west . . . we're looking west. That's where the enemy is. The river . . . is east.

The motion in the tree line was sudden and surprising, a flag first, then hats and faces, and slowly, the chests and legs coming up as well. The rebels were climbing up from the ravine Bauer had crossed, seemed to rise up from the earth itself. They were tired, angry men, suffering the same weariness as the men they pursued. Down the line, a musket fired, then another, one rebel returning fire. The lieutenants shouted out, stopping it, making the effort to hold the men as one, keeping control. In a few seconds the rebel line had emerged up from the woods, had gathered itself, facing the men in blue less than a hundred yards apart. Bauer stared at them, staring back at him, and now the drums were louder, driving more of the rebel troops before them. Bauer felt the panic again, the weakness, helplessness, the musket too small, useless, and now the order came, from both sides, the muskets rising up, a massive eruption of fire and smoke across the narrow space.

The rebel volley took away pieces of the line around him, but there was no time to look, the order coming to reload, while the line of men behind Bauer fired their volley in quick succession. The routine was automatic, and he didn't notice any of it, knew only that his musket was reloaded. Across the flat ground, the rebels still held their line, but many men were down, some twisting in the short grass. The volleys had no rhythm now, scattered bursts, and Bauer raised the musket, frantic, his hands shaking, fired again, heard the shouts of the lieutenant, "Aim low! Fire at will! Aim low!"

Bauer heard the hard concussion in his ears as the muskets behind him fired, the muzzle blasts too close, deafening. He flinched, struggled to load the musket again, dropped the cartridge, fumbled through the box, grabbed another, the routine repeated. He raised the musket, thick smoke, no targets, waited, the musket heavier in his arms. The smoke was drifting, thinning, and he saw an opening, aimed, thought, *low,* saw legs, pointed there, fired, more smoke blinding him. There were shouts down the line, and the lieutenant was moving closer to him, a strange cheer.

"They're pulling back! We drove them off!"

The musket fire continued, but it began to slow, scattered pops, the smoke drifting away again. He caught a glimpse of men, dropping down, hidden by the slope, the rebels pulling away into the trees. Men began to cheer, hats in the air, but Allen was there, his shouts drowning them out.

"Stand ready! They'll be back! See to the wounded! Make sure every man standing has a musket!"

The colonel spurred the horse, moved farther down the line, repeated the order. Bauer looked to the ground on both sides, a half-dozen men down, a bloody scalp, one man holding his shoulder, soft cries. Another man dropped low, tending to the wound, and he ripped the man's shirt from his back, swift efficient motion, wrapped the wound. Bauer looked at the others, another man motionless, two men rolling him over in the grass, then backing away, the wound obvious and deadly.

Now the drums came again, startling him, and the lieutenants resumed the shouts, Allen again, moving past quickly, and suddenly Allen was down, tumbling, rolling on the trampled ground. Bauer felt a hard shock, but the colonel pulled himself up, an aide, others, rushing to him. Bauer saw the horse now, blood in a gush from the horse's chest. From somewhere behind, another horseman came, jumped down, handed the reins to the colonel, and in a few seconds, as though the change of mounts had been rehearsed, Allen was up again, in the saddle, slapped his hat against his legs, jammed it back on his head.

There was no need for orders, the woods coming alive with movement again, but more this time, not just in front, but down to the left, more flags, horsemen. In front of Bauer, the flags came as well, the figure of a horseman, and immediately muskets began to fire near Bauer, the horseman falling away. But the rebels came as before, rising up in a heavy line, and Bauer glanced down to the left, more rebels coming from that way, many more. There was scattered firing from that end of the blue line, the rebels too far away, a voice in his head guiding his eyes straight ahead. He looked again to the front, toward the rebels coming up closest to him, ignored the lieutenant, watched until they were in full view, raised the musket, aimed at legs, slow and steady rhythm, and he saw muddy boots stepping toward him, fired. The others around him did the same, more of the blinding smoke, but there was no return fire, and quickly the second line opened up behind him, more smoke and the sharp ringing in his ears, but still no response from the rebels. He hurried the reloading, furious at the smoke, raised the musket, waited for a target, painful seconds, and now a man was there, close in front of him, running hard toward him, a sharp scream, the bayonet . . .

Bauer pulled the trigger, the man tumbling down, but the smoke could not hide the others. They moved toward the blue line in a rapid wave, and now there was a new sound, rising above the roar of the muskets, a high scream rolling over them from an enemy who had different orders, who did not form up and fire their volleys in neat succession. Bauer saw another man running at him, a knife in the man's hand, huge and deadly, and Bauer dropped down, the man's momentum carrying him over, and Bauer stood quickly, the man falling hard behind him, screaming out suddenly with a hard cry, and Bauer saw a bayonet in the man's chest, the grim face of Willis pinning the man down. The bayonet emerged now, a squirting fountain of blood, Willis staring down, red fury in his eyes, and Willis jammed the bayonet into the man again, pressed his foot into the man's stomach, pulled it out once more. The lieutenant was there now, moving past, a hard shout into Bauer's face, "Too many of them! We're flanked! We have to pull out! *Retreat!*"

The screams were close and manic, rebel troops lunging straight into the blue line, while to one side, another battle line rose up from the ravine there, a surge of bayonets pouring hard into Allen's left flank. The orders came in hot shouts, but to the men in blue who had tried to stand tall, to hold their ground, the orders meant nothing at all. The weight that came over them crushed and dissolved the blue line, and those men who could run began flowing back through their camp, their own tents, moving eastward, toward the hot glare of the sun.

## CHAPTER TWENTY

# SHERMAN

He understood now just what was happening. The high-pitched scream of the rebel troops was everywhere, rising up from every low place, spreading through the fields and thickets of trees across his entire division. Almost immediately, Appler's 53rd Ohio had broken, streaming past him in a panic that brought more of the terrible memories of Bull Run. Their eyes told the story, madness infecting every man as though each one felt his own devil in close pursuit. As the rebel attack pressed closer, Sherman sent his couriers all along the lines, trying to keep some sort of communications with his brigade commanders, but very quickly the front line was no line at all. For an hour or more, the roar of the firing seemed to surge in and out like the twisting body of some great bloody snake. He had heard nothing at all from Hildebrand, but the chaotic scamper of men from that part of the field was a message all its own. He had always known that Hildebrand was no leader, a gasping frustration that Sherman knew he could have changed, that there had been time and enough doubts for him to replace a man who had no business on the line. From all that Sherman could gather, Appler's regiment had fled the field completely, led by Appler himself, a gaping hole in Hildebrand's line that was spreading panic through that entire brigade, a brigade that was supposed to hold the center of Sherman's position.

He kept three staff officers close to him, rode quickly through the trees, emerging into another of the smoky fields, stopped, stared, nothing to see but masses of troops, sheets of flame from a thousand muskets, his ears ringing from the hard thunder of his own batteries. He saw one of them now, a cluster of six cannon spread out among a stand of tall trees, shouted back to his staff, "That way! We need every battery up here! Anchor them in line with those men! Move!"

The courier moved away, orders Sherman could only trust, had no idea himself where more of the batteries would be. But someone would know, someone farther down, someone who had not yet tasted the panic of the forward lines. They rode toward the trees through smoke that made him cough, the steady clip and zing of the musket balls in the air, like so many deadly bees. Out of the smoke came a horse, riderless, as panicked as the men who followed it, scampering back through the battery Sherman was trying to reach. The horse nearly collided with his own, seemed to be blind, bloody eyes, sickening, his own horse rising up, as though sharing the beast's agony. Sherman pulled hard on the reins, slapped the horse's neck, forced a low voice, "Easy. We're good here. I need you to do the job."

The horse seemed to calm, responding to his control, the one hand holding tight to the reins, his wounded hand wrapped in a bloody white handkerchief. He tried to ignore that, felt no pain, the bandage a bulky inconvenience, little else. The staff was close behind him, and he avoided their faces, did not want to see any sign of panic, knew that even the veterans, Sanger, Hammond, any one of the couriers could suddenly come apart, unable to hold away the terror from the men who continued to run in scattered chaos across the open ground. He searched the smoke for the battery again, saw the guns firing in unison, good work, men standing together, no panic there.

"This way!"

He led them into the trees, the artillerymen oblivious to him, focusing instead on some target Sherman couldn't see. He saw their officer, a very young lieutenant, the man off his horse, running back and forth, orders shouted to his men, the officer obeying his own commands, assisting his men, the guns loaded quickly, erupting again. The lieutenant saw Sherman now, no salute, just a sharp nod, fire in the man's eyes. Sherman knew he had to keep moving, to find the other commanders, their couriers, but something held him, the power of these guns, the efficiency of the men who worked them. He moved the horse behind the battery, halted the animal, the horse leaping upward when the guns fired again. Smoke blanketed the open ground, but through the gaps he could see movement, a thick cloud of dark forms, coming toward them through the smoke. He said aloud, to no one, "It's them. They're coming."

He shouted now, caught the attention of the artillery officer, who turned to him, impatient, work to be done.

"Keep up your fire! I will find you reinforcements . . . infantry! You must hold here!"

"We will hold!"

The lieutenant spun away, the gun crews loading again, ramrods and bags of powder and iron shoved hard into red-hot barrels. The lanyards came up now, each gun with a man at the breech, waiting with desperate impatience, no one needing the order. The guns erupted one more time, near-perfect rhythm, a vast sea of flame and gray smoke blowing out into the oncoming rebels. Sherman was blind again, stared into nothing but screams, but the sounds were closing, the enemy still advancing. There was a fresh chorus of the sharp, high yell, what could only be an all-out charge. He searched for the lieutenant, saw him manning one of his guns, standing over the body of his own bloody crewman, the lanyard in the officer's hand. The rest of his crew worked furiously to reload their gun, and Sherman could feel the man's impatience, urged them on in his mind, *Hurry up, damn you,* couldn't help a furious anger even at these men, men who had done nothing but fight. The crewman with the ramrod stood aside, the gun ready, the lieutenant tightening the lanyard, and the man seemed to shudder, curling over, falling, still gripping the lanyard, his fall pulling it taut, the gun erupting. Sherman stared for a long second, absorbed the scene, the man's crew pausing, motionless, one man bending low, a corporal, touching the officer's shoulder, a brief look, disbelief, shock, then the corporal was up again, shouted to the crews, taking command, more of the orders they already knew.

Through the smoke, the rebels were closer, and Sherman saw a dense

line of men no more than fifty yards away, advancing toward the guns.
They seemed to pause, uncertain, stepping over their own dead, and
Sherman stared at them, orders racing through his mind, what should
be done, if only there was infantry . . . order them forward, right now!
The enemy is shaken, exhausted, afraid, maybe their officers are down.
But the guns in front of him fired again, a jolting surprise, and the mass
of rebels vanished, their high-pitched yell suddenly silent. He stared
through the smoke, ordered it away with hard profanity, had to see,
*must* see . . . and now, the air clearing, and all across the muzzles of the
guns there was a mass of filth, heaps of shattered men, some squirming,
many others in pieces. Yes! Damn them! We will kill every damn one
of them!

The gun crews kept to their duty, men scampering back to the limbers
behind Sherman, bringing up more of the powder, more lead, and now
a new sound, off to one side, coming closer, faster. It came from far down
in the woods, a place he couldn't see, no time to look, the shriek coming
down with a shimmering whistle, a shell toppling downward, impacting
behind him, the limber igniting, a hard blast that threw Sherman forward, jolting his horse. The horse dropped to its forelegs, and Sherman
reacted with instinct, knew to jump aside, that the horse was going to
topple. He rolled away, the horse coming down close beside him, a thick
blotch of blood on its torn flank. Sherman looked away, would not see
the death of the animal, felt hands under him, helping him up, shouts
from his aides. Several of the horses from the limbers were loose now,
and quickly one was snatched close, one of the couriers jumping from
his mount, climbing up on the horse without a saddle. The man's own
horse was given to Sherman now, and he nodded a sharp *thank you*, saw
the man fumbling with the leather straps of the draft horse, making do.
Sherman looked again to the gunners, fewer now, some shot down, others simply . . . gone. Those who were left began to back away, one man
grabbing the horses at another of the limbers, yanking hard on the bri-
dles, pulling them forward, closer to his gun. Sherman knew what it
meant, that the man was trying to hitch the lone cannon, a desperate
attempt to save at least one of the artillery pieces. Sherman looked to his
staff . . . help him . . . but the man stared out toward a new line of rebels,
advancing quickly, and Sherman felt a stab of fear, the same fear that had
spread through the gun crews.

The artilleryman seemed to understand his own helplessness, the danger immediate, and so the man released the horses, disappeared as well, a quick scamper back into the trees, making his escape. Sherman pulled back on the horse's reins, nothing else to do, a last glance to the front, empty cannon pointing at ground spread thick with the bodies of the enemy. But still more were coming, stepping past their own, some of them stopping, one group staring at the cluster of blue-coated officers. Many more could see only the guns, were energized by the prize, made a glorious dash toward the precious cannon that were theirs for the taking. The musket fire blew past him, and Sherman turned the horse, spurred hard, the animal responding, the staff following as he sped into the cover of the trees. They climbed a narrow rise, a vantage point, and he halted the horse, spun around, the others reaching him, gathering. He ignored them, more fury in his brain, thought of Buckland, now the center of his division. He will hold. He *has* to hold. But Hildebrand . . . the left . . .

"How far to General Prentiss?"

No one responded, and Sherman looked at them now, Sanger reacting.

"A half mile or more, sir! If he's holding!"

Sherman stared that way, blind again, trees and ravines and brushy thickets, no vantage point good enough. *Prentiss.* Good man, I hope. If you break . . . we are flanked completely.

"Sir! A rider!"

Sherman ignored the call, had seen too many riders, most of them moving the wrong way. But the man reined up close to him, dirty sweat on the man's face, a young captain.

"Sir . . . respects from General McClernand. He has ordered a brigade to fill the gap to your left. The general believes you require assistance in maintaining a solid front. There is an opening between your left and General Prentiss—"

"Shut up, Captain! I know where we are, and I know what's happening on my left!"

He was angry at everyone, everything, hated McClernand for so many rumors of the man's drunkenness. But his brain absorbed the young captain's words, and he forced himself to understand, had no idea what was happening with Buckland, where Prentiss's flank began. The words rolled through his brain, a flash of clarity. McClernand was doing exactly the right thing.

"Where is General McClernand?"

The captain flinched at the fury in Sherman's voice, as though expecting Sherman to hit him.

"I don't know, sir! Back . . . there! He has observed the collapse of your lines . . ."

The words struck Sherman like a heavy fist.

"My lines are holding, boy! You tell McClernand that we will make our stand or die trying." He paused, realized he was shaking, his hands pulling hard on the reins, the horse protesting with a hard shake of its head, a stab of pain piercing Sherman's wounded hand. He glanced at his staff, saw his own couriers, said to Sanger, "Send word to General Prentiss! Make sure he knows we have secured his right flank!"

He saw uncertainty, questions, knew what was coming.

"I don't know where the hell he is! Just find him!"

He turned again to the captain, saw the man looking past him, toward the sound of the fight, louder now, and Sherman looked that way, could not help staring into the spreading roar of a new assault. Damn them! Damn them to hell! He looked to the captain again, said, "Return to General McClernand. Offer him my respects and tell him . . . *request* that he maintain his vigilance. We may require more . . . assistance." He paused, the roar of the battle still growing, closer, massive noise. "Tell General McClernand he should prepare to receive the enemy."

The man saluted him, Sherman returning it, already looking away, searching for something, getting his bearings, a glance at smoky sky.

"We will return to the church! There may be couriers all over these damn woods looking for me. That's where we have to be, the headquarters." The words came fast in his brain. That's where we *have* to be. It's where we *have* to hold.

SHILOH CHURCH

APRIL 6, 1862, 10:00 A.M.

The fighting continued, steady rumbles of artillery and musket fire, but Sherman had received word from McDowell that the right flank was battered but holding. But the rebel assault seemed to spread out now in a wider arc, much more sound coming from the left, what he had to assume was Prentiss's lines, and the piece of ground blocked now by McClernand's men.

In the woods close to the church, more of his men had fallen back, the rebel pressure too great, what seemed to be waves of muskets with no end. More of his artillery was working close by, anchored on good high ground, and to the right, Sherman knew the deep ravines in front of McDowell's men were thick with dense underbrush, ridiculous places for anyone to move at all. The fugitives from his center streamed back through his tents, some pursued by their officers, trying to rally the unstoppable flow. Sherman watched the action, like some bizarre play, men on horseback chasing men on foot, swords up, voices giving sharp commands to men who would obey nothing. There was courage in the officers, some of them trying to form their men into a piece of a line, some kind of organized defense. But still the musket fire came, a burst of rebels down to the left, rising up from a ravine, emerging from trees, and just that quickly, the blue lines dissolved.

At the church itself, the tents were still up, what Sherman now began to see as a symbol, his own defiance, but too many of his troops were rolling back through his camp, and he sat on the horse, stared into the smoky trees close by, more thoughts racing, General Grant, orders, mortal anger toward Hildebrand, toward anyone who had lost control of their men, the men themselves, their courage draining away at a horrifying rate. The staff had spread out, some of them trying to halt the flow of terrified men, what Sherman could see was a hopeless task. From the road to the right, he saw the rider before anyone else, the man searching, spotting him, a last rapid gallop, the horse bouncing to a halt in a near collision with him.

"Sir! Colonel McDowell offers his respects, and reports that he cannot hold the right flank. The brigade has broken, sir! We have made a valiant effort to hold them in line, but the enemy is pressing us with extreme vigor!"

Sherman looked at the man, a sergeant, gray hair, hatless, the formality of his words not masking the man's obvious terror. He thought of McDowell with a burst of rage, old man, lines breaking, *you useless son of a bitch*. He wanted to kill the man, strangle McDowell with his hands, jam a cigar in the man's bloody eye. He fought the image, brought himself to the moment, saw another cluster of bluecoats emerging from the woods, blood and fear, one man calling out, "They're right behind us! We're done for!"

Sherman ignored the man, nothing he could say, looked toward the courier.

"Has Colonel McDowell withdrawn with his men?"

"Yes . . . yes, sir!"

Sherman looked up that way, knew McDowell's right was the northern flank of the entire army. Behind him, Sanger said, "Do you require a map, sir?"

He ignored Sanger, didn't need the maps, knew the ground in his head, thought, the far right . . . bordered along that flank by Owl Creek. Heavy swamps, impassable. Damn him! McDowell was in no danger of being flanked. He just broke.

He looked to the courier again, had nothing to say, no orders, nothing that would prevent any of this, anything that had already happened.

"Stay with me, Sergeant. I may need you."

He turned to his staff, saw an officer on horseback galloping past, close to the church, the man staring ahead, avoiding Sherman purposely. Sherman put a hand on his pistol, thought of shooting the man, but the officer was quickly away, followed by another, and then, another riderless horse. Sherman felt the shaking again, a wave of the awful feeling he knew so well, but he forced his mind to focus. You are in command. *Be in command.* He stared out toward the woods west of the church, the battle rolling closer still, the musket balls splitting the air overhead. The artillery was still firing, but much of it was *out there,* the sky and trees down to the left torn with the familiar shrieks, thunderous impacts on the ground. He glanced at the tents, the *symbol* now utterly ridiculous. Turning the horse, he looked to his staff, saw cold, grim eyes, good men, men who would follow him anywhere. Well, he thought, this might be as bad as anywhere can be.

"It is time to go, gentlemen. We must withdraw what we can salvage of this division, and make every effort to form a new line. We must retreat."

———

With McClernand's help, Sherman's officers pulled and gathered and rallied every man who would still fight, and formed a new defensive line nearly a mile back from their original position, a mile closer to Pittsburg Landing. Against the right and center of the Union position, the rebels continued their push, sweeping through the rugged underbrush, driving across open ground and deep gullies, in pursuit of a stunned and demoralized Union army. But not all the men in blue were panicked, and in many of the fields and low ravines the fighting was more brutal and bloody than any of the troops on either side had yet experienced. In those places where the Federal troops stood tall, where their guns and muskets stopped their attackers, or drove them low into thick cover, even the bravest men found that their victories were short-lived. Through the worst ground imaginable, the rebels continued to come, fresh battle lines joining the fight, pulling their own battered troops up out of their cover, pushing forward. No matter the resolve that inspired many of the Union officers to hold their ground, the surprise had been too complete, the wave of rebels too overpowering. By late morning, rebel troops had driven into and past the vast fields of white tents, those neat rows of canvas left intact alongside the Federal food and supply wagons, fire pits and pots of burnt coffee. The camps were vivid testament to the shock and terror that had gripped the men who had once occupied these peaceful fields, men who had endured the drudgery of their routine, their sergeants, weeks of drill and training and bad food. Like Sherman, their primary duty had been to bide their time until the orders came for a grand and glorious campaign, what was now a fantasy, swept away with the tide of fugitives who ran far back from their own camps, their own officers, their own comrades, many not stopping until they reached the only barrier that could halt them: the Tennessee River.

## CHAPTER TWENTY-ONE

# GRANT

The first sounds of artillery had reached him at seven that morning, a distant rumble that had alarmed the men stationed outside the headquarters mansion, word brought to Grant that there might be some hint of trouble upstream. Grant had heard the thunder already, had left his breakfast behind, and his first order had gone to the captain of the *Tigress,* to fire the boilers of the compact riverboat that served Grant as a floating headquarters. Within minutes most of his staff was on board, along with their horses, Grant following, hobbled by the crutches, still nursing the painful injury from the tumble of his own horse.

The sounds of the cannon were too distant for him to judge just where the assaults were happening, whether at Crump's Landing, his first assumption, or farther upstream, at Pittsburg. Crump's had seemed the most logical, and his greatest fear. The Federal forces there, a single division under Lew Wallace, were assigned to protect an enormous stockpile of supplies and transport boats that would certainly whet the enemy's appetite. Grant had long given up any notion of secrecy, and he knew that assembling his army so close to Corinth would be interpreted exactly for what it was. If the enemy were to make any effort to prevent that assault, surely they would strike in some kind of small-scale raid that would disrupt the supply lines, or cause havoc in the weakest part of the chain Grant's army now held along the river. Wallace had believed that as well, had made several efforts to probe westward, hoping to break up any assault before it could begin. But the enemy had shown little inclination to challenge Wallace's troops, and just as the Federal commanders had experienced farther south, the enemy seemed content to harass Wallace with cavalry raids and brief and hesitant skirmishes. This morning, Grant had heard nothing from Wallace to hint that something larger was afoot. And yet . . .

The boat finally cast off its lines, easing out into the river, the traffic there making way. The flow of supply boats had been ongoing and impressive, and Grant knew that the rebels must surely be observing the buildup of men and equipment. But none of that explained what he was hearing now, the echoing thunder still too distant to provide details of just how large-scale the engagement had become.

The cool breeze offered no help, only masked the sounds of the guns. He stood on the second deck of the *Tigress* in his usual place, observing the river itself and the boats that were always moving past. Grant was impatient with the injury to his leg, tested it now, setting aside the crutches for a brief moment, tried to stand without help. The pain shot hard through his ankle, and he fell forward slightly, tried to hide it, knew that Rawlins was close behind him, watching, as he always watched. But Rawlins had the good sense to stay back, allowing Grant to slide the crutches back under his arms. Walking is out of the question, he thought. But I can still ride a damn horse. Rawlins will have the entire staff ready to assist me. I should be grateful. He glanced down at the leg, wrapped in thick cloth, an attempt by his doctors to offer a means of support. He knew that the horse had been more fortunate than its rider, and there could be no blame. The weather that night had been gruesomely awful, the blackest night he had ever seen, steady rain and roads that were rivers of mud. The horse had simply lost its footing, tumbling to one side, coming down precisely on Grant's leg. The only good fortune was the mud, softening the weight of the horse's impact, which Grant knew had possibly saved his leg altogether. He thought of Smith now, the old general still bedridden, the festering sore above his ankle growing worse, infuriating Smith as well as the doctors, who seemed helpless to offer a cure. If there is a fight, he thought . . . a general engagement . . . we shall miss him. William Wallace is a good man, a veteran certainly, but if there is some difficulty, I would feel comfortable knowing Smith is out there. He glanced back toward the wharf at Savannah, already sliding out of view. Heal, dammit. This is a weaker army without you.

He stared to the front again, the *Tigress* passing a larger vessel, hands waving, sailors mostly, greeting their own. He ignored that, didn't care for the moment what cargo had been aboard the larger boat, still thought of Smith. You warned me to move closer, he thought. I did travel to Pittsburg nearly every day, did my job by making myself visible and available to every one of my officers, ready to solve any problem. That was a lesson straight from Smith's West Point classroom, but until this morning, Grant had felt no reason for urgency. Once ashore, there was really nothing else he could order his generals to do, beyond those directives he had passed on from Henry Halleck. Anything else would be little more than meddling in the daily routines of men who should know better, who would likely see Grant's intrusion as more aggravation than help. Every one of the division commanders knew why he was in those camps, every one of them preparing the only way they could for the eventual attack on Corinth. At the landing itself, most of the problems involved tedious arguments between officers who inflated their own importance, disputes over which boat had priority, whose men should be allowed to go ashore before the others, who should get the shipment of new muskets.

The breeze slackened slightly, and he caught a fresh wave of thumps, from upriver. Yes, Smith warned me. You're too far away. Move out of that damn mansion and make your headquarters at Pittsburg. I always intended to make the move. But now . . . someone is letting me know that I should be there already.

He looked down into the muddy water, the boat making slow progress against the river's current. It had been one more bit of punishment from the weather, the river swollen from so much rain, the flow of water lengthening any trip southward. He pushed against the rail with his hands. Dammit, I have to know. If there is some failure here because I was a few miles from where I needed to be . . . He thought of Halleck. Yes, you will know that very soon. He was certain that Halleck had the means to plant his own eyes everywhere, that some of the staff officers who served any one of the division commanders might be seeking favor with the Western Theater's commanding general by making their own discreet reports, possibly embellishing anything Grant might order them to do with tales of inefficiency or some insinuation that Grant was being insubordinate to the clear instructions Halleck had issued weeks before. Grant knew that any whiff of displeasure that emerged from Halleck's headquarters might inspire the same kind of astounding lunacy that had nearly cost Grant his entire career.

He tried to light the cigar, but the crutches kept him immobile, preventing him from shielding the small flame of the match. Rawlins would be there, offering to help, but Grant had already stared the man down, keeping him back, the unspoken message: *Stop being so damn helpful.* He lowered the unlit cigar, Rawlins wisely keeping his distance. Grant stared forward, couldn't escape the image of Halleck, an image that appeared far more often than Grant would have liked. But the man's very being had infiltrated every move Grant made, and he thought of the ailing Smith again, the basic lesson of command, staying close to your army. Well, then, Henry old boy, why in hell don't you come down here and run this show for yourself? There's not anything going on in St. Louis that requires the *Big Man* to stay neatly tucked away in his office. He knew the scene well, Halleck at his desk, puffy eyes under a raggedly receding hairline, a chinless martinet whose vanity oozed out like the mud that stirred beneath the riverboat. One of these days, he thought, there will come a time when Henry Halleck stretches too far his belief in his own magnificence. There will be some mistake, something only he can be faulted for, and by God, his *genius* will be seen for what it is, the imagination of a small, frightened scoundrel, who runs his army the way a child plays with toys. Right now, I am just that . . . one of his toys. Grant shook his head, stared at the passing riverbank, sought any kind of distraction. It is unholy to feel such hate for anyone, he thought. Julia would not approve of that, not at all, would lecture me from scripture, as though I should need to be reminded that God will judge me by how I judge others. Even Halleck. Grant stuffed the cigar back into his coat pocket, tried to summon her face, the soft scolding. But the artillery was still there, louder now, the boat rounding another bend, no other boats crowding out the sounds. He thought of the boat's captain, I should ask him . . . but no, we shall reach Crump's soon enough. I will find out something there. Wallace must know something. He can certainly hear what is happening more clearly than we could.

He glanced back, nothing to see, Savannah a mile or more behind, and he thought now of Don Carlos Buell. Buell had arrived at Savannah the night before, ahead of the bulk of his oncoming army. One division of Buell's army had arrived as well, men who belonged to General William Nelson, one of Buell's more capable commanders. Grant had ordered that division southward, keeping their march to the east side of the river, and so staying clear of the congestion around Crump's and the flow of boat traffic on the river itself. Nelson had obeyed him with hesitation and a touch of insolence, something Nelson had wisely tried to hide, but Grant knew exactly why Nelson reacted that way. It was perfectly logical that Buell's generals had been well indoctrinated by their commander to believe what Buell certainly believed himself, that he should supersede Grant's authority over this entire campaign. Buell had arrived in Savannah with barely a hint to Grant, and there had been no effort by Buell to find Grant, though Grant knew with absolute certainty that Buell had received Grant's request for such a meeting. It was infuriating, but he had swallowed that, knew that Buell had once been a virtual equal in authority to Halleck, and that Grant was on thin ice as it was. The meeting had been scheduled for today, and Grant had wondered if Buell would dress him down for having the audacity to order Nelson's Division upriver without first seeking approval from Buell. Once Grant felt the urgency of moving south, he had sent word to Buell that the meeting would wait.

He let out a long breath, filled his lungs with the cool, damp air. The artillery continued, just a bit louder now, steady and consistent, and Grant thought, surely Buell will hear that. Surely he will hasten the rest of his men this way. Or must I order him, demand he obey? That will inspire a protest, certainly, some hot letter to Halleck, or a tirade to an eager newspaperman, who will make certain that Buell's admirers know how slighted he has been. It is so tiresome, these men who fight more for themselves than for what we are trying to accomplish. He will obey, for now, no matter how inconvenient that is, because he believes I am only a temporary annoyance. He stared hard to the front, measuring, the distance of the ongoing shelling still masked by the wind. Grant glanced to the side, the boat's first mate approaching him, the man pointing ahead.

"Sir, Crump's is just around that bend. It does not seem as though the artillery is that close."

Grant absorbed the obvious, said, "No, Lieutenant, it does not. We must continue on to Pittsburg without delay. We can put one of my aides ashore quickly to communicate with General Wallace. But we must not hesitate."

The man backed away with a mild "Sir . . ." and Grant could see the first of the great horde of boats anchored at the landing. Within a short minute, the wharf was in full view, a jam of steamboats lashed together along the shoreline, no gap, no place to slide the *Tigress* anywhere close to shore. But he could see a scramble of uniforms on one of the boats, the traffic on the river carrying rumor as well as supplies, his arrival already expected. Well, of course, he thought. They can hear those damn guns better than I can. The sounds of the fight were steady, louder now. He had an uneasy feeling, cursed himself. Smith was right. You should have been closer. I've got too many men camped out here in enemy territory to be so complacent, to spend my mornings drinking coffee in a mansion, while God-knows-what is going on in these woods. He looked up toward the banks, high above the river, could see tents and crude buildings, surrounded by scores of wagons. He felt a hint of relief, thought, at least they didn't hit the supplies. We were vulnerable here. But Pittsburg . . . he shook his head again, the thumps and thunder ongoing. What the hell is happening out there?

Grant focused now on the uniforms emerging onto the deck of a larger supply vessel, men gathering along the rail at the closest point Grant's boat could reach. One man stood out, the wide hat, thick bush of mustache, the lean handsomeness of Lew Wallace. Grant felt relief at that, too, pleased that Wallace would receive him without Grant having to disembark.

The sailors around him were in action now, ropes tossed out, men on both boats pulling together, the *Tigress* sliding in closer to the larger boat. They were only a few feet apart now, and Wallace stood tall, straight, saluted him, said, "General, welcome to Crump's Landing. We seem to have something of a conflict upriver."

Grant waited for the boats to draw tight, nearly touching, their hulls kept apart by thick pillows of canvas. He leaned closer, felt a sudden need for discretion, too many ears, too many crewmen and aides he didn't know. Wallace responded, leaned out across the railing, close to Grant's face, and Grant said, "What kind of conflict, General?"

He hoped for more than a casual response, but Wallace shrugged, surprised him.

"Not really sure, sir. Broke out about dawn, been going on since at a steady rate. Seems to be something of a general engagement, if I may offer the observation. With all respects, sir, I must state that I certainly share your confidence in the division commanders you have placed there. Any problem they encounter will soon be eliminated."

Grant turned, looked upriver.

"Sounds to me like the only damn thing being *eliminated* is artillery shells."

Wallace said, "Sir, I have put my men into readiness. My division is prepared to march toward those guns on your instruction."

"Good. Keep them ready. For now, you will hold your division here, and await my orders. I must learn just what we're facing. I will send for you if needed."

"Of course, sir. We will march on your order."

PITTSBURG LANDING

APRIL 6, 1862, 11:00 A.M.

There was space along the shoreline, a short distance from the mass of boats already moored there. Some of those were in motion, pulling away, making a wide turn in the river, starting their journey back toward Savannah. He ignored that at first, too many boats in this crowded waterway to warrant any serious attention. But there was a difference now, something catching not his eye but his ear. He looked out toward a larger vessel, slipping closer beside the *Tigress* as it moved away, and on the deck he saw them, uneven rows of men, some wrapped in white, some with filthy uniforms, made more filthy by their own blood. He knew what this meant, the decks crowded by far too many men for some simple skirmish. The sounds from the boat came to him with perfect clarity, a sound he had heard before, in every place there had been a fight. Among so many wounded, many of the men were screaming.

On the vessel, there were others in motion, doctors, the unmistakable aprons of men who were doing the dirtiest work of all, the men who sawed the limbs and plugged the bloody holes. One man looked out toward Grant, a distant stare, no recognition of Grant, just staring away, as though escaping the moment, a brief rest. But he returned to his duty, knelt low, doing something to one of the soldiers Grant couldn't see. There was nothing for Grant to do, no calling out, no questions. Along the shore, more boats were loading the wounded, men hauled up gangways on stretchers, others limping on their own, makeshift crutches, some helped by other soldiers. From every deck on every boat came the sounds, the horror of their suffering. Grant scanned the boats, the same scene across every deck, felt a stirring inside, knew there would be more belowdecks, out of sight, and in time, many of those men would be dead, stacked somewhere else, out of the way, to make more room for the steady flow of men who still might have some chance to survive.

"What in God's name is happening? What have they done?"

The words came from Rawlins, his aide close beside him now, no more skulking behind, no need for discretion. Rawlins was answered by a new burst of the sounds from the artillery, and Grant had no trouble now guessing the distance, two miles, maybe three, the thunder coming in a wide line inland from the landing, the battle obviously spread across the camps of most of his army.

Grant looked up at the bridge of the boat, thought, I must get ashore . . . but the captain was already anticipating the urgency, the boat shifting its way through the gap, aided by men on other boats, ropes tossed quickly, men straining to slide the boat into place, anywhere a plank could be laid. Grant felt the rumbling beneath his feet suddenly grow still, the belching smokestacks silent. The roar of the fight was magnified now, unmasked by the quiet of the boat's engines. He stared at the shore, ravenously impatient, turned awkwardly on the crutches, pushed past Rawlins, hopped down the short stairway to the lower deck. He expected to see the gangway already in place, the flat, wide planking, but onshore, men were tussling, one man down, fists flailing, another grabbing the plank, tossing it into the water. More men were in the water now, some swimming through the short gap to the riverboat, grabbing for the sides, one man shouting obscenities, another, his words reaching Grant with a shrill high-pitched voice: "Let us on! We have to get away! We are all dead!"

More sailors rushed along the shoreline, fighting through crowds of soldiers, officers understanding just who had arrived. The tussles and fistfights were more one-sided now, army and navy men, guards and provosts, shoving and punching their way through men who were obviously exhausted, whose energy had been spent trying to reach the river. The gangway was pulled from the river, guards holding away the men who still made the effort to reach it, and quickly, the planking was laid in place against the opening in the railing of the *Tigress*. Onshore, men on horseback moved through what Grant could see was a growing mass of soldiers, the officers raising their swords, drawing pistols. Gradually the area close to the gangway was cleared, and Grant saw his horse, led forward from the stern of the ship. Rawlins shouted through the din, "Sir! You may ride now! The ship is secured!"

Grant stared at the raw chaos along the shore, thought, secured from what? These are our men . . . my men.

He took the reins from Rawlins, another of the aides holding the crutches, the men boosting Grant into the saddle. The horse seemed to surge toward the plank, as anxious as any land-loving soldier to leave the boat. Grant fought with the reins, eased the horse down slowly, his staff following behind on their own mounts. He moved away from the river, expected some kind of greeting, some official welcome of his presence, saw officers still grappling with the surge of men who seemed to pour down from the higher ground in a steady wave. He felt a stinging helplessness, a brief moment when he had no idea what to do, forced the thought out loud.

"I am General Grant! Who is in charge here?"

The words were consumed by the noisy panic around him, more men pushing past, leaping into the water, some trying to climb aboard the other boats, the sailors hauling the planking upward to prevent the men from making the climb to the decks. Behind him the sailors of the *Tigress* did the same, the gangway pulled away from the bank, a chorus of shouts and curses directed their way. Grant nudged the horse forward, could see farther down the shoreline, the high embankment that bordered the river pockmarked by caves and hollows, places the river had gouged from the rock and dirt. In every hole, men had gathered, packed tightly, dirty faces and ragged blue uniforms, more men trying to shove their way in. Where there was space, the men disappeared into the mob, but others were tossed out, fists flying, some knives drawn, furious men striking out. Grant absorbed it all with a sickening horror, realized that the men were mostly weaponless, no muskets at all. Above him, more of them added to the growing crowd, some in the roadway cut through the bluff, others just tumbling down over the edge, all of them heading to the river.

"We're done for! They's right behind us!"

Grant watched the man slide past him, stumbling about in a daze, staring at the river, another man beside him, looking up at Grant, shouting, "We gotta get away! Get to the boats! They whipped us!"

His staff had surrounded him, obvious protection, Rawlins close to him.

"Sir! We have to get up the hill, away from the river. It is not safe here!"

Grant looked at him, saw Rawlins's usual concern, everything in its place, every bow tied precisely. But there was nothing precise here. Grant shouted again, "I must find what is happening! I will ride forward, but keep some of the aides here, have them locate someone in authority! I must know what is happening!"

A horseman came down the steep passageway through the rocky embankment, pushed his way through more of the fugitives, aimed his way toward Grant. Grant recognized him, an aide to General Hurlbut, and the man drew up close, shouted, "Sir! It is good you are here! We must move inland with all haste!"

Grant saw a hint of panic in the man, said, "What is happening here, Major?"

The man seemed to ignore the flood that continued to pour down onto the riverbank, as though this scene had been playing out for a while.

"Sir, if you please . . . we must move inland! The enemy has engaged us across our entire front! There is much confusion."

Grant felt a spring uncoil in his brain, fury at the man's obviousness.

"Why is there *confusion,* Major? Who commands these soldiers? By damned, what is happening?"

The man offered no response, his attention caught by a horseman close by, Grant seeing a young lieutenant waving his sword, striking hard at the shoulder of a man who ran past. Downriver, the scene was repeated, officers making some attempt to control the mob, hard shouts for the men to return to duty, to make a stand. But the panic in the men swept away the commands, more calls from the men who came down the hill, a chorus of terror and despair, that all was lost, every man doomed. Grant spurred the horse, had no more need of the major, could see too clearly that his army had been struck by a blow that had ripped away their spirit, their hearts, their ability to fight. He pushed the horse up the hill, past the wagons, saw the two small buildings, run-down cabins, wounded men lying there as well, more coming, too few doctors to help them.

Grant rode farther along the road, saw horses standing about, no riders, wagons untended, teams of artillery horses jogging past, linked together, trailing leather straps, no sign of their limbers or the artillerymen who had manned the guns. Through it all, the sounds of the fight continued to roar across the ground in front of him, distant yet close, unceasing, a fight that seemed to grow wider and louder, as though swallowing his army completely, a fight he had never expected.

# CHAPTER TWENTY-TWO

# JOHNSTON

NEAR SHILOH CHURCH
APRIL 6, 1862, 10:00 A.M.

From first light he had stayed close to the front lines, brief and
frantic meetings with his commanders. The fight had grown
chaotic almost immediately, the plunging strike into Federal
forces destroying most of the organization of the neat lines of battle. The
confusion had more to do with the lay of the land than the defense put
up by the Yankees, the treacherous ravines and thickets preventing any
kind of order. In every part of the field, regiments were splitting apart,
their individual companies losing touch with one another, men fighting
in small pockets wherever their enemy happened to be.

It was obvious to Johnston, as it was to Hardee and Bragg and anyone else up front, that the attack thus far had been an astounding success. Johnston had seen for himself what the cavalry had reported for
more than a week, that the Federals had made no preparations to receive an assault. There were no trench works, no abatis, the Federal
troops thrown into line often in complete disarray. Those fights had
been the easiest, the Confederate troops driving their enemy back in
a complete panic, Federal officers as well as their men scampering
away with the first few volleys. But others had held their ground, and
Johnston saw that as well, vicious firefights, often yards apart, men
shooting through thickets where the enemy was only a flicker of move-

ment, artillerymen aiming cannon toward clouds of smoke, the only hint they had where the enemy might be. On both sides, the artillery seemed to be accomplishing the most effective work, and the big guns were soon targeting the enemy's artillery as much as enemy troops. All across the fields, batteries were dueling batteries with horrifying results for the men and their horses. With the help of the infantry, cannons were captured, lost, recaptured, and often the men who had manned the guns were long gone, shot down or swept away in a panic, while the fate of their guns had become one part of an enormous bloody contest.

Johnston had spent his first couple of hours close to Hardee's men, had heard for himself the great push that had driven back Sherman, and then Prentiss, the enemy prisoners never hesitant to reveal who they served. The Federal troops had made efforts in every part of the field to find a new position of strength, backing to another ridge, another thicket, where their fight could begin again. It was completely expected that the men in blue would not do what so many had predicted, those mindless claims of their utter cowardice, that no Union man could make a stand against the raw dedication of the man in gray. Johnston knew better, saw it now, in every ravine, on every hill. While many of the blue-coated men had chosen escape, a great many more had stood up to fight, and many of those had fallen on the ground where they had made a stand, dead and wounded spread across every piece of ground where Johnston's men had made their push. But there was no mistaking that, so far, most of the dead were wearing blue, and some of those had not been in the fight at all. The Confederates had shoved hard right through the camps of the Federals anchored farther to the west, Sherman's Division in particular, and so, many of those men had not had time to gather into effective formations to receive the assault. Some had been in the midst of breakfast, some still in their tents, the sick and injured still in their bedrolls. Some made the effort, but the Confederates had every advantage, swept through and past the unprepared enemy with brutal efficiency. The message was clear now to Johnston, and to anyone else who saw the standing tents. This attack, the tactics and strategy of the great surprise, had worked.

———

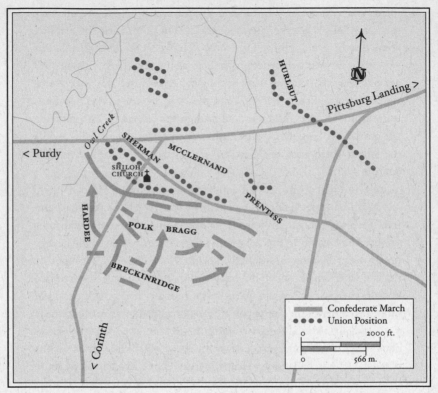

**THE CONFEDERATE ATTACK, AS LINES SPREAD OUT**

The fighting closest to him was scattered, sudden bursts of musket fire through smoky brush, men on both sides stumbling into their enemy, blinded by smoke and thickets of briars and vines. Johnston could hear the whistle of the musket balls, looked back toward the trailing line of horsemen, most of his staff following, some of the men reacting to the sound of the firing with lowered heads.

"Careful, gentlemen. I want no casualties here. If you see the enemy, move quickly away!"

He followed his own order, ducked low beneath a broken tree limb, could smell the spent powder in the air around him, sulfur burning his lungs. He knew the staff would stay close behind him, and he spurred the horse hard, jerked the reins, saw a massive flash of fire in front, artillery erupting very close. He had no idea who they were, pulled away, putting distance between his staff and the guns, thought, ours, certainly. Has to be. We have not yet ridden anywhere the enemy is in force. But still . . .

He led them up a knoll, saw officers, a cluster of horses and flags, felt a glimmer of relief, grateful for the calming presence of Leonidas Polk. Polk saw him coming, stepped the horse out toward him, a smiling salute.

"A glorious Sabbath, General! May I say, this army is performing in a most excellent manner. Most excellent, indeed."

Polk's smile was usually contagious, but Johnston felt a stab of something very uncomfortable.

"It is the Sabbath?"

"Yes, of course. Surely you knew . . ." Polk stopped, seemed to realize that Johnston had no idea. "It is all right, Sidney. God does not fault us for victory. And from what we have accomplished, a victory seems assured."

It was a strangely optimistic statement, and Johnston's discomfort turned to alarm. Polk seemed to sense where his words had taken his friend, the smile fading.

"I'm sorry, Sidney. But there is no harm in striking your enemy when the cause is just in the eyes of God."

Johnston didn't respond, looked past Polk's staff to a rising cloud of smoke, more hard thumps coming from a nearby hill, batteries firing eastward, Polk's batteries. The muskets began again, more distant, and in the low ground to one side, the rebel yell exploded in a chorus of terrifying passion, a surge of men Johnston couldn't see, pushing their way up the hill, toward an enemy somewhere beyond the next rise. The fight consumed everything around him, smoke and noise, deafening and magnificent, and he tried to feel Polk's optimism, the pure joy of a victory, his army seeking their triumph so close to him. But there was something still rattling hard through Johnston's brain, a scolding, the lesson from his grandfather, so long ago, a young boy who sat spellbound while the old man preached to him of hell and damnation and the wrath of the Almighty, all those lessons that terrified the young. The old man had died nearly forty years ago, but some of those fearful lessons had stayed with Johnston, and he thought of it now, felt a wave of new sadness. This is Sunday. We should not be making the fight . . . this day. Polk should understand, he thought. It was all of the delays . . . the interminable rains. I did not consider the calendar, the days of the week. We could have waited one more day. He knew that wasn't true, the voice of the general taking command of his wits. We took great risk as it was. One more day . . . and the enemy might be driving into *us*.

Johnston was drawn by a new round of volleys, farther out to the left, Polk's men again, still coming forward, more of the rebel yell.

"Yes, pray for us all, Bishop. This day is not yet done, and the enemy is still very dangerous. We must not become overconfident."

The fight close by seemed to fade, musket fire in slow pops, more yells from the men as they crested the far hill, in pursuit of a retreating enemy. Polk had his field glasses up, said aloud, "We have driven them back once more!" He turned to Johnston again. "You see? The Almighty watches us, our every move, and He strikes our enemies with the punishment they have earned. This is glorious, Sidney. Glorious!"

Johnston wanted to feel that joy, could not escape the scolding of his grandfather.

"Perhaps. But remain vigilant, remain aggressive. The wagons must maintain pace with your advance. Ammunition can become a problem, and I want these men supplied!"

Polk responded, "Of course. I shall see to it. But you had best put those wagons to a gallop! We are driving for that river, Sidney! God is providing the path!"

Johnston turned his horse, was still unnerved by his friend's overwhelming cheer. He turned to Major Munford, closest to him, said, "We will move farther to the right. If General Bragg can be found quickly, I would speak with him. I must know if progress on his front is as it is here."

He spurred the horse, did not look back at Polk, felt nervous, agitated, thought, it cannot be wise to assume God is standing with your men, that God wields the weapons that will drive the enemy away. We are still men. And this fight is being made by men on both sides who are dying for their honor. Which of those men has God's greater blessing?

There was another firefight in the trees before him, a fresh line of troops moving up from the right. He saw the flag, Arkansas, men pushing through the brush with another wild cheer. They passed by him, unseeing, their focus on where the enemy might be. From far to the left, the brush erupted into a single burst of smoke, Federal troops lying in wait, the volley punching through the Arkansans, men collapsing within a few yards of where Johnston sat. He turned away from that, realized he was in a very bad place, that the woods could disguise anyone, anywhere. The staff needed no instruction, followed as he dipped down into a gulley, riding through a narrow creek bed, away from the smoke. They climbed up into clear ground again, and across the field he could see another battle line, Texans this time, another advance, at least a full regiment, their far flank disappearing into a thick stand of trees. Men saw him now, and muskets rose, the cheering directed toward him, whether they recognized him or not. What they saw was a commander, sitting tall, and now their own officers appeared, one man riding toward him at a rapid trot. Johnston knew the man, tried to recall his name, the insignia of a colonel.

"Sir! With all respects . . . this is not the place for you! You are exposed to the batteries of the enemy! Please, sir, withdraw. The Yankees are on that ridge . . . there!"

As the man uttered the words, the ridgeline in front of the colonel's men burst into a furious cascade of firing, the sharp whistle of the shells impacting all across the field, punching great fiery gaps through the lines of men. The colonel turned, attentive to his men, a quick glance back at Johnston. "Sir! Please!"

Johnston waved the man away, the colonel needing no instructions, the man now following close behind his men, the entire line dropping away into low ground, disappearing into a billowing fog of gray smoke. More artillery came down now, a half-dozen blasts, and Johnston turned the horse again, shouted to his staff, "That was excellent advice! Let us retire beyond those trees!"

He led them again, pushed through a stand of thinly spaced hardwoods, saw more of his men coming forward, a fresh line, some of the men making way for him to pass. He searched for their flag, had to know, saw Alabama now, grim-faced men who acknowledged him with calls and shouts. Their officers rode up close, fought their way through the timber, but Johnston did not stop, had no need to halt men who were marching forward. There was nothing these men should care about a general riding where he should not be. Unless they falter, they do not need me to tell them anything.

————

The shooting had seemed to roll away, farther east and north, the ground closer to him clear of any kind of fight. As he moved past smoking hillsides, stands of cracked and shattered trees, the evidence of the fight was there, in every hollow, every hillside. The dead and wounded of both sides were mingled together in a horrifying smear of gruesome color, some men falling on top of their enemy, some of the men in pieces, shattered by the blasts of artillery.

As he moved among the lines, he had spoken to officers of every stripe, the men who served Hardee and Bragg and Polk, the commands now jumbled together in complete confusion. Any sense of order had been swept away, making a mockery of the carefully designed plan, what was so neatly drawn on paper by Beauregard and his minion, Colonel Jordan. Though Polk's exuberant optimism had not set well with him, Johnston had seen the same kind of joy in many of the others, officers and their men cheering Johnston as he moved past, some reacting as though the day had already been decided, the enemy whipped, crushed, driven into the depths of the river. But farther to the front, the fighting continued, Federal troops making new stands in new fields, and close by, smaller eruptions of fire came from the endlessly uneven ground that kept some men in place, shielded from orders, or simply lost where they stood. There were still fights off to the north, toward Owl Creek, but those were not many, and the reports that had reached him had confirmed the optimism he met along the lines, that Sherman's Division had mostly been routed, shoved backward in pieces. Farther to the right, the troops of McClernand and Prentiss were falling away as well, though their resistance had stiffened, the farther back they were pushed. But still, Johnston's troops seemed to be advancing in nearly every part of the field, no matter the difficulty of the land or the enormous number of casualties. At the crest of each rise, it was plain to him that a hard fight was still raging farther to the right.

He led his staff up another brushy hillside, needed to push forward, to move close behind his men, to be certain that no one gave way. There could be no failures of command, not now, not when the advance still inspired so many. It was not all perfection, of course, and he had seen at least one of his regiments break, a scampering flood of troops that poured down a hill, their flag too distant for him to identify. But those officers did their work, rallied the shaken and panicked men, and if some of those men continued to run, others found their composure, fell into place with other units that advanced past them, and returned to the fight. He absorbed that scene, knew that panic was something you could not predict, that good men could be infected by a single coward, an entire line dissolving by the sudden collapse of an officer. It kept him moving forward, sliding to the right as he rode, as though he would see them all, every regiment, every company, would do whatever he could to inspire them, if not by his orders, then just by his presence.

The trees opened up to a wide field, flat ground, and he halted the horse, amazed at the sight spread before him. The field was one of the Federal encampments, a great formation of tents in neat rows, some of them ripped down, flattened, others standing as though nothing at all had happened here. Scattered throughout the camp were men, his own men, some emerging from tents carrying all manner of goods, one man parading in a blue officer's coat, a show for his friends, who saluted him with raucous laughter. Others were sitting in a circle around a campfire, bottles passed around, more laughter there. There were horsemen moving through, officers shouting obscenities, ordering their men to continue the advance, but Johnston could see the paralysis, the temptations of the Federal camps too great. Many of his men had not eaten since the night before, and they could not pass by the Federal larders without taking advantage. Some men were doing only that, sitting cross-legged, eating something, anything, as though there were no battle at all.

He scanned the faces of the officers, tried to find someone familiar, but the horsemen were moving quickly, frustrated and furious. Some of them were successful, rallying their men back into formation. But many of the troops seemed utterly at ease, a celebration of the spoils of the fight they seemed to have forgotten. Johnston spurred the horse, shared the anger of his officers, shouted toward the men with the bottles, some of them turning toward him, still laughing, oblivious to command, certainly drunk. Others were pushing into the tents, exploring, ransacking, more tents collapsing, some ripped open with the bayonet. Trunks were everywhere, men dragging personal effects into the open, rummaging through letters and clothing, mementoes of men who were long gone. Others were admiring abandoned muskets, some shouldering bedrolls, replacing the rags they carried. To one side he saw a man pulling on a new pair of boots, covering bare feet. Johnston stopped close to one cluster of men, heard whoops of laughter as they read through a stack of letters, exaggerated playacting for some lover's show of affection.

"That's enough of that!"

They turned to him, some of them reacting to his authority, others seeming to test if he would do anything to them at all. From the closest tent an officer emerged, weighed down with clothing and other treasures, more than the man could carry without stumbling. Johnston saw the insignia of a captain, felt a surge of outrage, pointed a finger at the man, his voice rising, uncontained fury.

"No! We are not here for spoils! Resume command of your soldiers! Return them to the fight!"

The officer looked at him, seemed frozen, dropped the bundle, no words. Johnston could see a hint of shame on the man's face. Yes, good. You know this is not why we are here.

Others were beginning to stand now, responding to Johnston's presence, and he could see that they were gathering themselves, hearing him, some moving closer, as though seeking his authority. But others went about their business, and he fought the helplessness of that, dismounted, made a gesture to his staff to keep them back. Close to a smoldering campfire he saw a tin cup, bent low, retrieved it, made his way quickly back to the horse. Some of the men were watching him, and he took advantage of that, held up the cup, said, "There! This shall be my spoils from this fight. It is all I require, and it will be my reminder of this magnificent day! We need nothing more!"

He spurred the horse, saw the captain move to his own horse, climbing up, a hard shout to the men close by. More officers moved close, rallying their men, and Johnston moved forward, through the tents, past more of the men, displayed the cup, repeated the brief call. Close around him, some of the troops began to form up, a makeshift line, the captain, others on horseback pulling them together.

"Good! Now . . . make your way forward! There are good soldiers out there who require your assistance, who expect everything you can give them! The enemy is on the run! Do your part to keep them running!"

It had worked, at least for some part of those so distracted by the Yankee bounty. Johnston listened again for the direction of the firing, the hardest sounds coming from the right, and he made a quick motion to his staff, rode hard out of the field, toward the next place he might be needed.

They had come to a halt at the edge of a small field, drawn by the waving hand of a galloping officer, Samuel Lockett, Bragg's chief engineer. Johnston knew the man well, had hoped to hear much more from Lockett by now. The day before, the engineer was the one man sent far to the right, to scout the river, making note of the enemy's strength. But Lockett had not made his report until early that morning. He was trailed by one other soldier, a sergeant, and they reined their horses close to him, the engineer removing his hat in a quick salute.

"Sir! The enemy appears to be massing in force, and is threatening our right! There is word from that part of the field that the bluebellies are seeking to turn our flank, sir!"

Johnston stared hard at Lockett, knew him to be a capable man.

"Are you certain of this, Captain?"

Lockett hesitated, something Johnston did not want to see.

"It appears so, sir. The enemy troops are in evidence far out beyond our right flank."

"How many troops, Captain? Are they advancing?"

"The reports I have received suggest they could be. We could be in some danger there, sir."

Johnston knew how to interpret the man's words, heard more uncertainty than anything concrete.

"Does General Beauregard know of this? An hour ago I received a report from him that stated precisely the opposite, that the greatest crisis is on our left. I have ordered General Breckinridge to advance his reserve corps in that direction, and now you tell me that it is the *right* that is threatened?"

The air overhead split with the shriek of a shell, impacting in the trees behind them. Johnston held back his curse, another shell impacting to the left, in the open field. Behind him, Munford called out, "Sir! We are in the open here!"

Johnston pulled the horse around, said, "Down into that ravine. I will offer the enemy no careless opportunity."

The staff and Lockett followed him down, the woods around them mostly quiet, the shelling seeming to move away, Federal guns seeking targets they could see.

Johnston halted the horse, felt a rising wave of frustration. Messages like this had been flowing toward him throughout the morning, many passing first through Beauregard's hand. Johnston stared angrily to the ground, thought, this is idiocy.

"Allow me to make this clear, Captain. An hour ago, General Beauregard tells me we are in trouble on the left. From every report I had received before that message, I had been advised that the enemy there has been driven back in disarray. But I had to respond to General Beauregard's message as though he knows something I do not. He is, after all, positioned to receive couriers from all parts of this field. So, what am I to believe?" He saw the engineer glance downward. "I depend on you, Captain. If what you are saying is accurate, it could mean disaster."

"Sir, I observed enemy troops in the dense woods close to the river, the far left flank of their position. It appeared they were in a battle line, and I had to assume the worst. If I had ignored them . . . would that not have been the greater crisis?"

"How many? A division? We have not yet accounted for Hurlbut. Could you see their flags?"

"No, sir. I did not want to risk capture."

Johnston understood now, one fantastic error. Lockett had been sent to scout the enemy's flank nearly on his own, no cavalry, no show of force to draw the enemy outward. He stared out to the right, a gesture of frustration, looked toward Lockett again. He could not disguise his impatience, thought, why did you not push toward the river?

"Captain, you will ride to General Breckinridge. Offer the general my respects and communicate to him my direct instructions to shift his troops toward the right of the line. He is to disregard my previous order to move to the left. You will lead him into position yourself. Do you understand?"

Lockett seemed to appreciate the direct order, the precision welcomed by an engineer's mind.

"Immediately, sir!"

Johnston pointed to the left with a sharp gesture, but he knew that Lockett would find the way, that Breckinridge would not hide himself. The engineer made a quick salute, galloped away, and Johnston looked at Preston, the others, saw the concern.

"Yes, gentlemen. I know. There was a failure to properly scout the enemy's left flank, the ground closer to the river. Turning that flank, driving our forces between the enemy and his base at the river . . . that must be our goal, it should *always* have been our goal. Was I not clear to General Beauregard?"

Major Munford moved closer, Isham Harris beside him. Munford said quietly, as though keeping his words from the junior officers and the couriers who trailed out behind them, "Sir, we will drive away any threat. General Breckinridge will do his part."

Johnston looked at Harris, saw a sharp nod, confidence in the governor's eyes. He knew that Harris carried enormous respect for Breckinridge, who had, after all, been vice president of the United States. Harris's seriousness broke Johnston's gloom, and he reacted with a small laugh.

"You would naturally assume, Isham, that it would fall upon a politician to save this army from destruction?"

Harris seemed to draw back, embarrassed.

"Not at all, General. We have many capable men . . ."

"Never mind. We shall see what kind of crisis we are facing. Thus far, the only *crisis* has been placed squarely at the feet of General Grant. I wish to keep it that way. I must accept fault for not stressing to General Beauregard that this attack should have pressed harder to the right. The plan as drawn called for us to drive straight into the enemy's camps." His gloom returned, carried with the thought of Colonel Jordan. "We may have made an error, gentlemen. A grave error. We must do all we can to correct that. If the opportunity is there, we must drive as much force as possible between the enemy and the river and cut him off from his base." He looked at the staff, measured them. "I will not wait for Captain Lockett. Bragg is out there, and he must be informed, if he is not already aware." He turned the horse, hesitated, tried to hear anything from the right, the battle still scattered far across the ground, a steady roll of thunder. Most of that seemed to come toward him from straight in front of him, what should have been the center of the Federal position. "Let us find General Bragg. I am certain he would know if the enemy had struck his flank."

Munford responded, "Possibly, sir. But this confounded ground . . ."

"Yes, I know. There is no time to waste, gentlemen. General Bragg will surely understand that we must strike the enemy before he strikes us."

## CHAPTER TWENTY-THREE

# JOHNSTON

SOUTH OF DUNCAN FIELD
APRIL 6, 1862, 1:00 P.M.

The roar of the newly opened fight had spread across a half mile of ground, and Johnston had kept moving that way, protecting himself only by the cover of the trees. All through the woods, spent shells were slicing through the leaves above him, a demonstration of the sheer volume of fire being poured into his men by some force Johnston could not see. He was feeling the usual frustration, had to find a better vantage point, another, taller hill. The maps had become useless, the success of his army's push taking him far beyond where the cavalry and the engineers had been able to make their detailed sketches. He eased the horse to the edge of the trees, saw volleys of musket fire from several directions at once, the smoke disguising any high ground, or any place where Bragg might be observing what Johnston could clearly see was a struggle to drive the enemy away. He was disgusted by his blindness, motioned to his staff to follow, pushed the horse down into a gulley. He drew up quickly, surprised to see men there, realized they were his own. He saw now, a half dozen of his troops sitting calmly, some in a curled position, knees tightly under their chins. More were evident now, farther along the deeper ground, some sitting alone, weaponless, hatless, one man with a wound, the others just . . . sitting.

There was no mystery now. He could see it in their faces, the utter despair, the look of men who had no fight left, who might never have had it in them at all. His instincts told him to rally them, to shout them to their feet, but something held him back, soft faces, empty eyes, men who would be of no use now to anyone. He said nothing to them, pulled the horse up the far hill, away, would not look at them, understood what every commander knows, that when the fighting is hot, some men will simply fade away, some by themselves, others in mass, entire lines. He had not expected to see it in his own men, but he knew that was fantasy, that no army was made up entirely of the brave. Behind him, no one spoke, following his lead, moving past the shirkers, the soldiers who had lost their will.

The job for Johnston had become considerably urgent. There had been no great eruption of enemy troops along the river, at least not yet, but the retreat of the Federal center had seemed to slow, then halt, their lines strengthening, reinforcements perhaps, a great many of the enemy returning to the fight. The marvelous advance of so many of Johnston's troops had ground down, some by the geography and the exhaustion of his men, but in the center, where Braxton Bragg's Corps had maneuvered into line, the assaults had been halted by a stout resistance Johnston had begun to believe would never happen. He accepted now what had stuck far back in his mind, that it was foolishness to expect the entire Federal army to simply collapse. The wild optimism that had so inspired his men that morning was being replaced now by the rugged acceptance that this was to be a fight that would drag on all day, perhaps longer. On the left, what remained of Sherman's troops seemed able to make their stand farther back, some of those Federal troops closer to the protection of the swamps along Owl Creek, others finding new strong points along ridges and wood lines closer to their base at Pittsburg Landing. Out here, to the right of the lines sent forward by Hardee, and then Polk, Bragg's men had made the same kind of progress, sweeping through what proved to be Prentiss's camps, driving the blue-coated men back into the same desperate retreat that had seemed to crush Sherman. But now Prentiss had certainly rallied his men, and the progress of Johnston's men here was almost completely halted. He had to find Bragg.

---

Bragg was cursing loudly, shouting into the face of an officer, the man on foot. Johnston could see it was Colonel Gibson, one of Bragg's most able brigade commanders, the man enduring the withering tirade without comment, his expression betraying a temper that could easily match Bragg, but wisely, the colonel kept that to himself.

"I expect you to carry out my orders, Colonel! What I have seen here suggests a want of leadership! You will break that line, and you will destroy the enemy! I will not hear of casualty counts! You will gather whatever troops you can find, and send them across that field!"

Gibson stared back at Bragg with the look of a man who knows he must absorb anything his superior tells him, no matter if the insult to his honor is accurate or not. Johnston knew that Gibson was one of the most educated young men in the army, and surely Bragg's tirade came more from his own miserable temperament than anything Gibson had done. Johnston rode close, ignored by Bragg, held his words, waited for Bragg's explosion to end. Gibson glanced at Johnston, a hint of acknowledgment. It was not the time for pleasant greetings. Gibson backed away, Bragg's fury exhausted. Gibson saluted, said, "We shall obey your orders, sir."

"And find yourself a damn horse!"

"My horse was killed, sir. My staff will provide a new mount."

Gibson's tone was admirably restrained, and he moved quickly away. To one side, Johnston could see a dense line of troops spread far along the edge of a wood line, keeping in cover, with a wide field to their front. Gibson disappeared into brush, and Bragg seemed to notice Johnston now, said, "Abject cowardice! I will not tolerate that! This has been a disgrace! We have advanced against those far woods three times now. Three times! Colonel Gibson . . . all of them have shown no desire to crush that enemy, no desire at all. I have determined that there are gaps on both the enemy's flanks. Both flanks! We seem unable to drive through those spaces, and now that opportunity is being lost. Every report I am receiving tells me that the enemy is bringing people to this line, extending it, plugging his own holes!"

Johnston stared out across the field, less than a half mile to the woods where Bragg pointed. In the woods behind him, a horse moved close, and Johnston was surprised to see Captain Lockett, the engineer. He felt

a stab of relief, said, "Captain! Have you brought . . . is General Breckinridge accompanying you?"

Lockett seemed to shrink, shook his head.

"No, sir. But it is not necessary, so I was told. The general has already
been ordered to this flank of our position by Colonel Jordan. The colonel has made it known that he has the authority to order the disposition
of our troops, and is doing so. Your Colonel Preston was with him, could
only offer the suggestion to me that Colonel Jordan's orders be obeyed.
General Breckinridge is making his advance in this direction now, and
Colonel Jordan ordered me to report that to General Bragg, and to you,
sir."

Johnston stared at the engineer with a mix of grateful acceptance and
utter disbelief. He thought of Preston, his own good staff officer, sent to
Beauregard's headquarters, now at the small church that had once been
Sherman's headquarters. Preston was to act as a conduit for Johnston,
keeping him informed of any significant orders Beauregard was issuing
to shift the flow of the attack. But Preston was with . . . Jordan? That had
to come from Beauregard, and it could only mean that Jordan was moving along the lines, as Johnston had done. Giving orders?

Bragg sat silently, deferring to Johnston, who said, "I must ask you,
Captain . . . how did General Breckinridge respond to receiving a direct
order from Colonel Jordan?"

Lockett seemed to search for the correct response, said, "Colonel Jordan issued the order in *your* name, sir. General Breckinridge did not
hesitate to comply."

"*My* name . . ."

Johnston didn't know what to say, would not show his anger to the
captain, or to Bragg. Bragg would have an explosive reaction of his own,
and it came now, Bragg unable to resist.

"It was wrong from the start. I held my tongue, but my men are paying a dreadful price."

Johnston was confused, said, "What are you speaking of?"

"This plan. Sending our corps in one behind the other. We should
have kept to the original strategy and attacked the enemy in one great
mass. Their panic would have been absolute, the surprise even more effective than it has been. Look at the result! My men marched straight
into the backsides of Hardee and Polk and I had no alternative but to

shift my corps's position, to attack the enemy more to the right. If I had not done so, we would have created a disaster of our own making! As it is, commands are in a jumble, no cohesion between brigades. There has been firing between our own men! Casualties! I have ordered Colonel Gibson to take his men across this field, and there has been great cost, our efforts uneven, poorly executed. Over there, the enemy has strengthened themselves, they have good, thick, well-disguised ground, and somehow the panic I kept hearing about has instead become a show of bravery our men cannot equal! That position is strengthening as we speak, and I can only assume that the enemy is bringing every man he can find to make his stand right in my front! In the meantime, units are advancing into my position from God-knows-where, belonging to God-knows-who. There are regiments coming into formation here I have never seen before, Polk's men, most likely. I have no means of sorting through them, and I will not waste time by organizing an attack that, I was told, had been organized already. I must assume these same conditions exist to my left as well! Or am I being impudent to suggest that all is not *perfection*?" Bragg paused, seemed to run out of steam. "With all due respect to you, General, it seems there is a colonel, a staff officer to General Beauregard, who is making every effort to place himself in command of this entire army. Perhaps he has his ambitions set on *your* position, General. Or perhaps he has assumed that already. If I were to suggest, sir, perhaps a firing squad is in order. I shall be pleased to arrange that at your discretion."

Johnston wasn't sure if Bragg was joking or not, but his anger was very real, and Johnston understood for the first time that much of what Bragg was saying could be true. But there was no time for this kind of game, for casting blame on the confusion that had clearly surrounded Bragg's assaults. Jordan had, after all, given Breckinridge the correct order. And with the success gained that morning, it was entirely possible that Jordan had done the same everywhere he had been.

"I will address this matter with General Beauregard at the appropriate time. This is not that time. Is it your plan to continue your attacks against the Federals across this ground?"

"That's where the enemy sits, sir. That's where he must be beaten. I *plan* to do just that."

Bragg turned to the open field, a sudden eruption of artillery passing

overhead, coming from Bragg's own lines. The firing came back immediately from across the way, far down both Federal flanks, and now,
closer to the center. Bragg shouted over the din, "You shall see our intentions straightaway, General. I mean to destroy the enemy where he sits,
and if he retreats, I will pursue him until he is destroyed."

Johnston waited for a lull before responding, some kind of pause in
the deafening thunder. But no lull came, the guns aiming their fire all
through the woods on both sides, seeming to know exactly where their
enemy lay. A pair of shells came down close in front of the generals,
Johnston's horse bucking, and Johnston knew his staff would expect him
to pull back, a safer place. He shouted close to Bragg's ear, "Do you know
what is to your right flank? Has the enemy made any movements closer
to the river?"

"I have observed nothing that way. I have too many concerns right
here. With all respects, sir."

Bragg seemed impatient and Johnston suddenly felt out of place, as
though Bragg wanted him out of the way. He had no patience for that,
not now, shouted again, "General Breckinridge can offer you considerable support. If he is indeed closing up on this line, the added strength—"

From close in the woods all around him, the sudden burst of the rebel
yell took away Johnston's words, the men surging out of the trees in a
great wave, marching in a slightly uneven line into open ground. Johnston felt the wind drain from him, had seen this so many times today,
knew he was close to what might be Bragg's victory . . . or something
else.

The men were moving away in a line far wider than Johnston could
see, made their advance through the smoke of the artillery, no musket
fire, not yet. He watched them go with a familiar churn in his stomach,
thought, if the enemy is in those trees . . . if indeed they have the good
ground, then they will wait. I would wait . . . until the right time. He
glanced at Bragg, saw him staring out, standing tall in the saddle, a furious glare, his mouth saying something, low words blanketed by the ongoing artillery. Johnston drew back, pulling the horse behind, but he
could not leave, had to see, had to know what Bragg already knew. Could
it be, he thought, could they break the enemy, right here?

The great battle lines pushed forward, marching over trampled grass,
the same ground they had advanced across already, time and again.

Johnston saw the bodies now, men down in the grass, revealed as the troops stepped past them. Few stopped, no one tending the wounded, their attention on the woods to their front. Bragg raised his field glasses, and Johnston did the same, felt his heart beating furiously, tried to focus the lenses, his hands quivering. Bragg's men were very close to the far wood line now, stepping through thickets, some disappearing into lower ground, and Johnston stood in the stirrups, as Bragg did, tried to see any sign of the men in blue.

It came in a shattering burst of fire and smoke, the wood line exploding with a volley from artillery first, and quickly after, a vast eruption of musket fire. There was nothing to see of the men, the smoke obliterating everything, and Johnston sat back in the saddle, knew he could only wait. Bragg was shouting now, and Johnston ignored him, knew it was too late for bluster. The din of the fight was steady and horrific, flashes of fire flickering through the dense smoke, and now, men appeared, moving back toward them, all along the line. Johnston raised the glasses again, heard more cursing from Bragg, shouts of encouragement that would encourage no one now. From the dense pockets of smoke, more men were coming back, some tumbling down, shot as they retreated. The artillery kept up its fire, but most of that was Federal, the Confederate guns silent, no gunner willing to risk shooting through his own men. The shells were ripping through the field, plowing through the men who were trying desperately to pull away. To one side, Johnston heard a fresh volley, distinct, realized it was flanking fire, slicing down the men who were out in the open. From the Federal artillery, the canister screamed toward them, a spray of scorching metal that wiped the men away in one quick motion. More emerged from the smoke, some rising up from the low places, and Johnston knew what was happening, that there had been no great triumph here, that Bragg would launch yet another tirade at his commanders, the good men like Colonel Gibson, who understood that, in this place, the enemy was too strong, too well fortified for the kind of full-out advance Bragg was ordering them to make. Johnston felt helpless again, knew he could order Bragg to hold his men back, knew with a sickening jolt that Bragg had fewer men now, perhaps many fewer, that the bodies he could see in the great wide field were stacking on top of one another, some from the earlier assaults, more from this one. Johnston backed away, would not order Bragg to stop, could not, that no matter the cost in blood, Bragg was right. The enemy was there, was holding ground that was keeping the plan from being carried out. They will break, he thought. They *have* to break, as they have broken to the left. Bragg will do that, he knows how, and he has the officers to carry it out. It must be done.

He was startled by a tap on the shoulder, jerked his head around, pulling the horse with him. Munford was there, seemed to force himself not to look past, at the field where the vicious fight was playing out.

"What is it, Major?"

"Sir! A messenger has come from General Breckinridge. He has been directed to the right flank of General Bragg's position, and is moving into place there now!"

"Then we must go there! We must be certain that those troops determine the Federal flank, and turn it with all haste. If the enemy is gathering strength in *this* part of the field, he could be vulnerable closer to the river. I must communicate that to General Breckinridge."

Johnston saw the messenger now, a very scared boy who saluted him weakly, ducking from the sharp sounds of spent musket balls in the air around them.

"You! You will lead me to General Breckinridge!"

The boy nodded, desperately frightened, tried in vain to gain his composure.

"*Now, soldier!*"

## CHAPTER TWENTY-FOUR

# BAUER

SOUTHEAST OF DUNCAN FIELD,
NEAR THE PEACH ORCHARD
APRIL 6, 1862, 2:00 P.M.

He had kept as close to the color bearer as he could, one of those lessons that had become instinct. Through the misery of the retreat and the rolling terrain, the flag was, after all, the most visible symbol they could follow. There were officers scattered among them, some on their horses, some still willing to lead their men, but many more were either down or as lost as Bauer was.

The troops of the 16th Wisconsin had done as so many of the other regiments had done, had fallen back from the sudden and irresistible pressure of the surging rebels. Many of the Federal troops had kept some kind of order, withdrawing under the commands of their officers, but many more had seen the retreat as something more desperate, a mad dash through every kind of barrier, fallen timber, thickets of vines, thornbush, and muddy creek bottoms. The ones who stumbled out onto roadways seemed to draw a second wind from that, the going much easier, and so their escape was easier as well. The most terrified men moved along the roads with renewed energy, certain that escape was only a matter of reaching the river. But few bothered to ask which way the road might run, whether any route was the right one. The men added to the congestion that now included wagons and horses, many of those driven away from the fight as rapidly as the traffic would allow. But there would be little progress now for anyone, some of the mobs moving back to the landing halted by guards, or by their own exhaustion.

The congestion was made far worse by those wagons and artillery batteries attempting to move forward, those men not yet in action, not yet infected with the terror of those who called out to them, warning of certain death, breathless shouts describing the hell that was the fight itself. The most cowardly seemed to justify their own terror with extravagant claims of how their army had been thoroughly crushed, and some of the teamsters who tried to push forward caught that fever and disappeared, abandoning wagons right where they sat, one more barrier to any movement on the roads. Some took the time to unhitch horses, riding back toward the landing, shoving madly through crowds of men as they went. The ambulances that sought the river soon created the worst horror, drivers dropping down with the tide of running men, leaving behind their human cargo, wounded men packed in tightly against the bodies of some who had already died, others adding to the chorus of terrified voices by screaming, their fear and pain mingled with the cries of the men running past, certain that death was pursuing them with relentless determination.

For the first hour, Bauer had been among them, but something had drawn him out of the stark mindlessness. It was the sight of the flag, a color bearer making an astonishing effort to hold back the tide of men by standing tall, waving the flag, calling out to the Wisconsin men to rally around him. Within seconds of seeing the man, Bauer had been horrified to see him shot down, the flag wavering, tumbling down. But another man was there, the flag up again, and something in Bauer had responded to that. The flag was only a symbol, but even the cowards had once understood the power of that, and Bauer understood it now. He had stopped his retreat, moved to the flag, watched as more musket balls sprayed through the lightly spaced trees, the second color bearer cut down as well. Others fought to replace him, men competing for the honor of becoming the regiment's most sought after target, and Bauer had closed up with them, stood ready, officers finding them, bringing more order to the turmoil in the woods and fields.

Bauer had turned toward the flow of men, had shouted to them himself, joining in with a growing number of sergeants, others as well, furious attempts to halt the panic. Some of the men had rallied, seemed only to need some sign of order, of someone in command. But there were others who could not be stopped, and Bauer had seen familiar faces among the flow of many men, some from other regiments, other states. Horsemen rode among them, and there were swords held high, swords striking men with the flat of the blade, some men responding only to that, absorbing their own shame, finding some bit of courage in themselves to join the gathering lines of men, all those who rallied to their flags.

The officers spread them out along a wooded depression, protecting them from a shower of musket balls ripping the air overhead. In the low ground, Bauer could feel the determination in the men around him, beaten men who were no longer whipped, who were becoming soldiers again. He searched the faces, saw Sergeant Champlin, pushing men into line, many of those crouching to one knee, catching their breath. The lieutenants were there now, few of them giving orders, seeming to know that before any kind of advance could be made, the lines had to be drawn close, strengthened, all the while the fight out to the north was increasing, punctuated by the thunderous roar of artillery. Bauer stared up toward the ridgeline that protected them, wondered if the rebels were coming, would suddenly pour down on them, but for now most of the fight seemed to stay where it was, a couple hundred yards beyond the low ground. Around him sergeants spoke to lieutenants, horsemen arriving in greater numbers, the lieutenants seeking them out, seeking information or commands, one more ingredient that made these men an army. Bauer heard the call, a bugler, the call to formation, unnecessary now. Through the woods beyond the low ground, men continued to come, some led by officers, some simply moving toward the fight, stumbling down into the low ground with surprise and relief, joy at finding a thickening line of troops.

From one side, Bauer saw another of the horsemen, realized it was Colonel Allen, and Bauer wanted to cheer the man, call out his relief that the colonel was still alive. But it was not the time for cheering, and Bauer still felt the burn in his lungs, kept silent, knew that the colonel would give them the orders, would know *something* of what they were to do, what was happening out beyond the ridgeline. Bauer could see now that Allen was furious, his instructions to the officers around him short and loud, recapturing his command, one eye seeming to look to the ridgeline, as though Allen expected trouble.

Allen moved past him, and Bauer saw another horseman, knew him, Lieutenant Vail, from Company I. The man was shirtless, his arm wrapped in bloody blue, and he rode among them with soft words, orders that few could hear, the words of a dying man. Bauer saw his eyes, saw the man's calm, could see the blood dripping from Vail's fingers, more flowing out on the flank of his horse, a wound in the man's side. Allen was there, turned his horse, a silent moment as the colonel watched Vail waver in the saddle, his head down, the man now sliding off the horse. But Vail's foot hung in one stirrup, and Bauer heard the crack of the leg bone, saw it twist in a sickening curl as Vail's face impacted the mud, attached to the horse by the awful grasp on the man's leg. The horse moved slightly, dragging Vail with him, but the animal was as drained as the men around him. Bauer felt sick, stared at the man's leg, and he broke ranks, moved closer, others doing the same. Bauer reached the horse quickly, grabbed the lieutenant's foot, the boot wedged tightly. Another man dropped down close to him, lifting the officer's body, releasing the weight, and Bauer unhooked Vail's foot, eased it down. More men came forward, those who knew the man, who had trained with him, and now another soldier moved through the gathering, and in one quick motion climbed up on the horse. The colonel rode up beside the man, stared down at Vail for a long moment, but Allen didn't have the luxury of grieving, looked out toward the men now, shouted out, "Get back in line! Form up! Check your muskets! Load now if you have to! No bayonets, not yet."

Bauer looked at the man who had mounted Vail's horse, felt exhausted fury, *how dare you* . . . but he saw now it was another officer, a captain, the man just doing his job, and that job required a horse. The captain looked down at him, and Bauer saw an older man, grim experience, and Bauer felt the need to say something, the only thing that came to mind.

"Company A, sir. Are you in command?" The captain glanced down at Vail's body, then nodded slowly, said, "Yes. You were under Captain Saxe. He's gone. Sorry, boy. Fall in with me. The rest of you . . . anyone from Company C or A . . . D or I, stay with me."

Allen came back now, and Bauer heard the colonel say the man's name, *Patch,* remembered now, yes, Company C, and Bauer watched as a few more men shifted position, moved together, a half dozen, then more, coming together for their captain. Bauer thought of Company D, Captain Pease, a good man, friends with Saxe. Bauer wanted to ask about him, thought, Patch would know, would have a reason for calling Pease's men to his own. But no one would care about a private's questions, not now. Bauer backed away, fell back into formation, another look at the shirtless lieutenant, mud jammed into the man's nose and eyes, the body bloody and lifeless. Bauer said a short prayer, saw another man drop low, one of Vail's own, heard sobs, and now the voice of Allen.

"Wisconsin men! The fight is that way! Good men are holding that ground, and we shall help them! Do you hear me?"

Bauer had no voice to respond, but there were others, and he saw the flag again, the color bearer very young, familiar. Others along the line began to call out, a chorus suddenly rising from men who moved close, seeking answers from the man in command.

"Michigan, sir! Twenty-first! Where do we go?"

"Twenty-fifth Missouri!"

Allen waved them closer, held up both hands, an attempt to calm them.

"We will find your commands later. Right now you will march with us! There is honor in all of you! Find that now! We must hold the enemy back! We were driven back this morning, but we are here now, and it is the enemy who will know what kind of men we are . . . all of us!"

Bauer was surprised to see a new wave of men coming down from the ridge back behind them, some slipping down, stumbling through the vines, gasping and sweaty, drawn to the scene by the sight of order and strength. Bauer saw another flag, Missouri, was astonished to hear men cheering, gathering around their own color bearer, each man giving them a bit more pride, each musket making them stronger. Allen moved the horse farther down the ravine, then climbed up, reached the ridgeline, sat for a brief moment, scanning with his field glasses. He turned, waved toward another officer, pointed out to the north, and Bauer could hear it as well. The fighting was slowing, and in less than a minute the musket fire seemed to stop altogether. The only sounds now came from artillery, batteries in every direction continuing their fire. The colonel disappeared beyond the crest of the rise, and Bauer heard the bugler, the call to advance. Immediately the men responded, the entire line moving forward, climbing up the leaf-covered hillside, moving out into a thin stand of trees. As they had done so many times, they followed the officers who marched in front, were prodded by the sergeants behind them. Bauer tried to see how many there were, looked out both ways, saw two lines, each two men deep, the lines stretching far out past the field. The trees here were small, thin, but on both sides the woods grew thick, and many of the men were hidden, but still they advanced. Bauer was in the open now, walked at the pace of the lieutenant to his front, gripped the musket, glanced back, Sergeant Champlin close behind him. Bauer had a fleeting thought of the beast, Sergeant Williams. Gone. He tried to force that image away, the horror and disgrace of that morning already a foggy memory. Champlin is a good one, he thought, knows what to do.

The order came to halt, Colonel Allen there, talking to another officer, a staff nearby, more flags, the Stars and Stripes, *brass*. Around him there was motion, the lines closing up, and suddenly there was a hand on Bauer's arm, startling him, the man slipping close to him, low words, "You better be up here. I looked all over hell for you. Thought you'd skedaddled away like the others. I'd have kicked you in your man parts if you'd have deserted."

Bauer felt a surge of joy, wanted to grab Willis by both shoulders, but Willis wasn't smiling, their reunion deadly serious, one more piece of the company, the regiment, one more man Bauer knew he could trust.

"I started to run, Sammie. Not gonna run now. Swear to you."

"I'll be watchin' you. It's about to get nasty up there. You wait. That fight we heard weren't no church social. I done shot down a dozen of those devils, killed most of 'em right where they stood. They try to crawl off, I fix that, too. This is my third musket. Damn things get fouled." Willis paused. "It's gonna start all over again, or we wouldn't be standing here. You load your musket?"

Bauer knew he had, but looked at the percussion cap, the sign the weapon was ready to fire.

"Yep."

"Good. Remember to aim low. Shoot at their knees."

Bauer had heard that too often, but he knew that Willis was right, knew, too, that they would hear it from the officers.

Behind him, Champlin.

"Shut up! Wait for orders! Be ready to advance!"

Bauer was desperately happy Willis was there, no matter the odd display of energy for the fighting, for the *killing*. Willis's words stirred something uneasy inside of him, but the cold came again, the fear and the shaking in his legs. The entire formation seemed to pulse, anxious and tired men staring ahead across the small field. They were blind to what lay to the front, more of the woods they had learned to despise, and they stood in line with a hum of growing anger, fear, and fury, waiting for the order to march toward whatever might be in front of them.

Allen rode closer to them, one aide close behind him, the other officers and the great flag riding away. The colonel looked down his lines of men, the hasty gathering, no real organization at all. He seemed to measure them, and Bauer saw confidence. He drew his sword and pointed the way.

The new fight exploded to the northwest again, past distant trees to the right of them, as though the enemy had no idea these men were here at all. Bauer stared that way, the men around him doing the same, saw a low haze of smoke swelling up, maybe a quarter mile away. But the sergeants were acting like sergeants again, their orders passed along by the lieutenants, and Bauer heard Sergeant Champlin, moving along the line, directly behind him.

"Watch that ground in front of you! Nothing to see over there!"

Bauer tried to obey, but the fighting was growing more fierce, just as before, a clash of armies that seemed to swallow the air around them. Bauer wanted to know, to ask what was happening, who . . . but he knew better, looked ahead at the trees, thick brush, silence, shivered, thought, soon enough. They're coming. Sure as hell.

The bugle sounded again, Allen and the captains leading them forward. The flags were many now, and Bauer saw a small pond, rusty water, thin trees and heavy brush beyond. The lines shifted to slide around both sides of the pond, and Bauer saw a fence line, Allen ordering forward the first line to pull down the rails. Bauer was there, helped by others on both sides, the fence only pieces now, the men continuing to move forward. Bauer looked to the right again, the fight still there, heavy artillery in every direction, shells shrieking toward what seemed to be a single patch of ground. In front of him, the officers were shouting, pulling the men forward, and Bauer saw one lone farmhouse a couple hundred yards to the right, saw the men that way drive past it, their officers keeping them from bunching up behind it in the obvious cover. He cleared the brush line, and in front of him was a grove of peach trees, thick with white blossoms, small gnarled trees, their flowers like so many tents pitched a foot above the ground. The men were ordered down, beneath the peach trees, and Bauer was crawling now, Willis close to one side, Champlin behind him, pushing them, keeping every man in line. Now the order came to halt, and Bauer was directly beneath a single white canopy, hundreds of white flowers close overhead. He caught the fragrance, sweet and amazing, a small flicker of decency in the great horror that seemed to grow even louder down to the right. An officer crawled out in front of him, Company C's captain, Patch. He sat upright, beside a lieutenant Bauer didn't know, Patch's voice hoarse and ragged, just loud enough to be heard over the din.

"You see that brush out past these trees? That's where they're gonna be coming from. Hold your fire until you hear the lieutenant's order! No sooner! Any man shoots too soon gives us away!" Patch paused. "Give 'em hell, boys. They're just rebels, and this morning they dragged your flag through the mud. Time to get some revenge! But hold your fire! And dammit, shoot low."

The volleys to the right were quieting, that fight exhausting itself yet again. Bauer peered up, nothing to see but flowers and flattened men, the peach trees hiding any sign of what had to be a vicious confrontation. There were single pops from muskets, and now the artillery began again, but only a few, batteries mostly back behind them, some very far away to the right. Bauer curled his knees up slightly, rested his musket against the crooked trunk of the tree, measured the tree, no more than four or five inches, not much protection. The artillery was slowing now as well, a few thumps coming from far across the ground in front, ground he couldn't see. He stared at the brush, thought, fifty yards, maybe less. Awful close.

And now he heard the drums.

The men around him grew silent, faces forward, even the officers quiet. The drums beat in a slow, steady rhythm, and far out beyond the brush they could hear shouts, orders, the same calls of the sergeants and lieutenants that followed them into every march. Slowly, Champlin moved up beside Bauer, said to as many as could hear the hard whisper, "Wait until you *see* them! Aim low!"

Bauer leaned the musket hard against the tree, a steady aim, nothing to see yet, no targets. The drumming grew louder, and now he saw the tips of flags, close, the crunch of brush under the footsteps of marching men. His heart beat furiously in his chest, men around him making small nervous grunts, every musket forward, every man taking aim. The brush began to stir now, flecks of color, the voices continuing, one man calling out, "Keep forward! Prepare to fire!"

The rebels stepped closer, the brush giving way to a dense line of men, every type of uniform, no uniforms at all, an officer on horseback, flags, the drums louder, and from one side, Bauer heard the single command.

"Front rank! Fire!"

The front line of men beneath the peach trees emptied their muskets in one crashing eruption, smoke and flame bursting straight into the lines of rebels. Bauer pulled the trigger, too quickly, no target, but the smoke blew thick in front of him, filling the low trees. Another order, "Second rank! Fire!"

The second volley blasted past him, men behind with few targets, just firing into the smoke. But the enemy was too close and too many, and even the poorly aimed shot found its mark, the sudden screams of wounded men blending in with the order for another volley. Bauer felt the shock of a musket firing close behind him, the deafening roar driving a sharp pain into his ear, smoke engulfing him. Bauer cried out, but no sound could measure what now swirled around them, the rebels responding with volleys of their own. Bauer stayed behind his one small tree, struggled to reload the musket, rolled over flat on his back, could hear the cracking slaps against the trees, the rebel muskets mostly shooting high, oblivious to their targets lying so close, flattened out only yards away. He fought to pour powder into the barrel, tilting the musket up slightly, felt a burst of splinters against his arm, a musket ball blowing through the tree. He pulled the arm tight to his body, but the musket was still not ready, and he raised the barrel again, with a desperate hope that the powder had stayed inside. His hands were shaking wildly, and his fingers gripped the lead minié ball, and with a single rapid motion, he stuffed it into the muzzle, then slid the ramrod out of its cradle. Beside him the ground was punched by a ball, and he felt a sting in his arm. He pulled his arm in again, tried to make himself smaller, looked at the tear in his shirtsleeve, a small trickle of blood. He tried to ignore that, jammed the ramrod into the barrel, then pulled it out, set it aside, no time for the one-two steps of the field drills. He fumbled for a percussion cap, mashed it down hard on the nipple at the musket's breech, let out a hard breath, rolled over to his belly, tried to keep his head behind the tree. Through the smoke he could see the rebels, very close, some standing, aiming into the peach orchard, many more down, some firing prone, as he was. Others were just bodies, heaps of dead men offering some help to the living by providing a shield of flesh.

Through the moving smoke he saw one man aiming straight toward him, and he rolled again to his back, behind the tree, the musket ball slicing the air directly above his face, a dull crack behind him, a man crying out, then squirming, twisting wildly on the ground. Bauer froze, stared at the man's agony, felt the terror grabbing him, and he looked to the side, saw others firing through the twisted trees, reloading, firing again. The muskets of the rebels responded, sheets of lead slicing through the peach trees, churning the ground. All around him, he watched as the white blossoms were cut down, a steady shower that seemed to drift down on the soldiers. He stared at one man, Willis, his filthy blue coat flecked with the small flowers, the flowers on his hat, and Bauer's paralyzing fear began to change, something else calling him away, the bizarre and beautiful image, so many men doing their deadly work, and yet there was a peacefulness, the firing so steady it seemed like a hard wind, and all the while, the air around them seemed to bring that piece of home. It looked like a snowstorm.

He stared for a long moment, saw Willis reloading, another man beside him lying still, blood on the man's head. The musket fire continued, and Bauer fought through the terror, yelled at himself, a long loud cry, driving away the demons that kept him from moving. He rolled back over to his belly, his face close to the tree, slid the musket forward, took aim again. Men were still standing, as though invulnerable, oblivious to the threat, and Bauer chose one, the man loading his own musket, thoughts screaming through Bauer's brain, not this time! No more for you! He aimed low, at the man's waist and pulled the trigger. The rebel

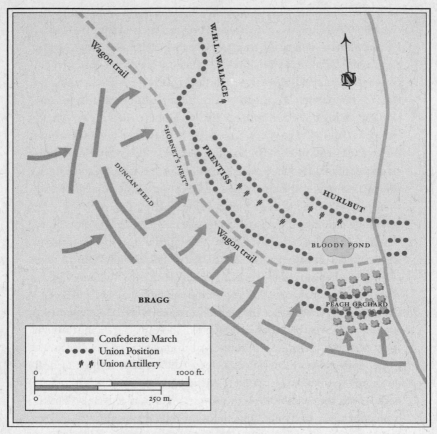

**ASSAULT ON THE "HORNET'S NEST" AND THE PEACH ORCHARD**

lurched backward, his limbs splayed out, his musket falling slowly down across him. A voice, close to him, Willis, "Good shooting! You got him!"

Bauer looked for the man to move, and for a brief second, he hoped the man was alive, felt a strange horror, get up . . . *just run away.* He noticed now that the firing had slowed, and then, voices, all around him, Willis again, others, calling out.

"They're running! They're hauling it holus-bolus!"

More men took up the call, some muskets still seeking a target, and Bauer could see through the smoke now, the dense brush trampled flat, saw the backs of men, some in a full run, one man turning to fire, a wild shot, suddenly cut down. The orders came now, behind them, and then, in front, "Up, men! Bayonets! Charge them! Don't let them get away!"

Bauer slid forward, clear of the shattered branches of the tree, stood, saw more men around him, up, ready, bayonets fixed, and out front, the rebels, some still trying to form a line, officers on horseback, one falling, flags waving, someone's feeble attempt to rally their men. The charge began, the men in blue driving forward from the orchard, but it was weak, no order, no time to form a hard line. Some of the Federal troops broke into a run of their own, chasing down their enemy, the slower rebels caught, the work of the bayonet, others just knocking the rebels down, tackling them, lunging fists and muskets swung like clubs. Bauer jammed his bayonet onto the musket, pushed out of the orchard, but the charge seemed to end before it began, men already coming back, some hurrying, as though understanding that the enemy might come again, the soldiers seeking protection in the orchard. Out front Allen was there, sword high, but the colonel seemed to understand what his men already knew. For now, this fight was over.

Bauer felt a surge of emotion, as though he had missed something, the enemy disappearing into far trees. Some men in blue were still far out in the field, but their fight was over as well, and they drifted back, shouting out a final curse, challenges and taunts. One man suddenly dropped, cut low by a far distant musket, and many of the others took the meaning of that, quickened their pace, once more to the orchard.

Allen was riding to one end of the orchard, northward, beyond the farmhouse, now riddled with holes. After a short minute, the colonel returned, the sword still high, waving slowly over his head, his words coming now: "Prepare yourselves! They'll come again! Get ready! Reload!"

Bauer watched him as he rode past again, toward the other end of the orchard, then beyond, more men far beyond what was left of the peach trees, protected as well by thickets of brush. Bauer slipped back through the peach trees, searched for his own tree, and he saw Willis now, kneeling, tending to a fallen man, Willis moving away, and Bauer saw the man's face, the hat, Michigan, saw a black, bloody hole in the man's forehead. Bauer looked away for a long second, noticed now that so many of the peach trees had been stripped and blasted by the shower of lead that had ripped the limbs to splinters, and beneath them, more of the dead and wounded. Throughout the orchard, the flowers had covered much of the ground with a carpet of white, some men seeing that as he did, sharing the odd peacefulness that seemed suddenly to settle on them all. Bauer looked again to the dead man close to him, began a prayer, but something stopped him, and he turned to the front, where the brush had been, the grass and briars replaced by a thick mass of rebel troops. He stared for a long moment, a voice close to him, Willis.

"Fine shooting, Dutchie. We took all they had and it weren't enough. They went scamperin' back to their mamas."

Behind them, the sergeant called out, "Whiskey and gunpowder, boys! That's what their generals feed 'em. Only thing that makes those damn secesh fight like animals. Well, not here! We took care of a pile of those devils!"

Bauer ignored Champlin's bravado, stared out across the wide rolling field, the deep grass waving in a slight breeze, hiding the bodies that had fallen there. Bauer felt a sudden urgency, stared farther, to the dense woods beyond, where the rebels had retreated.

"They'll be back."

Bauer's words came in a slow monotone, but Willis slapped his back, more joyous cheer in the man than Bauer had ever seen.

"Not all of them, Dutchie. Would you look at what they left here? We took half their strength, I bet. They wanna send out the other half, fine with me. But I bet they ain't got the stomach for it, not for this!"

Bauer looked down, the musket in his hands, began the automatic motion of reloading, stopped, stared at the cartridge in his fingers. The words came out quietly, barely a whisper, to no one.

"How can they do that again? How many more times? This won't end until we kill every damn one of them."

Willis moved close to him, stared into his eyes, said, "Yep. That's why we're here." Willis paused, studied him. "You all right, Dutchie? You ain't fixin' to go runnin' off, are ya?"

Bauer pulled himself to Willis's eyes, a brief glance, and he looked again to the musket, finished the job, the weapon quickly reloaded. He was prepared again.

"I'm all right, Sammie." He tried to feel the cheer that was spreading around him, men calling out across the open field, more taunting, the joyous boasting of the victors. But the colonel was there, other officers, sharp calls, ordering the men into silence. Bauer saw Captain Patch, red-faced anger, the man pointing his sword into the orchard.

"Get down! Their artillery hasn't found you yet! But that will change! You think this is over? They been charging our men to the right all day long! Get ready to receive another attack!"

The men responded with grumbles, curses, some still shouting across the wide grassy field to whoever might hear them. To one side, another horseman, brass, aides trailing behind, and Allen rode that way. Bauer watched them, always curious, and the colonel seemed to do the listening, gave a salute now, the higher-ranking officer moving away to the right.

He turned, whispered toward Willis.

"Who's that? Some general. Doesn't look like Prentiss."

"None of our concern, Dutchie."

Bauer watched as Allen rode closer to Captain Patch, the other officers on horseback coming up. Bauer stepped forward, close to the edge of the orchard, could hear the officers clearly, the colonel not hiding his words.

"They're moving out farther to our left! No idea how many. Get everybody ready. I'll ride to the left, make sure our flank's protected. There are some Indiana boys down that way, and we need to stay hooked up close to them. Do the job, gentlemen. They're coming again. Count on that."

Bauer stepped deeper into the orchard again, found his place, saw the top of his tree shot to pieces. He knelt, could see the impact of musket balls that had split the tree in a half-dozen places, most just above where he had lain. He looked toward the dead Michigan man, still there, no time yet for stretcher bearers. Beside him, Willis hunkered down, checked his musket, said, "You hear the colonel? Hot damn, they're coming again!"

Bauer ignored his friend's strange enthusiasm, knelt down, checked the musket one more time, heard big talk filtering all through the peach trees, men marveling at their own victory, at the stunning surprise the blue troops had given the rebel advance. Some men had moved out in front of the orchard, as though counting the rebel dead, but the lieutenants halted that, the men ordered down, back into cover. Bauer lay low, suddenly remembered the wound in his arm, had forgotten completely, made a frantic motion, raising the arm, studied it. The shirt was torn, but not much else, and he rubbed his dirty fingers across a bloody scratch on his elbow, the small amount of blood already dried to a thin crust. He let out a breath, thought, close. Too close. Lucky . . . this time. No, don't think on that.

He slid the musket up beside what was left of the peach tree, aimed, realized he was staring straight toward the man he had shot, could see the man's legs still splayed out, one hand cocked upright in a grotesque curl, the rebel musket lying across the man's leg. Bauer lowered his head, did not want to see that, said the prayer he had begun awhile ago. He scolded himself now, thought, stop this. This is why you're here! That's just one man, one damn secesh who would have shot you dead. You got him before he got you, that's all. You probably got two of 'em. That's what you're supposed to do, ain't it? And now, there'll be more. The officer's words came back to him now, *Hold your fire, aim low.* Yep, it worked. He laid his head down, his hat pressed against the base of the tree, saw the odd white carpet beneath him, the blossoms matted, dirty, churned up by the men and the fight. He closed his eyes, desperately tired, saw a rush of images through his head, Willis, the dead Michigan man, Colonel Allen, the captain, the vast mound of dead so close in front of them, the rebel falling . . . his rebel. One thought came now, pushing it all away.

God help us all.

## CHAPTER TWENTY-FIVE

# JOHNSTON

SOUTH OF THE PEACH ORCHARD
APRIL 6, 1862, 2:30 P.M.

He was guiding many of Breckinridge's men himself, showing the brigade commanders where to place their men, gradually extending Bragg's position farther to the right. The artillery fire had been furious all through his movements, guns on the Southern side softening up any position of strength where the Federal troops lay. Across the way, Federal guns were sweeping the field with relentless destruction, men and horses in every one of Bragg's advances cut down like so much bloody wheat. Johnston had spent more than an hour pulling the reserve troops into position, knew that by shifting Breckinridge forward, he was eliminating the reserves altogether. The reports flowing from Beauregard and from Johnston's own staff had convinced him that there was no need for added strength to be sent to assist his left, that the Federal lines closer to Owl Creek were spent, offering little except defensive fire. What was now the center had become a bloodbath that Johnston had never expected, Bragg continuing to send troops across the open fields straight into a stubborn Federal position.

There had been no great coordination to the assaults, Bragg seeming to piece together whatever units he could grab at the moment, launching them forward to fill the space where already the casualties had been horrific. Johnston had observed several of those assaults himself, could see that Bragg was trying to break what had become a stalemate, that the Federals had planted themselves into good, strong ground, their lines far stronger than he or Bragg had anticipated. But farther to the right, the river wound along the flank of the entire battle like a great inviting serpent, a siren call to Johnston that he could not ignore. The closer he rode toward the river, the louder that call became, and the scouting reports seemed to disprove anyone's theory that the Federals were massing there for an attack against Johnston's right flank. To be sure, there were blue-coated troops in those woods, but the going there was rough, the thickets more dense, the ravines deeper, boggier, swampy creek beds that Johnston now understood could suck men down into immobility.

He would not order Bragg to change his tactics, the attacks at least serving the valuable purpose of drawing other troops from the more distant Federal positions to move to the center, offering assistance to the battered troops who repeatedly drove Bragg away. Already the gaps that Bragg had targeted on the flanks of Prentiss's Division had been filled, word coming from prisoners and Bragg's own scouts that Prentiss was receiving considerable help from the Federal divisions of Hurlbut and William Wallace. Bragg continued to insist in the most violent terms that he would eventually break the Federal position, but if Bragg had hopes that Breckinridge would send his corps in to assist that effort, Johnston had other ideas. Breckinridge was ordered out to the right of Bragg as far as he could maneuver without pulling a mass of Federal troops his way. It was Johnston's effort, finally, to turn the Federal left flank. No matter what Colonel Jordan had drawn out on paper, it was clear to him now that this should always have been the plan, to drive in along the river and sever the connection the Federal troops had with Pittsburg Landing.

He rode now holding that thought in furious silence, directing the reserve troops out to do the job that should have been done by Hardee and Polk from the first skirmishes that morning. He had not seen Beauregard, knew only that the man was still suffering from his illness, had moved in an ambulance to the place the maps showed as Shiloh Church, what was now the army's headquarters. But Johnston had no time for consultation, knew that if he were to meet with Beauregard right now, there would be an explosion that rivaled anything on this field. He despised that about himself, that he had the capacity for such anger, had almost never revealed it to anyone at all. But throughout this day, that anger had festered and swollen, made so much worse by the obviousness of the mistake. He fought to avoid thinking of Jordan, the colonel who even Bragg had suggested was pulling the Creole's strings, the weakened Beauregard little more than a dancing marionette. It was an unwise and indiscreet observation from a subordinate, but he could not explode at Bragg, knew the man had to be allowed to do his job. After two hours of observing the carnage that Bragg seemed unable to stop, Johnston had left the man to his duty. Riding out in front of Breckinridge's approaching troops, Johnston could not escape the sense that by leaving Bragg to batter himself against Prentiss's stout defense, Johnston was making his *own* mistake.

No matter the earlier successes that had come on the left flank, Johnston had become obsessed with the right, that the final success of this day could come in only one place, and that was where he rode now. Breckinridge's men had marched out into the same kinds of open grassy fields as the entire army had done all morning. They pressed forward through artillery fire, seeking safety behind ridgelines or dropping down through deep cuts choked with briars and vines. But this time, no matter what the Federals might do to counter the move, Johnston would not hold back, would not offer a *plan* for anyone's discussion. This time his troops would smash the Federal flank and open a clear passage that would drive a stake northward, closer to the river, that would sever Grant from the heart of his army. Even Breckinridge understood he was no longer the reserve. He was the fist that Johnston would use to decide this fight, a fight Johnston knew could end with Grant surrendering his sword.

"Who is that on the far flank?"

Johnston stared to the right with his field glasses and Munford responded, hesitation in his voice.

"General Chalmers, sir, I believe. There is much confusion."

"No confusion there. Chalmers is Bragg's man. Bragg sent him out there to feel for the enemy's flank, and I don't hear anything but scattered fire. That can only mean the enemy is not yet in strength there. We must occupy this ground to support him. Is General Breckinridge moving with haste?"

"Yes, sir. The orders were specific, and the general agreed to put his men to double speed. Statham's Brigade is already moving into place to the right of General Bragg's main position and General Bowen is following. They should both be in position very soon."

Johnston turned, looked back through the woods, a field beyond, away from the ongoing Federal fire. He saw them now, fresh lines of troops coming forward, their drummers keeping time, their flags flying with brisk snaps in the breeze. A cluster of officers moved forward, and Johnston knew the man who led them, Winfield Statham, his brigade mostly from Mississippi and Tennessee. Many of those were green troops, no experience at all, but Johnston had confidence that Tennessee men in particular would fight this day, that no one among them would mistake the cause that brought them to this field. They were, after all, driving the invader from their own soil. Johnston focused again to the front, scanned a wide cotton field, one log cabin on the far side, and to the right of that, a peach orchard.

"Major, ride back to Colonel Statham. Request in the strongest terms that his brigade move into position so that he may advance toward that peach orchard. Bragg's people have done no better there than they have against Prentiss."

He saw a horseman, one of Bragg's couriers. The man reined up the horse, saluted him, said, "Sir, General Bragg offers his compliments and reports that the enemy has been compelled to withdraw from that peach orchard, and has established a defensive position farther back in those far woods. General Bragg wishes you to be informed that he is pleased with that progress, sir."

"Well, I am not pleased, Sergeant." Johnston stopped, thought, this is not the time. "Sergeant, does General Bragg know who is in command over there? What enemy are we facing?"

"General Hurlbut, sir. According to the prisoners."

Johnston looked out toward the distant tree line.

"Yes, I know him. Southern man, from South Carolina, I believe." He glanced back at Munford. "We lost that one, Major. We shall make General Hurlbut pay for his unwise decision to fight against his own people.

General Bragg is facing a stalemate, and I have no patience for stale-mates. I much prefer checkmates. Major, you will instruct Colonel Sta-tham to attack across this field as quickly as possible. Is General Bowen close behind him?"

Another of his staff spoke up, Colonel Preston.

"Yes, sir! I have just returned from that position, sir, behind those far woods. He is on the road that leads out that way, closer to the river."

Johnston raised the field glasses to his eyes, searched the woods to the right of the peach orchard, nothing to see.

"It appears the enemy has withdrawn to thick cover. It is a position of strength. We must drive them away, turn that position, or I will be com-pelled to order Bragg to halt his attacks. There is no purpose to crushing our army against a stone wall unless that wall will break. Colonel Pres-ton, return to General Bowen and order him to link his left to the right of Statham. I want a coordinated attack against the enemy's position, and I will not accept failure. General Prentiss has shown a stubbornness I did not expect, but I will not believe that General Hurlbut will stand up to us, not if we strike him hard, and in concert."

Preston rode away quickly, and Johnston still watched the field, thought of Bragg. So much confusion, and Bragg is an impatient man. We could not move in concert against such a scattered enemy, and Bragg's impatience caused him to attack with whatever he had at hand. Piecemeal assaults. Well, there will be nothing piecemeal about what will happen now.

The attacks had begun as Johnston hoped, a hard-driving wall of power that stormed the Federal position in one great wave. Al-ready the Federals were pulling back farther from their dense brush lines, the protection of the blasted orchard near the lone cabin. The blue-coated troops had endured so many assaults that the added strength now sent against them forced a retreat, Hurlbut's men drawing back into dense woods and gullies that would make any fight or any re-treat that much more difficult. As Breckinridge's troops did their work, filling between Bragg's forces in the center, the two brigades Bragg had sent toward the river launched attacks of their own, exactly what John-ston knew was needed to end the repeated carnage in front of the enemy

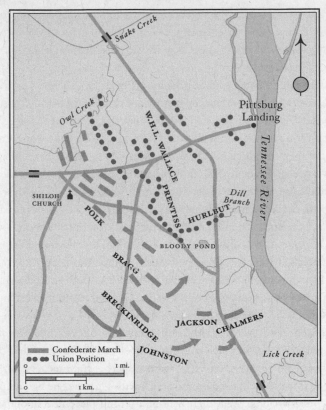

**JOHNSTON PRESSES HIS RIGHT FLANK**

forces commanded by Prentiss. But the reports came that Prentiss was mostly holding his ground. Johnston could see for himself that Prentiss's left was beginning to turn. But there seemed to be no great panic in the Federal lines, their withdrawal slow and methodical. Even in retreat, the Federal troops continued to fight, and so, for both sides, the cost was horrifying. What Johnston could not see, he could hear, the astonishing storm of musket fire matched by a torrent of artillery shells, launched by both sides. He continued to move to the right, stayed up close behind the lines of Breckenridge's troops. The progress of Breckinridge's assaults, along with the advance of Bragg's brigades under Chalmers and John Jackson, were opening up the gap nearer the swampy ground that bordered the river. Johnston heard it all, could feel the army moving as one great beast, seeking the opportunity he knew would decide the fight, to slice Grant's army away from its base.

He pushed the horse up a slight rise, his staff behind him, couriers and aides riding in and out with a steady flow of messages and orders. Johnston was aware of their progress with as much detail as anyone could provide him, and through it all, the excitement was building inside of him, the *adventure* of it. He would not show that to the staff, or the troops who marched past him, the units just arriving, still adding to the fight. He had offered them no grandiose cheer, thought, they will fight for themselves, not just for me. It is the Cause that is important, not the commander.

Behind him, protected by the fall of the hill, a horseman approached, one of many, and Johnston knew that if it was important, the staff would tell him. But he heard the voice, turned, was surprised to see Breckinridge.

"General Johnston, are you well this fine day?"

There was nervous exhaustion to Breckinridge's words, a kind of agitation Johnston had not often seen. Breckinridge was every bit the portrait of a general in the saddle, straight-backed, his reputation secured by a family pedigree that would be difficult to match in either army. But there was more to the man than the experience and the ambitions of a politician, or the slickness that made mockery of so many who had made claim to a general's stars. Johnston saw the agitation in the man's eyes, said, "Is there a problem, General?"

"Sir, I hesitate to express my displeasure . . . but one of my Tennessee regiments will not advance. They simply will not fight, sir!"

To one side, Johnston saw Isham Harris, knew Harris would absorb this news with more than casual embarrassment. Harris moved closer, said, "General, please show me this regiment. If they are indeed Tennessee men, I shall put them to the task!"

Breckinridge seemed apologetic, clearly meant no insult to the governor. Johnston appreciated the decorum in both men, but the time was *now*. He said to Breckinridge, "Let the governor go to them. I share his confidence."

"Very well, sir. Governor, if you will follow me."

The men rode off, over a slight rise, dropping out of sight now. Johnston felt a twinge of fear, knew that Harris was riding into a situation he might never have experienced. The firing in that part of the woods was ongoing and severe, and Johnston rode forward a few steps, an effort to see them, felt suddenly protective, and beside him, he heard a low voice.

"God go with them."

The words came from Preston, and Johnston forced a smile.

"Governor Harris will not accept that his own men have failed us. He will inspire them."

Harris had returned, exhausted and furious, and Johnston would not allow the governor's pride to prevent him from making his report.

"Did they advance, Isham? Were you successful?"

Harris looked down, still catching his breath, shifting in the saddle, uncomfortable from the rapid pace of his ride.

"With some reluctance, sir. I had hoped they would respond to my presence with a bit more patriotism. I fear that some are crawling into cover even now. It is very difficult there, sir. I have never seen such a fight. It is likely my own fear showed through, despite my oratory. I do not envy the foot soldier."

Johnston saw the shame in Harris's face, completely unnecessary.

"We do what we can, Governor." He paused, the roar and thunder opening up farther to the right, deeper in the woods.

"See? Another confrontation. We are pressing them back in every position. Do not be concerned. I, too, do not envy the man with the musket. We must always remember that *they* carry the weight here, *they* pay the ultimate price."

He felt awkward, dissatisfied with his attempt to buck up Harris's spirits. He stared out toward the new fight, said aloud, "We must move that way. All of you, stay close. We are engaging a new enemy position, and I must know what is happening. Who is in command there?"

Munford responded, "Jackson, and possibly Chalmers, sir. I believe we are close to General Breckinridge's right flank. It is hard to keep order."

"Yes, I imagine it is hard for them as well. If that is Chalmers, he is farther north than before. It means he is driving deeper past the enemy's flank." He absorbed that for a moment, could see nothing of the fight, just a thick haze of smoke, and the constant sounds of men firing weapons in enormous numbers, close together, volleys echoing through the dense thickets in a steady, horrible chorus. The excitement continued to build inside of him, and he rose in the stirrups, frustrated he could see so little. He tried to see James Chalmers in his mind, another good man who had to endure Bragg as a commander. There will be no complaint against you this day, no haranguing you for some minuscule failure. Bragg has his own difficulties to answer for. But not right now.

He crested another ridge, so much like the last, never-ending folds in the ground, more woods bordering a small field, and to the left a trio of farmhouses. There officers were pulling troops into line, organizing another advance. The troops had the look of men who had been in a fight already, small wounds, and worse, some lying flat behind the formation, cared for by one older man, unfamiliar, the man doing all those things a doctor would do. Johnston nodded toward the man, a gesture of respect, but the doctor paid no attention, was moving quickly through the row of wounded. Johnston thought of his own doctor, usually riding with his staff. That morning, they had passed through a group of wounded, many of them Federal prisoners, and Johnston would not ignore that. There seemed to be no one there equipped to care for the desperate wounds Johnston could see, so he ordered his own Dr. Yandell to remain behind, to make some attempt to establish a field hospital. Yandell had protested, but Johnston would hear none of that, had ordered the doctor to treat the men who required it. It was, after all, a luxury Johnston knew was excessive, too much like a martinet to have his own surgeon trailing behind him just in case Johnston stubbed his toe.

Johnston still watched the doctor in the field, the man kneeling in front of what seemed to be no more than a pile of remains, blood and torn bits of uniform. The doctor lowered his head, moved on to the next man. Johnston turned away, thought of the blood he had already seen this day, so many fallen men, disfigured and broken, so many beyond the reach of anything a doctor could do. I cannot see that, he thought. I cannot mourn, even for a moment, the loss of a soldier. It is my duty, after all, to regard this army as a single force, a single being. The whole, always the most important thing. *That* was the great failure of Beauregard's plan, not making proper use of the *whole*. It is why Bragg is so frustrated, gathering up units as he can find them, pounding against the wall that General Prentiss has placed in his front. It is why I am out *here,* and not sitting comfortably in a sickbed, reading messages, pretending to know all that is happening, all that must be done.

The firing seemed to roll toward him from farther away now, northward, deeper into the woods where Chalmers must be. He focused, sharp attention, the uneasiness that it could be the Federal counterattack, the great mass of blue troops that the engineer, Lockett, had feared. But the firing seemed to move to the left, as though his men were pushing the enemy farther from the river, exactly what Johnston had hoped. If my staff is correct, he thought, if that is indeed Chalmers and Jackson, it means that the Federal flank is that much closer to turning, that even the gallantry of General Prentiss cannot prevent what will happen next. The single word came to him again, the meaning so clear, that simple stroke of glory, what Johnston could feel inching toward him, so close to his grasp. *Checkmate.*

"Sir, General Breckinridge has returned!"

Johnston turned, saw more of the frowning concern, his concentration shattered by the discouraging glare from Breckinridge.

"What is happening, General?"

"The brigade . . . re-forming into line. Those men have been in a stiff fight. Some are claiming they have done all they can. General Bowen insists with much regret that they will not fight, that their day is done. I fear, sir, I cannot compel them to make this attack."

Johnston held in his anger, had only limited confidence in Bowen, the man commanding his brigade for a short few weeks. But he never expected Breckinridge to show such defeat.

"Yes, General, I believe you can compel them."

"But I have tried . . ."

"Then I will help you."

Johnston turned, saw Harris, the governor suddenly coming to attention, expectant now, waiting for the inevitable order.

"There are Arkansas men out here, Isham. Perhaps you can inspire them as well as you do your own. You will assist us. General Breckinridge will move his staff to the left, you to the right. I will assume the center position, and together we will show these soldiers the way to the enemy."

Johnston didn't wait, rode forward, down into the field, could see the thick lines of men, officers on horseback, just . . . waiting. Breckinridge rode farther down the line, toward the farmhouses, and Johnston maneuvered his horse through the men, halted directly in front of the lines. He had a small burst of inspiration, reached into a saddlebag, retrieved the tin cup he had picked up in the Federal camp. He held it up, removed his hat, wanted them to see him clearly, no mistaking who he was.

"This cup is my only reward, my only piece of the spoils from the enemy! There is much more to be accomplished here. I have tasted victory, and on a day such as this, there is no greater gift to be had. That victory is in your hands, right now. You must obey your commanders, and march forward to complete the task we have begun! The enemy is retreating even now, and with your help, we can finish the job!" He edged the horse along the line, men flinching slightly, as though expecting some kind of blow from his sword, but the sword was in its scabbard. He was not here to scold or shame these men; there was no need for a dramatic gesture. The soldier closest to him stood firm, and Johnston reached out, his hand slapping gently at the man's bayonet. "The enemy has proven stubborn today! *These* must do the work!" He rode farther along the line, his hand still out, touching more of the weapons. "We must use the bayonet! And I shall lead you!"

He looked down the line, saw Breckinridge watching him, following his lead, moving out with his staff in front of the brigade. Johnston looked the other way, saw Harris down off his horse, standing in front of the men with his pistol in his hand, ready as well. Johnston glanced back at the captain nearest him, made a sharp nod, the man understanding the order, the order passed quickly to the right, where General Bowen gave his own command. In seconds the drums began, shouts all along the line, and with no hesitation the brigade began its advance. Johnston kept the horse in a slow gait, allowed them to move up close behind him, and then, past. He called out again and they responded to him, cheers, the kind of cheers that drove men to a fight, that carried them toward the guns of the enemy, the confidence in their commanders and in themselves that would bring them victory.

----

The fight exploded throughout the woods in front of him, the men on both sides suddenly confronted with an enemy at close range. Johnston stayed close, could see glimpses of Breckinridge, the man's staff still with him, leading that part of the fight. The smoke was thick, blinding, and Johnston struggled to breathe, could hear shrieks and zips in the air around him, felt a tug at his side, glanced down, saw the tear where the ball had sliced his coat. He pushed that away, focused on what he could see, and more, the energy he could feel from the driving advance of Bowen's Brigade. No matter what reluctance they had before, only a few men were dropping back, and Johnston ignored those, no time now to gather up the few whose courage had failed them. He pushed onward, glanced to the right, no sign of Harris through the smoke and clusters of trees. He thought of moving that way, could not avoid concern for his friend, but his attention was drawn by a glimpse of blue, a line of Federal troops breaking, falling back. He felt another rip along his arm, glanced down, no damage to anything but the cloth, but the horse suddenly jerked, seemed to slump slightly, struggling to right himself. Johnston patted the horse's neck, felt another jolt just behind him, against the horse's leg, the horse shifting from the blow.

"Fire-Eater, this shall be our day. Just stay with me! Stay in the fight!"

Johnston was surprised to see Harris riding up, the man wide-eyed, a mix of terror and pure joy, and Johnston started to speak, felt another punch against the bottom of his boot. The horse staggered again, and Johnston pulled his foot from the stirrup, saw the sole of his boot completely shot away. Harris saw that as well, said, "Sir! Are you all right?"

Johnston raised the damaged boot, laughed, said, "I am fine, it seems. But these boots are of little use."

"Did the ball injure your foot?"

Johnston shoved his foot back into the stirrup, flexed his toes, said, "It seems not."

Close to one side, an artillery battery suddenly opened its fire, brutal shrieks passing close overhead, the screaming of canister, tearing through the far flank of the Confederate line. Johnston couldn't help a flinch, thought, very close . . . and very dangerous.

"Governor, Colonel Statham is in that vicinity. Go there, find him, and order the colonel to move troops toward that battery. It must be silenced."

Harris said nothing, no salute, rode quickly away, the terrifying excitement stripping away the governor's newly acquired military protocol. In front of Johnston, the soldiers kept up their march, more volleys blowing through on both sides and Johnston felt another tear in his coat, ignored it, no pain, the ball missing him yet again. He laughed again, could feel the triumph of the men before him, jabbed his fist into the air, could not hide an overwhelming joy. He spurred the horse lightly, the animal responding obediently, and Johnston tried not to think of that, would not yet look to the horse's wounds. He patted the horse's neck again, more low words, a sudden wave of affection for this servant that had carried him so far.

There was more firing now, a pocket of blue suddenly rising from a deep trough, their fire answered by a fresh volley from men right in front of him. The two groups rushed together, shouting, all through that part of the line, the fight too close for muskets, and he saw men grabbing one another, knives and bayonets flashing through the smoke. The fighting seemed to swirl around him, the smoke from more artillery blinding him, and he saw a new flash of fire, close to his right, men in blue bolting away, his own in pursuit. Johnston pushed the horse up a low rise, crested the ridge, could see the fight more plainly now, saw another volley from a line of blue, that line giving way, offering its final defiant blow. Johnston felt a slight tug at his knee, glanced down, nothing to see, felt no pain, just a tingle in his leg, a hint of numbness. He ignored that now, rode forward again, down along the ridgeline, still following his men, more of them in a rapid chase to catch the Federal retreat. The horse slowed, lowering its head, and Johnston tried to avoid the pain of that, raised the field glasses, tried to see something, anything. In every part of the open ground, his own men filled his view, the last of the Federal position driven away. The firing slowed, but there were new volleys farther to the left, more artillery, the thunder of the shells wiping away the cheers of the men who had so bested their enemy. He wanted to cheer with them, but they were still moving, leaving him behind, and he felt a strange weakness, as though sleep was coming, lowered the glasses, his mind drifting, the sounds of the battle rolling into a soft hum, like music, deep bass drums, a chorus of violins. He closed his eyes for a brief second, to shake the nonsense away, and he fought to breathe, weakness there as well. He opened his eyes again, saw drifting smoke, men far away, and now hoofbeats, a voice, Isham Harris.

"General, your order is delivered. Colonel Statham is in motion."

Johnston felt himself starting to fall, nothing to stop it, and suddenly an arm was holding him, keeping him upright.

"Sir, are you wounded?"

Johnston tested his breathing, still felt no pain, just the numbness in his right leg, wetness in his boot. He looked down, tried to focus, realized his boot was filled with blood, saw blood spilling out.

"Yes, Isham. And I fear seriously."

Johnston felt the sleep coming, could not stop it, his hands releasing the reins, but Harris was close beside him, holding Johnston's horse close to his own, and Johnston could feel movement now, the slow, lurching rhythm. He seemed to wake, felt hands on him, supporting him as he fell, but it was slow, gentle, the hands laying him down. He tried to talk, to ask, felt the hands on his body, tugging on his clothes, coolness on his chest, realized his shirt was open, his chest exposed. His mind was carrying him farther away, and he struggled against that, heard voices above him, faces mostly a blur, but Harris . . . his staff . . .

"General, do you know me?"

Johnston forced his eyes open, saw treetops and blue sky, a face, Preston, felt a hard tug on his leg, his boot pulled off, more of the voices, pieces of words, "Bleeding . . ."

He didn't respond, the energy gone, his eyes closing again, a single thought, that he could hear nothing of the fight, the silence strange, alarming. But the panic passed in a single moment, drained away, his mind engulfed by a strange, cold silence, and he saw her standing in the orchard, sweet Eliza smiling, tending to the beloved trees, and behind her, the ranch house, smoke from the chimney, soft lights in the windows . . . home.

## CHAPTER TWENTY-SIX

# HARRIS

"His heart has stopped! It cannot be . . . it is such a small wound."

Harris was on his knees, felt Johnston's face, already growing cold. Colonel Preston stood above him, others from the staff gathered close, low words. Harris could feel their despair, felt it himself, sickening grief, a horror of disbelief. He ran his hand down Johnston's leg, felt the thickening blood, his fingers finding the hole behind Johnston's knee. But it was barely a hole, more of a gash, a deep scratch. Preston saw what he was doing, was down beside him now, and Preston said, "Dr. Yandell should have been here. He would be alive. A simple tourniquet would have stopped the bleeding."

Harris thought of Yandell, the man so vigorous in his protests that he should stay with the general. Harris spoke through tears now.

"He did not believe he required a surgeon. I suppose . . . none of us believe that. None of us expects . . . this."

"You are wrong, Governor. I mean no disrespect, understand me. But a soldier must *always* expect this. The general knew that, certainly." Preston was sliding his hands into Johnston's pockets, removing papers, anything official. He suddenly withdrew a small strip of cloth, stared at it for a moment, showed it to Harris.

"My God, Governor, he carried one in his pocket. A tourniquet. He just . . . he must not have known of the wound. There must have been no pain, no sensation at all."

Harris blinked through the tears, glanced at the tourniquet. He lowered his head, said, "He was directing the fight. There was nothing else that mattered. Look, his coat. He was struck by several balls. Death could have come at any time. It did not matter to him."

"What's this?"

Preston had removed Johnston's coat, one hand deep inside a pocket, withdrew a small bundle. He cradled it carefully, and unwrapped it, and Harris caught a stinking smell. He looked away, had seen the bundle before, said slowly, "It is a sandwich. It's the parting gift from Mrs. Inge."

Couriers had continued to come in, and the staff had done all they could to shield prying eyes from the identity of the fallen officer. Preston had kept his calm, doing the job, taking command of the staff, and despite the grief that was so hard to disguise, every man knew that Johnston's death had to be kept from the troops who were still pursuing the fight. Even more important, General Beauregard had to be notified. Harris felt no joy in the sudden realization that Beauregard now commanded this army. But that judgment had been made by others, and Colonel Preston recognized that with perfect clarity. Preston had sent a courier on his way, a message for General Breckinridge that said nothing about Johnston at all. Preston moved closer to Harris now, pulled him by the arm, away from the others.

"Governor, we are faced with two very important tasks. I shall supervise the transport of the general's body to headquarters. We must remove him from the field, so that nothing . . . unfortunate should occur. He must not fall into enemy hands, certainly. But you must precede me to headquarters as rapidly as you can. Ride to that church with all haste, and notify General Beauregard what has happened." Preston looked back toward the others. "Who among you has been to the headquarters?"

Several men nodded, motioned with their hands, and Preston pointed to one, Captain Wickham, the man attempting to wipe away tears.

"Captain, you will guide Governor Harris to the army's headquarters.

Make haste. Orders must still guide this army. It is possible that General Beauregard is unaware of the progress we have made on this flank. He must be informed. General Johnston would insist . . ." Preston stopped, seemed to choke on his words.

Harris walked slowly toward Johnston's horse, his legs weak, trying to gather himself. He put a hand on the saddle, supporting himself. He turned toward Preston, said, "Colonel, I will do as you instruct." He looked past Preston, to the others, saw the grief, the sadness on all of them. He could not remain silent, felt the need to ease the pain.

"We will endure this tragedy, gentlemen. We must. It is just . . . one more challenge we face."

Harris didn't believe his own words, felt his despair widening into a vast chasm of depression. He looked out toward the fighting, distant now, moving farther to the north and west. He turned, stared toward the river, and Preston moved closer to him, Johnston's coat still in his hand. Preston seemed to struggle to control himself, to keep his composure in front of the staff.

"You share my thoughts, Governor. The river is a short distance from here. It would have been appropriate if the general had been allowed to make good on his promise."

"Promise?"

"To water his horse in the Tennessee River."

Harris patted the horse, said, "Well, perhaps that will happen still. My own horse is badly injured. I shall ride Fire-Eater to headquarters. He is a swift animal, strong."

Harris climbed up on the horse, but the animal seemed to stagger, and Captain Wickham was there now, moving around the horse, examining, said, "He is badly wounded, sir. Three legs have suffered. Respectfully, sir, he is no longer of service."

Preston tried to maintain his stoicism, said, "The orderlies . . . back there. They have other mounts. Use one of those, Governor."

Harris stayed up on the horse for a moment longer, felt the added grief for the horse's injuries, thought, they will wait for me to leave, and then his suffering will be ended. It has to be. He swung his leg over, dismounted, saw where Preston had pointed, the orderlies and several horses standing back in the trees.

"Go now, Governor. There can be no delay. I will follow behind, as rapidly as the general's body can be transported." He glanced at Wickham, then back to Harris. "Tell no one of this, *no one,* until General Beauregard is notified."

Harris understood Preston's urgency, but he hesitated, looked down one more time at Johnston's face, saw perfect peacefulness, the serenity of a man whose burdens are lifted. He took a long breath, said a silent farewell, a new flow of tears, and moved away.

SHILOH CHURCH

APRIL 6, 1862, 4:00 P.M.

Beauregard was standing tall on a cut tree stump, a column of men moving past him with joyous waves, shouts, which Beauregard acknowledged with a hearty wave of his hand. Harris rode close, tried not to look at the general's smile. On the long ride, his grief had festered into anger, made worse by the painful gait of the horse he had never ridden. Captain Wickham had led him well, passing behind most of the troops, avoiding the vast fields of wounded, the farmhouses where rumors could have spread, where questions might be asked. As Harris came into sight of the church, and now Beauregard himself, the pain of the ride gave way to the pure misery of the job he had to perform. Beauregard saw him, seemed to puff up, kept to the stump, and Harris knew the trick, so familiar to a politician, the petite man doing anything he could to appear larger, a portrait that was more about image than anything else. Harris dismounted, Wickham as well, the captain keeping behind him.

"Well, Governor, are we faring as well to the right as we have over the rest of the field? Have you come to tell me of a great victory?"

Harris heard infuriating sarcasm in Beauregard's voice, couldn't avoid a growing hatred for the man. But the duty came first, the obedience, what now had to be absolute. He glanced around, no one else within earshot, but still he moved close, stood beside the ridiculous stump, and after a long breath, Harris said, "Sir, it is with deepest sadness that I must report the death of General Johnston."

Beauregard seemed to flinch, jumped down from the stump, stared hard at Harris, a glance toward Wickham.

"Are you certain? Well, of course you are." Beauregard seemed ready to burst with questions, kept them inside, and Harris saw nothing that resembled sadness. Beauregard nodded now, a strange gesture, said, "It is a tragic loss for our army and our nation, Governor. Tell me, how is the fight progressing in that part of the field?"

Harris felt a dismal calm, the grief drained from him by Beauregard's casual need for facts.

"The fight is progressing extremely well, sir. The general . . . at the time of his death . . . was supervising the rapid advance against the Federal left flank. It was the general's supreme wish that we drive between the enemy's position and their base at Pittsburg Landing. If I may offer the observation, sir, it seems we are accomplishing that very success."

"Yes, I know the general's *supreme wish*. I designed this battle, if you recall." Beauregard paused, seemed suddenly deep in thought, and he motioned for Harris to follow, began to move toward the small church. Harris noticed the building for the first time now, crude logs, a single doorway. He expected more, something larger, knew the churches in Nashville for their grand façades, the tall steeples that graced the skyline he so deeply missed. But there was nothing of Nashville, or even a village here. All around him, narrow roads led away, each one choked with the debris of the battle, wounded men, ambulances, men pushing through on horseback, some men doing . . . nothing at all. Close beside the building was an ambulance, what Harris assumed to be Beauregard's place of rest. He followed Beauregard up the low steps into the church, the single room dark, lit only by a lantern. He studied the Creole for the first time now, still saw hints of the man's illness, but Beauregard carried a new energy, his voice clear, purpose to his steps. Beauregard sat, no other chair for Harris, and Beauregard seemed to study papers on the small table beside him.

"At this moment, General Polk's people are doing good work against the enemy's position, and on his right flank, Bragg is performing well. There is considerable lack of organization, however, and many of their units are inexorably tangled. In that regard, General Hardee is no better off. At least, on our left, he seems to have secured our flank. But I am not yet concerned with the reorganization of the overlapping commands. That is a problem I will confront when the time is right. If you are correct that we are turning the enemy's far flank . . . well then, the battle may as well continue."

Harris waited for more, but Beauregard went silent. Harris said, "Yes, sir. I believe that is the best course. General Johnston would most certainly agree."

Beauregard ignored that, studied a piece of paper, and behind Harris a courier suddenly appeared at the door, staff officers moving in without a knock. Harris felt a new wave of despair, not for Johnston, but for what he was seeing now, the business of this army moving forward as though nothing had happened, nothing had changed. He fought the urge to just . . . leave, to climb up on the horse and ride away, felt suddenly as though his usefulness to the army had ceased to exist. He thought of Corinth. I should just . . . ride, inform Mrs. Inge, certainly. But Colonel Preston might not approve. There is no need to alarm civilians, no matter the magnitude of the tragedy. And they will learn soon enough. What good can I do here? He stopped himself, thought of Johnston, the long talks, the friendship. *You* are still alive, and the general would not approve of this kind of melancholy. There must be someone, some command who can make use of me.

Beauregard's staff officer was reading from a paper, a message from Hardee, that all was going well, the enemy making no attempt at a counterattack. Beauregard seemed immensely satisfied by that, and Harris still felt as though he was in the way. He fought with himself for a long moment, to leave or not, tried to stay out of the way as men passed by him. Beauregard was clearly drawn to other matters, and Harris thought, I *chose* this duty. I did not come to this army just to serve one man, to serve a friend. And you know what Sidney would tell you to do. And it would not be a *suggestion*. He waited for the conversation to pause, a quiet moment, then said, "Sir, with circumstances as they are now, it is appropriate that I offer my services to your staff, if you will have me, sir."

Beauregard looked up at him, rubbed a hand on his chin, nodded slowly.

"Yes, that would be acceptable. You have a horse, so make use of it. Keep me informed of events on the right. You will find me here at all times. This is, after all, the army's headquarters."

Harris backed away, had endured all he could of Beauregard's utter lack of humility. More staff officers were moving in, past him, Beauregard hidden by the clean gray of their uniforms. He stepped out into cool air, saw Wickham, wet sadness on the captain's face. Harris moved to the horse, stopped, looked upward, blue sky flecked with white clouds, stared for a long moment, the sun settling slowly into the treetops to the west.

## CHAPTER TWENTY-SEVEN

# PRENTISS

NORTH OF THE PEACH ORCHARD,
NEAR THE POND
APRIL 6, 1862, 3:30 P.M.

The rebel artillery kept up their fire, directed mostly to the right now, a new surge by troops against his flank. For a long while, that part of Prentiss's position had been wide open, a deep gash in the overall Federal lines that had attracted waves of attackers, coming up out of the trees not more than a quarter mile away. But the gap had been filled by the magnificent response of William Wallace, who had recognized the critical importance behind Prentiss's desperate call for help. Now Wallace's troops had filled the gap to the west completely, and farther that way, Wallace's flank was partially protected by McClernand, the man who had given assistance earlier that morning to protect what had once been the left flank of Sherman. Throughout the day, as the disastrous impact of the rebel attack spread throughout most of the Federal forces, no one had been immune. Prentiss's men had fallen back with the same chaotic scramble that affected Sherman, driven away from their own camps. But Prentiss had been able to rally many of his regiments from complete collapse, had made good use of the lay of the land to pull many of his units together into what had now become a hard barrier that had finally been effective in holding back the rebel advance. The rallying point for many of Prentiss's men was a wagon trail, an old roadbed that wound across the edge of Duncan Field, then out in both directions, curving through the woods, past more patches of open ground. The trail was old, worn, and much of the way was lined by dense thickets of overgrown brush that produced perfect cover for the troops. The roadbed extended even into Wallace's lines, and the men in blue who formed up along the road had responded to their new protection with desperately needed confidence.

Once Prentiss understood the sheer mass of the rebel assault, and once the rebel advance had eliminated any communications he had with Sherman, Prentiss began to understand that his division was virtually severed from the rest of the army, that retreat was the only viable option. The first indication he had that the rebels were coming in force had been sent to him much earlier that morning from Colonel Peabody, the brigade commander seeing firsthand the sheer bulk of the rebel advance. But, like Sherman, Prentiss had doubted the reports he had received from the picket outposts, had engaged in a heated discussion with Peabody, who Prentiss believed had exaggerated just what was happening to the west. He knew that Peabody had taken serious offense at the challenge to his skills at observation, and Prentiss would hear none of that. But soon after the magnitude of the rebel attack became clear, Peabody had of course been vindicated. Prentiss had seen for himself that most of his entire division was engulfed by a far stronger assault than anything Prentiss expected. But there would be no opportunity for Prentiss to offer his apologies to the outraged Peabody. By mid-morning, Peabody was dead.

As Prentiss struggled to re-form his division along the old wagon trail, he had expected the rebel assault to continue with the same energy he had seen earlier that morning, the kind of energy that even a good defensive line might only contain for a short while. But that kind of full-out assault never came. Instead the roughly four thousand men he managed to put into line were attacked by lines of rebels who were fewer in number than he was. Instead of one massive envelopment of his lines, which Prentiss and his officers had feared, the rebels had come at them with a *series* of attacks, each one nearly the same as the one before, usually brigade strength, perhaps more, marching in slow, neat lines across Duncan Field, or farther to the right, in the woods that kept the rebel lines from keeping any kind of order. The results had been the same in nearly every attack the rebels sent forward. The thick cover along the wagon trail had proved to be a significant disadvantage for the rebels, the Federal troops disciplined enough to wait in their blind cover for the rebels to approach within point-blank range. For the Federal troops, it was the first real advantage they enjoyed all day. The results were devastating for nearly every rebel unit who made the quarter-mile march across Duncan Field, as it was for the others who had stumbled blindly through the woods. Even worse for the rebels, Prentiss had been able to shift artillery batteries from Wallace's positions on the right, many of those guns anchored into deep woods, their sights now perfectly ranging the Confederate flanks. The artillery had added their devastating canister to the sheets of flaming musket fire that came from Prentiss's infantry.

Prentiss wasn't sure just how many assaults the rebels had made, perhaps a dozen, perhaps less, but in every case the combined fire of the Federal troops had been shattering. Every attack concluded the same way, the rebels pushing directly into a mass of Federal firepower, then pulling back yet again, leaving many more of their troops in the field. Across Duncan Field, where Prentiss could see the far woods clearly, the entire stretch of open ground had become a carpet of dead and dying men, almost all of them rebels. With each new assault, Prentiss had wondered if his men would finally be overpowered, driven away by the same kind of overwhelming panic that had spread through his division that morning. But so far his lines were holding firm, and Prentiss began to receive reports that the worst problem affecting his men was a shortage of ammunition.

Despite the amazing willingness of the rebels to attack Prentiss's position with what seemed to be piecemeal efforts, the sheer volume of fire on both sides was taking its toll. Rebel artillery was doing their work as well, and all across his position, rebel shells poured down with relentless efficiency. Unlike the foot soldiers, the artillerymen didn't have to see their targets to be effective. After several of their failed attacks, rebel artillery commanders knew with perfect precision where to direct their fire. As the day wore on, a new tragedy erupted, mostly for the wounded on both sides. The brutal storm of shell fire had ignited several patches of thick brush in front of the Federal position, fires carried on the breeze that spread quickly through the woods and across the grassy fields, engulfing anyone unable to move out of the way. The screams of burned men only added to the horror that every man in the field was experiencing, Prentiss among them.

Benjamin Prentiss was not a West Pointer, had instead gained experience during the Mormon conflicts in Illinois, and later in the Mexican War. Originally a Virginian, he spent most of the 1850s practicing law in his adopted home of Quincy, Illinois, but the eruption of the war brought Prentiss back to the army. Though he had remained active in his local militia, serving as colonel of his local regiment, it was Ulysses Grant who had some familiarity with Prentiss's good experience under Zachary Taylor, more experience than many of the professional soldiers who had staked their claim to command. Throughout 1861, Prentiss did nothing to discourage Grant's well-placed confidence, and served efficiently in Cairo, Illinois, guarding the crucial junction of the Ohio and the Mississippi rivers, and later, protecting the rail lines in war-torn Missouri. When Grant's army was mobilized for the drive toward Corinth, Grant had no hesitation in suggesting Prentiss, now a brigadier general, for division command. Like Sherman, Prentiss had been assigned to lead a division of raw recruits who had never seen combat. In the weeks following their encampment west of Pittsburg Landing, Prentiss had tackled the same tasks as Sherman and the other division commanders: drill and train men who had most likely never seen a rebel soldier. Now, by the chance positioning of his Sixth Division more southwesterly from Pittsburg Landing, Prentiss had become the center of the entire Federal position, the first to receive the rebel assaults. As much of a chore as it had been to train so many green soldiers, Prentiss had every reason to feel a distinct pride that his men had rallied just enough to keep the rebels from driving straight through the Federal army, to Grant's base at the river.

Though William Wallace's Second Division had rushed forward to protect Prentiss's right, there was very little order to the placement of troops, no time for any neatly drawn out battlefield planning. The jumble of commands was as confused now as it had been since early that morning, and as his position solidified along the wagon trail, Prentiss found himself commanding regiments from Wallace's Division, as well as his own. Some of Prentiss's units had disappeared altogether; some were mere fragments of their former strength. But thus far, after so many Confederate assaults, and a withering storm of fire from rebel artillery batteries, those lines had held. Wallace knew as well as Prentiss that it made little difference which officer stood to your backside while the guns of the enemy were tearing into your ranks. Not only was Prentiss grateful for Wallace's unquestioning assistance, he actually liked Wallace. He couldn't say the same for some of the others in the Federal command, had no great affection for either Sherman or John McClernand. But right now, personal opinions had nothing at all to do with what was happening around him. And down to his left, in the vicinity of a peach orchard, the tide of the battle was not nearly so static, the defenses not quite as complete.

There the morning had begun with a yawning gap a half mile wide, which separated Prentiss's Division from the single brigade of Colonel David Stuart. Stuart's men, who were actually a part of Sherman's Fifth Division, had been sent far out beyond Prentiss's left flank almost as an afterthought, someone's revelation that the dense woods and gullies closer to the river should at least have some token force there, more as observation than defense. Prentiss could not worry about Stuart, had no idea if those troops were even in the fight at all, not while waves of rebels were striking Prentiss from the southwest. Stuart's meager presence notwithstanding, Prentiss had to believe he was now the left flank of the entire Federal position.

As the morning passed into afternoon, Prentiss could see that the rebels had discovered that gap and were shifting their troops eastward, bringing up fresh regiments to exploit the opening that might turn Prentiss's left and cut off Stuart altogether. With the rebel assaults threatening to envelop his flank, Prentiss had made a desperate plea for the closest Federal forces to do anything they could to fill that gap. That call had been answered with admirable speed by Stephen Hurlbut's Fourth Division. As had happened on his right, Hurlbut's rapid and disorderly advance had resulted in a jumbled mess of overlapping and confused commands, entire regiments stumbling through woods and thickets, some marching directly across the firing line of other Federal units or wandering blindly into pockets of advancing rebels. Many were now fighting under officers they had never seen before, soldiers moving into line beside men from other states. As the day wore on, and the attacks shifted eastward, it had become evident to Prentiss that his division, and those who had rallied to his aid, were confronted by an enemy who was nearly as jumbled up as the Federals.

He rode quickly, avoiding the bursts of incoming artillery, maneuvering his horse through shattered trees, past clusters of men who were hunkered down in whatever cover the woods provided them. For the past hour, he had heard what many of his officers had heard, their attention directed eastward, toward the river. The sound was unmistakable, so different from the artillery shells the rebels were throwing toward them. From near the landing, one of the Federal gunboats had begun shelling what their crews must have presumed to be the vanguard of the rebel advance. It was an honest attempt to hold the rebels away by launching the enormous shells of the naval guns onto the enemy's position. Instead, as Prentiss could see now, the shells were falling more into his own lines than doing anything to hold back the enemy. Besides cursing the navy, the Federal troops had absorbed the incoming fire the only way they could, by keeping low, and holding to the desperate hope that the shells would fall on someone else, or that someone in command might inform the gunboat that the enemy was *over there.*

Prentiss had heard the distinctive explosions from the beginning, but the ongoing assaults from the enemy had kept his attention focused more on what was happening to his front. But still the shells came, and he heard another one, much closer, stared up helplessly, the shell arcing down, the men shouting out their warnings, their voices quickly drowned out by the blast. It impacted in the woods a hundred yards to his front, launching a fountain of dirt and debris, and he cursed along with his men, spurred the horse that way, knew there could be casualties. His staff followed closely behind him, and suddenly, in the midst of the dusty cloud, he saw the slow fall of a massive oak tree, dropping to one side with a thunderous crash. More dust and dirt rose up, showering men who made a desperate scramble to escape being crushed. Through it all the rebel artillery continued to scream overhead, their shells falling at random, most impacting far behind his men. He pushed the horse into the dust, knew that if anyone had been caught by the tree, there was little he could do to help them.

The rebel batteries seemed to be shifting their ground, more shelling coming from the left, farther to the east. It confirmed what he already believed, that the enemy was changing their tactics, had perhaps chewed themselves up more than they had expected against the mass of his well-hidden troops. He turned the horse, moved around the great thicket of the fallen treetop, slow progress, the woods a jumble of shattered limbs, and now a crushed fence. Through it all were wounded men, many of those pulled back from the forward positions. He halted behind the fallen tree, doing as his men did, taking advantage of a three-foot-thick wall of impenetrable cover. He waited for his staff to gather close, looked around, sought out an officer, could see no one on horseback. He shouted back to his staff, "Have we heard anything from General Hurlbut?"

There was no positive response, no surprise, and he stared out to the left, spurred the horse again. Farther out through the thick woods came a new burst of firing, not what he wanted to hear, that message too clear. The men he saw now were not his own units, and their volleys were aimed at an enemy who was clearly out beyond what had once been his left flank. He pressed the horse on, moved along a narrow trail, saw officers shifting their men into good cover, and Prentiss moved past, acknowledged those who acknowledged him, knew to let those men do their jobs. He was among Illinois men now, no mistaking Hurlbut's command, saw a Wisconsin flag, then Indiana. One officer rode out to greet him, and Prentiss was surprised to see Ben Allen, of the 16th Wisconsin. Allen was trailed by a single aide, saluted him, and Prentiss said, "Colonel, I did not expect to find you down here. Are you holding up?" Allen seemed exhausted, and Prentiss saw the hint of a bandage beneath the colonel's coat. "You're wounded. Are you able to continue here?"

"Yes, sir. No one will remove me from my men . . . with all respects, sir."

Prentiss appreciated the defiance in Allen's voice, but there had been too much of that already.

"Colonel, you may of course remain with your men, for now. But we have lost a great many officers today who were admirably stubborn. Colonel Peabody is down, and presumed to be dead."

Allen lowered his head for a brief second.

"I had not heard that. He made a most favorable impression on my men."

To the east, a new burst of firing spread through the trees, and Prentiss felt the urgency of that, had no time now for conversation.

"Colonel, have you spoken with General Hurlbut? Do you know his location?"

"He placed us here, sir. The last I saw him, he was farther east. The general was able to summon ammunition wagons, to our great relief. My men have refilled their cartridge boxes. That has added considerably to our morale. We had been positioned in that peach orchard, out toward the enemy, but the rebel artillery compelled us to fall back."

Smoke blew past them now, some from the burning timber Prentiss could see in front of their lines. Allen pointed that way, said, "The brush-fires have been something of a blessing, sir. The enemy is reluctant to advance through burning grass. But that will not last."

"Hold your position, Colonel, as best you can. Maintain your connection to the units on either side of you."

Allen saluted him again, and Prentiss moved away, toward the direction where Hurlbut might be. Ammunition wagons, he thought. Hurlbut must have more influence than I do. Or perhaps my couriers never made it to their destination. If my men aren't able to fill their cartridge boxes, the fires may be all I can rely upon to hold the enemy back. If I can find Hurlbut, perhaps he can send those wagons my way.

A volley of musket fire opened out in the field nearest him, men closer to him, his men, returning fire. Behind him, an aide stammered aloud, "Sir, we must move back. This is not the place for you . . ."

He ignored the man, his horse already in motion, chewed on the irony of the aide's words. The question would go unasked. Just where is *the place* for me?

He glanced back, saw his flag held low, a flash of good sense from the color bearer. He ducked beneath a cracked tree limb, heard voices, his staff, could hear urgency. He halted the horse, saw a rider to one side, a lieutenant, very young, one of Wallace's men, and the man bounced close on the horse, saluted, said, "Sir! General Wallace . . . is down, sir. All I know is what Captain Luman saw, sir. The general was struck in the head, most probably by a musket ball, sir. This is a tragedy, a horrible tragedy."

Prentiss did not hesitate.

*"Is he alive?"*

The man lowered his head, feeling the impact of his own news.

"It seems unlikely, sir. We could not retrieve the general's body. The enemy was driving on our position . . . General Wallace was attempting to rally our troops."

*"You did not retrieve his body?"*

There was fury in Prentiss's words, disguising the horror of what the man was telling him.

The man was clearly shaken, Prentiss's anger not helping the man's composure.

"Sir, the enemy overran our position. There was no time."

Prentiss closed his eyes, tried not to see Wallace's face. But the man's words came to him, unavoidable, one of those jokes passed around the camps of the commanders, Wallace's surname matched of course by another of Grant's division commanders, Lew Wallace. Prentiss had laughed, as they all had, certain that in the army's post office, there was confusion among the clerks, no doubt causing *great waves of profanity*. Prentiss looked at the lieutenant, a shine on the boy's cheek, no hint of a beard.

"Who is in command there? Who is senior brigadier?"

"Colonel Tuttle, sir. He is attempting to re-form the men. But the enemy is driving us back. We are in danger of losing our own camps!"

Prentiss looked hard at the man, no expression.

"You are still in possession of your camps?"

"Well, of course, sir." The man seemed suddenly to understand the stupidity of his pride, was silent now.

Prentiss held the thought to himself. Will Wallace died the only general on this field who had his possessions, his trunk intact. I suppose . . . he would be pleased. He looked again at the lieutenant.

"Return to Colonel Tuttle. Offer him my respects and instruct him to hold his lines at all cost. If he is unable to keep the enemy from disturbing your *camps* . . . I must be informed. He is my right flank . . . he is possibly the right flank of what remains of this army."

The lieutenant was quickly away, and Prentiss pushed away the grief, had no time for that, not now. Tuttle . . . not sure about him. Met him, maybe. Hope like hell he knows how to put men into line.

He saw a pair of wagons, far back in the trees, rode that way, a clearing, and nearby, a cluster of officers, their color bearer holding the Stars and Stripes: Hurlbut. To one side, a single artillery shell came down with a monstrous splash, and he pulled up, realized he was at a pond, a place he had been before. It had been the anchoring point of his left flank, the peach orchard out beyond it, but any sense of order to that was long gone. He moved forward again, saw Hurlbut looking at him, a quick wave. He pushed the horse past the pond, the smoke giving way, and now he saw the pond itself, was surprised to see rows of wounded men on the ground, most close to the water's edge, completely surrounding the murky rust-colored water. Doctors were moving among the fallen and Prentiss saw bodies to one side covered with cloth, those who had not survived. He halted the horse, forced himself to see this. Scattered around the men were a dozen or more horses, dead and broken animals, guts and limbs smeared over the open ground, blown into pieces by the artillery. Close to the pond, one horse lay among the men, the rows of wounded arranged around it, the horse mostly intact, one leg blasted away at the hip. The horse's blood flowed out of the gaping wound directly into the pond, the water growing more red. The pond was a logical place to treat the wounded men, the doctors using the water to clean wounds. The blood of the soldiers was soaking into the muddy edges of the pond, mixing in with the blood of the horse. Close behind him, he heard a man retch, the sight too gruesome for one of his aides, and he tried to ignore that, fought the contagiousness of the nauseating sight.

He felt an uncomfortable fury, not for the fallen men, the men who had chosen to make this fight. He had always felt far more disgusted by the death of the horses, the helpless innocence, regal beasts whose service was so crucial to everything they did. He had wondered about pain, if the animal felt it as man did, if there was suffering. So often, the wounded horses seemed strangely calm, as though accepting their fate with far more peace than the soldiers. It had been like this in Mexico, and he would never admit to General Taylor or anyone else that the horses affected him with far more grief than the men, even the men in his own command. The dead, he thought, are with God. That is the human way, the thing that gives us comfort. Is there salvation for the beasts? He had fought with this question in every fight he had seen, but there was no time for that luxury now, and he slapped the reins on his own horse's neck, moved toward Hurlbut.

Stephen Hurlbut was a few years older than Prentiss, seemed always to keep his hat on, as though hiding what everyone knew to be his baldness. Prentiss knew he had much in common with Hurlbut, both men coming out of the South, settling in Illinois, both men practicing law. Unlike Prentiss, Hurlbut's military career had been brief and uneventful, serving for a time in Florida during the Second Seminole War. But Prentiss respected the man, as did Ulysses Grant, and already Hurlbut had proven himself capable, a part of Grant's victory at Fort Donelson.

Hurlbut moved out to meet him, his staff keeping back, and Prentiss saw no surprise on Hurlbut's face. Hurlbut said, "Glad you're here, Ben. We have a handful of slop out this way. The enemy is shifting to our left, and I don't have the strength here to move with them, not without losing contact with your flank."

Prentiss could hear ongoing musket fire, could tell from the direction that Hurlbut's flank was already turned. He paused, formed the words, said, "Will Wallace is down, Stephen. His staff thinks he's dead."

"Oh, dear God. We cannot replace him."

Prentiss still tried to avoid the sadness of the loss, said, "Right now, we cannot replace anybody." He paused, knew his tone had been harsh, but Hurlbut seemed to understand. Prentiss continued, "Do we know anything of Stuart's Brigade? Can they be of help?"

"I have heard nothing from Stuart, and I suspect he has chosen the wise path, and has withdrawn toward the landing. Or he has been driven back. Either way, my flank is not strong enough to hold away the enemy."

"We cannot fall back this way. It will open a direct route along the river."

Hurlbut showed his frustration now, a hard glance back to the east, said, "I already have, Ben. Had no choice. You hear that?" The thunder from distant artillery rolled past them, much of it coming east of where they were now. "I can make a stand back there, those woods that run behind this pond. It's good high ground, and thick as the devil. The enemy won't see us until they're in our faces, and we can give them a pretty tough surprise. But I don't know how many they are, or how many more are behind them. We heard from some prisoners that General

Johnston is out there himself. Johnston knows what he's doing, knows if we give way . . . well, I'd be doing the same thing he is. He gets between us and the river, and we have no place else to go."

The words came from Hurlbut in a matter-of-fact tone, and Prentiss knew he was right.

"Stephen, we have one duty here. We have to hold as long as we can. That's it. That's all we can do."

Hurlbut reacted to a new series of volleys, turned that way, then back to Prentiss.

"I have to get out that way, see to my Illinois boys on the flank. They're veterans, but not sure how much of this they can take. We break out there . . . well, I'll do what I can. Any chance we can get help from the landing?"

"You mean, Buell? Haven't heard a damn word about reinforcements. The last thing I heard from General Grant was that they were *on their way*. So far, I haven't seen a single flag from Ohio."

Hurlbut shook his head, and both men knew they had little else to discuss. The task at hand was clear to both of them.

Hurlbut said, "God be with you, Ben. Keep your head down."

Hurlbut moved back toward his staff, shouted an order, led them quickly away. Prentiss did the same, glanced back at the pond, saw more wounded coming in from the woods, men on stretchers, others walking slowly, drawn by the water in the bloody pond

H e had gone back toward the center, and the couriers came one behind the other, Hurlbut keeping him informed of what was rapidly becoming a disaster on the left. Hurlbut's lines had finally curled back, an arcing hook that had stretched out in a perpendicular formation to Prentiss's own lines. But Prentiss could not hold his center position, either, some of his units forced back away from the protection of the wagon trail. On his right, with William Wallace gone, that command seemed to unravel, no one there with Wallace's strength to hold the line. Facing a renewed assault by troops from Leonidas Polk's Corps, the protection for Prentiss's right flank soon collapsed. On the left, with the pressure from Breckinridge, and from the two bri-

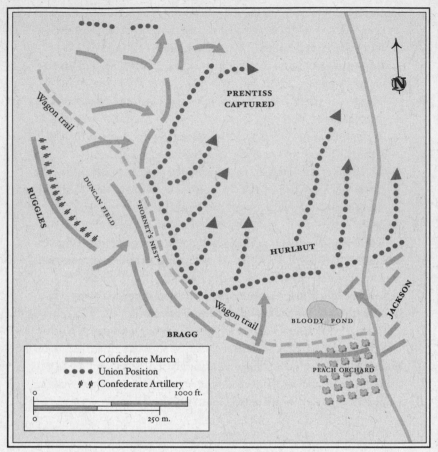

**PRENTISS COLLAPSES**

gades of Bragg's troops under Chalmers and Jackson, even Hurlbut's veterans gave way. By four o'clock, Prentiss was holding a fragile line that had virtually no flanks at all. The enemy was on three sides of him.

T he word had come from the officers that something new was happening across Duncan Field. As he rode forward, he passed by the men who had held the line, could see the weariness, the worn faces, dirt and spent powder coating every man. Many of the wounded had been taken away, but many more had not, and they mingled with the dead, with troops who had taken the worst the enemy had given them, shattered bodies, pieces of men cut apart by artillery. Others lay where the musket balls had found them, some with no weapons anywhere near them, those muskets now in the hands of others who fought close by. The line was thinned as well by those who were gone, not wounded, but panicked, some of the men enduring as much as their courage would allow, the continuous assaults finally besting them. As he moved forward, the men who were left were watching him, empty stares, no cheers, no one seeming to care that their general had come up to see what it was that had so caught the attention of those few lieutenants who still stood with their men.

He had left the horse behind, moved out toward Duncan Field with binoculars in his hand. Down to one side was a burned thicket, peppered with the charred bodies of men. Some of the grassy patches remained but not many, most of the cover obliterated by the advances of the enemy or by the swarms of musket fire that had sliced and chopped and ripped through any vegetation that rose up in the way. The officer who had led him forward had fallen back, and Prentiss looked behind him, saw the man drop down, slumping against the ragged stump of a fat tree, the man's energy gone, his duty performed. Behind Prentiss, an aide stayed close, a young sergeant who seemed to absorb with a growing terror all that lay around him. Prentiss said nothing to the man, had seen too much of this himself, and by now he didn't care if the sergeant ran away or not. Prentiss stepped forward over every kind of obstacle, was surrounded now by men with muskets, some sitting with their backs to the enemy, most in some kind of cover, stumps and broken timber, all that remained of the stands of hardwoods. Some curled up in man-made holes, dug with bayonets, seemed paralyzed with exhaustion, some of them actually sleeping.

He reached the wagon trail, saw a fence line where rebel soldiers had fallen, some bringing down the fence rails where they fell. Some of his men were using those bodies to form their own wall, leaning against stacks of rebel corpses, protected now by sacks of dead flesh. The smoke had drifted away, and Prentiss knew it had been nearly an hour since the last attack on this part of the line. But still the stink was there, artillery, spent powder, churned soil, and then, something different, unfamiliar, the astounding stench of burned corpses, those lumps of black in the charred grass, one fire that had kept thankfully to the far side of the wagon trail. To the right, the ground dipped down, and he saw bodies strewn across a creek bed, some his own men, many others the enemy, one officer in gray, the man's sword still in his hand. Prentiss was in the trail, felt no danger, no reason to duck low. The field was strewn with bodies, some moving in a slow crawl, no one on his side of the line seeming to care. He raised the glasses now, searched the far woods, what the officer had told him to see. He expected nothing at all, just an exhausted soldier's imagination, blinked through the lenses, struggled to focus his eyes through the dust and grime that clung to every part of his face, digging into his eyes. He took a breath, tried to steady the weakness in his hands, eased the glasses from side to side.

· As his eyes fought to see anything through the distant line of trees, he saw a reflection.

He perked up, focused again, scanned the woods more carefully, slowly, the reflection again, another to one side. He felt the surge of his heartbeat, could see enough of the shape to know he was looking at a cannon barrel. The questions came now . . . so close to the edge of the woods? Why would they put a battery . . . now he saw more of the reflections, the low angle of the sun revealing more brass, more barrels, some standing in the wide open. But as his eyes adjusted, picking out what he was searching for, he could see the artillery pieces spread out in a long row, stretching out into the trees, hidden there, then appearing again, another clearing farther down. There was movement as well, teams of horses, more guns brought forward, put into line. Down the line beside him, other officers were standing, staring out as he was, some of them calling to him. He did not respond, but he knew what was coming, lowered the glasses, stared for a long moment, the thought tearing through his brain, the tactic that would actually work.

The Confederate general was Daniel Ruggles, commanding a division under Braxton Bragg. Like so many of the rebel commanders, Ruggles had become infuriated with the grotesque inefficiency of pouring men across the open ground into a position no one had been able to move. Ruggles had his own answer to what his commander had not yet solved. On the southwest edge of Duncan Field, Ruggles placed artillery pieces drawn from every battery anywhere near that part of the rebel position. As Confederate troops looked on expectantly, Ruggles placed into line a total of sixty-two cannon. When they were ready, their crews completing the task of positioning and loading the pieces, Ruggles gave the order to fire.

The shower of shells erupted mostly behind the Federal lines, the men across the front doing what they had done all afternoon, keeping low, praying desperately that their makeshift cover would offer them protection. But unlike before, the cannonade did not stop, there was no halt while lines of infantry began their march across the deadly field. This time the artillery kept up their assault, and what remained of the trees were shattered, along with the men unfortunate enough to be perched anywhere close. Prentiss had ridden back to his usual position behind the line, but that was very quickly the wrong place to be. As so often happened, the gunners were aiming too high, overestimating the distance to the Federal front lines. If the men were protected by the miscalculations of the rebel gunners, behind them the supply and ammunition wagons, the ambulances, the fields of wounded men were not. In minutes the barrage from Ruggles's guns had obliterated most everything behind Prentiss's lines, including nearly every artillery battery in the Federal center. At the same time, those few staff officers who dared brave the onslaught brought Prentiss the worst news imaginable. On both sides of him, rebel troops were pushing forward their advance, closing the ring around the last stronghold of Prentiss's Division. That attack had completed the task that had begun hours before, shoving Wallace's Division and Hurlbut's men completely away. Prentiss attempted the only remedy open to him, calling forward reinforcements from behind, the desperate hope that someone could pour fresh troops, or reposition their forces to come to his aid. But the couriers either disappeared or returned with word that the rebel forces had cut off the last route open to him, ending any hope that reinforcements could reach Prentiss at all.

CLOUD FIELD
APRIL 6, 1862, 5:26 P.M.

The cannonade across Duncan Field had grown quiet, the rebel gunners understanding that what they had not yet destroyed, Prentiss had withdrawn. But from the rear, blasts of canister were ripping through those men who were pushing that way, the one road Prentiss himself was trying to reach. With his men pouring back toward him from the sudden outburst of artillery, Prentiss halted the horse. He sat motionless for a long minute, a handful of his staff still with him, no one speaking, the staff waiting for the next order he would give them. He stared at the woods, thick smoke pouring through the trees, more of his men falling back. It was not what he had seen before, no typical retreat from an overwhelming force of the enemy. These men were retreating from behind him, were running from rebel batteries that now had closed the last gap he could use that would allow any of his men to escape. He tried to feel the energy, to rally them, to put men into position, knew there were officers doing just that, doing what they were supposed to do. But he felt something else, a kind of despair he had never experienced, had never hoped to understand. More of his men were flowing into the field, some gathering near a pair of log houses, seeking shelter. But the musket fire was reaching them now, and there was no shelter, no place for any of them to hide. He closed his eyes, wiped away what he knew was in the textbooks, that what officers were taught had no meaning to him at all. The thought in his mind now was clear and vivid. If I continue this fight, I will lose every last man. We are surrounded.

He turned, the staff looking past him, seeing all that he had seen, and gradually they looked toward him, some of them understanding what the next order would be.

"Gentlemen, we have no other options. We must not sacrifice these men who have fought so well this day. I will not see them butchered."

He reached back to his saddlebags, could not avoid the shaking in his hands, the emotion tightening his throat. He pulled out a white shirt, a spare he always kept close, the officer's decorum. But there was only one act of decorum now. He looked again at the men around him, at the soldiers in the wide field, pulled his sword, attached it to his shirt, began to wave it over his head.

## CHAPTER TWENTY-EIGHT

# BAUER

SOUTHWEST OF PITTSBURG LANDING,
NEAR CLOUD FIELD
APRIL 6, 1862, 5:00 P.M.

His last shot at the enemy had come at point-blank range, a blast straight into the face of a rebel who lunged at him with a bayonet. But there was no chance to reload, the lines around him collapsing completely. Bauer had no choice but to follow the others, the entire regiment pulling away, much more of an orderly retreat than they had experienced that morning. The officers had kept them in control, the sergeants holding the lines at least partially intact, some men firing a random shot back toward the advancing rebels, a meager attempt to slow their pursuers. For a while, the rebels seemed to stay with them, more scattered volleys as both sides crushed through thickets and dense brush, stumbling over fallen limbs and the remnants of shattered trees. Along the way, they slid down into gullies, falling over the bodies of their own men, those shot down before them, some of the wounded who had been pulled back to a *safe place*. In every ravine, the men forced themselves up the far sides, becoming targets for the enemy who might be close behind, taking the time to fire a volley from the ridge behind them.

There was panic in some, always, but Bauer kept his focus on the men around him, felt the strong presence of the sergeant who pushed him from behind, Champlin keeping a tight hold on the discipline and order of the men closest to him. All along the line it had seemed to work, their retreat methodical and orderly. Bauer struggled to climb yet another ridge, struggled in soft dirt, and to the front, a lieutenant, someone Bauer had never seen, ordered them about, to turn, form a line, give the pursuing rebels a volley to slow them down. He wanted to obey, but the wave of men continued past the officer, Bauer moving with them, even Champlin understanding that the time for a neat battle formation had passed. Bauer could hear the struggles of the men around him, harsh breathing, some stopping for brief rests, then moving on, and Bauer shared the exhausted determination to keep going until they could finally reach that *safe place,* every man searching frantically for that next ridgeline, the next field, where there would be solid defensive lines, batteries of Federal artillery, a place where *order* would mean more than a young officer's desperate hopefulness. After a while, the pursuit by the rebels had seemed more distant, less dangerous, the enemy as exhausted as the men they chased, maybe more so. The blue-coated officers had rallied around that, the men on horseback who guided the lieutenants, who were now convinced that the rebels would not continue their pursuit until they re-formed, found order of their own.

The officers knew that when the enemy came again, and they would come, if the Federal troops could form that line, good high ground, protected by the brush, the enemy might repeat what they had done so often that day. They might charge blindly forward into yet another massacre. But most of the blue soldiers had seen enough of that already, and when the rebels slowed their pursuit, the men around Bauer slowed as well, more of them catching their breaths, some staying in the gullies, a desperate tumble into any creek bed that held water. Some kept to the low ground, a lesson from earlier, that in the deep ravines, rebel artillery wouldn't find them. But others, Bauer included, had learned that those same gullies could become death traps, rebel infantry pinning men down in places where escape was impossible, enfilade fire from one end of a ravine that might sweep the low ground with deadly effect.

After a lung-crushing run up a long incline, pushed still by Sergeant Champlin, Bauer had broken out into a wide field, was surprised to see the familiar formation of a camp, rows of so many tents. Rebel artillery had found the camp as well, and clearly there had been fighting in the area, some of the tents cut apart by musket balls and canister. He stopped, Champlin not pressing now, and Bauer sat on a wooden crate, noticed a headquarters flag, a Stars and Stripes flying over a larger tent. Federal artillery was positioned there, a single battery who watched the oncoming troops with a hint of panic. The artillerymen were bringing forward their teams of mules, and Bauer could see that they were less interested in seeking targets than in preserving their own guns. In short minutes, the cannons were hitched to their limbers, their single officer leading their retreat out of the field.

Bauer saw Champlin sitting as well, others taking advantage of the obvious lull, but the officers wouldn't allow much of that, and quickly, men on horses rode through the tent rows, ordering the men to their feet. Bauer looked back toward the low ground he had crossed, thick trees hiding anything beyond, watched as more of the retreating men climbed up into the open field. Some slowed to a staggering march, some were bandaged, walking wounded led by officers whose horses carried wounds of their own. Bauer stood, but his legs wouldn't go, and he leaned against a naked flagpole, glanced down at the empty musket in his hand, the image of the last dead rebel still with him.

There had been too many horrors that day, no way to erase any of that, his ears still ringing from the astounding volume of musket fire thrown across such tight spaces in never-ending waves, a steady hum and roar like some ungodly swarm of hornets. On the retreat, the men who littered the ground were nearly all in blue, and it was impossible to ignore the gut-twisting sight of so many pieces of men, severed arms and legs, corpses chopped in half by cannon fire, some shredded by canister. Many faces were unrecognizable, gone altogether, but some men were still intact, their bodies twisted in grotesque shapes, untouched but for a single wound, a barely noticeable speck of blood, a small hole in a man's head. So many had their eyes open, and Bauer could not escape that, either, the dead seeming to watch him as he moved past, the eerie notion flowing through his mind that even in death, they were seeking something, an answer, an explanation, some kind of relief he could not offer them.

As the blue troops retreated farther, there were fewer of those men, fewer pieces of bodies, fewer smears of blood on broken trees, fewer pits of smoking ground. But there were even more wounded, the men who had crawled back out of harm's way, seeking the rear of a battleground where the *rear* had ceased to be. Many of those were out there still, no one to help them. That settled into him worst of all, the men who screamed at him as he passed, but there could be no stopping, the sergeant making that profanely clear. There were no ambulances here, no stretcher bearers. He had told himself he would go back, they would all go back, that the wounded would be found, cared for. Even if the rebels got there first, Bauer felt some hope in that, had understood finally that those men were not devils after all, that surely they would not slaughter the men they had injured. With every new assault, the enemy had become much less beastly, the death of so many of them so close in front of the peach orchard and the wagon trail taking some of that aura away. The rebels had come to them in perfect waves, what became an obscene rhythm to their attacks, one line after another driven back with amazing loss. Each time, there seemed to be a perfect pause, giving time for the men in blue to reload, to prepare. Then, when the new wave approached, it happened just as before, that the rebels would walk toward them again, so close that Bauer could see their expressions, terror and ferocity, the rebels stepping closer through what remained of the brush and timber, until the men in blue wiped them away, obliterating the lines once more.

The men were starting to move, prodded by officers, the sergeants doing their jobs again. Bauer spied a canteen near a collapsed tent, begged silently that it not be empty, picked it up, felt the heft, at least half full. He drank, ignored whatever liquid it was, felt a sharp sting from something alcoholic. Champlin was there now, others who had seen his good fortune, and he offered the canteen, said only, "Liquor."

One man grabbed it from his hand, seemed not to care at all, and across the field, he saw others rummaging through the tents. Bauer looked again at the Stars and Stripes, hanging limp, and he looked around, thought of Hurlbut, the general he had never seen before, had barely heard the name. The flag hung above a headquarters tent as though nothing at all had happened, and he convinced himself it had to be Hurlbut's camp. Makes sense, he thought, since it was Hurlbut who took us out of that fight. He had no idea where General Prentiss was, had heard the astounding rumor pass through the lines that Prentiss was gone, killed perhaps, most of the rest of his division captured by the rebels. He wouldn't believe that, knew only that the 16th Wisconsin was mostly right here, familiar faces around him now, rallied by their own flag, held upright by a young man on foot, who stood now with a gathering of officers on the far edge of the field. Bauer's brain had scrambled so many of the awful images, but the men who flowed across the field were seeing what Bauer saw, seemed to move toward the flag as though by instinct. It was the training to be sure, but more now an aching need for camaraderie, for being with their own, friends seeking friends.

Through much of the fighting, there had been orders shouted at them from behind, the lieutenants who screamed out the ridiculous commands no one needed to hear. One stuck in Bauer's mind now, *Aim for the officers,* and he wondered why any lieutenant would hope for the death of his counterpart. Bauer had ignored that, as had most of the riflemen around him, Willis in particular calling back to the lieutenant that it wasn't officers who were shooting at *him.*

In the pauses between assaults, Bauer had marveled at the rebels who still came, not to fight, but to drag away friends, or hoist up the wounded, giving aid to anyone who needed it. A few of the men around him, Willis included, had no such admiration, and shots took those men down as well. But Bauer would not participate in what seemed to be a different kind of slaughter, something indecent. He couldn't avoid a surge of respect for men who cared less for themselves than for another who had fallen. Bauer had tried not to think about Willis, had no idea where he was now, what might have happened to him. He felt hesitation still, wanted to stay out in the open field, searching the faces, knew that Willis would not leave the line, that no matter Bauer calling to him, Willis had kept up his musket fire, had even ignored the captain's order to pull back. There were always those men, the ones who wanted one more look, one more kill, but the enemy was pouring toward them in a wave that, finally, they could not hold back. Damn you, Sammie, he thought. Sometimes *retreat* is the right thing to do. You can kill more of them tomorrow, but today . . . we've done all we can. He still searched the faces, many familiar, many more not, Illinois men, Indiana, Iowa. Hurlbut's men. Maybe we belong to him now. *Prentiss.* Always heard good things about him. Wish I'd have known him. Need to find out more about him, for sure. Hell of a thing to be led by a man you never see. Maybe he's out there, just like Sammie, still finding a way to fight the secesh.

He fell into a loose column, moved along a narrow rutted trail, paid more attention to the sergeant than any horseman. He looked at the others around him, the ones following the flag, a hundred or more from the 16th, asked himself, how many are we now? How many ran like hell this morning? Well, you did, for one. He suddenly thought of the loudmouth, Patterson, shot down in the first minutes of the dawn. Where would he be now? He wouldn't have lasted a single minute on the line out here. Good thing Colonel Allen was able to gather us up, send us back out there, joining up with General Hurlbut's men. I guess it was a good thing. *Allen.* Dammit, him too. He had seen the colonel go down, a hard wound that knocked Allen from his horse, a shower of musket balls that killed yet another horse beneath him. The colonel had been treated, bandaged, had shouted down a doctor who had tried to have him hauled back behind the lines. But the wound was bad, and Allen had finally succumbed to the weakness of that, was finally taken away on a stretcher. Dead? Bauer didn't want to think of that, either. He tried to focus on the backs of the men who walked in front of him, wished now he could have stayed back, still wanted to find Willis. Come on, Sammie. You're already a hero. To me anyway. You're a better soldier than I am, for certain . . . but there's a time to give it up. The damn secesh were just too many, and if General Prentiss is gone, and Colonel Allen . . . we didn't have a choice but to move it holus-bolus out of there.

"Let's move, soldier!"

The order came from one side, a lieutenant standing against a tree, seeming to hold himself up. The man wore the insignia of the 41st Illinois, the unit that had been to the right of the 16th Wisconsin. Behind Bauer, a man spoke up, obviously familiar with the officer.

"Where we headin', sir? Where they leadin' us?"

"Only place left, Private. Pittsburg Landing."

PITTSBURG LANDING
APRIL 6, 1862, 6:00 P.M.


Bauer marched up onto the flat high ground at the landing with openmouthed marvel. The hustle of activity was noisy and chaotic, the plain above the landing surging with men and wagons, some giving way to a column of artillery pieces. The Wisconsin men were pulled into line between rows of cannon, orders coming that they were to plant themselves in a brushy ridgeline, which curved out away from the landing, a sweeping S that bordered low ground on both sides. Despite the order, Bauer moved out of line, stood in awe, watching cannons unlimbered, teams of horses and mules worked with ruthless efficiency by the men who were organizing what seemed to be one solid row of artillery. He glanced out toward the river, saw a column of blue troops marching up from the water's edge, could see the smoke from the transports, as familiar now as it had been weeks before. But the troops he saw wore clean uniforms, were led by men with fresh horses, officers wearing a look of smug confidence, and Bauer realized through the fog in his brain, these men haven't fought anybody. They haven't even seen the enemy. Not one of those officers has had his horse shot out from under him. But . . . who are they?

The lieutenants were moving the Wisconsin men out past the gathering line of artillery, marching them farther out on the snaking ridge. Bauer heard the order, moved that way, saw the ground in front of the artillery falling steeply away to a rough thicket below, what looked to be a wide, swampy bog. He felt a hand on his shoulder, pulling him along, and he followed, slow automatic steps, saw Champlin, a hoarse bark of a command, the slower men gathering together along the crest of the ridge. Directly behind them, the artillery continued to pull into line, more officers, loud, impatient commands. Champlin released him, moved back to gather up those who had staggered to a halt, and Bauer took advantage, knelt down, heard an officer shout out to the men something about loading their muskets, once more, those horrible words . . . *get ready to receive the enemy.* He felt for his cartridge box, maybe a third full, gave that little thought, the fog in his brain taking over, the end of the march turning his legs to jelly, and the rest of him as well. He stared out to the road that came up from the landing, the column of fresh troops, the word coming to him, *reinforcements.* But there was no excitement in that, no sense of relief. You're no better than we are, he thought. He wanted to say it, to leave the ridgeline, move back out through the wheels of the cannons, to walk up to the closest officer he saw, a major sitting high on his horse, a ridiculous plume in the man's hat. You'll be the first one they shoot, you stupid . . . but the thought drifted away, no energy left for that kind of anger.

He looked to his musket, blinked through a desperate need for sleep, felt a hard growl of hunger, a cavernous hole in his stomach, had not even thought of food. Most of the 16th was out on the ridge now, but still others came out from the trail, marching up the road toward him, filthy, ragged, exhausted. Some just stopped, as he had, watched the procession of these clean new troops, some using their last bit of strength to shout out curses and ridicule, insults for their clean uniforms, for the shine on their muskets. Bauer was too tired to join in, looked again to the major, the man waving his troops along the roadway with perfect confidence. The major turned now, only a few feet from Bauer, seemed to catch Bauer's stare, looked at him with curiosity. He smiled now, odd, unnerving, and Bauer had no energy to respond, the training too ingrained, that it was not his place to respond at all. He studied the man with the last bit of focus he had left, saw the gold oak leaf on the man's shoulder. But the hat caught his eye again, the enormous idiotic feather, and Bauer saw the insignia of Ohio. The major spoke to him now, a blur of words Bauer tried to sort through: "It's all over for you boys. Nothing to worry about. General Buell's pulling your bacon out of the fire."

Behind Bauer, a voice.

"Only fire around here is the one we fed the enemy. Hate to see you mess up that fine hat, sir."

It was Willis.

The major sneered at the insult, spurred his horse, made a show of raising the hat for his own men. Bauer's brain cleared, a burst of joy, and he spun around, saw Willis moving along with the last group of Wisconsin men. Willis saw him now, a weary smile.

"Well, Dutchie, I knew they wouldn't catch *you*. You run faster'n any rabbit I ever saw."

"Sammie . . . where you been? Looked all over hell for you."

"Well, that's where I was. Used up a half-dozen muskets fightin' my way out. Would ya look at these parade ground boys, now? Gotta be a regiment. One single damn regiment. Like that's all we need to scare those secesh clear out of this country. What kind of fools are they sending us?"

"Watch that mouth, Private."

Bauer saw the officer on horseback, Major Reynolds, one of Colonel Allen's most senior adjutants. Willis said, "Sorry, sir. Didn't mean no disrespect. I hear you're in charge of us boys now, Major."

Reynolds nodded, didn't seem pleased about that, said, "Colonel Allen, Colonel Fairchild, both wounded pretty bad. Until the army tells me any different, the 16th is under my command."

Some of the Wisconsin men had heard Reynolds, some gathering closer, the nearest lieutenant silencing the others. Reynolds was popular with the men, but seemed to have a serious conflict with Allen that inspired a raft of rumors that Reynolds was set to be court-martialed. Bauer looked up at him, knew nothing about any of that, and right now, he didn't care. At least he knew who was in command. Bauer felt the words come out in a dreamlike mumble.

"We're ready to go again, sir."

"I doubt that, Private." Behind Reynolds, the rumbling din of the artillery teams and more of the gathering of troops was flooding Bauer's brain, driving him even closer to dropping down right where he stood. Reynolds seemed to notice that in all of his men. He raised his voice now, said, "You boys move out there, and settle in right along that ridge. The enemy's still out there, and we haven't done a damn thing to stop their advance. These Ohio boys with their clean long johns are supposed to be some kind of salvation for us, but there aren't enough of them to matter, not yet anyway. You boys find whatever cover you can, and stay just back of the crest. Check your muskets. If the enemy comes at us, it'll be right up these steep hills. That's all you need to think about, for now. Dark in an hour or so. Won't much happen after that. Just remember . . . aim low."

## CHAPTER TWENTY-NINE

# HARRIS

SOUTH OF PITTSBURG LANDING,
SOUTH SIDE OF DILL BRANCH
APRIL 6, 1862, 5:30 P.M.

The governor had found Bragg, the corps commander seeming to do what he could to fill the awful void caused by the death of Johnston. With the surrender of Prentiss, Bragg turned his attention to the right, where his own brigade commanders, Chalmers and Jackson, continued to press onward toward the ultimate goal, Pittsburg Landing.

Harris rode with Bragg's staff now, knew his orders from Beauregard had suggested that the governor keep in motion, riding back and forth from the field to Beauregard's headquarters to report on the successful progress close to the river. Though Harris carried the grief of Johnston's death with him still, he knew that obedience to the army's new commander was a responsibility he had to accept. But riding back across the tangle of woods and roadways had no appeal to him now, not after seeing Beauregard's cavalier attitude about the death of Beauregard's superior, and Harris's friend.

More of Beauregard's considerable staff had taken to their horses, and Harris had to respect that the army's new commander was at least seeking information from every part of the field, and would certainly use that information to maneuver the army into the best position he could

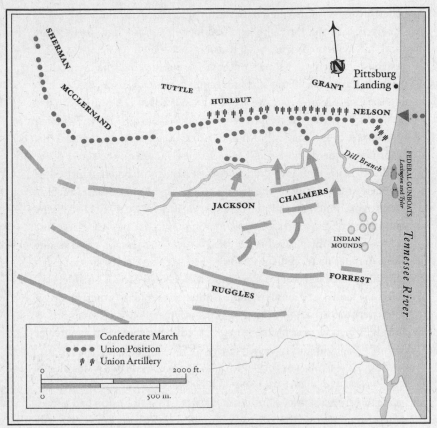

**GRANT'S LAST LINE OF DEFENSE**

to finish the day's work. The disposition of the army was still a confused and chaotic mess, but there were exceptions, and with Prentiss's final collapse, Hardee had taken advantage by driving his troops even closer to Pittsburg Landing on the left flank, pushing back the Federal forces who still tried to maintain some cohesion. When Hardee's men finally confronted what Hardee concluded was an unassailable line of Sherman's beleaguered defenders, he was within a half mile of Pittsburg Landing. With Prentiss gone from the center, Polk, now commanding a complete mishmash of units from every corps on the field, brought his troops forward as well, pushing through the heavy woods with Hardee's men, closing the arc that seemed destined to accomplish Johnston's cherished goal of driving Grant's army into the river. The last piece of that puzzle lay on the right, as it had for most of the day. There Bragg had shifted his command, but it took Bragg a good hour before he could establish himself on that part of the field, and the chaos he found there played straight into Bragg's furious temperament for discipline.

The Confederate troops who had routed Hurlbut's Division, who had crushed Prentiss's left flank, were now mostly bogged down, whether exhausted, or too smitten with their own success. As had happened that morning, some of those soldiers had focused more on the spoils of the Federal camps than they did on whatever Federal troops might still be to their front. Many of the troops tossed their smoothbore muskets away, replacing them with the far superior Federal weapons, and taking advantage of the stores of fresh ammunition. As they rode into the camps of what must have been Hurlbut's regiments, Harris could see the men plundering more than weapons. Most of these men had not eaten anything since well before dawn, and the enemy's collapse had left behind the kinds of rations few of the Confederate soldiers could ignore. If they were too tired now to load up on booty, many of Bragg's and Breckinridge's men were definitely going to feed themselves, a much greater priority than pursuing a beaten enemy.

Though Harris knew very little of tactical maneuvering, it was plainly obvious that, no matter the pause in their bloody advances, the Confederate forces had hemmed in Grant's army exactly as Johnston had hoped. There was only one thing left to accomplish, and with Bragg furiously reassembling whatever units he could gather, putting them back into line for the last great push northward, Harris shared the thrilling exuberance that, before this day was over, Bragg would drive his forces straight into Grant's last stronghold.

T he tents were mostly in shambles, and Harris absorbed all he could see, trunks of the officers, every kind of utensil for cooking, coffeepots and mounds of tin plates. The weapons were there, but not many, Bragg's men grabbing up most of the discarded swords and knives. Harris was shocked to see bodies as well, scolded himself for that, knew that should have been no surprise at all. There had been talk from some of the troops, reckless boasting that Harris could not help overhear, how any wounded Yankee would be cut to pieces where he lay, that there were sick men in the tents who would die in their own blankets. With his usual furious bombast, Bragg had put a stop to that wherever he could, but still, Harris could see the blood-soaked blue coats, an outstretched arm, a few Yankee soldiers cut down while still in their tents. Harris moved close behind Bragg, prepared to do whatever Bragg asked of him, but so far, Bragg had spent his energy gathering up the wayward troops, his staff and subordinate officers pulling every available man back into some kind of formation. Flags and unit designations meant very little now. The most urgent job at hand was to put a hard advance together before they ran out of daylight. Even Bragg seemed to have a tolerance for looting, as long as the primary mission was accomplished first. Once Grant's sword was in his hands, Bragg had made it clear to the men he pulled together that the spoils of this fight would be theirs for the taking.

They moved now into woods, and Harris saw men doing what Bragg had ordered, forming up their lines, officers shouting men into place. Out front, there was still musket fire, but it was slow, inconsistent, pockets of Federal troops dueling with the farthest advance of Bragg's men. Bragg had given Harris a map, seemed to realize that the governor might be more useful in a less military role, something Harris had no problem with at all. Bragg pulled up now, blind woods to the front, the congested ground falling away to one side. The men were mostly silent, and it wasn't all from exhaustion. They seemed to know what Bragg was about to do. Bragg leaned close to Harris, held out his hand.

"The map, Governor."

Harris obliged, the worn paper unrolled in Bragg's hands, and Bragg looked behind him, appraised the gathering of troops. He glanced at Harris now, the same scowl Bragg seemed to wear no matter what was going on around him.

"Dill Branch. It's wider than most of these infernal creeks, but it's the last low place before we reach the landing."

He looked to the side, waved one of the aides closer.

"Captain, you will locate General Chalmers with all haste. He holds the position closest to the river. Insist in the strongest terms that he press forward. Every movement must be forward! You hear me? *Forward!*"

"Yes, sir!"

Bragg looked to another of his aides, a young lieutenant, said, "Go to General Jackson, and give him the same order! If their flanks are in contact with each other, more the better. If not, that cannot be an impediment." Bragg looked at the map again, nodded, as though confirming his order to himself. "Both brigades must push through the low ground to their front and assault the enemy's position. The Yankees are confused and panicked and will give way in short order. I will order General Withers and General Ruggles and every other unit I can send their way, to support their assault as rapidly as possible. Now go!"

The two aides saluted, moved out together into thick woods, disappeared quickly. Bragg looked toward Harris, returned the map, and the governor was surprised to see a hint of a smile.

"It is close, Mr. Harris. Very close. Your friend General Johnston predicted we would be triumphant here, and I will make it so."

They charged down through the muck and swampy grass, slow going in the face of what now seemed to be a powerful wall of Federal artillery. The musket fire came as well, most of it from a long, steep rise, Federal infantry protected by sharp ridges the Confederate troops could only hope to climb. The ground was far steeper here than most of the rugged terrain Chalmers and Jackson had already conquered, high embankments that required their men to use both hands, keep flat to the sloping ground, while their muskets were passed up from the men behind them. But even then, the targets above them were few, protected by the angle of the ground.

Where it flowed into the river, Dill Branch yawned wide, a flat, soggy swamp, and there the Federal gunboats slipped into position, firing at anything that dared cross the open ground. The noise from those shells was as terrifying for Bragg's men as it had been for Prentiss's hours before, some of the Confederates unable to keep their courage, falling back from any sight of the boats themselves. Farther inland, Dill Branch made a sweeping curve, hiding the men from the big guns, and it was soon apparent to Bragg and his officers that as long as the men kept away from the river's edge, the gunboats could do very little damage at all. The sounds were terrifying to be sure, but the angle of the tall riverbank meant that the guns would have to fire higher still, and so most of their shells flew far above and beyond Bragg's men. No matter the fear that infected some, the troops who hugged the steep hillside just below Pittsburg Landing understood quickly that the greatest challenge to their advance would not come from the heavy artillery on the river. On the ridges above them, hidden in thickets, or lined up along the many wooded ridgelines, Federal artillery was pouring out a blistering wave of shot and shell, canister and grapeshot, keeping Bragg's men mostly pinned down. But Bragg made good on his promise, and to the south, more of his troops were pushing their way forward, nothing at all to slow their progress but the miserable lay of the land. As long as they kept out of direct sight of the gunboats, there was little to stop a growing number of Confederate troops from adding to their final surge across the boggy creek.

As Harris rode hard with Bragg, shifting and directing the flow of men toward the fight, they began to see a radical change in the larger units. Despite Bragg's aides spreading his order for any brigade or regimental commanders to drive northward, those gatherings of troops suddenly seemed to stop, many of them actually pulling back. It was not from anything the enemy was doing, no shelling reaching them in the thick woods, nothing violent to halt their progress. It was an order from Beauregard.

Harris had been sent to General Ruggles, carrying Bragg's order that Ruggles's Division advance with as much speed as possible. But Ruggles wasn't advancing at all, and Harris could see from the expression on the general's face that something was very wrong. Harris halted the horse, saw another officer close beside Ruggles, a colonel, slightly familiar, from Beauregard's staff. The man carried an expression of perfect arrogance, the smugness of a man who knows he carries *authority*. Ruggles glanced toward Harris, but Harris saw little of the man's furious temperament, the man's shoulders slumped as he sat limply in the saddle. Ruggles said, "Governor, I assume you have come from General Bragg?"

Harris could not look away from the other officer, said, "Yes, sir. The general offers his respects and orders you to advance your troops at the double-quick. General Bragg believes that one last push can overcome the batteries the enemy has placed in our path, and their infantry is badly beaten and will not resist us for long." He paused, still drawn by the smirk on the colonel's face. Harris felt uneasy, but he had a job to do, had to deliver the order as Bragg had instructed him. "Sir, General Bragg insists that the additional strength from your forces combined with any-one else you may gather . . . will end this day in our favor. General Bragg also requests in the strongest terms that you send a courier to General Breckinridge and communicate the urgency of moving whatever forces he can put into motion, to support your efforts. I must admit, I have never seen General Bragg so animated . . . in such a positive fashion."

Beauregard's staff officer seemed to wait patiently for his moment, politely allowing the governor to deliver his message. He spoke up now, soft and fluid, the familiar smoothness of a politician.

"Governor Harris, with all respects to you, I bring orders from Gen-eral Beauregard that this day's fighting has already been concluded, by his order."

Ruggles still looked at Harris, said, "You must return to General Bragg. He must be informed of this. Surely the general expects me to obey his orders, but I cannot disobey General Beauregard."

Harris was enormously confused, felt prickly anger toward the colo-nel, who reminded him too much of those men in Nashville whose ef-forts suited only themselves. Harris said, "You bring this order from General Beauregard? I assure you, sir, this day is hardly *concluded*. There is considerable fighting taking place to the north, as you can hear. If I may suggest, perhaps you should return to headquarters and inform General Beauregard how close this affair has become. General Bragg is in position to drive straight into Pittsburg Landing!" Harris's words seemed to have no effect on the colonel's smug self-assurance, and Har-ris had an uneasy thought now, was suddenly suspicious.

"May I ask, colonel, who you are?"

The man seemed surprised at the question.

"Certainly, Governor. I am Colonel Augustin, one of General Beaure-gard's senior adjutants. We have met before. But that is hardly the im-portant issue here. The general has issued an order that is being delivered to every commander in every part of the field, that their forces are to withdraw out of range of the guns of the enemy, and seek whatever shel-ter they may find, presumably in the very camps the enemy has abandoned. The enemy has generously graced us with substantial amounts of ammunition and rations, and our men can find adequate shelter in the enemy's own tents! General Beauregard is confident that his officers can use this evening to sort through their commands."

"But . . . *why*?"

It was a question only a civilian could ask, and the colonel looked at Ruggles now, smiled.

"The governor is not accustomed to following orders. I suppose that is to be expected. However, General Ruggles, you are. As is General Bragg." He looked again at Harris. "Governor, I must admit to some surprise at your reaction. I am aware that you have been near the front lines most of this day. Surely you have observed how completely we have bested the enemy. This is a day of triumph. But this army has done all it can for this day. General Beauregard is deeply concerned by the number of stragglers he has seen near his headquarters, and he is very well aware, as are you, sir, that this army is in something of a tangle. We must reorganize as quickly as possible on the morrow, and then we shall complete the job. If I may dare to quote General Beauregard, upon issuing his orders to those of us in the saddle, the general stated with great pleasure that we have General Grant right where we want him. I should think you would be greatly pleased, Governor. Your friendship with General Johnston is well known. Is this not the most positive result we could have hoped for?"

Harris would not think of Johnston, that effort made simpler by the bursting disgust he felt for this colonel. He thought of Bragg, could still hear the firing close to Pittsburg Landing.

"I must report this . . . to General Bragg. This is—"

"This is General Beauregard's order, Governor. If you wish to convey that order to General Bragg yourself, that would be appreciated. However, I shall accompany you. I am under the strictest of orders to communicate the general's disengagement order to every senior commander I can locate, and to be sure they pass that order along to their subordinates."

Harris saw a glare from Ruggles, so much like Bragg. Ruggles pointed skyward now, said, "Colonel, we have a full hour of daylight still to come. Does the general not wish us to complete this task . . . today?"

Augustin smiled, shook his head.

"I do not question the general's orders. Nor should you. Now, excuse me, gentlemen. I must continue my mission. Governor, shall we ride? We must make every effort to communicate this order to those men who are engaged up that way. That firing must cease."

Ruggles looked at Harris, seemed struck speechless. After a long moment, he said, "Governor, you must return to General Bragg. He must certainly be questioning why I am not moving up in support. I do not envy you the task."

The colonel raised his hat, a salute, as though he were in a parade.

"General! Governor! You seem to feel that this is some sort of tragedy! I assure you, as will General Beauregard . . . this is a glorious day! We have a victory here, and if you are concerned about proper recognition, I am quite certain General Beauregard is well aware of your accomplishments here! Tomorrow will be General Grant's final day in the field. The general is certain of that! A celebration is in order!" Augustin lowered his voice, as though passing along a privileged secret. "If I may, gentlemen . . . as I left our headquarters, I heard General Beauregard making arrangements to communicate this magnificent news by wire to President Davis. Soon this entire nation will know of our triumph!"

## CHAPTER THIRTY

# GRANT

PITTSBURG LANDING
APRIL 6, 1862, 6:00 P.M.

He watched as they came ashore, men moving with purpose, but not nearly fast enough to suit Grant. He had chafed at that kind of slowness all afternoon, but Buell's men had not been the worst offenders. By late morning, Grant's order had gone back to Crump's Landing for Lew Wallace to put his division into rapid motion, to march along the road closest the river, adding his seven thousand men to a fight that had clearly gone the way of the enemy. Grant could only expect that Wallace would do exactly that. He could vividly recall the man's assurances from their meeting early that morning that Wallace's Division was prepared to move at the first order they received. The distance between the two landings was less than ten miles, and given the urgency of Grant's order, he had fully expected Wallace to make that march in no more than two hours. Yet by early afternoon there was no sign that Wallace was anywhere near Pittsburg at all.

For much of the late morning and early afternoon, Grant had ridden close to some of the most furious fighting, engaging in short meetings with Sherman, Prentiss, Hurlbut, and any other commander whose men were facing what could only be interpreted as bloody repulses in nearly every quarter of the field. Thus Wallace's failure to appear had been that much more infuriating, especially since Grant had expected Wallace to appear on the right flank close to Pittsburg, exactly where Sherman's men were being driven back and exactly where a fresh division of blue troops was most required. By mid-afternoon, Grant's fury with Wallace's absence had become absolute. Grant could only dispatch two more of his senior staff to ride northward, to find out just how long it would take those critical troops to reach the field. By late afternoon, with most of Grant's army falling back on itself around Pittsburg Landing, Wallace had still not appeared. By then, Grant had too many problems close at hand, was faced with too many retreating men to organize, and the mammoth task of organizing some kind of defensive position that would prevent the rebels from driving straight into his last remaining strong point at the landing itself. All he could hope for was that Wallace might arrive in time to be of some assistance.

P ittsburg Landing was as congested as it had ever been, but Grant was at least able to organize a line of artillery to face the draws and rough country where the enemy's advance seemed most certain. The task had fallen to Colonel Joseph Webster, Grant's chief of artillery, and Webster had performed with the kind of speed and efficiency Grant had hoped to find in all of his subordinates. On the high plain that made up the landing itself, Webster had gathered every available artillery piece, and had positioned those guns in a solid line, their crews ordered to prepare for the enemy's assault certain to come from the south, the boggy ground closest to the river. Already the collapse of the left flank had brought most of the infantry from the left back toward the landing, and Grant had ordered them put into line, that any man who was still equipped to fight be put into place in support of the artillery, spread out on the many wooded ridgelines that snaked along the swamps fed by Dill Branch.

To the west, Sherman and McClernand had continued to strengthen their positions, so much so that the enemy had mostly halted their attacks. It was obvious to anyone at Pittsburg that the greatest efforts by the rebels were now coming from the south. Grant knew of Prentiss's collapse, and the talk had reached him of Prentiss's capture, and the loss of what might be as many as three thousand men. Grant had no real facts about Prentiss's whereabouts, or even if the man was alive. But Prentiss's failure had provided the Federal forces with a magnificent gift, the gift of time. Though the flanks protecting Prentiss on both sides had given way, Prentiss's Division had held back the rebel advances for several precious hours, time that Grant's commanders had used to shore up and improve their lines in a tight arc around the landing. Grant had not yet considered who Prentiss's replacement might be. Until the ragged remains of his army could be sorted out, Grant had no way of knowing just how much of Prentiss's Sixth Division still existed.

The tide of fugitives had continued to flood back toward the river, thousands of men carrying the disease of panic and hopelessness. Every transport boat, every supply boat had been met with the same challenge, each one settling against the wharf, only to confront a violent attempt by hordes of men to force their way aboard the vessel, as though that boat would carry them to some other place, some place where there was no enemy to pursue them. Grant had tried to rally pockets of those men himself, with no more success than any other officer. As the enormous crowds of men packed along the bluffs of the river, their desperation forced them farther, some taking hold of timbers or anything else that would float, a feeble and usually hopeless attempt to cross the river on their own. Grant had heard of that as well, dozens of men swept away by the current, presumed drowned, their final escape.

As the daylight began to fade, Grant had seen the vanguard of Don Carlos Buell's men arriving at the landing. The march by Nelson's Division had finally brought them opposite Pittsburg, and the smaller transports had begun to ferry those men across. The progress of the crossing was agonizingly slow, made more hazardous by the mobs that awaited the boats. Nelson's men had employed the bayonet, and when the troops could finally push their way ashore, they were met with the same cries the sailors had heard all day, that any man who joined this fight was doomed, that slaughter would be their reward. To Nelson's credit, most of his men pushed past that, their officers keeping them focused on the job at hand. The imminent danger was close at hand, and Grant made certain that the fresh troops were put into place to hold the line alongside Webster's artillery.

————

He lit another cigar, watched as Nelson's men thickened their lines overlooking the deep gash south of the landing that spread out into the swampy ground split by Dill Branch. The fight there had already begun, rebel artillery first: probing, aimless shots that did very little harm. The infantry had come then, and Grant had seen for himself that the ground the rebels had to cross would be a disastrous advance in the face of the strength he had assembled there. But still they came, a surge of troops that rolled toward the massive power of Webster's guns with that same yell that the enemy seemed to bring with them into every fight. But this rebel yell was muffled, not only by the lay of the land, with most of those men far down in the broad expanse of swampy bottom, but drowned out as well by Grant's own guns, and the thunderous firing from the gunboats on the river.

He rode nervously, ignored the pain in his leg. He tried to hear anything from the west, if the rebels were driving into Sherman the way they were pressing the defenses close to the river, but Sherman's lines were mostly quiet, and Grant watched the sun, settling far into the trees, knew that if the rebels did not come very soon, they would likely have to halt and await the new dawn. That was a luxury he could not yet enjoy, the sun seemingly frozen in place, no darkness coming for an hour at least. He chewed the cigar, moved the horse again toward Webster's guns, then held back, knew that no matter his nervousness, he had to let Webster be, no orders necessary, the artillery commander understanding exactly what he had to do. From a distance, Grant watched the colonel revealing his own nervousness, pacing his horse back and forth along his gathered assembly of guns, every variety, every size. Some of those gunners had already begun seeking the targets that stubbornly shoved toward them from the hidden ridgelines in the south.

Grant watched the thick smoke flowing out toward the river, saw a line of troops fire a volley, someone making out targets on their own, the first surge of rebel infantry close enough to be seen. Grant wanted to ride forward, to see that himself, couldn't avoid a strange admiration for those men making the effort to do what so many of his own troops had feared, the effort that had succeeded for most of the day, that had driven a disgusting number of his men away from the field in utter panic. He didn't know yet the casualty counts, assumed he would not know for many days, but already the officers who had come back to him reported losses to both sides that were staggering. But, so far, the collapse of his lines had given Grant a great advantage. With the enemy's successes, Grant's lines were now compacted, tightly woven into a much more powerful defense, with interior lines of communication and supply, allowing orders and materiel to flow to any point that had the most urgent need. He could not help thinking of a book he had read, knew that the author was out there, William Hardee. Hardee would know better than anyone on the field that no matter the earlier defeats, Grant's position had become much stronger, the ground now favoring the defender. But still . . . Grant could not escape the tension. Other than Prentiss, not one of Grant's division commanders had shown they could hold back the enemy's relentless advances, and for the rebels to push across the low ground of Dill Branch would require a relentless attack indeed.

Grant moved closer to the big guns, his ears ringing from the firing. He tried to see his infantry, saw a thick line of fresh uniforms, Nelson's men, firing down toward the ground out below them. Above Grant the whistle of musket balls passed high, the enemy close enough to return fire, and Grant felt the certainty of what they faced, that whoever was out there, whoever commanded those men had to know that this was their last, best opportunity to shatter the defenses that protected Pittsburg Landing. They could do it, he thought, and he glanced around, felt enormously guilty for believing that. Already the new recruits that made up so much of his army had succumbed to that rabble, led by the rebel officers who had betrayed their flag, who dared to believe they could destroy this nation by first destroying its army. He tossed the spent cigar to one side, focused on the smoke and the sounds of the fight, felt the gut-twisting anxiety of the moment. He stared hard at the backs of his own troops, and Nelson's, half expecting that horrible sight, any one of them suddenly leaping to his feet and running away, joining the uncontrollable mob at the river's edge. It was the most horrifying sight of a horrifying day, those men who had already brought shame to themselves, to their general, to their country. They were still there, thousands of them, no officer able to encourage more than a handful to rejoin the fight. He had kept away the thoughts of what to do with them, if anything could be done at all. Grant focused now on the men out on the ridgelines, hidden by the smoke of their own muskets, the men still fighting, who kept their courage, who had absorbed a vicious, bloody day and still kept their ground. As the sunlight faded, he felt a wave of tearful emotion, clenched his fists, spoke aloud, his words swept away by the growing roar of the fight.

"Hold on, men. For God's sake. You have to hold. Today, this is all we have left. It's my last line."

He stayed in place, nowhere else to go, a glance at the darkening sky. And then, the firing seemed to slow, the smoke clearing, the big guns gradually quieting. The infantry quieted as well, some scattered musket fire, single pops far out in the woods, a few more out to the right. Men began to call out now, some toward the enemy, others just cheering, as though something glorious was happening. He eased the horse forward, close to Webster, who noticed him now, shouted out toward his gunners.

"Be ready! There's time yet! They'll be coming back! Clean those barrels! Prepare to reload!"

The order was repeated all along the line, his men doing their job, the big guns made ready again. Out on the ridgelines, the infantrymen checked their muskets, sergeants and officers keeping the lines together. For a long moment, there was no sound at all, just the agonizing anticipation, men keeping to their positions, his troops preparing for what they had seen all day long, awaiting yet another screaming wave of rebels crushing themselves into anything the Federal troops could throw in their way. With daylight still hanging over them, the men in blue stared out through the darkening trees, searching for a new surge of movement in the swamps below, some focused farther out on the brush across distant ridgelines, waiting for the next wave, the next assault. But it never came.

## CHAPTER THIRTY-ONE

# SEELEY

For most of the day, he had watched the great assaults commence while perched up on horseback, standing in line with the rest of Forrest's men. But their job was simply to keep to the rear, none of the corps commanders seeking out Forrest's cavalry, as though the infantry and artillery were perfectly adequate for the job. From Seeley's perspective, the series of attacks had seemed like thin waves, repeated assaults that washed noisily into the Federal center, mostly Polk and Bragg launching their troops into dense thickets of brush. But that brush had proven to be a far stronger wall of Federal power than the generals had realized, and the effects, particularly on Bragg's men, had been clear enough. Throughout the day, Colonel Forrest mostly chafed impatiently, a growling temper Seeley had seen before. With nowhere in particular to go, and none of the senior commanders paying much attention to Forrest at all, the horsemen had spent most of the afternoon maneuvering through various parts of the field, seeking out opportunity or crisis, or finding at least one general who might authorize Forrest's cavalry to do their own kind of work.

The horsemen shared their colonel's frustration, especially as they witnessed the slaughter of too many lines of infantry. To his own men, Forrest preached what he saw to be obvious, that his horsemen could accomplish far more than the foot soldiers, that rapidly moving cavalry could slice a gap through the stubborn enemy defenses, and possibly re-create the chaos that had swept through the Federal lines that morning. But no matter. No one Forrest could find would authorize anything of the sort. After suffering through hours of furious frustration, Forrest had finally seen enough, and he accepted the responsibility for leading his men all by himself, orders or not. Seeley had been a part of that, the horsemen launching a screaming attack alongside the infantry of Benjamin Cheatham's Brigade, part of Leonidas Polk's Corps. The charge had punched into the Federal position to the left of the ground where Prentiss had eventually offered his surrender, but Forrest could take no credit for Prentiss's collapse. Whether any general besides Cheatham even noticed, the cavalry charge had proven as frustratingly ineffective as most of the piecemeal attacks made by the infantry. The difficulty came mostly from the ground itself, soft earth giving way to mud and thickets that halted the horsemen far more effectively than anything the Federals had thrown in their way. Worse, Federal artillery batteries had observed the cavalry attack rolling into motion, and the horsemen had endured punishment from guns they could not even see. Though one Federal battery had fallen into Forrest's hands, that was, after all, not their primary goal. Scavenging for Federal equipment was hardly satisfactory to the ambitions of their colonel, and unless they could carry a strong position and hold on to it, thus giving serious aid to their beleaguered infantry, the horsemen were too vulnerable to the enemy's big guns to slog their way slowly forward through deepening muck.

For the rest of the afternoon, the cavalry had pushed and probed, mostly toward the river, where the activity remained hottest. Even there, the opportunity for driving some attack into a vulnerable Federal position had been thwarted by the ridiculous difficulty of the ground, and then by the setting of the sun. But with darkness came opportunity, and once more Forrest was inspired to take responsibility for issuing his own order. Near the day's end, the cavalry officers had observed the army's bizarre withdrawal, Beauregard's order obeyed by every other commander on that part of the field. To Forrest and his men, what seemed at first to be a mystery soon began to feel like someone had backed away from a fight that was all in their favor. There was no counterattack from the Federal position, no sudden burst of reinforcements driving the army back from the captured Federal campgrounds. Like so many of the other field commanders, Forrest had driven closer to the river believing the final fight would come there, that with one rapid shove, the Federal army could be driven hard to the swamps to the north, or, as had happened to Prentiss, once the bluecoats were surrounded, they would have no alternative but surrender. It was there, close to Bragg's final assault, that the cavalry had heard the devastating news that General Johnston was dead. Every effort had been made to keep that news from the troops, but no army keeps its most brutal secrets for long, and that rumor was seeping through most of the units near the river. From all that Forrest could see, it was clear that Beauregard was giving the orders, a graphic confirmation of the rumor. Still, Forrest had kept his men in motion, had tried to avoid the retreating infantry, men whose glorious victory seemed to have been stripped away from them by what must have been a storm of confusion at the army's highest levels. All through the fields south of Dill Branch, Forrest had rejected this new rumor, passed hotly between regimental commanders, that somewhere back there, *a general* had lost his nerve. All Forrest could do was keep his men moving forward, avoiding any kind of contact with the enemy, thus obeying the order.

But the cavalry's great advantage was mobility, and the one advantage of the miserable geography was that a scouting party could move close to their enemy and, if they were cautious, remain undetected. And so there would be another mission that no one had authorized, another responsibility that would fall solely on Nathan Bedford Forrest. No one among his command questioned the wisdom of that, and every man seemed eager to volunteer, to see firsthand just what was happening along the Federal position. The last great fight had broken off very close to the river, just south of Pittsburg Landing. To Forrest and his officers, that seemed to be the most logical place for the cavalry to go. Though some of his officers made meager suggestions that word should be sent back to someone higher up the chain of command, informing them just what they were planning to do, Forrest had no intention of making any noise, either toward the enemy or anyone in the rear. For now, all he wanted to do was see what the enemy was up to. And besides, with the darkness fully over the field, it was unlikely any of his couriers would have the first notion just where any of those generals might be.

## SOUTH OF DILL BRANCH
## APRIL 6, 1862, 9:00 P.M.

They crept forward slowly, soft leaves on soft ground, no sounds at all but the nervous breathing of two dozen cavalrymen. The horses had been left behind them in a thickly wooded ravine, caution against accidental discovery by some Federal patrol. Seeley led one of the four squads, moving through thick darkness in the deep crevice of what could only be a muddy trough, high banks on both sides, thickening mud on his boots. He felt the tension from them all, knew that what they were doing was supremely dangerous.

Forrest had provided them with captured blue coats, and they wore them now, for one very good reason. If the Federals had indeed shifted forward, farther from the landing, they could be anywhere at all. At least these men would have the single advantage of hesitation, should they stumble into the unexpected Yankee outpost.

The blue coats emerged from the saddlebags only when the men were low in the deep woods. Seeley welcomed that, had begun to feel the chill of the damp muddy bottoms, their own coats left behind. But that didn't do much to aid the tension. Seeley knew, as did all of them, that capture in a blue coat meant a very brief and very brutal interrogation, likely followed by their execution.

The ravine was thicker now, low brush, a creek flowing alongside him, and Seeley kept his men in line behind him, using the water as his guide. Parallel to him, more men stepped slowly forward, mostly invisible, few sounds at all. To the front the ground seemed to flatten out, yawning wide, and he could begin to see reflections. He halted his men, stepped forward with the other officers, knew that Captain McDonald had led the way, would be somewhere in the dark waiting for them, would already know what they were supposed to find. Seeley was breathing heavily, pulled at the dark coat, had avoided thinking who might have begun the day with this coat on his back, if there were any telltale holes, or where that enemy soldier might be right now. He kept his stare to the front, the reflections more obvious now, dancing and rippling on the wide expanse that was the Tennessee River. He took a few more steps, realized that where the ground flattened out, the deep draw hadn't been so deep after all, the surface of the river well below him. The reflections of light on the water came from the left, and he looked that way, downriver, a vast spray of lanterns and torches, the lights of Pittsburg Landing.

He was surprised to hear a whisper above him, knew the voice of the captain.

"Climb up!"

Seeley tried to make out the shape of the ground close to him, realized it was a distinct mound. The distant lights showed more of those close by, spread out in the flat ground. He turned back to his own squad, a soft command to remain in place, their job more to serve as guards for the few officers who were there to make the observations, who would answer the questions posed by the colonel. Seeley dug his boots into the soft ground, climbed a half-dozen steps up the side, the crest of the mound only a few feet square. But the perch was perfect. In front of him lay the river, and farther downstream, a far better view of the strings of lanterns that marked the wharves at the landing. Captain McDonald was kneeling, stood now, close beside him, staring through field glasses, and Seeley waited, knew the captain would tell him what to do. As he waited, he touched the grassy ground beneath his feet, no mud, the hilltop nothing like he had seen in these swamps. His curiosity took over now, and he whispered to the captain, "What is this? The river do this?"

"Indians."

Seeley absorbed that, had no idea what McDonald meant.

"Indians? Where? At the landing?"

McDonald lowered the glasses and Seeley could feel the captain staring at him, had seen enough of that in the daylight to know he must have suggested something stupidly obvious. Or just wrong.

"Indian mounds, Lieutenant. These are Chickasaw most likely. This whole bottom area is covered in 'em. Right now it's a good vantage point. Indians did us a favor."

Seeley stared down, nothing to see, felt suddenly uncomfortable.

"They buried here? Like tombs? We standing on bones and such?"

McDonald stared through the glasses again, and Seeley heard a low laugh.

"No, Lieutenant. These mounds are usually ceremonial places. Probably had their meetings here, weddings, promotions, whatever else Indians do to each other. No ghosts here, son." After a long moment,

McDonald's voice came again, higher, a hint of excitement. "Holy Mother of God."

Seeley waited for more, was completely confused.

"You . . . uh . . . praying, sir?"

"Look out there, Lieutenant. That's why we're here, ain't it? Watch those boats."

Seeley obeyed, still shuffled his feet, not altogether certain McDonald knew enough about Indians to know this hill wasn't somebody's grave. *Chickasaws.* They the good kind or the bad kind? He brought the glasses up, stared toward the lights, saw a boat in motion, crossing the river, moving away from the far bank on the right, a short trip to the landing itself. His attention was all that way now, making out shapes, catching movement, trying to identify just what he was seeing. That was, after all, the assignment. Below him, the other lieutenants had come up close, and McDonald acknowledged them with a sharp whisper: "Move out over there. There's more of these mounds. Every one of you, get a good look. Make note of any details you can see. This is exactly what the colonel wanted to know." He turned now, called out in a hard whisper, "Evans?"

There was a scramble down below the mound, a voice responding, "Here!"

"Go back to Colonel Forrest. He needs to see this for himself. I'm not taking responsibility for this . . . too damn important. Move fast. Bring him back to this spot!"

Seeley could see the shadow of Sergeant Evans, the man McDonald most relied on for his own missions. It was a short jog to where the horses were being held, and Evans was gone quickly, Seeley knowing that McDonald's confidence was well placed. His own sergeant, Gladstone, was somewhere with Seeley's squad, standing watch, and Seeley wondered if Gladstone knew about Indian mounds. He certainly knew enough of swamps.

McDonald seemed to be talking to himself, making his own observations, and Seeley began to feel the man's excitement, still wasn't sure why. He stared out again through his own glasses, another boat crossing the river, several more seeming to sit in a line to one side, spread along the far, eastern shore. He caught a flicker of motion, much closer, from the center of the river, realized now there was another boat there, dark and very large, realized with a jolt it was one of the Federal gunboats. He wanted to say something to McDonald, but the captain was looking that way as well, said in a low voice, "There they be. Like two she-devils, spittin' fire. Wonder when they'll start shootin' again. Those boys ain't sittin' out there catchin' catfish."

Seeley's heart was jumping. He knew exactly the power of those craft, so close offshore. By now the entire army knew that the Federals had anchored two of their powerful gunboats, the *Lexington* and the *Tyler*, with their heavy artillery sending enormous shells out toward some part of the fight, usually with more fury than effectiveness. He scanned each of those, saw only a hint of lantern light from inside, glimpses of movement on the decks, sailors going about their nightly routine. He felt an itchiness, whispered to McDonald, "We could pick those boys off from here. Never know what hit 'em."

McDonald was staring again toward the landing.

"You cannot possibly be that dense, Lieutenant. They'd see the flashes of our muzzles, and we'd have barrel-sized shells falling on us in a half second, and a regiment of Yankees hustling down here to chase us away. I don't care a whit about those two gunboats. Look at the landing, and across, the other side of the river. Those boats are going back and forth, like some kinda ferry crossing. The colonel's gotta see this. He'll know exactly what this means, and he'll bust a horse's gut to tell the generals about it."

F orrest knelt on the peak of the Indian mound, stared out through his glasses toward the landing. Beside him, McDonald crouched low, Seeley just behind both of them. They could hear bells now, different tones, rhythms, and Forrest said, "They're signaling each other. Easier than shouting your lungs out. Something like, make way or I'll ram you." Forrest lowered the glasses. "That's the only thing we didn't want to see."

Seeley couldn't contain his curiosity, said, "Sir, forgive me. What are they doing? They pulling their people out of here? Everybody says we've got 'em whipped."

Forrest seemed to have much more tolerance for the lieutenant's questions than McDonald did. He sat, let out a breath, seemed to stare out toward the river, the gunboats still anchored right offshore, the bustle of activity continuing downstream at the landing. Forrest turned toward him slightly, said, "Not leaving. They're arriving. Those are Buell's men. The Army of the Ohio. They'll be crossing over to this side of the river all night long, until every one of them is planted in line next to Grant's people. We whipped some of Grant's boys, no doubt about that." Forrest stood now, a tall shadow outlined by the distant lights. "We had our chance. By God, we had our chance." He paused, seemed lost in thought for a long silent moment. He looked around, began to ease his way down the side of the mound, said, "Captain, pull your men back to our camp. I have to get word of this to General Beauregard."

Forrest slipped down the side of the mound, moved to a waiting horse, and quickly was up and gone, soft hoofbeats in the wet creek bottom. McDonald started down as well, the men gathering, a shadowy line, waiting for their orders. Seeley heard pattering taps on his hat, looked upward. He blinked, water in his eyes, lowered his head again, heard the others reacting as well, and now the patter became heavier, the trees around them peppered with rain, a whistle of wind beginning above, the rain spreading past them, spreading out into the river. Seeley gathered his own squad, heard the cursing, the grumble from Sergeant Gladstone. He still had questions, wondered about Buell, the same blue-bellies they had harassed weeks before. Now . . . they're here. I guess . . . that's really bad. But he had only one job now, lead his men out of the swampy ground, mount up and pull back to the south.

As they reached the horses, the rains grew heavier still, the ground beneath them already churning into mud. McDonald led them away from the river, but not far, the men on a trail that led them along higher ground, a ridgeline. The captain kept them just below the crest, no outlining the men in silhouette, even though, as the rains grew heavier, Seeley knew it was unlikely anyone could see or hear them coming. They trusted the captain's instincts for direction, followed in column, the horses moving at a slow pace, the trail parallel to the river, McDonald keeping them out of the deeper ravines.

Farther inland, the Confederate troops who had been ordered to sleep on their arms struggled mightily to find any kind of cover. The fortunate ones had been positioned directly in the captured Federal camps, and even the wrecked tents offered some kind of shelter. But many more of Beauregard's army had nothing to shelter themselves but their own coats and the limbs of trees, and so thousands of men curled themselves into whatever small space they could make, beaten down by the kind of storm they had seen before, cold and relentless. Fires had been forbidden, the commanders knowing any light could draw sniper fire, and that surely the Yankees had slipped sharpshooters out close to their position. But that mattered very little now, since any Federal soldier who intended to remain in these woods would be as miserable as the men he was sent to observe. Those men had certainly withdrawn to the relative luxury of the camps at Pittsburg Landing, where many found shelter beneath the cannon, the limbers, and wagons, many piling into the hastily arranged tents, brought onshore from the boats that ferried the Army of the Ohio to their side of the river.

All across every part of this enormous battleground, wounded men of both sides lay in helpless agony, the wet darkness blanketing them all in complete blindness. There was little chance any of them would be pulled back to the makeshift hospitals. If a man was still mobile, he could seek some kind of shelter, but too many had sought the safety of the deepest troughs, what had offered them protection from the deadly sprays of canister, or the random flurries of musket balls. Now, as the storm continued, those bottoms grew wet, creek beds swelling, swirling water through the darkness, mud and debris engulfing the men who could not move at all, whose wounds were too severe. Some of the wounded welcomed the rain for the relief it brought to their desperate thirst, but then the shivering chills came, their soaked clothing stripping many of their last bit of energy. The one blessing came from the sound of the storm, wiping away the soft, horrible cries of men in pain, of men terrified of dying, of men calling for loved ones, or one another. For the men without wounds, the soldiers who had been ordered to endure this night, to renew their fight at dawn, the rains at least kept away those awful voices, the cries of the helpless.

And then, out on the river, the *Tyler* and the *Lexington* began a new mission. If they could not obliterate the rebel troops, they could at least prevent Beauregard's army from having any kind of peace at all. With perfect clockwork precision, both gunboats began to launch their shells aloft, the thunderous roars streaking through the rain. There was no aim, no targets. It was simply noise, minute by minute, man-made thunder and lightning, adding to all that came from the skies.

F orrest made his ride. From General Chalmers to General Breckinridge, the only response he drew was the suggestion that he take his observations to General Beauregard himself. Riding to Shiloh Church, Forrest found that Beauregard had changed the location of his headquarters, and no one who had holed up around the church had any idea where that new headquarters could be. But Forrest kept moving, located General Hardee, related what he had seen to the one man in the army who would appreciate its meaning. But Hardee had seen too much slaughter on this day, and so he would not pay heed to Forrest's urgency, would not even invite the colonel into his dry tent. Once again Forrest was ordered only to pass his information directly to Beauregard. And so Forrest continued the ride, the infuriating gallop through blind woods, over roadways where no guide could help him, where no officer could give him direction. After hours in the saddle in a storm that seemed to have no end, a different kind of storm fired through Forrest's brain. He had witnessed the arrival of a full Federal army, an army that possibly doubled the strength that Grant now had packed tightly into his position at Pittsburg Landing. To his furious astonishment, no one in the entire Confederate hierarchy seemed to care. And worse, the man responsible for issuing the orders, for making the preparations for the new day's challenge, was nowhere to be found.

## CHAPTER THIRTY-TWO

# SHERMAN

PITTSBURG LANDING
APRIL 7, 1862, MIDNIGHT

Sherman had come back to the landing through the driving rain, had hoped to find Grant there. He was unsure whether Grant would return downriver to Savannah. He had prepared himself to be angry at that, that Grant should not leave this army for the comforts of that damn mansion, that across these woods and fields, an army had suffered as badly as any army could, and by damned, a commander should see that, understand what kind of price these men had given. Along the way, Sherman had allowed his temper to blossom, imagining every kind of curse, the indiscreet blasts into the face of a man who had done so many things wrong. But Grant had surprised him, had drained away Sherman's fury by a fury of his own. It was the one reaction Sherman did not expect, and the one he most respected.

He had found Grant close by a log dwelling at the landing, the place Grant had intended to use as his own headquarters. But the place was a hospital now, a grim necessity not even the commanding general could object to. They sat on horseback, close beneath the spread of a fat oak tree. Sherman kept his coat as tight around him as he could, but the rain found its way inside, always, and he fought the shiver, could see enough of Grant's expression in the glow of the lanterns that Sherman felt as though a great muzzle was engulfing him, holding him silent. Clearly Grant had something to say.

"He's here. He's finally here. How in hell did it take him so long to make that march? Rawlins tells me that Wallace sent his people out on the wrong road, and then he countermarched them. But instead of turning them around where they stood, he shifted their whole damn position, brought his vanguard all the way to the front of the line, like turning around a big damn snake inside a narrow pipe. All he had to do was march them tail first, save three hours. I'll find out why, before this is over. General Wallace says I wasn't definite enough, that my order wasn't urgent. It's the same thing I heard from Nelson, that his division didn't know there was any need to hurry it up. And of course, Buell is backing *him* up. No surprise there. That's what Halleck will hear. A hatful of bellyaches from men who sat out there all damn day and listened to more cannon fire than any of them have heard in their lives. And they didn't think there was *urgency*?"

Sherman saw Grant struggle with something in his hand, realized it was a cigar, no chance of lighting it. Sherman felt that need as well, but it would have to wait. Sherman had been as desperate as anyone on the field for the arrival of Lew Wallace's Division, a division that had only arrived with great fanfare after dark. As Sherman absorbed the overwhelming punishment on his right flank, he had wondered if Wallace might suddenly appear, might so stun the rebels that a sharp flank attack along Owl Creek by thousands of fresh troops might drive them back completely. But Wallace had never arrived, not even a hint of where his division could be. It was not up to Sherman to launch any kind of fury at Wallace, and obviously, Grant was carrying enough of that to go around. Sherman said, "He's here now. I've seen his people moving up on my right."

"Yes, he's here *now*. A great many men lost their lives today . . . because Lew Wallace is here *now*."

Sherman let it go, knew that any problems caused by Wallace's delay had been solved, at least for Sherman. Whether Wallace had caused a greater problem for himself was not anything Sherman could address, at least not publicly.

He glanced down, saw a reflection off a badly bent scabbard lying against Grant's leg.

"I heard you were wounded. Is the leg—"

"It's fine, dammit. Wandered right into a mess, nearly got myself killed." Grant reached down, held the scabbard in his hand. "Hurt like hell. Could have been worse. Wonder if the damn rebels even knew who they were shooting at." He looked toward Sherman's fat bandage, pointed.

"How's the hand?"

"Hurts. Not bad. Damn nuisance trying to hold the reins. Hard to shoot the pistol without falling off the damn horse."

"Then don't shoot the pistol. You've got no business leading your troops into a fight. What the hell's the matter with you?"

The fury in Grant's voice was unusual, more emotion than Sherman had heard before.

"You're right. But there were times today . . . when there was no alternative. The damn rebels rolled right over some of my lines. We had flanks just fall away, like leaves blowing in the wind. The enemy took full advantage, and I had to pull some of my people out of good strong ground, pull 'em back, form up as best we could. Only brigade that held up was Buckland. He needs a promotion. The rest of 'em . . . they need a firing squad."

"And what do I do with *you*? You're their commander. It's your responsibility, after all."

It was a difficult question, but Sherman knew the answer already. He waited, knew there was no good response.

"We're here. We held 'em back. Finally. Cost us too many men, and we gave them too much ground. But we held 'em back. I'll file my report, and I'll not hold back on the names. Heroes and cowards. Smart actions and stupid ones. Plenty of both."

Sherman saw Grant looking at him, no words, knew exactly what Grant was thinking. Yes, Sherman, how much stupidity belongs to *you*? Sherman waited for more, Grant silent, and Sherman said, "Learned a lot today. Learned something about my men . . . about the enemy. They came to fight. No mistake about that. They pushed regiments through the worst ground you ever saw and came out the other side with muskets in our faces. Took everything we had, and gave it back to us. Yep. Learned something today. Lots of mistakes. Lots of blundering." He looked at Grant, as though trying to convince him. "Won't happen this way again. If I'm allowed to keep my command."

"Shut up, Sherman. Only one likely to lose his command is me. This fight isn't over, and once it is, there's people with bigger britches than you or me who'll make those decisions. Damn them to hell."

There was another silent moment, Sherman feeling the awkwardness, his brain seeking another road. He peered out past Grant, to the cabin, saw the horror of a stack of severed limbs, saw a naked leg suddenly appear, tossed through a lone window, tumbling down the pile. Inside, a sharp scream rolled out, muffled only slightly by the rain. Sherman shifted in the saddle, had no need to hear this, had heard too much of it all day long. But Grant was planted firmly beside the tree, a hint of shelter from the storm, and Sherman would endure. Grant seemed to study him, pointed back toward the cabin.

"Damn mess . . . the hospital. No place to shelter the men. They laid a bunch of wounded under some canvas back over there, and a damn undertaker's wagon starts picking them up, the crew thinking they were dead. You never saw so much of a commotion. Scared hell out of everybody involved. The wagon . . . I don't know where they ended up." Grant paused. "We're putting as many wounded on the boats as we can fit, but Buell's commandeered a good many of those for his own purposes. He's hauling his people over here as fast as he can, and I can't object to that. Those men . . . they're moving in here like we don't even matter. At least they're getting a taste of this infernal weather." Grant paused, peered at him under the brim of his hat, tilted to one side. "This was not a good day, Sherman. Not for any of us. It was a near thing." Grant seemed to stare past him, said again, "It was a near thing."

Sherman thought a moment, felt the need to defend at least . . . something.

"Not so near. We drove 'em back, time and again. Took a hell of a toll on those graybacks. They'll not likely do that again."

"They'll try. They have to. No other reason for them to still be out there. That's why they came up here, to knock our teeth down our throats. They damn near did." Sherman heard the anger in Grant's voice, felt like he had to say more.

"We made mistakes. We had too many untested troops. In the wrong place."

"There's never a right place to put untested troops, not in a fight like this."

Sherman felt a generosity in Grant's statement, shook his head.

"They were the first line of defense. Wrong place."

"Oh hell, Sherman, it's only the wrong place because we know *now* it's the wrong place. You didn't expect this fight, and neither did I. I have some explaining to do about that. Maybe you, too. Maybe every damn one of us. Lew Wallace goes on a flower-picking jaunt around Crump's, instead of bringing his people where we need 'em. Buell takes his sweet lovely time bringing his people toward the sound of what he damn well knows is a fight he should be a part of. Whether either one of them did that for a reason . . ." Grant stopped, and Sherman knew that wasn't an accusation he could make lightly. Sherman felt the need to change the subject.

"I guess you know . . . Prentiss is gone, captured. Will Wallace is gone, dead or captured. His own staff says they had to leave him behind, and he was in bad shape out there. Horrible thing."

Grant lowered his head.

"More horrible. Ann Wallace is out there on one of the boats. Arrived this morning, looking to see her husband. All perfume and lace and romance."

"Does she know?"

"Do we? We had to give her all the news we had, and what the hell do we know? Her husband is out there somewhere, maybe drowned in the mud, maybe with half his head shot off. And you know what she's doing? Right now? She's out there on that river helping the doctors, stepping those petticoats through guts and pools of blood. No place for a woman . . . not a general's wife. She should be back home sipping tea in her parlor. What the hell was she thinking, coming down here? Who the hell authorized that?"

Sherman had met Ann Wallace only briefly, the perfect picture of an officer's wife. He couldn't picture the image now, blood on her dress, hands covered in . . . everything. He stared out into the rain, more ambulances coming in, making their way in deep muddy ruts toward the hospital. Sherman saw a man emerge from the cabin, walk into the rain, not wounded at all. He saw the man's apron now, a massive bloody stain.

"One of the doctors . . ."

Grant glanced that way, turned back, stared down at the landing, a fresh column of Buell's troops making their way up the slope.

"There have been a few . . . just leave their posts."

Sherman bristled at that, stood higher in the stirrups.

"Well, to hell with that! I'll round him up, send him back to do his job."

"No you won't. If he can, he'll come back. Some of 'em, they're done. Seen that before. So have you. Only so much you can make a man do, even a doctor. By tomorrow maybe, he'll be back, pick up the saw, do what he has to do. But right about now, he's sitting under a tree, pulling out a bottle, trying to make it go away. It won't."

Sherman felt the image of that too close to a dangerous place in his own mind. He had heard most of the fight out to his left, once his own lines were fairly secure, once the rebels had exhausted all they could seem to do to drive him back. He tried to add a hint of cheer to his words, said, "Prentiss saved our bacon."

"I suppose he did."

Sherman had never had much to do with Prentiss, no great affection between them, was fairly certain Prentiss disliked him altogether. Prentiss wasn't alone. Sherman realized he might never see the man again, and thought again of Ann Wallace. Does Prentiss have a wife? Children? Somebody will have to tell them about this. He looked at Grant. Yes, you.

Grant removed his hat, slapped away a spray of water, put it back on his head.

"I've heard that Sidney Johnston is dead."

Sherman was surprised.

"You certain?"

"No. Not certain of anything. But there were several prisoners, brought in over on the left. Said he was wounded, died leading some Tennessee boys." Grant looked at him, again from under the brim of the hat. "*Leading.* I'll not have that nonsense, not in this army."

Sherman tried to ignore the scolding.

"The left? That's where I sent Stuart's Brigade. Wonder if it was his boys that did the deed."

"Doesn't matter. None of that matters. Only thing we need to be thinking about right now is what happens tomorrow."

With the setting of the sun, Sherman had been comfortable with the position of his remaining troops, was much more comfortable now that Lew Wallace's seven thousand men had filed up against his right flank. But Sherman also knew that he had lost several of his commands altogether, regimental leaders who had collapsed, an entire brigade coming apart. Some of those men had been gathered up, rallied around different officers. But the rest . . . he knew of the fugitives at the river, wouldn't go there, not yet. But he couldn't avoid the certain knowledge that some of those men belonged to him. He glanced up, no sign of a slackening of the rain, said, "For tomorrow . . . you have orders for me yet?"

Grant seemed to ponder that.

"Some of the rebel prisoners say we're whipped. Say they're coming after us to finish the job, to shove us into the river at first light."

"I've heard a little of that."

"You think it's true?"

"Not likely. This rain will slow down any assault. With all respects, sir, I'm hoping you will allow us the privilege of a counterattack." Sherman looked again toward the landing, more troops marching up through deep mud. "Buell's whole force here?"

Grant shook his head.

"Not yet. Maybe by morning, I guess. Buell hasn't seen fit to meet with me. He's marching in here like he's taking over the entire operation. He wanted that from the beginning, and he's making it pretty plain that he's not bowing down to my authority one bit. My own staff had to poke around down there just to find out that Buell intends to launch an attack in the morning, whether we join him or not. You think he might have told me that? Or am I just to assume that Buell believes what we're hearing from the rebel prisoners, that my poor damned army is whipped, worthless, tails tucked hard between our legs."

Sherman was surprised, had spoken to Buell earlier that night.

"Um . . . sir, he came to me, a few hours ago, told me of his plans. I thought you would have known all about that. My apologies."

Grant said nothing for a long moment. Sherman was truly embarrassed now, knew that Buell had stepped over a line . . . or perhaps he didn't. Perhaps, Sherman thought, this is what Halleck intended all along. Grant takes a beating, and Buell comes in to be the damn hero. He scolded himself for that. No. No one could have known what was happening here. Hell, *we* didn't know. But this is foolishness. Buell should at least follow some kind of protocol. Grant spoke now, seemed resigned to the absurd.

"I am assuming Buell told you his boys are ready to rip trees out of the ground, that his troops are making all kinds of talk about showing the rebs what a *real* soldier is, all that stupidity."

Sherman bristled, had no interest in Buell or anyone else ridiculing his men, no matter their failures.

"He didn't really say, sir. But we did a poor job today, and no matter what Buell intends to do, that will change. The men in my lines now are the best I've got, and they'll rip a few trees up, too. Begging your pardon, sir."

"Beg all you want. This isn't some parade ground, and if I have anything to say about it, this fight will not be about whose trousers carry the greater manhood. Buell might not accept my authority, and I know damn well he wanted this show to be his. Halleck's watching me every time I spit, and today I allowed the enemy to shove this army into a latrine. But everything has changed, *everything*. You want a counterattack? We'll do a hell of a lot more than that. Right now, the enemy is out there drowning in this rain, and by morning, they'll be tired, hungry, and, God willing, they'll have had enough of this. They can shout out all they want about how badly we're whipped, but I know damn well they took casualties as badly as we did, and their commanding general might be dead. We've got four fresh divisions marching in here. We've got rations for the men, and fresh ammunition for their cartridge boxes. The artillery is restocked, fresh horses are coming ashore alongside Buell's troops. No matter what Buell thinks, and no matter what any damn rebel thinks, this army is a long damn way from being *whipped*."

Sherman could feel Grant's energy, more now than ever before. He looked again to the columns of fresh troops, saw artillery drawn by their teams of mules, men sitting high on their limbers, their boasts and shouts only muffled by the misery of the rain. Sherman tried to see his pocket watch, no chance of that, but he knew it was very late, well after midnight. Farther upriver the gunboats still thundered out their shells, a rhythm so consistent, Sherman had stopped hearing it. He thought of the enemy, all that Grant had said, felt the energy rising up inside of him. There was none of the nagging fear, the curse of uncertainty that had plagued him so many times before. All throughout the day, the extraordinary fight had erupted so close to him in so many places that all he had done was react. In the brief quiet moments, he had tested himself, couldn't avoid thinking of Bull Run, of the disabling fear, but there had been none of that, the job at hand so desperate, so critical that the paralyzing terror seemed to be erased once and for all.

His focus had been outward, combating the enemy as he waged war with the panic in his men, working to maneuver and retreat and doing all he knew how, to put men in the best places they could be. He had seen it all, the death of his own, and the sweeping collapse of the enemy's lines, then more lines, rising up from the low ground in screaming waves. It was the very thing that separated the cowards from the good soldiers, and he had seen all of that, on both sides. Right now, he thought, the best men I have left are out there waiting, just like I am, just like Grant is. Buell's men have more experience, all their bragging about being veterans. But right now, the men out there, Buckland, the others, *my* men, no matter what kind of men they were yesterday . . . tomorrow they'll be veterans, too.

He felt the gnawing need to ride back out there, a pair of staff officers sitting far to one side, waiting for him, men who would know how to find the tent that was now his headquarters. He couldn't sit still any longer, and he said aloud, not to Grant, not to anyone but himself, "Get this damn night over with. I'm ready for more."

## CHAPTER THIRTY-THREE

# BAUER

The rains had stopped before dawn, and the order had gone out to every division commander in the Federal army, passed down to their men, that this day would begin with an advance, not of picket lines and cautious observation posts, but by the entire force. Though a good many of Grant's troops still suffered the scars and bruises from the day before, Buell's troops were almost entirely fresh, and when the first bugle calls opened the day, Buell had already positioned more than fifteen thousand of his troops on the line, with more advancing as rapidly as they could be ferried across the river. As Grant had dreaded, a nasty sniping rivalry had begun, some of Buell's officers making too much of the *salvation* they brought to the fight, rescuing Grant's beleaguered troops, the men who could not avoid the indignity of what had been done to them the day before. That sniping came all the way from the top, and though Buell was too discreet to say anything directly to Grant, Buell was very clear to his own staff, and to many of his senior commanders that this day would prove just whose troops were superior. Those units Grant had positioned closest to Buell's men, including the 16th Wisconsin, were hearing too much of that even before the advance had begun.

Once the massive counterattack was in motion, Grant's men began to feel a pride of their own. This time there was none of the hesitation, the carelessness and frustration of junior officers, whose nervous agitation had led to so much of the previous day's disaster. This was an entire army making its move, what these men had so impatiently hoped for since their first disembarking of the boats. Then, the target was to be Corinth. On this day, it was a battered rebel army spread out all through the countryside, an army that Grant's men in particular were confident had already given their best effort. To many of the troops of the 16th Wisconsin, who had reacted to the overwhelming rebel attack by scattering like rabbits, today they believed they would have their pride returned. Today, the *rabbits* would not be wearing blue.

The night before, when the rebel attacks wound down, many of Grant's men had spread rumors, born of wishful thinking, that the rebel army would simply vanish, abandoning the field altogether. Those who had seen so many men fall to musket fire had convinced themselves that the rebels had certainly absorbed too much punishment, that the sudden halt in the rebel assaults could only mean that the rebels had taken a far worse beating than they had given the blue troops. Among Buell's army, the rumors were very different, and even before the counterattack began, word began to spread that they had simply missed out on the adventure, that the rebels had escaped their due by running away before Buell's veterans had their crack at them. Naturally, Buell's officers assumed it was their very presence on the field that had drained away the enemy's will to fight. The hopeful euphoria of Grant's men and the annoyance from Buell's were short-lived. Though the rebels had backed away, they had conceded nothing.

No matter the utter lack of coordination with Buell's forces, Grant accepted that Buell's initial assault would be the signal to the entire army to start the attack. At first light, that attack began, an expanding arc, moving out from their compact base. As they had come across the river, Buell had positioned his people to the ground closest the river, to Grant's left. Grant, now strengthened by the addition of Lew Wallace's Division, had anchored the right, making good use of Owl Creek. Wallace held the far flank, and to his left was Sherman. Both men knew that their advance was tied to the advance of Buell's men, and so they waited for the first thunder from Buell's artillery, the signal that meant Buell was on the move. As Wallace drove forward on the flank, that end of the line soon made their first contact with the rebels. But it was no great barrier, no powerfully organized line. Instead the Confederate left was anchored by a single brigade under the command of Preston Pond, of Bragg's Corps. After a brisk exchange of volleys, Pond recognized just how badly outmanned he was, and wisely withdrew. The move exposed an enormous gap on the Confederate left, and exposed as well an enormous flaw in Beauregard's strategy. The night's dismal weather had left many of the rebel troops out of touch with anyone with the authority to improve their position, or anyone who could either locate or order forward their supply wagons. The Confederate commanders, Beauregard in particular, could only assume that their troops had been able to refill their cartridge boxes from the vast stores of ammunition believed to be found in the abandoned Federal camps.

As confident as Grant might have been, his adversary began the day with the same optimism. Beauregard had every expectation that this day would begin with a resumption of their successful advance the day before, with the expectation of driving a wedge between the river and much of the Federal army. Virtually ignoring his left, Beauregard focused most of his attention, and the attention of his senior commanders, on the center, the logical place to drive their first assault. Before the dawn, orders had been sent forward that the assault would begin at first light. In those places where officers could actually organize a battle line, that advance began as ordered. But, instead of empty woods and a weak, rattled Federal defense, the rain-soaked, hungry, and underequipped Confederates were soon confronted by the fresh troops of Don Carlos Buell. And, to Buell's right, Grant's troops, who had done so much of the fighting the day before, who quickly advanced over ground they had abandoned, learned that their wishful thinking was premature. Instead of a victorious romp to reclaim their camps, and drive remnants of a beaten rebel army away, they found what Buell's men found: an advance by entire brigades of rebel troops who didn't seem beaten at all. As the two armies came together, many of Grant's men found themselves confronting the enemy on the same ground that had seen some of the worst bloodletting the day before. From the peach orchard and the old wagon trail that had been so tenaciously held by Benjamin Prentiss, many of the same regiments who had given up so much faced one another again.

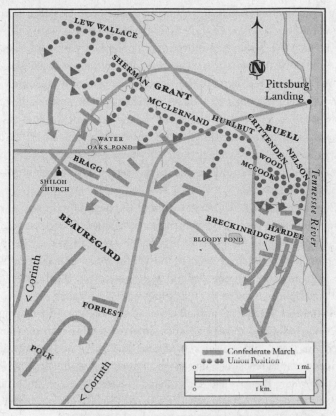

**GRANT AND BUELL COUNTERATTACK**

NEAR DUNCAN FIELD, THE OLD WAGON TRAIL
APRIL 7, 1862, 10:00 A.M.

With the first bugle call to advance, Bauer could feel the same optimism that affected much of the army, that this time they were moving *forward*. In the ranks, the sergeants were there as they had always been, but the orders weren't harsh, no need for prodding hesitant men who had no stomach for a fight, or green troops who had no idea what the enemy could do. Immediately the men learned that *advancing* was a far differ-ent and far more inspiring experience than they had suffered the day before. The horrors and the terrifying retreat were a far distant memory for Bauer, and no one around him spoke of that at all. If any of those men were likely to break, to repeat their stampede to safety, no one showed it.

The 16th Wisconsin had moved out alongside men from Missouri, many of them the same men who had fought on their flanks the day before, their last real stand in the wood lines north of what some were now calling the Bloody Pond. Bauer didn't know how much of the regiment stood in line, but anyone could see that the unit was most likely below half strength. Bauer knew that if most of those men were casualties, or instead, if some were gathered in shameless paralysis at the river, what mattered now was the number of muskets, and the backbone of the men moving forward.

Even before seven o'clock, the artillery had begun on the left, a scattering of fire that seemed disconnected, unorganized. But those sounds were increasing, and the farther forward the Wisconsin men stepped, the more they could hear waves of musket fire. Most of that came from the left and center of the Federal position, where Buell's men had marched right into the teeth of the renewed rebel advance.

As the 16th Wisconsin pushed closer to the sounds of the new fight, the woods that had tormented and protected them began to change. There was cover still, and thickets of vines and briars clogging the deep ravines, but the great sweeping canopy of treetops was mostly gone. Past the field where Prentiss had surrendered, the trees were mostly broken and shattered, enormous matchsticks tossed about in a haphazard jumble. Here the lines came apart, the men making their way through entirely new thickets, fallen limbs and treetops that broke down any organization. The officers were powerless to change that, and the orders were shouted out with a strange kind of hesitation, even the captains unsure what was waiting for them up ahead, or just how these men would react once they saw the enemy.

Buell's fight on the left had become far more intense, opening up in distant fields, the noise distorted by the woods and hilly ground in that direction. Some of that ground had not been as devastated, had not suffered the long hours of artillery barrages that had swept the ground where Bauer marched now. Where the lines could be brought back together, the men around Bauer reacted to the changes around them, the shattered trees spread over thick mud, the ground pockmarked by craters from the storm of cannon fire that had driven these men away the day before.

Around him, the talk was silenced by the effort it took to shove through the ruins of the woods. The land was far more open now, more visibility to the fields that spread out all around them. Some of the men stopped, focused on what they could hear, and Bauer heard it, too, the musket fire shifting direction, still to the left, but the right as well, a sudden burst to that side that made him flinch, ducking low, dropping to one knee behind the protection of a fat tree limb. Others were down as well, but the sergeants seemed to pounce on them like cats on a wounded bird, yanking men up by the collar, cursing hard into scared faces. Bauer saw Champlin screaming at a man who stared at the sergeant with wide-eyed terror, the man turning forward as though fearing more from Champlin than he did from the sounds of the fight. Bauer rose, didn't wait for the hard hand of the sergeant. But the terror was there, unavoidable, the musket fire and bursts of artillery still making him flinch. He pushed forward, helped by the movement of the men beside him, men who were no doubt helped by him. Champlin was shouting out still, and Bauer knew that the sergeant was doing exactly what he had to, but no amount of mouthy bravado could keep the fear away completely. The closer the men drew to the enemy, the more the memories would leap out, and the more they would need men like Champlin to hold them together.

Willis had stayed beside him, a bond that Bauer believed he needed. He drew strength from Willis's stoicism, the man not ever showing the kind of fear that Bauer fought along every step. Through the rainy night, the Wisconsin men had been grateful to share huge Sibley tents brought to the landing by Buell's supply officers. Willis had done as he had done every night, had pulled out that same letter, crumpled and worn now, then folded it, returning it to his pocket, no words at all. Bauer still would not ask, knew there would be no answers. But in the morning, when the bugles called them out, Willis was the same he had always been, as he was right now, and as long as Bauer carried the musket, he would make every effort to stay close to him.

The musket fire was spreading to the right, low mumbles from some of the men, orders called out from officers who led the way. Beside him,

Willis stepped over a log, tripped, stumbling into mud, righted himself, wiped mud from his hands. Bauer stopped to help, but Willis said nothing, stepped forward, glanced back at him with a hard glare that carried the message. *Move it.* Bauer struggled to keep to his feet, the entire line disorganized, the floor of the woods a carpet of ankle-breaking hazards, hidden muddy holes. All through the blasted woods, the going was slow, the musket fire and artillery thumps louder, the shouts of the lieutenants seeming to increase in pitch, those men just as unsure, just as scared, most of them ducking and flinching with the sheets of fire that tore through the woods to the right.

And now there were bodies.

He nearly stepped on the first one, realized they were everywhere, many hidden by the destruction of the woods. Others were finding them as well, low groans of the advancing men suddenly blending with the sounds of the wounded. The cries grew louder, the surprise of those men who had endured the long wet night, who had absorbed the relentless thunder from the gunboats, no different for the men in blue as it was for the rebels. The wounded seem to wake up, suddenly aware that soldiers were moving past them, and their cries began to spread, some of them from behind, men in cover so deep, Bauer and the rest had stumbled right past them. It was clear that some of those men were barely alive, their cries nonsensical, but others emerged from their holes with desperate pleas for help. Through the advancing lines, the orders still came, different now, the officers seeming to understand what many of their men did not, that they had to continue, to keep moving. There was no time to stop for the wounded. But some did stop, the sergeants exploding with profanity, dragging their men past the nightmarish sights, the tormenting needs. Bauer tried to ignore the wounded, but he saw now he was walking straight toward a man lying in the hollow of a shattered tree trunk, the man staring at him with pale white skin, hatless, a smear of muddy hair. The uniform was blue, washed by the rains, and Bauer hesitated, searched for some way around the man. Willis called back to him, out to the right, a narrow gap in the impassable timber where men were funneling through. Bauer caught the wounded man's stare again, and the man raised a quivering hand, pointed at his own head, turned, one ear completely gone, Bauer staring at a gash in the man's skull, a thick crust of dried blood. He realized that a piece of the man's skull was gone, torn away, the man's brains exposed. The man looked to him again, no words, seemed unable to speak, and Bauer looked away, a piercing thought: How can you be alive? Champlin had him now, a hard grip, sharp surprise, hot words: "Go! You can't help him!"

Bauer went with the shove, moved quickly through the gap in the fallen trees, more men falling in behind him, one man saying something about the wounded man, the words choked away by Champlin.

"Move forward! No talking! The enemy's close! He might be waiting right through those trees, so quiet down!"

Bauer focused on the sheer stupidity of Champlin's words, the sergeant doing plenty of shouting himself, loud enough for the enemy to hear, even above the gathering musket fire.

They reached the edge of open ground, a large patch of burned brush, and Bauer's nose curled up from the stink, different, the rain doing nothing to wash away the smell of what he saw now. Across what had been thickets of tall grass were dead, charred bodies, covering most of the ground, some in rows, lying where they had fallen, some of those twisted in grotesque shapes, many of them unrecognizable, no hint of a uniform, or a face. But others had crawled out after the fire, dozens of men who were dead now, who had escaped the woods, for reasons Bauer could not fathom, seeking water perhaps, their faces upturned, mouths open, drinking in the rain. Some were still alive, the mud and black soot on their clothes disguising which side they had fought. Some wore blue, were curled up next to men who did not, the dead and the barely moving. The bodies spread out far beyond the charred ground, but the black stubble lay directly ahead, and the lieutenants were waving the men forward, right across the sea of bodies. The lines wavered, the advance halting on its own, frozen by the nightmare in front of them.

Once more the wounded seemed to wake with a burst of energy, aware that help was at hand, rescue perhaps. The lieutenants continued their shouts, and the sergeants obeyed, pushing the men onward, hesitant footsteps even from them, the troops responding as they had to, stepping through and over the corpses, trying to avoid the wounded. Bauer closed his eyes, a bad idea, opened them again, picked his way past lumps of burned corpses, struggled through the smell. Close to him, one man moved his arm, waved, called out, and Bauer couldn't look away, saw the man's hand a stump of black, stripped of fingers. The mud was there as well, even in the stubble, and Bauer smelled that, too, thick on his boots, knew without looking it wasn't just mud. Some of the bodies were in pieces, one man sliced in half, perfect precision, the two parts separated by a foot-wide puddle. Bauer picked his way, the fury of the wounded driving a hole in his brain. One officer reacted his own way, calling out, "The ambulances are coming! They'll be here soon!"

Bauer wondered about that, saw the stare on the lieutenant's face, knew it was a lie. The officer could not possibly know anything of ambulances, or what might be coming up behind them. Bauer was moving past the burned stubble, into taller grass, wet, stinking, but still there were bodies, some of them pressed deep into the soft grass. Around him, some men were tripped by what they couldn't see, some jumping forward, past whatever sickening obstacle they encountered, making their way the best they could. By now all of them were staring downward, making their way forward by first searching the grass. Bauer could feel the wetness from the grass soaking through his trousers, but below his feet, the rains had a different effect. Much of the blood had washed into the ground, but there was a price for that, so many parts of bodies clean, a shining skull, stripped of skin, exposed bones, a rib cage, no head, a single leg, naked. There were many more still whole, no apparent wound but a rip in the cloth. In this field was a perfect mix of troops from both sides, and hidden in the grass were the weapons, a danger all their own, bayonets and knives, one man to Bauer's left crying out, stumbling, a sergeant moving quickly. The man stayed down, the sergeant saying something about a bayonet, then looking back, as though hoping the lieutenant had been right, that an ambulance might yet come up. Bauer stared down again, his feet pushing more carefully through the grass, thought of the newly injured man, Hopkins, from Madison maybe. Now Hopkins was their newest casualty, the newest member of this astonishing horror, this nightmare fraternity that spread out in the fields as far as anyone could see.

Bauer glanced toward Willis, saw him making his way with delicate care, staring downward, picking his way, making a long stride over a body. Around them were more calls from the wounded, men in every direction, hidden by the grass, the voices too many for Bauer to hear the words, one thought as he blocked them out: God help them. The slow trudging march seemed unending, and Bauer looked toward the far wood line, another blasted patch of wrecked timber. Officers were there already, a man on a horse, a sword pointing, guiding the closest men through a gap in the timber. There were more gaps, narrow openings that led them around and through the obstacles, the lines disorganized once more. He reached the tree line, waited his turn, moved through the gap, made his way over the obstacles, could see more dead, heard more cries. By now Bauer was growing numb to it all, his brain saturated. The bodies had become just part of the ground, pieces of trees alongside pieces of men, the smells blending together, mud and death. The shouts of the officers grew louder, the woods only a small patch, the field beyond one more carpet of horror. Out front, another horseman appeared, and Bauer welcomed the distraction, saw it was Captain Patch.

"Move those men out here! Double-quick! The enemy is in those far trees, and they're coming! Fall into line in cover . . . get ready! Aim low!"

Patch seemed to pause, realized his horse was stepping through the remains of the men who had gone down the day before. He said something Bauer couldn't hear, seemed to back the horse away. Another pair of horsemen rode quickly across from one side, and Bauer was surprised to see Colonel Allen, had wondered if the colonel was even alive. A few men acknowledged that, shouts, mostly subdued, but Allen spoke only to Patch, waved one hand toward the far woods, and Bauer saw the bandage, thick and heavy, wrapped around Allen's chest. Bauer felt a strange surge of emotion, the thought shared by men around him, low voices, all of them recognizing that the colonel had come back . . . *for them.* Allen looked across the line, said something again to Patch, then rode away, followed by his aide. Patch turned the horse toward them, another shout, "Find cover anywhere you can! Get ready!"

A voice behind him, Champlin.

"The colonel coulda stayed in the back. We'll follow him to hell, boys."

Champlin went to work, moved quickly out past Bauer, pointing out the cover, the best places for a man to lie down. Other sergeants down the line were doing the same, but the men were already dropping low. Bauer backed farther away from the edge of the field, heard a wounded man behind him, a desperate rasping cry. Bauer hadn't seen him before, wouldn't see him now. He saw a gap between two logs, slid down, wet mud beneath, brought the stock of the musket against him, the muzzle pointing up close to his face. The mud was soaking up into his pants, and he tried to ignore that, but couldn't, one hand reaching out below, feeling for something . . . human. He glanced at the hand, saw mud, only mud, once more the quick prayer in his mind: Thank God.

He heard horses, turned, was surprised to see an artillery battery, the teams of horses pulling limbers and four guns up close to the edge of the woods behind them. Men were calling out, low cheers, and Bauer felt that, the sudden surge of confidence, added power to the position. He watched as the gun crews unlimbered the artillery pieces, wheeling them about. One officer stepped through them, pointing out past the men in the trees, toward the woods far across the field beyond. The guns were positioned a few yards apart, their crews adjusting the elevation, nudging each gun to one side or the other, what Bauer could only guess was the effort to aim at some target only the gunners knew, where rebel batteries were positioned, or where the rebel infantry might be moving right now. He stared with excited admiration, watched as the crews loaded each gun, and Bauer tried to see the projectiles, but the men moved too quickly, no way for Bauer to see if they were using canister or solid shot. Canister, he thought. If the rebs are coming . . . we need canister. He glanced out toward the field again, saw Willis close to one side, staring out to the field, not interested by the battery. Willis had his musket up, resting on a log, and Bauer looked again to the big guns, saw the aim of the barrels just above them, thought, keep your head down, that's for sure. The crews stood back now, ready, and Bauer knew to brace for it, expected the battery to open fire immediately, the blasts that would throw thick clouds of stinking smoke right over them.

But the first shell came from the other way, from the front. It tore through the jumble of tree limbs with a sharp scream, the blast coming down close behind him, tossing splinters skyward with a deafening burst. He ducked low, farther into the mud, the thick limbs on two sides of him, a V shape, pointed out toward the field. He glanced back, saw a shred of blue, smoke engulfing him, blinding, choking, tried to see the ripped coat . . . who? But there was no time for that, the next shell coming in with a different sound, a tumbling whistle, impacting farther back, where the battery was positioned. He kept low, the shells coming in a screaming chorus, one to his right, then more, a shower of roars, impacting behind . . . *the battery.* A half dozen more split the air to one side, coming from another place, somewhere to the left, all of them exploding where the cannons had been placed. He covered his ears, fought the sounds, harsh ringing in his ears. But the shelling seemed to slow, a pause, silence, then one shell out front, far short, in the field, dirt and debris tossed in the air.

The silence came again, a long pause, nothing at all. He waited still, slowly dropped his hands from his ears, took a breath through the dense sulfur smoke, shook his head slowly, the silence not changing the ringing pain in his ears. The rebels guns were firing somewhere else, nowhere close, and he rose up slightly, turned, looked back. The battery was completely destroyed, all four guns broken, blasted, smoking heaps of wreckage. The smoke was clearing, but still, one limber was on its side, burning, black smoke. Where the guns had been were only broken wheels, timbers, one barrel stabbed straight down into the ground, another cracked, split lengthwise. He rose higher, drawn by a stunned curiosity. He saw the crews, what was left of two dozen men, shreds of blue cloth, bodies and pieces of men scattered through the wreckage . . . and dead horses. They lay in pieces as well, steaming piles of ripped flesh, guts in heaps. He felt sick, still stared, a last flicker of hope, that someone would have survived, that one gun would still be there, ready to help. But there was nothing left. The men around him stared as he did, raw silence, a short moan coming from the wounded man, still unseen, Bauer hating the man, furious now, furious at everything.

"Get ready!"

The voice came from some other place, barely audible, the ringing in his ears numbing his brain, but the voice came again, closer, familiar.

"Get ready! They're coming! Aim low!"

A pair of shells came in one behind the other, the ground jumping beneath him, a shower of thick splinters blowing into his back. He cried out, the shock, saw a man lying across a broken tree, the shell finding him, pure chance. He ducked again, curled up as tightly as he could, thought of Willis, where? Champlin, the others . . . Captain Patch. But his brain pulled him back, another jolt under him, a remnant of a tree to one side swept completely away. Every part of him was shaking, a hard shiver in his gut, the musket held tightly against him. The shells came again, another series of four, then two more, not as close, the aim of the gunners shifting, seeking targets farther to the right.

"Everybody up! Get ready! Aim low!"

He glanced up, his eyes barely above the fattest limb, sat upright now, was amazed to see Captain Patch moving his horse directly along the line. Patch had a strange fire on his face, a hard, cold steel as though fighting through the horror in his own mind. But there was a job to do, and Patch was drilling that into his men. Bauer shifted his knees, rose up, could see now what the job was to be. Beyond the carpet of bodies, the woods were in motion, a wave of color, men coming at them quickly, no more than three hundred yards away. He stared, hypnotized, but around him men were shifting position, finding a place to aim the musket. The sergeants were clambering over the fallen timbers, quickly, sliding snakelike through the men, their own muskets and carbines settling into the good place, seeking protection in the cover. To the left, a volley of musket fire erupted, too soon, someone's nervous impatience, the line of rebels not affected. All along the line, both directions, the calls came, but the men knew what to do, had done this before. The rebels came on, the only sounds now coming from them, the volume of their voices rising, a great wave rolling forward. A musket fired, close to his left, terrified impatience, and Bauer tried to fight that, angry at himself, shouting silently at the shaking in his hands. He had a different panic now. *Is it loaded?* He glanced down, saw the percussion cap, yes, good! The roar of voices was closer still, strange, unreal, something in his brain giving way, a story he heard, campfire at night, *the scream of the Banshees . . .* and he fought that, pushed back at the terror, the desperate need to leave this place, to stand up, drop the musket, run . . .

"Fire!"

The muskets around him blew out their charges, and he stared at the smoke, had done nothing, no aim, his finger fumbling for the trigger. The men behind him fired now, more smoke, the blasts close above his head, men all around him scrambling to reload, more useless shouts from the sergeants. He aimed, cursing the smoke, the shaking in his hands slowing, waited, some glimpse, the order to one side, "Fire at will!"

The chorus of shouts coming toward them was louder still, and he saw them through the smoke, a man with a thick black beard, strange floppy hat, red shirt, twenty yards. He pulled the trigger, musket jolting his shoulder, smoke in a burst in front of him. He didn't wait to see, the routine taking over. He dug frantically into his cartridge box, shoved the musket down beneath the log, the barrel toward him, paper in his teeth, ripping, the taste of powder, pouring it into the barrel, the ball, shoved in, the ramrod, push . . . hard, pull the musket up, roll it over, hammer back, percussion cap in place. He looked out, saw a man step up on a log, a small gray hat on the man's head, gold braiding, gold buttons on his chest, the man holding a pistol, looking back, waving it, then forward again, pointing, firing, to the left. The man seemed to search, looking manically, his eyes finding Bauer, but Bauer's search had ended. The pistol moved, a single smooth motion, the man aiming, and Bauer pulled the trigger, the musket making an odd sound, belching smoke. He grabbed for another cartridge, began the routine again, saw the rebel officer standing fixed, looking down, the pistol gone, his hand moving to his chest. Bauer saw it now, the ramrod, *his* ramrod, driven through the man. The officer stepped back off the log, then dropped to his knees, still stared at the arrow that had impaled him, then fell to one side, disappeared into the debris of the timbers.

"They're pulling back! Fire at will!"

Bauer felt an odd panic, no, what did you do? His hand searched frantically, the ramrod not in its place, nowhere around him. He looked out to the field, saw the rebel line pulling back, men still dropping, shot down from the muskets of the men close to him.

"Up men! Charge them! Don't let them get away!"

A dozen men closest to him took the call, rose up from their good cover, stepping forward awkwardly, stumbling, moving out into the open ground. But an officer held them up, forming them into line, and Bauer stood, tried to climb out of his hole, his legs stiff, frozen, and he looked out again into the field, fresh bodies in the grass, men stacked on top of men. Close in front of him, he saw the ramrod, pointing straight up from the debris, forced his legs out over the log, eased himself that way, hesitated, his brain holding to the image of the man's pistol, the black hole of the barrel. He held the bayonet ready, peered quickly over the debris, saw the officer, blood in a small stain on the man's gray coat, the ramrod halfway buried in the man's chest.

"Well, pull it out! Let's go!" Willis was there, rapped him hard on the back. "You practicing archery? Here, I'll do it."

Willis grabbed the ramrod, put a foot on the man's ribs, gave a tug, the thin steel sliding out, a small fountain of blood following it up from the hole. Willis laughed.

"You do that again, just remember . . . there's plenty of these damn things lying around here. But it ain't the smartest way to kill a reb. You mighta bent this one a little. C'mon. Load your damn musket. We still got work to do."

"Move! Advance!"

Champlin was there, gave Bauer a shove in the back, noticed the rebel officer now.

"Well, look what you got here. A captain. Good shooting, Private."

Willis slapped him again.

"Yeah, he's a regular sharpshooter."

"Let's go! Join up with those fellows over here. Form up!"

Bauer followed, looked again to the graycoat, heard Willis say something about the man's pistol . . . *a keepsake.* Bauer ignored him, stared out to the field, the men forming into line, Captain Patch again, more men down the way, more strength, the line stretching all along the edge of the woods. The men were stepping forward, picking their way through the bodies, and Bauer felt that as well, some odd logic, the rebels just killed not as respected, Bauer stepping on a fresh body to avoid an older one. He slid into line, saw a small wound on the captain's horse, heard Patch call out, "Look at it, boys! Look at how many we are! Brigade front! We're going after those damn rebels! The colonel's damn tired of this! We're not waiting for 'em to come to us!"

Patch waved his sword, the bugler giving the call from somewhere down the line, and Bauer began to step through the scattered and heaped bodies, stared down at the mass of flesh around him. He avoided what he could, saw men farther out in the field, wounded rebels, some trying to crawl away. Bauer suddenly absorbed Patch's words . . . *we're not waiting for them to come to us* . . . and one thought rolled through his brain, one question:

*Why not?*

———

They had moved forward again, past another field littered with dead. Bauer squatted low, a nervous shaking stare at the line of rebels who stared back at him. Behind him, more men were standing, and now the order came, Captain Patch to one side, still on the horse.

"Fire!"

The entire line erupted, and down to the side another order was given, another volley. Across from Bauer, the rebel line seemed to waver, too many men going down, some pulling away. The musket fire came toward them now, sharp zips that tore the air in all directions. Behind Bauer, the second line fired their volley, while Bauer reloaded, the bend in his ramrod ignored, the bloodstain from the rebel captain long wiped away. Across the field, the rebels began to melt away, many of them down, falling still, a third volley tearing their lines, Bauer joining into that, searching the smoke for anyone standing, the aim at the legs, the jolt into his shoulder. The smoke hid the rebel retreat, most of it, some men still standing tall, but not for long. Bauer had seen that too often, at the peach orchard, near the awful bloody pond, and now, in the open fields. They stood as though deaf to the sounds of the lead in the air, as though on the parade ground, fire, reload, fire again. But the strength in the Federal lines was far too great, and the brave rebels, the men Bauer had begun to admire, were far too few to hold back the wave of blue that poured toward them.

The order came now, a hoarse shout through the lull in the firing.

"Advance, double-quick!"

Bauer obeyed, as they all did, their line strengthened by a fresh regiment coming out of the woods behind them, moving up quickly. Few turned to see them, no one really caring who they were, what state, what flag. As Bauer stepped forward, he breathed in the smoke, his eyes and lungs burning. But no one held back, few ran away, the sergeants keeping order without the brutality, the cursing jerks on the coat collars. Bauer appreciated that moving forward was a far simpler maneuver than pulling away, that if there was any kind of contagiousness spreading through these men, it was the best kind, the certainty that they were driving the enemy back, that they were *winning*.

They drove through another stand of timber, more of the cracked and broken trees, obstacles and cover, slowing the line. But the men around

Bauer were used to this now, filed through the openings in good order. Bauer fought the watery eyes, the coughs, ignored the others around him, suffering the same ailments he was. He pushed past a wounded man, a rebel with blood on his face, a quick glance, searching for weapons in the man's hand. That was new, the wounded still dangerous. As they pushed past more of the fallen rebels, some of those men had suddenly taken their last chance, a bayonet lunging upward, a pistol discharging the last round. If there had been pity before, there was none now, and many of the men who marched beside Bauer stepped past the wounded with a flash of the bayonet, no one stopping them, the wounded not wounded any longer. Out front the officers kept up the pace, one lieutenant suddenly stumbling, a single sharpshooter making good his last round. The fallen officer caused a roar of anger that spread through the men who followed him, draining away a small piece of their exhaustion.

In the field, the rebels waited, but they were not many, and Bauer fought to breathe, pain in his ribs, the exhaustion of yesterday returning. He slowed, others near him doing the same, the line of rebels taking aim, a volley blowing out toward them. Bauer had seen the rebels aiming, had dropped low, simple instinct now, the balls flying high, one man crying out, the one man who reacted too slowly. They were up again, the sharp command, the rebels drifting back, leaving more of their own in the field. Bauer tried to keep the pace, but no one was moving quickly, many men stopping, as Bauer did now, staring out with blackened faces, powder-coated shirts, some with small wounds, torn shirts for bandages. The officers knew what their men had done, how far they had come, and so the orders didn't come, the men on horseback focused more to the front, seeing what so many of the infantrymen could not. In the woods beyond, where the backs of the rebels showed one more retreat, the field was speckled with white. Some of the tents were still standing, though many more were ripped down, either by the rebels or by the artillery fire the Federal batteries now poured toward the rebel lines.

Bauer leaned on his musket, didn't know if he had reloaded, and for the moment, he didn't care. The enemy had faded away in front, and in some weary place in his mind, he knew they would stand up again, face them again, the next field, the next patch of forest. He saw Willis, down on one knee, but there were no words, nothing to say, no energy to say it. The artillery continued out to the right, a hot fight, but in a few short minutes, that quieted as well. The sudden lack of firing seemed to catch them all by surprise, the men standing again, few speaking, and heads began to turn, Bauer with them, hearing the chatter and thumps far to the right, where the other Federal divisions had driven their way forward. No one around him, none of the officers, not even the colonel had any idea what was happening on those far distant fields, in the ravines and gullies and stands of blasted trees. But here the officers knew they had to get their men up and moving, had to keep the pressure on the retreating rebels. Bauer saw Patch ride out in front, saw the sword come up again, could see the other horsemen, the line stretching to both ends of the field. He saw motion, far to the left, the end of the field, the woods there suddenly alive with blue, another line rolling forward, coming at an angle into their flank. For a long moment, the two lines halted, officers in a gallop toward each other. The meetings were brief, and Bauer saw a larger flag, the breeze showing the Stars and Stripes, *brass,* someone who must know what was happening. Colonel Allen rode back toward his men now, Patch and Captain Pease close beside him, aides trailing behind, blood on the flanks of the horses. The men around Bauer knew what was coming, and they hoisted their muskets, Bauer doing the same, a quick glance at the percussion cap, knew he had reloaded, no memory of that. Behind them, the bugler was there, ever present, the man Bauer almost never saw. The call came now, Patch's sword pointing the way, and once more, the blue lines, feeling the strength, the power brought to them by so many fresh troops, obeyed the order and began to march.

PART FOUR

# DESPAIR

## CHAPTER THIRTY-FOUR

# HARRIS

BEAUREGARD'S HEADQUARTERS TENT
APRIL 7, 1862, DAWN

The governor had stayed close to Braxton Bragg, and Bragg had succeeded where Colonel Forrest had not. He had not only located Beauregard's new command center; Bragg had slept in the same tent. But both men had been called out, responding to the surprising sounds of a fight.

The first artillery fire had come to them from the left, and Harris knew little of what Beauregard had done to secure that flank. But Bragg went into motion immediately, Harris following. Before Bragg could reach the rugged terrain where his own brigade had been the point of that sword, word came from Preston Pond that he had been forced back. An infuriated Bragg did what Bragg had always done, shifting his men where the fire was most severe, doing all he could to support Pond as he withdrew to a new position. But the assaults began to come more to the right, and Bragg had gone back to Beauregard, reporting that the Federals must have decided to offer a last desperate gamble, that perhaps Grant had ordered Sherman and Hurlbut and the other commanders to drive from their defenses in a mad suicidal dash. It was the kind of theory Beauregard seemed entirely willing to accept.

Harris had been sent out toward Pond's new position, had seen the first of the prisoners brought in, a scattering of Yankee troops who had been caught up in a dense brush field that separated them from their main force. The surprise came when they identified themselves, a proud declaration that they weren't fighting for Sherman at all. These men were a part of the Union Third Division. They fought under Lew Wallace.

Harris understood enough of what was happening to know that this information had to be sent back to Beauregard. With a growing sense of chaos spreading all across the left flank, the commanders there had mostly exhausted their couriers, staff officers focused more on keeping their lines together, shifting units where the Federal surge was starting to blow through. Harris had no choice but to return to Beauregard himself.

Harris was amazed to see a broad smile. Beauregard sat straight in the saddle, showed few signs of the months-long ailment that had put him on his back through so much of the planning. Instead Beauregard was energized, responded to the sounds of the fight on the left with a kind of enthusiasm that Harris had never seen in the man. Harris could not avoid the thought that, with so much at stake, and with a surprise assault exploding toward them, Beauregard was actually *happy*.

Bragg had already ridden away, was moving more to the center of the lines, a fight erupting there as well. Harris did the only thing that made sense to him: He rode close to Beauregard, ready to respond in the event the general required a courier.

Beauregard moved quickly, riding hard, his staff straggling behind, not used to the manic energy coming from a man who had barely crawled out of a sickbed. But Beauregard shared his enthusiasm with the men he met on the roads. They were scattered, pieces of regiments, small commands, most without officers. Whether they were shirkers, or simply lost in the confusion of yesterday's fight, seemed not to matter to Beauregard at all. He spoke to them all, short, eloquent speeches, rallying them, gathering a force that actually had weight. With Beauregard leading them, the assemblage took shape as a regiment all their own. Harris followed as closely as he could, the newly minted battle line rushing forward into what seemed to be a gap at one end of a brigade that belonged to Bragg.

Beauregard kept to one side, cheered them as they passed, the men returning that with a hearty cheer of their own. Beauregard searched his staff now, pointed at Harris, said, "Governor! You are witness to great deeds this day. Great deeds! You must ride back to General Polk, offer the bishop my most reverent respects and request that he advance his forces to this location. They must occupy any ground they find where the enemy threatens. Polk will know what to do, once he observes the situation."

Harris saluted, moved away. He knew that the night before Polk had been pulled away entirely, that whatever troops he could gather had been drawn so far back, they were well behind Beauregard's own head-quarters. Harris had not been privy to the conversation that produced that result. All he knew now was that Polk was clearly too far away from any place he should be.

"Governor, may I see your map? I fear mine has been destroyed by the storm."

Harris dismounted the horse, was surprised to see Polk without his coat. Behind Polk, just outside the opening of Polk's tent, a black orderly was removing breakfast dishes from a wooden crate, a makeshift table. It was obvious that Polk had just finished his breakfast.

Harris withdrew the crushed roll of paper from his coat, handed the map to Polk, the same map Bragg had used the afternoon before. The details were small, nearly unreadable now, the rain doing damage to that paper as well. Polk seemed to squint, shook his head.

"I know the roads. Used them too many times. You say General Beauregard wishes us to advance again?"

"Those are his instructions, yes, sir. There is some urgency to the general's request."

Polk turned, called out to his adjutant, said, "Major, go to General Cheatham. Have him put the men into motion with all haste. Respect-fully suggest that the general be certain his men have full cartridge boxes."

The man seemed to hesitate, responded slowly.

"Sir . . . there is very little ammunition. The wagons we found last night were mostly empty. We had hoped we would not require fresh cartridges today."

Polk stared at the man, now a quick glance at the governor.

"Why is that, Major?"

"Well, sir, if I may make the observation, last evening General Beauregard was most optimistic that this corps's services would not be required today. Was that not the reason for our withdrawal, sir?"

Polk pondered the question, and Harris heard him let out a long breath.

"I brought the men back here with every hope they could be fed, Major. They have performed with the might of the Almighty's sword, and, yes, I had hoped that by now, this battle might be concluded."

Polk looked at Harris now.

"Is it your understanding, sir, that the enemy is not cooperating?"

Harris began to absorb the mood around him, felt a stirring uneasiness.

"General Polk, the enemy is pressing hard into our left and center. There has been word that they are also emerging from the landing itself, far to our right. Though I am not a military man, I have observed General Bragg responding to that with considerable energy, and though General Beauregard seems unconvinced of a threat, General Hardee has shifted his troops more to the right, to drive the enemy back. I have not yet seen General Hardee, but if I may offer, sir, there is considerable concern in General Bragg's quarter. Any hope that the enemy would have surrendered . . . has been contradicted by what is happening right now. He has been reinforced on our left flank by the division of Lew Wallace."

Polk nodded, kept his reaction to himself.

"And what of General Beauregard?"

Harris began to understand more clearly now. Polk had not been told anything of the fight. He was simply too far away.

"Sir, General Beauregard remains confident that this day, the campaign is ours. If I may suggest, sir, at this moment, from all I have seen, General Bragg would not agree with that optimism."

Polk stared at him, sharp, stern eyes, and Harris knew the look, had often seen the same gravity from Johnston. Polk turned to his adjutant again.

"Go *now* to General Cheatham. Have all available troops put into column of march and advance to the enemy's positions at once. Follow the sounds of the fighting. General Bragg and General Hardee must be informed once we are on the field. They will know where we should be placed. There is to be no hesitation. Do you understand?"

"Most certainly, sir."

The major spun his horse around, was gone quickly. Polk showed a hint of frustration now, the first emotion Harris had seen. He moved toward the crate, sat. Harris kept silent, knew Polk was deep in thought, realized suddenly he was thinking of Johnston. Polk looked up at him, the steel in his eyes giving way to a soft sadness.

"Optimism is a curse, Governor. It clouds our vision, gives rise to carelessness. I am guilty of that, to be sure." He paused. "Sidney would not have been so . . . sure of himself. He would have swept that away from our conversation. And so he would not have removed my troops so far from the field. He must . . . be furious. He would have known what to do. He would know that right now."

Harris understood the meaning, that Polk would certainly believe Johnston was looking down on all that was happening. Harris felt a burst of anger, fought to hold the words back, but there was too much sadness, too much grief, his discretion too battered by all he had seen.

"Sir, with all respects, we cannot rely on the wisdom of angels."

Polk looked at him again, tapped his chest with one hand.

"The angels are here, Governor. They do guide us. But they do not make us infallible."

Harris heard a distant rumble, turned, Polk standing now, moving beside him. Harris said, "Artillery. Ours, I assume."

"Most likely. We will find out soon enough."

NEAR SHILOH CHURCH<br>APRIL 7, 1862, 11:00 A.M.

Beauregard was back closer to the church, but not by his own choice. The Federals had pressed their attacks hard into any units Bragg could send against them, and even Beauregard began to understand that he could not muster the strength he needed to hold them back. The left flank was mostly a chaotic mess, the same ground that had served the Confederates so well now working against them. The deep cuts and thickets gave the Yankees cover, and artillery batteries had kept up the pace, splintering the guns that Bragg's artillerymen had hoped would slow the advance. For every Federal battery destroyed, it seemed another took its place, and Bragg's commanders on that part of the field had no such luxury. The guns that still fired were facing another problem as well, a spreading shortage of ammunition. Throughout the long, dismal night, no one had sent forward the supply wagons or fresh limbers. The gunners were making do with what little ammunition they had left.

Harris reached the church with the vanguard of Polk's forces, stayed closer to Beauregard, was too uncertain just where Bragg might be to offer his help there. The fight had grown, Polk's men stepping into a new hell in the fields and wood lines through the center of the position. There they were tied on the right to Hardee and whatever force Breckinridge had gathered together. It was the same all along the lines, and well behind. The Confederate forces were too jumbled, too few officers in places they needed to be. As the Federals advanced, the Confederate infantry rallied around anyone they could find, staff officers, gunnery officers, entire regiments following the first captain who raised his sword.

Beauregard was still in the saddle, rode with manic enthusiasm, pulling men out of the woods, the deep gullies, doing all he could to inject courage into men who had given up the fight. Harris rode behind him, watched in amazement as men responded, soldiers rising up with Beauregard's call, some of those without weapons, some with wounds.

They rode close to the church, and Beauregard halted the horse, seemed to freeze in place, staring out. Harris did the same, heard the variety of noises, far more activity now coming toward them to the left, to the northwest. Beauregard spoke out loud, a pronouncement not directed at anyone.

"They have turned the left flank. Bragg has failed us. Who do we have who can save that position?"

He looked around now, the staff silent, no one with an answer. Harris saw a rider, a hard gallop on the road to the north, the horse wobbly, thick froth on its flanks. It was Lockett, Bragg's engineer.

"Sir! General Bragg offers his compliments and reports that General Ruggles has been unable to stem the tide. The enemy continues to sweep past our flanks!"

Lockett paused, turned, and Harris saw what caught his eye. Swarms of men suddenly appeared, far more than before. They ran toward the church, away from the sounds of the growing battle, refugees who had abandoned the fight. Beauregard ignored the engineer now, rode out to meet them, waved his hat, the horse rising up to its hind legs in a perfect parade ground maneuver. Harris saw the faces, the look of men who had nothing to give, who were feeling the panic, an infection spreading through them all. More came down the road, men stumbling out of the woods, more climbing slowly up from a deep thicket to the east of the church. Lockett rode close to Beauregard, the din of the battle closer to the east, shouted, "Sir! Do you have orders for General Bragg? Should he withdraw to this position?"

Beauregard spun the horse around, some of the men responding to him still, and he shouted out, "Good soldiers! Form a line! Form here! Weapons at the ready!"

Some of the men slowed their retreat, most others kept moving, pushing past Harris, blank stares, barefoot, and Harris felt a wave of helplessness. I'm a civilian, he thought. What do I do to stop this? He shouted out, joining into the chorus coming from Beauregard and his staff officers. The men were rallying, but not many, and Harris called out, the only words he could think of.

"Men of Tennessee! This is your ground! Fight to keep your ground!"

The men mostly ignored him, the flow still moving past, some disappearing into the woods to the west. He saw one flag, torn, two halves dangling from a pole, carried across the chest of a man with no other weapon. The flag was Arkansas, and Harris felt desperation, hopelessness, the fear building in him as well. They are not mine, he thought. I am nobody . . . I offer them nothing. In front of him, Beauregard grabbed Lockett by the shoulder, shouted, "These are your men now! This is your command! Lead them!"

Lockett stared back, shook his head slowly, but Beauregard looked away, a ragged line coming together, a hundred men, an anchor that seemed to gather up more of the stragglers. Harris saw a change in Lockett's face, the man accepting the duty, a man who had never led troops being told to do so now. Lockett shouted, waved a short sword, "Soldiers! Follow me!"

He rode forward, away from the church, pushed his dying horse down into a ravine, and Harris was amazed once more, the ragged line following him. Beauregard cheered them, more officers riding up, couriers, frantic messages. Beauregard turned toward him now, a stab of cold in the governor's chest, and Beauregard said, "Go! To the west! Find General Hardee! Tell him he must advance! He must keep moving forward! The enemy will break!"

Harris tried to understand, but it was not his place to ask questions. It was a simple command. He rode away from the church, a road that led to the west, the same road that had brought him to Beauregard the day before, the awful duty, the image of Beauregard's complacency coming back to him, the lack of emotion, whether or not Johnston's death meant anything at all. He kept to the road, knew it would lead him out to the south of the bloody fields, the worst fighting he had ever seen, the worst anyone in this army had seen. They had taken those fields, and much more, had pushed the Yankees completely away. But now the battle was there again, closer than he expected. To one side, an artillery battery came to life, startling his horse, and Harris struggled to stay in the saddle, the reins slipping from his hands. He gripped the thick hair on the horse's mane, searched for the straps of leather, grabbed for them, pulled back, a gentle slap on the horse's neck. The horse calmed, Harris righting himself, and he spurred the horse once more. He could see the battery now, three guns, manned by only a half-dozen crew, all that was left. Around them, he saw what remained of their limbers, dead horses, dead men, but still the small crew swarmed over the three guns, loading each one, then firing all three at once. He halted the horse, fought the smoke, could see through broken trees a vast open field. It had been one of the Federal camps, a place where some of Beauregard's men had spent their night. But those men had withdrawn, some of them coming toward him even now, the retreat orderly, officers pulling them away with barely audible commands. The men still faced the enemy, that peculiar trait of soldiers who refused to die with a bullet in the back. Their muskets came up, another order, some firing, others just . . . standing, nothing in their muskets. Harris stared out through waves of smoke, saw no sign of anything they were shooting at. An officer rode past him at a gallop, suddenly jerked his horse to a halt, turned toward him, seemed lost, panicked, looked at Harris, no recognition, shouted to him, "Are you from Polk? Is General Polk moving this way? We need troops out to the right!"

Harris shook his head, could give the man nothing at all. The officer did not wait, spun the horse away, a hard gallop along the road toward the church. Harris started out again, quickened the pace, moved alongside another wide field, saw a pond to the left of the road, deep with grass, men standing on the near side, spread out in a line of battle. Officers were moving among them, preparing them, gathering them closer. He knew where he was now, the Hamburg–Purdy Road, the pond on the map, Water Oaks. To Harris, the gray line seemed strong, the men standing together silently, expectantly. Far out across the field, Harris saw their targets, a thick wave of blue. They were a quarter mile away, flags in the air, men on horseback leading them into the open ground. He sat, mesmerized, flinched at a sudden blast of artillery coming down very close to the men in front of him. More came now, one red streak in the air straight over his head, the blast in the woods behind the road. The officers were riding quickly, moving behind their men, offering encouragement, but some broke, one section pulling back, a dozen men in a frantic run right past him. An officer followed them, sword in hand, headed them off, turned a few, drove them back to the line, but others escaped, Harris watching them as they scampered away. He moved the horse toward the officer, saw a gleam of madness on a blood-red face, fiery eyes, the man seeing him, pointing the sword.

"Get out there! Help lead these men!"

Harris didn't know the man, saw the rank of major, said, "I am here from General Beauregard! I am to find General Hardee!"

The man seemed not to hear him, looked again to the oncoming enemy lines, and now Harris saw more of the blue, a heavy line emerging at an angle from woods on the right. The line halted, men on horseback riding among them, flags clearly visible, neat rows, the Yankee lines shifting position, straightening with the men already in the field. Harris watched the maneuver, shouted again at the officer, "General Hardee! Where is he?"

The man responded with a thrust of his arm, out to the right, directly into the fresh line of blue. The officer moved away, rode up close behind his men, and suddenly a bugler began his call, discordant notes through the roar of shelling, and the men close to Harris marched forward, some of them straight through waist-deep water in the pond. They pushed out into the field, incoming artillery peppering them, most falling behind, the Federal gunners overshooting. Harris watched in stunned amazement, the ragged line, no more than a brigade, a steady march farther into the open ground. The musket fire came now, the major's men firing first, and across the way, the blue line seemed to pause, and suddenly they backed away, disappearing into the woods. Harris could see it all, the charge by the major's men actually succeeding, and he felt a burst of excitement, of *hope,* thrust a fist into the air.

The brigade pushed onward, a thousand men even closer to the woods, but the smoke spilled over them, then a hard rattle of musket fire. Harris saw a glimpse of blue coming far beyond the men, to the left, out past the gray flank. It was another line of Yankees, orderly, a burst of fire into the Confederates on that end of the line. Almost immediately the line seemed to curl, bend, the charge slowing. For a long minute the musket fire poured out both ways, but Harris could see the blue mass, many more troops, could see enough through the smoke to see the brigade coming back, slow retreat back toward the grassy pond. It was clear in his mind now that these men had no chance at all. The Yankees were far too strong. He searched for the major, the man who had made the astonishing effort, the word in Harris's mind, something Johnston would know, would keep silent about until later. But Johnston would find the man, would talk to him in that slow, measured way, would tell the major how well he had done the job, might offer him the treasured words, that the man was a hero.

Harris held that thought, felt his throat tighten, wouldn't drive that away, not yet. But overhead, the musket fire was reaching him, the smoke in the field clearing away, the crumbling retreat of the major's brigade rolling closer, chased by artillery shells, the Federal gunners finding the range.

Harris thought of Beauregard's order, stared out to where the major had pointed, blue troops advancing, knew there was nothing he could do now, that even if Hardee was out there, the enemy had come too close, that surely Hardee had pulled back. He turned the horse, said in a low voice, "I cannot do this. I am sorry, Sidney. I cannot obey."

He pushed the horse back along the road, heard a scattering of artillery shells explode behind him, more piercing the air all around. He ducked low, useless gesture, pushed the horse harder, the animal responding, and he rode as fast as the horse would take him, back toward Shiloh Church.

SHILOH CHURCH

APRIL 7, 1862, 1:00 P.M.

The shells were falling in every direction, the stream of men coming through the woods increasing. Beauregard still tried to rally them, but the sounds of the fight were closer, the thunder from the shelling sweeping away his commands. Harris had made his report to the general, had apologized for his failure, but Beauregard had mostly ignored him, ignored him now. Harris felt the utter helplessness again but there was nowhere else to go.

He was surprised to see a cluster of horsemen, Colonel Jordan leading them, Beauregard's adjutant riding in from the same road Harris had taken. Jordan saluted, kept his demeanor as though nothing of concern were happening anywhere around them. Harris inched the horse forward, saw the same annoying confidence on Jordan's face, had tried to avoid him whenever he could. Earlier that morning, they had met, and it was unavoidable, Jordan riding from some place where the lines had failed, where the enemy was pressing toward them. Jordan had still kept the calm, his words matter-of-fact, that Bragg could not hold the left. But Jordan did not require anything from the governor, their talk brief, meaningless, Harris only a bump in Jordan's journey, a momentary pause in the inevitable.

Jordan said something to Beauregard, what seemed to be a calm, friendly chat. Harris pushed the horse closer, no decorum now, didn't care if Beauregard or anyone else ordered him away. Jordan said, "Would it not be judicious to get away from this place with what we now have?"

Beauregard still ignored Harris, kept his focus on Jordan, seemed to weigh the man's words. Harris saw something very different in Beauregard's face, none of the glorious optimism, none of the spirit for pushing the men into the fight. There had been so much sickness in the man, but it was not like that. Beauregard seemed pale, but there was something new, a look in the man's eye Harris hadn't seen before, a calm sanity, the bluster drained away, none of the airs of a man who knows *more* than anyone else. Around them the artillery still came in, some of the shells closer still, a burst of fire shattering a tree at the edge of the woods, more men pouring from those woods, desperate to make their escape. The musket fire was there as well, and Harris knew that sound, knew as much as the men around him what the musket balls could do. After a long moment, Beauregard nodded, looked around, seemed to notice his staff, glanced at Harris, held that for a moment, as though he suddenly remembered who the governor was, why he was here. Beauregard nodded toward him, unsmiling, formal, then turned to Jordan again, said, "I intend to withdraw this army in a few moments." He looked to his staff, the men anxious, sharp glances toward the artillery blasts.

Beauregard said, "Issue orders to all commands. Colonel Jordan will organize a covering guard. They will be placed in an advantageous location, with a view toward protecting our retreat, making every effort to halt the enemy's pursuit."

Jordan said nothing, nodded in agreement. Harris felt a strange stiffness between the men, as though the matter had been decided over a cup of tea. Jordan saluted, rode away, and Beauregard watched him leave. To one side, the staff went to work, senior officers sorting out the duties they had to perform, ordering the couriers on their way. Through it all, Harris still watched Beauregard, expected more, saw only a grim calmness on the man's face. Harris wanted to say something, anything, but there was nothing he could do, nothing he could give. It was cold truth, the sudden clarity that there was nothing anyone could do to change what was happening. Beauregard pulled on the horse's reins, but there was no urgency, and he moved past Harris without looking at him, the horse taking him out away from the church, into the muddy road, the road that led to Corinth.

# CHAPTER THIRTY-FIVE

# SHERMAN

In nearly every part of the field, black smoke rose high, drifting in a soft breeze. It came not from the fight, but from the destruction of most of the Federal camps. As the rebels had pulled away, they had committed as much destruction as they could, setting fire to the tents and wagons, a last hostile act by men who knew they would not see those places again.

Sherman stared at the tent, felt fortunate that his own headquarters compound close to the church had been spared, at least by those men who lit the torches. The other tents close by were mostly ripped down, ransacked. But his own had been left standing, an odd sight in a field where so much of the debris of war was scattered about. He dismounted, ignored the troops who streamed past him, men led by officers who continued to drive them forward. He eased his head into the opening, saw papers on the ground, not his. He bent low, picked up a handful, saw a Confederate seal, the orders and instructions for staff officers. The names were there as well, Beauregard, Jordan, Bragg. He studied the words, nothing of importance, not now. He noticed a bare space at the back of his tent, realized that the rebel commanders had not only used his tent for their own quarters, they had stolen his bedding.

"Savages. Damn savages."

He tossed the papers down, reconsidered that, thought, maybe Grant should see these . . . but there was nothing there, those orders now made meaningless. The rebel army was gone.

He stepped out of the tent, darkness settling on the field far too quickly, and he saw the thick clouds spreading over them, another storm coming. He moved again to the horse, climbed up slowly, the pain in his wounded hand still infuriating him. The dressing was filthy, rubbed through by the reins of the horse and he knew someone should see that, that a doctor would re-dress it, scolding him all the while. He looked to his staff sifting through their own belongings, scattered remains of back-packs and trunks, papers soaked by the rain, books tossed about, a shat-tered mirror. The men seemed stunned but Sherman was not surprised at all. The camps had been ransacked altogether, probably every Federal camp across this miserable ground looted for anything of value, and a great deal more of no value at all. He saw Major Sanger, staring at a handful of letters, raw emotion on the man's face, but there was no time for any of that.

"Major!"

The man looked at Sherman with red eyes, walked quickly toward him, the letters stuffed into the man's pocket.

"Sir?"

Sherman hesitated, had not seen Sanger this emotional before.

"You all right, Major?"

"They destroyed my wife's letters, sir. My photographs are gone. Why would anyone do that? What would it matter?"

"No answer to that, Major. Call it the spoils of war. One more kind of weapon. They have injured you. Was that not their goal?"

Sanger seemed to absorb that, nodded slowly.

"I suppose, sir, I can have her commission a new photograph. It will require some explanation. She will not be pleased. I do not share much of what we do in the field. Certainly not . . . all of this."

Sherman looked past Sanger, saw blue troops in the nearby road, coming out of the woods to the west. Alongside them were others, men who didn't look anything like soldiers at all. He left Sanger behind, dis-tracted, rode that way, could see they were rebel prisoners. He pulled the horse to the side of the road, focused on his own men, bandages and filth, blackened faces, hollow eyes. But it was those men who held the muskets, who prodded the rebels with the point of the bayonet. They noticed him now, but the energy was gone, the cheers few. The rebels looked up at him as well, men with the same look in their eyes, men who had given every piece of themselves. He was surprised by the faces, both sides sharing that common ailment. It was the aftermath of the worst experience of their lives, and the only difference between them was the uniform they wore. And of course, the muskets. He saw one uniform, gray, the insignia on the collar, but the buttons had been cut from the man's coat. Souvenirs, he thought. The final indignity. The officer looked up at him, seemed to know who he was, and Sherman felt the same way, a glimmer of recognition. The man tried to speak, but there were no words, the man's head dropping, the shuffling march continuing. Sanger had mounted his horse, moved up close behind him, and Sherman said, "I know that man. Baton Rouge, I think. Make sure the officers are treated with respect." He looked again toward his tent, the ridiculous abuse of his own personal belongings. My *bedding*? "Perhaps not too much respect. But care for their wounds, certainly. No matter what we may think of them, I will not have them think of *us* as savages."

"Yes, sir. I will see to it."

Sherman glanced skyward again, heard a low rumble, but it was not artillery. It was thunder.

"Ridiculous, damnable place. This will torture the wounded yet again. I want the ambulances sent out with all haste. There has been enough suffering for these men. The dead must be buried. Do what we can with the horses. Grant will order that, and I want the work under way before he has to tell me."

The line of prisoners continued past, seemed to stretch on as far as he could see. He turned away, had seen enough of bare feet and torn clothes. Sanger moved with him, the others mounting up, anticipating what might come next. Captain Hammond spoke up.

"Orders, sir?"

Sherman took a long breath, looked out to the west, the blanket of clouds hiding the sunset. He had already begun to think of the brigades, who the new commanders should be. He thought of writing that down, making his report to Grant, but he was feeling as tired as his men. Still the names came. Buckland . . . he'll have his own division, if I have anything to say about it. McDowell . . . old fool. But he has powerful friends. Hildebrand . . . I'll wring his neck, and make that decision a simple one. Stuart . . . not sure. He'll probably get his own division, too. Did good work out there. Wish I had been there to see it. If I'd have kept him here, alongside Buckland . . . He shook his head. I split up the division, weakened us. And yet, what might have been my most stupid mistake could have saved this army's left flank. Grant won't ignore that. Stuart will get a division.

He looked at the staff, shook his head.

"Nothing right now. See to your belongings, if they left you any. We must put this division back together as quickly as possible. I do not believe this fight is concluded."

Sanger responded, "Surely, sir, that is not the case. From all we have learned, the rebels have withdrawn completely. They are marching southward. Surely, sir, they will not come again. If anything, I had thought a pursuit was in order. With all respects, sir."

"Pursuit with what, Major? Look at these men around us. Go out to the camps and look at what we have left, who among the men is prepared to do this again. It can be no different in the other camps. Not even Buell's men can have much left after today." He paused, looked to the east, felt a cool, damp breeze. He knew they should have pursued the rebels, but already the Confederate commanders had placed a strong rear guard in their path, perhaps the only fighting men the rebels had left. Beauregard knows more about that than we do, he thought. Bragg, Hardee . . . they know very well that if we are careless, they can still give us a hard punch in the face. But there will be a pursuit. There has to be. That *man* in St. Louis will not understand what truly happened here, will not understand what this fight has done to us, to all of us. General Halleck will expect us to waltz right out of here and hammer those rebels like it's a walk in the woods. And if Grant does not comply, nothing we did here will matter.

"Gentlemen, I must go see General Grant."

ON BOARD THE TIGRESS,
PITTSBURG LANDING
APRIL 7, 1862, 8:00 P.M.

"I should send a wire to General Halleck, informing him of today's actions. I am quite certain General Buell has already done so." Grant paused. "There will no doubt be two *official* versions of the same event."

Grant sat on a small wooden chair, Sherman across from him, both men smoking the ever-present cigars. Sherman tried to distract himself from staring at Grant's injured leg, looked out toward a porthole into wet darkness. As Sherman had ridden eastward, the rain had come again, but not as bad, a steady light drizzle. He had not expected Grant to be back on the riverboat, but one look at Grant's leg told the story. Grant saw him looking again at the swollen limb, said, "They had to lift me out of the damn saddle. Thing is swollen like a barrel. Doctor gave me hell, as much as he had the courage to do that. After what they've been through, I let him blow out as much steam as he needed to. Still had blood on his hands. Hard to fault a man who spends his whole day in men's guts."

Sherman finished his own cigar, was suddenly nervous, kept his eye on Grant's leg.

"Is there some danger . . . ?"

"That they'll cut the thing off? I don't give them that much rope, Sherman. I just overdid the riding today. It's not a damn wound, no open sores. Not like General Smith."

Sherman had forgotten completely about Smith, said, "How is he? We sure as hell need him now."

Grant shook his head, one hand pressing on the injured leg, kneading, a grimace on his face.

"He's worse. No idea why. The doctors scratch their damn heads. My injury ought to have been worse than his . . . and they say if he doesn't improve soon, he might not improve at all." Grant looked over to him with a sharp glare. "That information is not to leave this boat. You understand? His division fought like hell out there, took casualties as bad as anyone on that field. I'll not have them reminded that their commander is sitting on this river being tended to by gloomy doctors." Grant pulled another cigar out of his coat, and Sherman did the same. Grant seemed startled by a thought, said, "Oh! Not sure if you heard. They found Will Wallace. The rebels wrapped him up in a blanket and left him by the side of some damn road. Damned if he isn't still alive. We hauled him back to his wife, out here on the river. I have to hand it to that woman. She held to her faith that he'd survive, that she'd see him again. Hell of a thing."

Sherman rubbed the dense stubble on his chin.

"I'll be damned. Pretty lucky there. I ought to go see him."

"Leave him be, for now. He's not all that well. Doctors say he might not last long. If he's awake at all, he's got his hands full of lace. If Ann says it's all right, then you visit. Otherwise, leave him be."

Sherman nodded, understood. He felt a sudden optimism, as though fortune was smiling on them all.

"Any word about Prentiss?"

Grant pulled at the cigar, the smoke rising.

"No. Prisoners say he's alive, taken back to the enemy's headquarters. Probably questioned by Beauregard himself. That's what I'd do, in his boots. They won't mistreat him."

Sherman thought of his own tent.

"If you say so."

There was a soft knock on the cabin door, and Grant tried to move, the pain in his leg shoving him back into the chair.

"Dammit. Yes, what?"

The door opened and Sherman saw Rawlins peering in, another stare at Grant's leg.

"Sir, General McClernand is here."

"Yes, good, send him in." Grant looked over at Sherman now, said in a low voice, "About time he got here. Hates the rain, I guess."

McClernand came in, removed his hat, another stare at Grant's leg, and Grant responded.

"Oh, for God's sake. The leg is fine. Just swollen up. Sit down, John."

John McClernand outranked Sherman, had already served as Grant's second in command during Grant's previous fights. Though he was capable on the battlefield, there was grumbling from some that McClernand was only in his position because he was a good friend of President Lincoln. Sherman didn't know whether that was true, but he had little use for the man, for reasons that came mostly from a bottle, though Sherman had conceded that he had never actually seen McClernand drunk. Whether the rumors were true didn't really matter right now. Sherman couldn't avoid what McClernand's First Division had done, holding on to Sherman's left flank through much of the fight, performing as well on the battlefield as anyone else in the army. McClernand smiled at him, a brief friendly nod, the perfect signal of the man's political skills. Grant held the cigar out toward McClernand, said, "We didn't chase them down today. I'll catch hell for that. Buell's probably told Halleck all about that. That's all right. I'll tell Halleck the same thing about the Army of the Ohio, if it comes down to that kind of schoolboy name-calling. Fact is, we didn't have it in us to chase anybody. You both know that. Buell does, too. He might still be out there in the field for all I know, trying to gather up half his army. Don't much care about that right now. What I care about is tomorrow. The enemy is beaten, and they know that. I believe that with a little pressure, we can scoop up a whole passel of those boys. The goal here is still Corinth, and Halleck will remind me of that the first chance he gets. I'm expecting that wire to get here any time now. I want you to choose the most fit men you have left, and march them out in support of Colonel Taylor's cavalry."

McClernand lost the smile.

"*Now?*"

Grant blew out a cloud of smoke.

"Easy, General. Not *tonight*. First thing tomorrow morning. The rebels can't move any faster in this rain than we can, and that's why I want the cavalry out there with you, pushing south until you can find whatever rear guard Beauregard has thrown out our way. Move your people after those boys as quick as you can. It won't be hard to follow the tracks of the rebs. Everything I hear says they're in a full retreat, and they'll be dropping off wounded men and any equipment they're hauling every step of the way. But no carelessness. That bee still has some sting, and we've taken enough casualties as it is."

McClernand looked at Sherman, as though reassuring him.

"We'll get the job done, sir."

Sherman said nothing, was rolling the units through his mind, just who might be able to make that march. Grant seemed to relax, the cigar in his hand. He massaged the leg again, said, "If you're lucky . . . maybe you can grab up the whole lot of 'em. Might be the only thing that'll convince General Halleck I deserve stars on my shoulder. It wouldn't hurt me any if Colonel Taylor rode his cavalry right into Corinth."

## CHAPTER THIRTY-SIX

# SEELEY

NEAR FALLEN TIMBERS
APRIL 8, 1862, 11:00 A.M.

Most of the Confederate army was already far to the south, the closest infantry a force of Breckinridge's Corps, which held a strongpoint on well-chosen ground a few miles closer to Corinth. It was the best solution Beauregard had, to place a hard line of infantry capable of putting up one more fight. Breckinridge agreed, both men understanding that the Federal army might march out on the same roads in an energetic pursuit. But Forrest had no expectations that the Federals would move quickly at all. Like many of the other cavalry units, he had dashed in and around the second day's fighting, had tried to assist anyplace horsemen might be useful, but on every part of the field, the astonishing number of casualties had been a clear sign that Beauregard's decision to withdraw had been the only possible choice. Though Beauregard had responded to the obvious power the Federals threw against him, Forrest assumed from all he had seen that most of the Federal troops were hesitant, jittery, and as worn-out as the men who had retreated. Forrest had convinced his own men that the only reason the blue troops still held their ground was that Confederate cavalry had been poorly used.

Seeley could only agree with his commander's assessment, had seen plenty of the horrors of the second day's fight. The Federal forces had seemed to come toward the Confederate infantry in continuous waves, as though their troops were created out of the air. When one blue line wavered, another appeared close behind, shoring it up, or falling in on the flank, adding to the power of a great blue fist the Confederate infantry could not hold back. Seeley respected Forrest, a feeling shared by the men around him, what seemed to be evolving into idolatry rather than simple obedience to the colonel's orders. There was an infectiousness to that, and Seeley was not immune.

Forrest had lined them up just back of a wooded ridge, with a clear view of a wide road, one of the primary routes that led toward them from the battleground. To one side were their hastily arranged camps, a scattering of tents and smoldering campfires, dampened by the constant drizzle of rain. Behind them spread a newly created hospital, a gathering of tents planted among a handful of ramshackle farmhouses. The smells were unavoidable, and Seeley had ridden past feeling a mix of wonder and sickening shock. He marveled at the dedication of the doctors, who had stayed in place, doing their awful work, even as their army left them behind. Not all of them had the luxury of an inside work space, and so the stretchers lined up outside as well, and Seeley could see them laboring feverishly over the torn bodies of more men than Seeley could count. The wounded were from both armies, soldiers and Federal prisoners, the doctors not seeming to notice uniforms at all. As at every hospital, the most horrifying sight was the growing pile of severed limbs, bloody and white, stacked beside every place where a surgeon did his work. Seeley had wondered about that, as much as he thought of the astonishing suffering of the victims. What happens to those? Are they just . . . buried, like the dead men, in their own graves? He had held back asking Captain McDonald, knew he would get that same stare, the response to yet another stupid question. Well, certainly they're buried. Everything is buried, even the horses. That can't be too hard. The ground around here is mostly mud anyway.

Forrest's cavalry was now the end of the line, the last to leave the area close to Shiloh Church, and so they did their work as usual, keeping hidden, observing the activity around the Federal positions, making sure the Yankees were not organizing massed columns to chase down the ragged men who stumbled toward Corinth. But there was no great surge. Instead the men who spread out across the churned-up battlefields were burial details, almost all men in blue. Most of the men Seeley saw were carrying shovels, not muskets, and he had watched with a painful admiration, knew theirs was a job he could not do. They dug long trenches mostly, directed by the commands of a sergeant, perhaps an occasional officer. In every case, the dead had been lined up beside the fresh trench like stacks of cordwood, and when the hole was thought deep enough, or the men too tired to dig any further, the bodies had been dragged in, one at a time. There were other kinds of graves as well, huge holes where the Confederate dead were placed, heaps upon heaps, mass burials with no markings, no way to preserve the identity of who those men were, no way for anyone's family to find them at all. It was one more sad piece of the tragedy, that the Confederate retreat meant that there was no time to collect their dead, and that many of the wounded had to be abandoned as well.

Leaving his own people behind had infuriated Forrest, but even the colonel's passions for killing the enemy had been tempered by the job the burial parties were doing. Seeley had only guessed that perhaps Forrest, like the other horsemen who followed him, had no stomach for handling so many bodies, no matter which side claimed them. It had not escaped Seeley that a quick and violent raid against those men would have been a slaughter, that the few Yankees who were actually armed would have been no resistance at all, would most likely have scampered away in the face of screaming cavalry. But for a while at least, burial parties were not soldiers, no matter their uniforms. Seeley had been grateful that Forrest shared that notion, that those men were somehow serving God, that even the mass graves were the first step toward a peace those soldiers had earned.

The cavalry along the low ridge numbered about a hundred fifty, but more were riding up, horsemen from other units sent back their way by Breckinridge, or other infantry commanders, who knew how important Forrest's men were. It was, after all, a line of defense, and hospital or no, they were all that stood between Grant's army and what dragged away behind them.

Seeley turned toward the sound of hoofbeats, saw what seemed to be several companies of cavalry coming up the road, moving slowly past the hospital. Beside him, McDonald said, "Texas Rangers. Good many of them. That'll help."

Forrest rode out that way, met their leader, rode alongside the man as they moved up in line, strengthening the horsemen already there. Forrest called out, "Gentlemen, this is Major Harrison, and these Texans are his men. Welcome them with a hurrah!"

The cavalrymen responded, a single cheer, as though perfectly rehearsed. Seeley knew of Forrest's annoyance with the cumbersome chain of command, that right here, Forrest was in command, and intended to keep it that way, and so Seeley picked up on Forrest's mention of the Texan's rank of *major,* no uncertainty among the Texans just who the ranking officer might be. Forrest had shared his disgust with his men the night before, that the clumsiness of their chain of command might have cost the entire army a victory that first night, close to the Tennessee River. The rangers moved up into line behind and to one end of Forrest's men, and McDonald said, "More than three hundred now. I feel a whole lot better."

Seeley looked back, a smaller group of cavalry coming up the same road, and McDonald saw them as well, said, "Well, hello. Better still."

Forrest rode out that way, the formality of command, and Seeley saw an exchange of salutes, then a brief handshake. The men carried carbines, not the usual shotguns of Forrest's men, and McDonald said, "I bet they're from Morgan. That might be Morgan himself. Wish he'd have brought more than a handful."

Those men rode up into line as well, and Forrest slipped out to the front, watching as the new men added to his formation. Forrest shouted out, "General Breckinridge has given us very specific instructions. We are to make every effort to delay any Yankee march in this vicinity. And we shall do exactly that. The general has offered to march a column of infantry back this way, should we require them. I am counting on you to perform any action, so those infantry may safely continue their march to Corinth."

Seeley stood taller in the stirrups, said to McDonald, "Captain . . . what's that?"

Forrest had turned, more of his men pointing out to the north. The field there was wide, cut by a single creek, was strewn with cut trees, a natural obstacle for anyone to cross. Two horsemen rode quickly, the scouts Forrest had sent out to observe anything that might be advancing along the road. They rode with perfect skill, slipping gracefully past the fallen timbers, through the muddy creek. That was no accident, Forrest selecting his best horsemen as advance scouts. They galloped up the hill, reached Forrest, saluted, gave their report, and Forrest turned back toward the men along the ridge, said aloud, "They're coming, boys. We have a job to do."

Seeley felt the rising excitement in the men around him, shared it, patted the horse, a brief show of affection, low words.

"You hear him? It might be time for a fast ride."

He heard muffled drums, the men along the ridge quieting, listening, and now, across the field, cresting a distant hill, they could all see the blue. It was a column of Federal infantry.

The Federal troops spread out quickly, battle formation, and Seeley pulled out his shotgun, the others doing the same, weapons loaded, checked, everyone watching as the Federals began their advance. Seeley could hear Forrest, nervous chatter to the other commanders.

"They see us. Probably see our camp. But I'm betting they're as jittery as squirrels. They have no idea how strong we are here, if we're backed up by a whole division. That's a huge advantage. Let's see what they intend, and we'll decide what to do about it."

The Federals continued their advance, and on the road behind them, another column crested the hill, a small gathering of horsemen and flags leading the way. Seeley watched the blue line making its way through the cut trees, felt the jitters himself, and beside him, McDonald said in a low voice, "Whole brigade. Maybe another behind them."

He raised his field glasses, and Seeley did the same, and suddenly Forrest was there, right in front of them. Forrest glassed them as well, said, "Ohio flag. Could be Sherman's boys. I can see a flock of cavalry behind them, whole herd of horses back in those trees. They're just watching us. That's their first mistake, Captain. Their horsemen ought to be leading the way. You see any artillery?"

Seeley scanned the trees frantically, heard McDonald say, "No. Not yet."

"If they intend to shove us away, there ought to be some big guns out there with them. Just depends how much they want us out of the way."

Forrest lowered the glasses, and Seeley watched him, saw the look he had seen before, the usual fire in the man's eyes, changing to something far more dangerous. The words came out in a low monotone.

"Let them get to the creek. Yankees don't like to get their feet wet, so they'll look for rocks, some shallow place. That'll slow them down even more, and their lines will fall apart, the officers will lose control."

Seeley felt the thunder in his chest, looked to the side, to his own squad, the men all staring out to the oncoming lines of blue. He pulled the pistol from its holster, checked the cartridges, a full load, saw his men doing the same, following his silent command, a brief check of the percussion caps. He stared again to the oncoming troops, no sound but the distant drummers, the troops forced to crawl and step over the fallen trees. They were almost halfway across the field, their lines already breaking up, disorganized, and now Seeley saw exactly what Forrest had predicted. In the lowest part of the field, the men reached the creek, and Seeley knew the waters were swift, the creek swollen by rains most of the night, rains even now in a thick drizzle. The Federal line seemed to halt, gaps appearing as the men sought a crossing, and the voice came now, the single word, loud and long, carrying to every man along the ridge.

*"Charge!"*

Forrest led the way, the horsemen surging up and over the ridge, a hard ride straight at the Federal lines. Seeley held the shotgun tight against his right side, the horse's reins in his left hand. He kept low, his eye on Forrest, stared again at the blue infantry. Smoke burst out from the Yankees, scattered volleys, and already men were stumbling into one another, utter confusion, some thigh-deep in the swollen creek, splashes as the men fought one another to back away. In seconds the horsemen were there, pushing through the creek without pause, the shotgun blasts and pops from the carbines erupting along the line. Seeley felt a scream coming out of him, some place deep and black, was surrounded by a panicked mob of blue soldiers. He released the horse's reins, a quick second, aimed the shotgun at a man's back, the horse moving him right up to the man who struggled with his musket, stepping clumsily over a cut log. Seeley pulled the trigger, the man punched down into mud and grass. He saw another man, facing him, trying to fix a bayonet, but the man seemed to understand the hopelessness of that, turned, running away. Seeley shot him as well, the man falling over another of the trees. The Yankees were still around him, a mad, desperate retreat, most of them offering no fight at all. *Squirrels.* Seeley jammed the empty shotgun back into its holster, pulled out his pistol, aimed, a man raising his musket, pointing out to one side, and Seeley shot, missed, shot again, the man firing the musket, then tumbling down, trying to rise, the wound on his shoulder. Seeley was closer now, a few feet away, the man looking up at him, terrified, and Seeley fired one more time, the ball striking the man's head. Seeley felt his hard breathing, his own terror blending with the raw thrill of the chase.

He rode forward again, another man running, the horse too quick, the pistol down, pointing at the man's back, another shot, the man crying out, down as well. Seeley turned, saw Yankees moving toward him, men he had passed, and they tried to avoid him, but one man had a pistol of his own, an officer, and Seeley saw the man aiming at him. Seeley ducked, from instinct. He rose back up, pointed the pistol at the officer, fired, missed, fired again, the officer doing the same. Both men missed, Seeley cursing to himself, the officer rushing past him. Seeley pulled the trigger, but the pistol was spent, six shots, and he looked at it, cursed his own shaking hand. The pistol went back to the holster, and he drew the saber, yanked the horse to one side, saw another man with a bayonet, and the horse jumped past a fat log, the saber coming down in a hard chop, ripping the musket from the man's hand, slicing a gash across his chest. The horse kept moving, and Seeley looked for another target, could still hear the crushing fire of the shotguns all around him, the ping and pop of carbines. Some of the Federal troops were trying to form a line, an officer holding a sword of his own, but the officer dropped to his knees, fell forward, the line dissolving, the men in blue still trying to make their escape. The horsemen pressed on, no one slowing, and from a small cluster of blue came a burst of smoke, a volley too quick, too high. Seeley was there now, the saber swinging wildly, a man's shoulder, another, Yankees running alongside him, shielding themselves with arms, Seeley hacking down, not looking at the result. Around him were screams and shouts, from all of them, the terror of the Yankees, the mad energy of Forrest's horsemen. It was one great chorus, the Federal line broken completely. Seeley searched manically for a target, still swinging the saber, slicing the air, felt a magnificent energy, pure raw adventure, the Yankees harmless, scattering like so many flies.

The horsemen had chased most of them back to the road now, and

Seeley saw blue cavalry, disorganized, the horsemen trying to advance. But the panic of their infantry drove right through them, and the horsemen didn't hold their formation, began galloping away, parting shots from badly aimed carbines. Some of Forrest's men had already reached them, the fight one-sided, the Federal horsemen struggling to retreat, Forrest's men striking them down, shotgun blasts again, the men who had taken the time to reload. Pistol fire rang out as well, both sides, but the blue cavalry were making their escape, men riding hard past their own fleeing infantry, scampering past another formation, another line of infantry. Seeley hesitated, pulled back on the reins, saw another mass of blue, a battle line deep and solid, spread out across the road. He saw the volley, the air around him ripped, torn, men tumbling out of the saddle. It was a shock, unexpected, and he looked down, saw his own man, Hinkle, rolling, writhing, his blood smearing the grass.

Seeley thought of the shotgun, but there was no time, the Federal line pouring out another volley, the air alive around him, a sharp *zip* close to his head. He suddenly felt helpless, weak, could see some of the fleeing Yankees falling into the line, more of the Yankees firing, another man close to him going down, the horse falling as well. The solid line was no more than a hundred yards in front of him, and Seeley searched for McDonald, knew the time had come, that they could not hope to drive back that many. But then he saw Forrest, waving the saber, calling out, pulling them forward. Forrest rode out straight toward the Federal line, the blue line wavering, the strange shock of Forrest's maniacal attack still pressing the scattered Yankees, the men desperate to reach their main line. Seeley halted the horse, held tight to the reins, held the saber, but there were no targets now, most of the Yankees back out to the road. But still Forrest chased them, a pistol coming out, Forrest firing, a man close to him rolling over.

The fight began to quiet, scattered shots, many of the Federals reloading, officers giving the commands, a cluster of horsemen close behind the main line, the Stars and Stripes. Seeley heard a command, loud and harsh, turned, saw the Texan, Harrison, waving the sword high above his head, motioning his men back. Others obeyed, and Seeley felt a burst of relief, could see what had to be a thousand Federals spread out along the road, more coming up behind, adding to their strength. The blue line threw out another volley, smoke and flame in a vast cloud, more of the horsemen dropping away. Seeley began to feel a panic of his own,

saw McDonald riding back, calling out, heard the Texan again, the single command:

*"Fall back!"*

Seeley looked to his own squad, one empty horse, his men watching
him, expectant, wide-eyed, and he turned the horse, pointed back to the
ridge, repeated the command.

*"Fall back!"*

Close by, he heard the voice of McDonald.

"Good God! What's he doing?"

Seeley turned, saw a single gray figure riding hard straight toward the
blue lines. It was Forrest. Seeley held the horse, his brain screaming, *no*!
Forrest still chased down the fugitives, slashed at the men around him,
firing the pistol again. The Yankees close to him seemed to understand
what was happening, that this one officer had ridden too far, had left his
own command in a one-man assault that had carried him straight into
the enemy. Seeley wanted to ride that way, to help, expected Forrest to
go down, McDonald shouting to the colonel, the infantry's muskets
aiming now at Forrest, who fought back with his pistol, then the saber.
But Forrest finally seemed to understand, realized he was by himself,
virtually swarmed over by surprised Federal troops. Seeley watched
with desperate horror as Forrest spun the horse around, drove hard
through the mass of blue, the saber lashing downward, clearing his own
way, bayonets and blue arms reaching up, grabbing at him, musket fire
still ripping the air. The word rolled again through Seeley . . . *no* . . . but
Forrest kept riding, coming back toward them.

For a long moment, the musket fire seemed to fade away, no danger
to anyone but Forrest, every weapon of the enemy all seeming to target
him, what they had to know was some *great prize*. But the main force
still obeyed their officers, and another volley whistled past Seeley, and
McDonald shouted out the order to retreat again, the men helpless to
aid Forrest. Seeley ignored the order, could not just . . . leave. Forrest was
still among a scattering of blue, bent low, hugging the horse's neck, no
fighting now, just survival. Seeley saw him ride close to a single man,
reach down, a blue soldier hoisted up by the collar, arms flailing, Forrest
pulling the man up behind him. Seeley saw that Forrest was using the
man as a shield, the enemy responding by holding their fire. Forrest
moved out beyond the last of the scattered Federals, kept the horse at a

hard gallop, released the soldier now, the man tumbling down in a rolling heap. Seeley waited another long second, saw a sharp grimace on Forrest's face, but he was closer, coming fast, *safe*. Seeley spun the horse, saw that most of the horsemen were already across the creek, making good their retreat, a few empty horses milling about, some standing above the fallen men who had ridden them. But most of the troopers reached the ridge, and quickly Seeley was there as well. He turned, gasping breaths, saw Forrest coming up behind him, bent over, blood on his side. Forrest dropped the saber to the ground, and Seeley saw the pain on the man's face, saw the horse with a pair of gushing wounds. There was mostly silence now, officers moving quickly toward Forrest, helpful hands, questions, Seeley sharing their stunned bafflement. Forrest tried to straighten, leaned to one side, the blood spreading. He removed his hat, held it high, a short quick wave, and the horsemen around him responded, offered him one more cheer.

Incredibly, Forrest was struck only once, but it had come at very close range, a musket ball driven into his hip, the ball lodging close to his spine.

Along the ridge, the horsemen waited still, the ailing Forrest keeping them in line. But a few miles to the south, General Breckinridge had heard the commotion of the fight, and almost immediately a courier had appeared, giving Forrest and his cavalry a direct order to retire, the order instructing them to move south, to strengthen the rear guard of infantry that Breckinridge now commanded. With the Federal troops still to their front, Forrest obeyed.

After a pause to regroup, the Federals pressed forward their advance, driven by a general who would not tolerate yet another utter collapse of a force under his command. They re-formed their brigade front and drove back out through the timbers, across the creek, and pushed on to the ridge. But the cavalry was already gone. Instead the blue troops and their red-haired commander found the camps that had been abandoned by Forrest's men. Beyond that, they also found the hospital, the doctors continuing to do their work, caring not who the soldiers or their general might be. The Federal troops were ordered to destroy the cavalry's camp, but the hospitals were allowed to remain. Without fanfare, the Confederate doctors were paroled, and the Federal troops added to their work by dragging up the Confederate horsemen who lay wounded in the field.

On this day there would be no further Federal advance. The brief fight at the fallen timbers had been enough for their commander, an embarrassment explained only by the complete exhaustion of the men driven out to pursue the rebel retreat. Now the Federal brigades began a brief retreat of their own, returning to the camps near Shiloh Church. Forrest's survival had come in plain sight of the general who commanded the Federal forces, who had ridden close enough to face the empty muzzle of Forrest's pistol. The man's fury was complete, and he knew that of course there would have to be an explanation, why fewer than four hundred rebel cavalry had driven back and panicked five times their number, and how a mass of blue troops could not find the point-blank aim to take down a single horseman. It only added to the disgust of the general who rode beneath the Stars and Stripes, on his way back to his own tent, the place where he had yet to replace his stolen bed.

The one-sided fight at the fallen timbers had accomplished just what the Confederate commanders had hoped for. Any Federal pursuit had been delayed for at least a full day, and the relief Forrest had provided the desperate soldiers who trudged toward Corinth was welcomed as nearly miraculous. Whether Colonel Forrest would ever make a one-man charge again was a question his officers kept to themselves.

Seeley rode past the ragged clusters of infantry, stragglers and walking wounded, some men already collapsed beneath shade trees, some foraging the woods for drinkable water, settling often for the muddy slop in rain-filled puddles. The cavalry units had gone their separate ways, the Texans and the others returning to where their senior commanders expected them to be. Still, they had a job to do, guarding the various routes the enemy could use to pursue. Forrest's men had watched their commander carried away, no amount of protest from Forrest allowed to contradict the doctors, and Breckinridge, that Forrest be moved quickly back to Corinth, to be treated in some place other than a roadside shack.

They stopped beneath a wide canopy of trees, McDonald and the other officers ordering them to dismount. The cavalry knew already what most of the army did not, that for now at least, there was safety. Seeley dismounted, felt a stiffness in his legs, examined the horse again for wounds, nothing, what he had to believe was another miracle. The men around him were mostly sullen, silent, every man having watched their commander survive what he should not have survived. But Forrest's wound was severe, and there was a dreadful expectation that came from that.

With the men down in the coolness of the shade, some sought sleep, and for others rations came out, but there was not much of that, most of their food left behind in their camp. Breckinridge could send them nothing at all, the infantry mostly without any rations of their own. Seeley had seen too many of those men. He sat alone, had already sifted through his pockets, a gesture of futility, nothing at all to eat. He was surprised to see Sergeant Gladstone, the old man limping, and Gladstone dropped down heavily across from him, kept his distance, chewed on what looked like a stick. After a moment, Gladstone broke the silence around them, his usual growl.

"Fun, weren't it?"

Seeley was feeling the weariness now, had a sudden need for sleep.

"What?"

"That there fight. I saw you with that saber. Chopped some of those boys into stew meat. Best part of it, being a horse soldier and all. You get to watch 'em up close. You wipe off the blood?"

Seeley recalled that now, a quick swipe against the horse's flank, returning the saber to its scabbard.

"Yes, I did. What difference does that make?"

Gladstone shrugged.

"It's a damn sight harder if'n you don't. Get it off while it's fresh. Get some on your hands, too. Healthy."

Seeley had no energy for this, leaned his head back, heard low talk from some of the others. He thought of the fight, the sounds still ringing in his ears. It was the first time he had done that, the first time he had been so close, had put a shotgun right into a man's back. And the saber . . .

He felt his heart suddenly racing, the sounds of the fight only a memory, but the images, the cries of the men, the horse driving right into them, the *saber*.

Gladstone seemed to read him, gnawing on whatever strange thing was in his hand.

"It were fun, weren't it?"

Seeley was annoyed at the man, thought, none of your business. He wanted to turn away, to find another spot, or easier still, order the sergeant to go somewhere else. Chewing that damned . . . what? Crazy old man. But the images still wouldn't leave him, and he glanced at his gloves, covering stiffening fingers, aching joints from holding so tightly to the saber, that marvelous weapon. He saw blood now, stains in the creases of the soft leather, wanted to pull the gloves off, waited, stared at the blood, thought of the shotgun again, right into that Yankee's back, both barrels, two men down. Dead, most likely. Had to be. *Right up close.* He looked at Gladstone, who nodded, smiling at him. Seeley knew he couldn't stay angry at the old man, knew, after all, he was right.

"Yes, you farting old chicken gizzard. It was *fun.*"

The heavy rains came again, and once more the roads that led out of Corinth became knee-deep troughs of stinking mud. The stink came this time from the refuse of the men too often left behind, the men who simply fell away, some dying from bloody wounds they could not survive. Any hint of order, of regiments and brigades, was mostly gone, the few officers who could command anything as desperately tired as their men. All along the road, every house had become a hospital, whether there was a doctor there or not. With an effort few knew they could still muster, they made the slogging march over the roads that had brought them to the fight, once more crossing swollen creeks, drinking filthy water, eating nothing at all. The shoes were mostly gone, backpacks and bedrolls and the muskets as well. But many of the men kept their legs in motion, inspired by the single thought, that they were still an army, still hated the Yankees, that their families and their officers still expected them to fight for the cause they believed in. Corinth was, after all, a great stout fortification, a place they had always expected to defend. The fight around Shiloh Church had come from the plans and ambitions of generals, and no matter the disaster of that, it was the foot soldiers who would still do the deed, who would be asked to decide the fate of the town, of the country, and more important to many, the fate of the men around them.

# CHAPTER THIRTY-SEVEN

# BAUER

SOUTHEAST OF SHILOH CHURCH
APRIL 28, 1862

General Halleck had arrived at Pittsburg Landing on April 11, saluted by his generals, mostly ignored by the troops, some of whom had been given the worst job imaginable, sifting through the wreckage of the battlefield, searching for anyone who had survived, burying the dead, and finally, burning the horses. By now most of the gruesome labor had been completed, the soldiers rested, but they expected more than what Halleck gave them. Instead of a rapid march to Corinth, to chase down and swallow up the battered remnants of the rebel army, Halleck kept them in their camps. The explanations stayed mainly with the senior officers, who already knew of Halleck's need for caution. It was no different now. To Halleck, rapid action meant a greater probability of mistakes. No matter what his soldiers expected, Halleck first had to examine the mistakes already made, sifting through reports and facing his senior commanders. Grant understood that mistakes must be answered for, and regardless of the retreat of a badly mauled enemy, Halleck would put all of his ducks in a neat row before anyone pursued another engagement.

Though many of the Federal troops expected to finish the job they had been given, to destroy the enemy by first destroying their valuable rail junction, many of the troops appreciated the respite Halleck had given them. There was impatience, to be sure, inspired by the same boredom that had plagued the army weeks before the battle had actually begun. As spring spread its hand over the Tennessee countryside, the fresh flowers and nesting birds could not quite disguise the grotesque scenery, bodies not quite buried, the continuous stench of bloody earth that not even the rains could cure. And the rains did make the effort. The life of the camps was no less miserable now than it had been throughout March, frequent storms, deepening mud, and a lack of adequate supplies. Though Halleck, along with Grant and Buell, recognized that supply boats had to be a priority, those supplies were slow in coming, the food and clothing distributed to the men in a thin trickle. It only added to Halleck's hesitation, that before this army could hope to drive southward, they must first be repaired. That repair required time.

Bauer sat alone, ate something he couldn't recognize, tried to ignore the taste that tormented his mouth and settled into his stomach like a sack full of rocks. He felt an enormous need for coffee, but that supply was exhausted hours before, had been just enough, he thought, to satisfy the cravings of the officers. Instead the men were using their canteens, water sought out from the various springs, those places where the water was still clear.

Immediately after the fighting had stopped, word had spread quickly that the army was issuing rations of liquor to anyone volunteering for the burial parties. The army's logic seemed to be that an intoxicated man might have far more tolerance for performing the awful task. The result, of course, was that a great many men had volunteered for the job. Bauer had been among those at first, had done what many had done, dug a hole or two, maybe a foot deep, had slid what used to be a man into the pit, covering with a few shovelfuls of dirt. Then they had gathered in small groups, bathed in whatever shade they could find, out of sight of the officers, who kept mostly to the camps. To Bauer, the liquor was nearly undrinkable, since he was not accustomed to alcohol in any form. But still he tried, and the burn and the dizzying effect in his brain had at least forced him to fall asleep, even if he suffered for that by the combined torments of a headache, poison ivy, and a plague of small creatures that attached themselves to the skin of any man who nestled into underbrush. Bauer knew something of ticks from his childhood in Wisconsin, and there were plenty now. But in Tennessee, the springtime offered up a new torment, virtually invisible to the men, some creature that delighted in burrowing under a man's skin, producing an itch that could only be cured by applying their liquor rations directly to the skin. To many that was a tragedy all its own. To Bauer, it was the final excuse he needed to retire from the burial detail.

Almost immediately after the rebels had gone, the men had reconstructed their camps, new Sibley tents arriving, to replace the ones ripped or burned by the rebels. They slept as before, more than a dozen men arranged feet to feet in a circle. If the liquor had brought at least some kind of peace, there was no peace in the tents. Even if Bauer could escape the incessant snoring, he could not avoid the nightmares. The sights and sounds of the fight were a part of him now, a part of all of them. Some, like Willis, seemed to absorb all that had happened by shoving it away into some hidden place. Bauer saw the images even when he was awake, could not seem to blow the stink from his nostrils, could not quite wash the blood from his hands. During the night, the battles were fought again, and he awoke with the same shouts and short screams that affected many of the others.

The platoons and companies were a jumble, too many officers gone, some units too small to be called units at all. But Bauer thought little of that. It was, after all, the army, and the army would do what it did best, put men into lines and figure out how to divide them up into some kind of order. Whether that order made any sense, or whether the officers who might suddenly appear were familiar or complete strangers, Bauer didn't care. It was his job to just . . . obey.

He tossed aside what remained of his supper, the darkness already spreading, no sunset, again, thick clouds and drizzle adding to the misery of his worn-out shoes. Few of the men had anything solid on their feet, and the curses toward the supply officers went mostly unheeded by the officers, who had worries of their own. It had been a relief to Bauer that Captain Patch seemed still to be in command of the company, though talk had spread, as it always spread, that Patch would be promoted, might get his own regiment. That same talk mentioned Colonel Allen, whose presence was still so reassuring to Bauer. The colonel wore the bandage still, but smaller now, a comforting sign that Allen would survive after all. Some of the rumors floating through the camps offered the most tantalizing of details, men satisfying their boredom by speculating on the fate of their generals. Halleck's arrival had only added fuel to the fire, that Grant or Buell would be dismissed, that perhaps all the generals would be removed, replaced by men no one had ever heard of. So far, none of that had proved true, something else Bauer was accustomed to. There had been one formal announcement, passed through by the senior officers, the army's way of convincing the men that the message was no rumor at all, but was actually true. The fight for Island Number Ten, one of the last great rebel strongholds on the Mississippi River, was a complete victory for the Federal troops. The officers cheered that as a monumental accomplishment. To Bauer, and most of the men around him, it meant nothing at all. Like so many, he had no idea where Island Number Ten was, or if in fact there was an Island Number Eleven, some battle yet to be fought.

He stood, fought the stiffness in his back, the rumble of unhappiness in his gut. The men around him ignored him, as they mostly ignored one another. Some of them were struggling through the rations, other just sat, staring into a campfire, some writing letters, or reading them. There was futility in that as well, the orders coming down in a very specific and very menacing way. No letters would be mailed from the camps at Pittsburg Landing until someone high up the chain approved that. Bauer saw no mystery in that at all. He had spent too much time wandering the battlefield with a shovel in his hands, had tripped over too many bones, seen too many blackened corpses, smelled too much rotting flesh and sickening horse meat. Bauer understood completely that the army didn't want these soldiers writing any of those details on paper and sending them home. It would be the perfect ammunition for newspapers, those who had some ax to grind against the army in general, or Halleck or Grant or Buell in particular. And most certainly, mothers and wives who read of those kinds of horrors might become energetically motivated to pressure their congressmen to call this entire thing off.

Bauer had contemplated that. He missed home, his parents, the lush green of Wisconsin, so very different than nature's various curses here. In some part of his logical mind, he knew there had been a mission that was not yet accomplished. The goal had always been Corinth, that talk coming from officers whose job had been to stoke them with enthusiasm for this campaign. Like Island Number Ten, it had never seemed to matter if the troops had ever heard of Corinth, where it was, or really knew just what they were supposed to do. They knew now. But the talk had changed, very little goading of the men for all the masterful ways they would crush the rebels, those men who had *spit on their flag*. Bauer knew that the officers still expected him to hate the enemy, but now, the reasons had changed. The enemy was not some mythical beast, to be brought down by the gallantry of the Union sword. They were an army, faces behind muskets, a horde of screaming soldiers who had just as much passion for tearing you in two as you were supposed to have for returning your flagpole to their local courthouse. The 16th Wisconsin had lost at least six of their color bearers, something the officers were already trying to use as some kind of emotional kick in the 16th's tail, a kind of inspiration for these men to seek out revenge. To Bauer, it meant that the flag he had followed had been more of a deadly target than he had ever thought. If there was to be any kind of fight in the future, he would keep his distance.

He moved toward Willis, his friend sitting on the ground, reading the letter again, the same rumpled scrap of paper, torn and ragged. Willis glanced up, then did as he always did, stuffed it into his pocket, self-conscious, mysterious. Bauer waited for the invitation to sit, never knew if Willis was in the mood for conversation or not. Willis leaned back against a cut log, looked up at him.

"You eat, Dutchie?"

"Tried to."

"Not me. I got the damn gripes again. I eat it, it just slides on through, stabs me like a thornbush all the way along."

Bauer felt his legs weakening, the long dreary day taking its toll. He sat down beside Willis, too tired to care if he was invited or not.

"You gotta see the doctor, Sammie. Tell them about it. They got potions and stuff."

"Yeah? You been back there? You seen those places? Not me. Somebody'll tie me down and cut my leg off, just for fun."

Bauer couldn't argue with Willis's reasoning, had his own fear of hospitals. There was no reason at all to go back to the landing, especially after what he had seen in the field.

"Guess you got a point. Few days back, I was out near that bloody pond. Just needed to get away from these tents. I hoped the bodies were all gone, but right down in some hole, I saw an ambulance. The smell told me plenty, but I found some of the burial boys, and they checked it out. The secesh had just left it behind. Guess they needed the horses for something else. But there were still men in there, and one of them was alive, right in the middle of a pile of dead. They were green, Sammie. *Green.* The poor secesh . . . he was shot in both legs, couldn't move at all. The smell knocked me to my knees. I couldn't imagine what that poor fella had to endure. We pulled him out, and pieces of the dead came with him."

"Shut up. Please shut up."

Bauer saw a hint of green on Willis now.

"Sorry. Won't do that again."

They sat in silence, and Bauer felt a chill, the relentless drizzle soaking through his coat. He looked toward the nearest campfire, nowhere to sit, the men gathered close with no gaps between them. After a silent moment, Willis said, "What happened to him?"

"Who?"

"The wounded secesh."

"They hauled him off, I guess. I didn't stay around there. Figured out I needed to stick closer to camp."

"You did your part. Wondered why you let them give you a shovel in the first place. Not me. They can fill me with *Old Misery* till I bust. I'm not burying pieces of anybody."

Bauer nodded slowly, saw a man by the fire drink from a brown bottle, said, "You remember Patterson? Big mouth, big head. He loved that stuff. Never understood that. Tried some back home, some *potion* my papa gave me. He laughed. I puked." He stopped, knew he had crossed into *that* territory again, glanced at Willis, saw his eyes closed, his head against the log. Willis said, "Yeah, and where is that big-mouth jerk now?"

Bauer tried to see Patterson's face, couldn't recall what he looked like. But the memory was there, that amazing day, the awful sight of Captain Saxe going down, the horse waiting for him to get up again. He shivered again, different this time.

"I'll never forget this, Sammie."

"Until next time."

Bauer hadn't actually thought of that, that there might be a next time. "No. This'll never happen again. They won't make us do this. Nobody wants to see this happen. Nobody expected this kind of . . . mess. That's all there is to it."

"Sorry, Dutchie, but you're wrong. We didn't do a damn thing this time. Didn't capture the secesh army, didn't cut that railroad they kept talking about. All we did was kill people, a whole lot of people. Both sides."

Bauer couldn't accept that, had seen too much to believe this wasn't one disastrous abomination.

"We beat the rebels, Sammie. We won. That's what they're all saying. I heard Captain Patch talking about that, something about General Halleck sending out big fat congratulations to the whole army, that he had sent word to President Lincoln how good we had done here. The captain said the newspapers back home are already crowing about this."

"Then how come we can't write letters?"

Bauer didn't have an answer for that, began to think that his cynical theory was wrong, that it wasn't just the horrors that might frighten his mother.

"Maybe they don't want us talking about it until we can get it right, I guess. We don't know everything that happened. Maybe the secesh are talking about surrendering. That's probably it. It's all secret, and they don't want none of us writing home, saying stuff we shouldn't say. The army's got its ways."

"Yeah, here's one of its ways: Nobody's gonna surrender a damn thing. The secesh are gathering up down there in that town, holding on to their damn railroad. We're gonna be up and marching soon, and they're gonna send us down there, and we're gonna fight that same bunch again. A whole lot of us are gonna die in that fight, too, and a whole lot of secesh. And, dammit, Dutchie, you know this ain't the only place there's a war. This is the whole country doing this. We're gonna keep killing each other until nobody's left. Maybe one soldier. There'll be some big final fight, and one soldier will walk away, the luckiest damn man in these United States. He'll be able to stand up and do all the crowing he wants . . . that *he* won the war. If President Lincoln is lucky, too, that man'll be wearing blue."

Bauer looked at Willis, baffled by the man's bitterness, could see the man's anger mixed with miserable sickness.

"You're crazy, Sammie. This can't happen again . . . not like this. Somebody's gotta know that. Both sides. The secesh ran away. They're whipped. They left thousands of dead men here."

"So did we."

Bauer said nothing, couldn't break through Willis's sour mood. At the campfire, a half-dozen men crawled to their feet, the man with the bottle staggering away. The darkness was almost complete, the chill growing, and he thought about moving that way, but the aching weariness held him in place. Out toward the next fire, he saw a man walking close, an enormous bandage on the man's hand. Bauer said, "Hey, that's Walbridge. Didn't think we'd see him again. See? I guess the hospital fixed him up."

Walbridge moved past the fire, came toward them, held up the hand.

"They left it on! Glory be! I thought they'd cut my arm off. Looks like you two made it all right. I heard they got Howe, a bunch of others. And Sergeant Williams."

Bauer grimaced at the name.

"Yeah, I saw it. I was there."

Walbridge moved on past, nothing else to say to them. He moved toward another group, the same words, the pure elation at still having two arms. Willis said, "He was the only man in the platoon who liked that stinking sergeant. Well, Patterson, too, but I don't count him as a *man*. I won't miss either one of them."

Bauer felt a twinge of guilt, recalled the stunned relief he felt when the sergeant went down. He didn't feel right hoping for any man's death, not even a brutal savage like Williams. Bauer said, "He's probably sent to hell."

"Maybe. All that matters right now is that he's dead, and we're not. Not yet."

Bauer was growing tired of Willis's gloom.

"We made it through this, Sammie. That's a blessing, for certain. I gotta believe we're gonna make it through all of it. After this place, maybe they'll figure we did plenty enough. Maybe they'll tear up those enlistment papers and send us home pretty quick. There's plenty of new boys up there who think this is a pretty fine thing. That's maybe why we're not sending any letters. It might scare some of those boys from signing up."

"Dutchie, you dream too much. Somewhere out on that river, those generals are patting themselves on the back that they made us *veterans* now. They need us. They'll send new boys down here for certain, but they're not sending us home."

Willis put a hand on his shirt pocket, seemed to drift into some other thought. Bauer stared at the hand, Willis lightly tapping the shirt. Bauer was more tired with every minute of darkness, more tired from Willis's mood, tired enough not to care about Willis's feelings.

"Dammit, Sammie, what's in the letter?"

Willis stopped tapping, looked at Bauer, his face reflecting the campfire. Bauer felt guilty for asking now, but Willis surprised him, pulled the letter out of his pocket, opened it carefully, read,

> *My Dear Son Samuel,*
>
> *We are overjoyed by the arrival of your first-born son. Mildred is doing just fine. The birth was not difficult, and the doctor says she should be recovered in a few days. The baby is a perfect image of his father, and Mildred has hoped you would agree to naming him in your honor, Samuel Junior. We hope you are well, and that you will share with us this joyous time by offering your thanks to the Almighty for this precious gift.*
>
> *Love, Mama and Papa*

Willis folded up the letter, put it back in his pocket. Bauer stared at him, his mouth slightly open.

"My God, Sammie . . . what wonderful news!" He paused now, utterly confused. "I thought . . . it was something awful. You always act like it's really bad news."

Willis sat silently for a moment, then said, "I will never see him."

"What do you mean? That's crazy. We'll be going home soon enough."

Willis looked at him, a hard glare, shook his head.

"*You* will. *You're* careful. *You're* afraid. You'll survive whatever fight we have to do."

"So?"

"Not me. I like killing those damn secesh. Trouble is, I like it too much. The officers order me back, I don't want to go. That surprised me at first. I had no idea how it would be, what I'd do when somebody shot at me. But . . . it was *fun*, Dutchie. I can't wait till we can do this again.

I'll do it until they get me. I saw their faces, those damn secesh. There are too many of 'em just like me. They're not gonna quit, and we're gonna have to kill every damn one of them." He paused. "God doesn't watch out for people like me."

The words were cold and matter-of-fact. Bauer stared at him, openmouthed. Willis leaned back again, closed his eyes. Bauer felt a burst of frustration, wanted to yell at him, to shake him, do anything to change what Willis had said. He couldn't accept that, had thought of what it would mean to have a family, a child, a *son*. Willis's letter had carved itself into his brain, the words so perfect, the *precious gift*. Willis didn't move, and Bauer was too tired to do anything, to protest or argue, to do anything to change Willis's perfect logic, and perfect despair.

Behind him, a voice, Sergeant Champlin.

"Hey, boys! Looks like we're finally getting out of this place! Got the word from the captain. First light, gather up your belongings, and get ready to march! Make sure your musket is cleaned and your cartridge boxes full."

Champlin started to move away, to pass the word to more of his men, some of them already hearing him, questions coming. Bauer felt a jolt, heard a single word from Willis.

"Finally."

Bauer stood, ignored the stiffness, moved closer to Champlin.

"Sergeant . . . begging your pardon . . . we're going home, right?"

Champlin turned to him, a short laugh.

"Hell, no, Private. We still got work to do. Tomorrow morning, we head south . . . to Corinth."

Bauer looked back toward Willis, who didn't move, his eyes still closed. Bauer felt a strange cold inside of him, beyond the chill of the air.

"But . . . we whipped 'em!"

"We whipped some of 'em. But word is, there's a whole lot more of those graybacks gathering up, still spoiling for a fight. You ask me . . . this thing's just getting started."

# AFTERWORD

*In numbers engaged, no such contest ever took place on this continent, in importance of results, but few such have taken place in the history of the world.*

—ULYSSES S. GRANT (*shortly after the battle*)

*No battle of the war—no event in Confederate history—has such a long list of "ifs" and "might have beens" as this battle of Shiloh; it is the saddest story of them all.*

—COLONEL E. L. DRAKE,
2ND TENNESSEE, HARDEE'S CORPS

In July 1861, the Battle of Bull Run (Manassas) shocks a nation with the raw violence that erupts from what many had believed to be a simple political dispute, a toothless rebellion that could be settled by little more than the threat of military force. The bloody aftermath of that fight drives home the reality that both sides of this conflict are willing to do whatever is required to secure their victory. But that battlefield is a short distance from the capital cities of both North and South. Thus photographs and vivid eyewitness accounts fill newspapers on both sides. The casualty figures greatly exceed what anyone on either side expects: in total, sixty thousand troops are engaged, producing approximately five thousand casualties. As mortifying as the conflict at Bull Run is to the citizens of this country, it pales in comparison to what occurs at Shiloh. Far from the eyes of either capital, one hundred thousand troops face

one another, at a cost of *twenty-four thousand* casualties. And yet, because of the vast distance from the great media centers, particularly in
the North, few newspaper reporters are on the field to tell that story.
Incredibly, given the volume of photographs taken throughout the war
by Alexander Gardner and Mathew Brady, to name just two, there are
virtually no photographs taken of the aftermath of the Shiloh battlefield
at all. Thus, in April 1862, our nation suffers its most costly military disaster to that time, a tragedy that many, particularly in the North, are
hardly even aware of.

The Northern newspapers do report a magnificent Federal victory,
their information supplied of course by the facts as Henry Halleck presents them. But recriminations fly as well, specifically aimed at the one
man who has so few political allies: Ulysses Grant. On April 11, when
Halleck arrives at Pittsburg Landing, it is for the specific purpose of taking command of a campaign that he believes has been poorly handled,
despite the Federal army's success in driving the Confederate forces
back to their stronghold at Corinth. But Halleck's own decisions that
follow do nothing to enhance his reputation.

Grant accepts much of the blame for the battering of his troops on
April 6, and assumes that once again he will be removed from command. But Halleck understands that Grant has won a victory at Shiloh,
and Fort Donelson has taught Halleck that removing a victorious commander is a gesture of foolishness that will not be received well in Washington. Thus Halleck names Grant as his second in command, though
for the rest of the campaign, Grant is virtually ignored.

Sherman's enemies pounce as well, and the newspapers, never Sherman's allies, begin to grumble about the near disaster suffered by the
Federal army, caused mainly by Sherman's denial to his own troops that
any rebel threat existed at all. It is an easy criticism to make that the first
morning's collapse was a result of Sherman's utter blindness to the possibility of a surprise attack. Long after the war, Sherman maintains he
was never actually surprised by the Confederate attack, but many of the
officers close to him at the time dispute that. Regardless of any failings,
Sherman's actions throughout the latter parts of the campaign wipe
away much of the stain of the first morning. Also in his favor, Sherman
continues to be a favorite of Henry Halleck, and so, with Grant as Halleck's scapegoat, Sherman is lauded as a hero, Halleck insisting to the

newspapers that it was Sherman who saved the day. Within weeks, Sherman is promoted to major general.

The other primary player for the Federal army is of course Don Carlos Buell. Buell supports Halleck's version of events, and supplies much of the fuel for Halleck's condemnation of Grant. For years after, Buell maintains that it was his timely arrival that saved Grant's army from utter destruction. That dispute is never resolved to either Grant's or Buell's satisfaction, nor do the advocates for either man accept the other's version. That disagreement continues to this day.

On the Southern side, the condemnation leveled toward Pierre Beauregard is predictable and, mostly, logical. Beauregard's reputation suffers considerably from his premature declaration of victory the night of April 6. That fire is fueled by the energy of Jefferson Davis, who continues to despise Beauregard.

Despite a number of mistakes attributed to the command style and decision making of Albert Sidney Johnston, his death erases many of those stains, and Johnston becomes, to many, a martyr for the Southern cause. By putting himself in harm's way on nearly every part of the battlefield, and by receiving his fatal wound near the front lines in the act of leading troops into battle, Johnston becomes a valiant symbol of military leadership, and thus is regarded by friends and some of his former critics as a fallen hero. But, as in the North, debates ensue. Johnston's son William Preston Johnston produces a memoir, which presents a great many personal accounts by officers and others who served with Johnston, including those who witnessed his actions at Shiloh. The younger Johnston's criticism of both Beauregard and Colonel Thomas Jordan is relentless. Naturally, Jordan disputes that interpretation and defends the decisions made by Beauregard. But Jordan receives a far more impartial critique from many of the senior officers who executed his amended plan of attack at the onset of the battle. There is debate whether Jordan's plan is the root cause of the Confederate failure. That debate continues among military strategists and historians into the twenty-first century.

Both sides claim victory at Shiloh, though of course, victory in war is most often credited to that army that maintains a hold over the battlefield. Thus, despite claims by some (including Beauregard) that the fight at Shiloh is a triumph for the South, on that point there is little to debate. With Halleck's arrival, and the additional Federal forces that follow him

up the Tennessee River (including the victorious army from Island
Number Ten, commanded by John Pope), the Federal forces that eventually march on Corinth increase dramatically, eventually numbering
more than one hundred thousand troops. In contrast, Beauregard's
army makes its withdrawal to Corinth, and occupies its fortifications
with an effective force *one-fifth* that number. Halleck has in his hands
the opportunity to destroy the South's best chance to hold back the Federal tide in the West.

After holding his army at Pittsburg Landing for three full weeks, Halleck begins his march to Corinth. The officers under his command are
fully prepared to find the enemy well fortified, well dug in, and well
prepared to receive the inevitable assault, and the Federal superiority in
numbers is an advantage the Confederate forces cannot likely withstand.
To the dismay of his commanders, Halleck reaches Corinth only to
order his army to dig fortifications of their own. Thus begins a siege of
Corinth that will last a full month. Though there are skirmishes and a
scattering of artillery duels, the worst tragedy of the siege is not military
at all. Lacking sufficient sources of clean water, and with neither side
providing adequate food and sanitary conditions, disease, especially
dysentery, consumes both armies. The cost in lives is horrendous. Pres-
sured by his generals to bring this campaign to its most likely conclu-
sion, Halleck finally agrees to send his troops forward. But the
Confederates, under Beauregard, are well aware of Federal intentions. In
the days prior to Halleck's order to attack, the Union troops can plainly
hear wagon and railcar activity in the town that suggests an army in motion. The day the advance is to take place, the Federal forces hear the
blasts from explosions that pour through Beauregard's ammunition
dumps and supply depots, Beauregard's efforts to prevent his stores from
falling into Federal hands. Halleck's generals do not share their commander's surprise, when, on May 29, Halleck finally rides into Corinth,
and finds no opposition at all. Beauregard and his army have escaped.

*The process by which the Union army worked its way to Corinth
has passed into history as one of the most inefficient operations
of the war. It involved an elaboration of strategy that now looks
a good deal like imbecility.*

—CAPTAIN LUCIEN CROOKER, 55TH ILLINOIS

Instead of making effective use of the enormous juggernaut the Federal army has become, Washington decides the army can be best used by separating, and driving toward a number of Confederate strongholds and strategic positions. That decision is debated as well, but with the advantage of hindsight, most historians agree that sending so many different pieces of Halleck's army in many different directions likely lengthens the war in the West.

## THOSE WHO WORE BLUE

### DON CARLOS BUELL

With the breaking up of Halleck's vast force, Buell once again commands the Army of the Ohio. His first mission is to press eastward, toward Confederate forces assembled south and east of Nashville. But Buell's plans are interrupted by a Confederate army under Braxton Bragg that invades Kentucky, an effort to reclaim territory lost earlier that year by the retreat of Albert Sidney Johnston. Buell must pursue Bragg, and in October 1862, the two meet at the Battle of Perryville, near Louisville. The fight is considered a draw, which seriously damages Buell's reputation in the North. Washington succumbs to the public outcry, and Buell is replaced by William Rosecrans. Buell never again is given any significant field command, and he resigns from the army in June 1864. After Ulysses Grant is elevated to command of the entire Federal army, he offers Buell the opportunity to return to service. But Buell, who had previously outranked Grant and Sherman, refuses to accept any subordinate position. Grant is disgusted with Buell's egotism, and the men remain estranged for the rest of Grant's life.

After the war, Buell serves as an executive in an iron and coal mining company in Kentucky and at the time of Grant's death in 1885, Buell is a civil servant in Louisville.

He dies in Rockport, Kentucky, in 1898, at age eighty.

### BENJAMIN PRENTISS

Released by his Confederate captors in October 1862, he is rewarded for his heroism at Shiloh by promotion to major general. Named to command of the army's Arkansas District, Prentiss feels his role in the success at Shiloh is being ignored, and that the new command is little more than window dressing. Thus, in late 1863, he resigns from the army.

Educated as an attorney, Prentiss returns to the practice of law in Missouri, and dies in Bethany, Missouri, in 1901, at age eighty-one.

### CHARLES F. SMITH

The man often saluted by Grant, Sherman, and many others who appreciated the value of his tutelage at West Point never returns to command of his Second Division. The leg injury Smith receives from making the jump onto a riverboat festers unmercifully, and on April 25, 1862, even before the Federal troops vacate their camps at Pittsburg Landing, Smith dies. He is fifty-five.

### LEW WALLACE

Despite earning a sterling reputation in the field prior to Shiloh, Wallace is never forgiven by Grant for his tardiness in reaching the Shiloh battle-field, and Halleck accepts Grant's judgments. As a result, Wallace loses his command, and in the fall of 1862 he is assigned to Cincinnati, to command defense forces there, a response to Braxton Bragg's invasion of Kentucky.

Wallace's reputation lands him a command as part of the defensive forces surrounding Washington, D.C., and in July 1864 he leads Federal troops to a defense against Jubal Early at the Battle of Monocacy, Maryland. Though Wallace's forces are defeated by Early, Early retreats, a debatable move in itself, and thus ends what could have been a critical threat to the capital.

After the war, Wallace, educated as an attorney, is part of the United States military commission that convicts and condemns to death the assassins of Abraham Lincoln. He also serves the government in the trial of Henry Wirz, the commandant of the Confederate prison at Andersonville, Georgia, thought by many to be the only man in the Civil War to be executed for war crimes.

Wallace resigns from the army in November 1865 and goes to Mexico, where he serves the nationalist forces that oppose the French puppet dictator, Emperor Maximilian. Contributing successfully to driving Maximilian out, Wallace is thus offered a general's commission in the Mexican army. Wallace gracefully refuses, and returns to his home state of Indiana to practice law. He later serves as governor of New Mexico and U.S. minister to Turkey.

Though Wallace's achievements are many, he is never able to erase the stain of his failure at Shiloh. Despite the relentless blame laid upon him, Wallace's civilian life is noteworthy for one other accomplishment: He begins a career as a novelist, and in 1880 he authors *Ben-Hur,* which comes to be the most successful American novel of the nineteenth century.

He dies in Crawfordsville, Indiana, in 1905, at age seventy-seven.

### WILLIAM H. L. WALLACE

After suffering a severe head wound, then left on the battlefield by the urgent retreat of his own staff, Wallace is inexplicably abandoned by retreating Confederates, who can only have assumed he was too near death to be considered a valuable prisoner. His survival throughout the dismal night of April 6 is considered miraculous by those who serve him, and his wife, Ann, welcomes her barely conscious husband to her arms at the Cherry Mansion in Savannah, Tennessee. For the next three days, Wallace passes in and out of consciousness, but according to his wife, he is very aware of her presence, and on April 10, he offers her his final words: *"We meet in heaven."* He is forty years old.

## THOSE WHO WORE GRAY

### PIERRE G. T. BEAUREGARD

After Shiloh, Beauregard's illness returns, and he embarks on a temporary leave in June 1862. But Jefferson Davis sees an opportunity to punish the man he blames for the great failure at Shiloh. Using the excuse that Beauregard has abandoned his post without permission, Davis replaces Beauregard in the West with Braxton Bragg, and orders Beauregard back to Charleston, South Carolina. Beauregard, who still relishes his public reputation as the *Hero of Fort Sumter,* is not altogether unhappy with the assignment, and performs adequately by defending the city from various assaults, primarily from the U.S. Navy.

While he is eventually given command of all Confederate territory up through southern Virginia, his command ceases where Robert E. Lee's begins, and Beauregard enhances his reputation once more on the Virginia peninsula by successfully confronting the forces of the inept Union general Benjamin Butler. In late 1864, as Grant's army presses southward through Virginia, Lee's command is expanded, and conflict erupts between Lee and Beauregard, who, during the war, are never friends. With Davis backing Lee, Beauregard's command, which includes Petersburg, Virginia, becomes subservient to Lee's. Despite the slight, Beauregard performs a masterful defense and maneuver that thwarts the first Federal attempts at capturing Petersburg. In October 1864, Beauregard is approached reluctantly by Davis to resume command in the West, and Beauregard, eager to reclaim the public's attention, accepts the post. But Beauregard's authority there is mostly ignored by both Richard Taylor in Texas and John Bell Hood in Tennessee. In December 1864, when Hood's army is destroyed by the twin disasters at Franklin and Nashville, Beauregard realizes the post Davis has given him has become virtually nonexistent. Beauregard moves east once more, and mobilizes an army to confront the rapid advances of William T. Sherman through Georgia. No longer in command of any theater, Beauregard accepts a subordinate role to Joseph Johnston in the South's final stand in the Carolinas. In late April 1865, both men participate in the negotiations to surrender to Sherman, concluding the war in the East.

Beauregard returns to New Orleans, and in 1866 he serves as president of first one, then a second railroad, but his arrogance makes enemies, and in 1876, he is removed by the railroad's dissatisfied shareholders. In 1877, he and Jubal Early share the duty of supervisor of the Louisiana Lottery, which elevates both men again into the public eye. But the job is seen by many as unseemly, promoting gambling in an era when the South's interests lie in rebuilding their economy.

From 1865 onward, Beauregard's reputation as a superb military leader is enhanced overseas, and he is offered positions of command in the armies of Brazil, Romania, and Egypt. Though tempted, he does not accept.

The dislike between Beauregard and Jefferson Davis boils into a full-blown feud, both men penning works that criticize the other. In

1889, when Davis dies, Beauregard refuses to accept the privilege of leading the funeral procession, replying to the invitation by saying, *"I am no hypocrite."* Beauregard remains sensitive to the criticism leveled at him for the failure at Shiloh, and he cannot completely escape the mystique surrounding Albert Sidney Johnston, though he attempts to do so by encouraging his former subordinate, Thomas Jordan, to write his *more precise* version of the battle. That work does little except fuel the debates.

He dies in 1893 in New Orleans, at age seventy-four.

### ISHAM HARRIS

Though harboring an intense dislike for Pierre Beauregard, Harris continues to serve on his staff, and when Beauregard is relieved of the command in the West, Harris accepts the same post with Beauregard's successor, Braxton Bragg. He continues in that role through the evolving commands in the Confederate West, serving as well on the staffs of John Bell Hood and Joseph Johnston.

After the war, Harris flees what he fears will be a brutal fate, and moves first to Mexico, then to England. As Reconstruction unfolds, and Harris understands that influential Confederates are not being executed en masse, he returns and settles into a law practice in Memphis. Always dedicated to public service, he remains a popular public figure in Tennessee, and in 1877 is elected to the United States Senate. He is reelected four times, and his influence and reputation land him the office of Senate president pro tempore in 1893, a post he holds for two years. In the 1896 presidential election, he campaigns vigorously for William Jennings Bryan, but the exertion of that effort, combined with the crushing blow of Bryan's defeat, takes a toll on Harris. He dies in Washington in 1897, at age seventy-nine, and is buried in Memphis.

### THOMAS JORDAN

Jordan continues his loyal service to Beauregard throughout the rest of the war, and after Shiloh, Beauregard secures his promotion to brigadier general.

As well as his own history of Shiloh, Jordan coauthors a biography of Nathan Bedford Forrest, and contributes mightily to the feud between

Beauregard and Jefferson Davis by attacking Davis in print at every opportunity.

He serves as editor of a Memphis newspaper, but his reputation among the Southern military hierarchy inspires an invitation from Cuban insurgents, who are struggling to free Cuba from Spanish control. In 1869, he accepts the post as commanding general of the insurgency, and is moderately successful in several actions against the Spanish army. But the job is not one he can complete, and after a year, he returns to the United States, settling in New York City. He dies there in 1895, at age seventy-six.

### JAMES SEELEY

The young cavalry officer continues his service to Nathan Bedford Forrest and participates in the planning for what will become Forrest's enormously effective raids through southern and central Tennessee. But he returns home to Memphis for a brief leave in late May 1862, and is thus witness to the naval battle in early June that results in the Union occupation of that city. Seeking to protect his wife and family, Lieutenant Seeley is captured attempting to flee the city, and is transported to Camp Douglas, near Chicago. In December 1862 he is released through an officer exchange, and returns to service in the cavalry under Nathan Bedford Forrest.

### THE LEGACY OF ALBERT SIDNEY JOHNSTON

*From all I have been able to gather, the conception, or plan of battle was excellent. It was a complete surprise; and at the moment of General Johnston's fall . . . we were successful all along the lines. The enemy was broken and routed and in full retreat. We were moving our commands toward the river with nothing in sight to oppose our easy march. . . . My conviction is that, had General Johnston survived, his victory would have been complete. . . . Sometimes the hopes of millions of people depend upon one head and one arm. The West perished with Albert Sidney Johnston, and the Southern country followed.*

—GENERAL R. L. GIBSON, BRAGG'S CORPS

*One more resolute movement forward would have captured Grant and his whole army.*

—GENERAL JAMES R. CHALMERS, BRAGG'S CORPS

*Commanding generals are liable to be killed during engagements; and the fact that when he was shot, Johnston was leading a brigade to induce it to make a charge which had been repeatedly ordered, is evidence that there was neither the universal demoralization on our side nor the unbounded confidence on theirs which has been claimed. There was in fact no hour during the day when I doubted the eventual defeat of the enemy.*

—ULYSSES S. GRANT

The debate continues.

The night of April 6, Johnston's body is first placed in Shiloh Church, until well after dark, and after General Beauregard's order terminates the day's fighting. He is then transported from the battlefield to Corinth, and placed in the house belonging to Mrs. Inge, who had been his hostess during his stay in the town. There the body is embalmed with whiskey, and thus prepared for burial. The army is officially notified of their general's death on April 10, after their arduous return to Corinth, though by then few had not heard the news.

Transported by rail to New Orleans, Johnston's body lies in state in City Hall, and is visited by enormous throngs of the citizenry. On April 11, he is buried in New Orleans's St. Louis Cemetery. But it is known by Johnston's family that his wish is to be buried in Texas, and so five years later, after considerable wrangling between the family, the city of New Orleans, and the legislatures of both states, the general's body is relocated to the Texas State Cemetery in Austin.

No discussion in these pages will solve the enormous "what-if" questions that follow Johnston's death, despite the lamentations of Jefferson Davis: "When Sidney Johnston fell, it was the turning point of our fate; for we had no other hand to take up his work in the West."

Or that of Confederate general Richard Taylor: "Had it been possible for one heart, one mind, and one arm to save her cause, [the South] lost them when Albert Sidney Johnston fell on the field at Shiloh."

Speculation will continue, both North and South, that the outcome of the battle, the war, and American history might have been changed entirely had Johnston lived. Regardless, there is little question that if Johnston had been on the field, the fight on April 6 would not have concluded the way it did. Either Grant's army would have been severed from Pittsburg Landing, thus forcing certain surrender, or the final Confederate surge would have been blunted by the mass of artillery and the increasing number of Federal infantry that lined the ground above the steep hillsides around Dill Branch and the landing itself. Regardless: Every war has its heroes, those who cement their place in the hearts of their countrymen. In the Eastern Theater of the war, no death carries the emotional power produced by the fall of Thomas "Stonewall" Jackson. In the West, that same power is unequaled by the death of Albert Sidney Johnston.

Following Johnston's death, command of the various Southern armies flows through the hands of a half-dozen men whose various successes and marked failures define the history and the outcome of the war. It is those peculiar moments and tragic accidents in every event that alter our history. The death of Albert Sidney Johnston is one of those moments. That a battle was fought at all around Shiloh Church is another.

Ulysses Grant's dismissal of the possibility of Southern victory at Shiloh comes directly from his memoirs, written very late in his life. In his earlier writings, he offers us something of a contradiction to that view: "I knew Albert Sidney Johnston before the war, I had a high opinion of his talents. When war broke out, he was regarded as the coming man of the Confederacy. I shared that opinion . . . but he died too soon, as Stonewall Jackson died, too soon for us to say what he would have done under the later and altered conditions of the war."

The Battle of Shiloh is one of the great tragedies of the Civil War. But regrettably, those stories are many, and the cast of characters enormous. When the men who serve Ulysses Grant are moved away from the great force assembled by Henry Halleck, they begin a new campaign, and a new chapter of the war that will end in yet another dramatic and costly clash of the armies, the commanders, and the men who carry the musket. That place is Vicksburg.

> *God grant that it may end soon, and yet I do not see any hope for its early termination. The future grows darker. Those persons who reason themselves into the belief that peace will soon come or at least that the war will soon cease, are blinded and mislead by their wishes.*
>
> —DR. LUNSFORD YANDELL, APRIL 21, 1862

Read on for an excerpt of *A Chain of Thunder,*
the next installment in Jeff Shaara's
exciting new Civil War series.

## CHAPTER ONE

# SPENCE

VICKSBURG, MISSISSIPPI
APRIL 16, 1863

The ball was a glorious affair, the Confederate officers in their finest gray, adorned with plumed hats and sashes at their waists. There was dancing and a feast of every kind of local fare, even the wine flowing with no one's disapproval. By ten o'clock, most of the older citizens had retired, the senior officers gone as well, offering the reasonable excuses that there were duties to perform, an early morning that would come too soon. Those who remained were the young and the unmarried, no one among them objecting to that. The music continued, more lively now, the quartet of violinists respecting the youth in the room, waltzes that brought the officers closer to the young women, hands extended, those girls who had caught the eye, whose furtive glances spoke of flirtation, the daring willingness to accept the invitation of a young man who had the courage or the skills to lead a dance.

As the night wore on, and the matrons drifted away, Lucy had allowed herself a single dance, had caught a beaming smile from a young lieutenant, one of the Louisiana regiments. She knew nothing of a soldier's life, what authority he carried, but the face was handsome, a firm jaw and bright blue eyes, clean shaven, the young man's hand extended toward her with smiling optimism, hinting of hope. She knew he had been watching her for most of the evening, and she had smiled at him once, was immediately embarrassed by that, quick glances to be certain that none of the others noticed. But now, as the energy of the ball rose with the youthfulness of those who remained, so too did her courage. And, apparently, his.

· The waltz they danced to had been familiar, the violins doing admirable service with a pleasing rhythm that seemed to intoxicate her, the young officer admirably graceful. The couple was one of a half dozen who moved with elegance across the floor, but it ended too soon. With visible regret, the lieutenant had done what was required, had properly escorted her back to one side of the room, where the ladies sat, the officers returning to their own station, closer to where the wine flowed.

She sat, maneuvering the wide hoops of her finest gown, and still glancing at the other girls, the rivalry they all observed. Such occasions were rare now. The welcome invitation had come from Major Watt, the officer spreading word that a gala was well deserved. But many stayed away, a gloomy acceptance that perhaps this kind of frivolity was not yet appropriate, not with the Yankees so close. For months now, the citizens had endured shellfire, Federal gunboats with the audacity to throw their projectiles into the city itself. Most of those boats were anchored far upriver, and the officers in the town boasted of that, that Federal sailors knew they could not match the enormous power of the guns dug into the hillsides across the riverfront. But still the shells came, and many of the civilians had heeded the advice of the army's senior commanders, had begun to move out of their homes, digging themselves into caves and caverns, most dug by the labor of Negroes.

The first serious violence had come close to Christmas, and the customary Christmas ball had been rudely preempted by one of the first great assaults, what so many of the townspeople described as the barbarity of the Yankees, their utter disregard for simple courtesy, for the sacred observance of Christmas ritual. Major Watt seemed to recognize that as well, and with the warmer weather came the army's gift to the town, driven by the kindness of this one major, who seemed to understand that the civilians would be buoyed by a party, a show of defiance toward the ever-present gunboats. Though the attendance was not as large as the major had hoped, the air of protest was there still, and like the others who attended the ball, the young Miss Spence thought it entirely appropriate that the townspeople make some effort to improve their own morale. Since Christmas, most of the people had gone about their business as though nothing were really happening upriver, as if the Yankees were there just for show, a protest of their own. Businesses continued to operate, the markets mostly able to stock their shelves, citizens freely traveling to the countryside. Even the occasional bombardments were part of the routine, and for the most part the damage had been minimal, the shelling more random than targeted. Like Lucy, most of her neighbors had sought the protection of Providence, that if a shell was to find them, it would be the hand of God and not the unfortunate aim of some devilish Yankee gunner. After all, the people of Vicksburg had done nothing to deserve such violence.

She watched her young lieutenant across the room, was disappointed to see a glance at a pocket watch. The music began to slow, and the atmosphere in the grand room was growing heavy with shared sleepiness. It was, after all, near ten o'clock, far beyond the bedtime of even the young.

Lucy felt the same weariness, suppressed a yawn, heard the talk around her, much as it had been all evening. The young women spoke of those things Lucy had kept mostly to herself: who among the men in their gray finery were the best dancers, the most handsome, who had embarrassed himself by enjoying a bit too much wine. She held quietly to the warm glow that came from the single dance with her lieutenant, that it was her young man who outshone them all. She wondered about Louisiana, not the swamps that spread out for miles across the river, but down south, New Orleans, Baton Rouge, sophisticated places she could only imagine. Surely he was from the cities, she thought, a cultured man, familiar with music and libraries, perhaps from a military academy. Her imagination was fed by the sleepiness, and she blinked hard, fought to keep anyone from noticing that, saw him glance at his watch again, a scowl on his face. Then he glanced toward her, and she looked away, then back, wanted to smile, held it, scolded herself. He was speaking to another officer now, a captain, both men showing regret that this one beacon of color and gaiety had to come to an end. He began to move toward her, and her heart jumped, a blend of hope and alarm that he might ask to escort her home. She felt a slight shiver, and he seemed to hesitate, gathering courage of his own.

And now came a large thump of thunder, a jolt in the floor beneath her feet, the chandelier quivering, the entire room suddenly motionless.

Another rumble came, but it was not close. She saw the lieutenant looking past her, and realized he was staring toward the river, where the army had anchored it largest guns. Now the firing thundered closer, the officers speaking up, calming voices, that it was their own guns, not the enemy. To one side, a door burst open, an older officer moving in quickly, searching, finding Major Watt, a quick word between them. Watt turned to them all, and had their attention.

"I regret," he said, "this ball has concluded. The Yankee boats are coming downriver, and you must retire to your shelters. Do not hesitate. Officers, report immediately to your posts."

There was authority in his words, and the men were quick to move, filing toward the wide entranceway, already disappearing into the darkness. She caught sight of the lieutenant, but he did not look back, and she pushed that from her mind, rose up with the other women, some of the officers lingering, standing to one side, allowing them to pass. There were questions, but no panic, so many of the civilians having experienced all of this before. Major Watt stood by the door, still their host, and offered a smile, pleasantries to the women, with the slight edge of firmness.

"Go on home, now. We shall deal with the Yankees. This has been a most pleasant evening. It shall be still, if our artillerymen have their way."

She passed the major, was outside now, a cool night, no moon, a hint of lantern light from the homes that lined the street. But quickly those grew dark, the usual caution, no needless targets offered to any Yankee gunner who might be telescoping this very place. She stepped onto the hard dirt, avoiding the ruts from wagon wheels, and heard the talk around her in hushed excitement. She felt it as well, that there was something different about this assault. She looked in every direction, still no shells coming into the town, the sounds all toward the river. The soldiers were mostly gone, only a few, the usual guards drifting past, offering assistance if any was required. Lucy saw a cluster of women moving uphill, not toward their homes, but toward the magnificent vantage point, what they all called Sky Parlor Hill. It was the highest point in the city, a knob of land the width of two city blocks, and during the daytime it was the most popular place for couples to gather, for picnics and courtship. For others, for the lonely, widows perhaps, the women struck hard by the pain of war, it was a place for solace, the perfect place to find comfort from gazing out toward the river, or across, to the flatlands of the Louisiana swamps. Lucy had climbed the heights often, enjoyed the silence, or the warm breezes that rose with the arrival of spring. More recently, her focus had been mostly northward, to where the Yankees had their camps, this high ground offering a perfect glimpse of a distant sea of white tents, and riverboats of all shapes and configurations. She had studied that with intense curiosity, had heard from the soldiers that the Yankees seemed only to be going about their business, more for a show of strength than for any real threat to the town. It was from upriver that the shelling came, though the Yankees had also positioned their guns straight across the wide river, as though taunting the town with their daring. The Confederates had offered daring of their own, the occasional raid, troops slipping across on small boats and rafts, harassing raids that drew pride from the civilians but seemed to accomplish little else.

She moved in line behind several others, most of them women, fumbling with the awkwardness of the ball gowns, helped along by a few old men, too old to be soldiers. The winding path led them higher still, and she was surprised to see a glow of orange light, beyond the hill, as though the sun was rising through a foggy haze, coming up from the wrong direction. She reached the top, breathing heavily, tugging at the hoops, adjusting her dress in the darkness, and realized it wasn't truly dark at all. All around her were curious faces reflected in the glow of what she saw now were a dozen great fires, great fat torchlights on both sides of the river. She knew something of that, the soldiers openly talking for weeks about their preparations if the Yankees dared to bring their boats within range of the big guns. The fires came from enormous mounds of oil-soaked cotton, barrels of tar, wiping away the darkness that would hide any craft that tried to pass on the river. And now she could see them, silhouetted, a parade of vessels spaced far apart, coming downstream in single file. The guns began again, startling bursts of fire down below her, some out to the north, upriver. Out in the river, the fire was returned, small bursts of flame from the gunboats, the impact of those shells against the steep bluffs. But more shelling came from the Yankees, streaks of red and white arcing up and over, coming down far out to one side of the great knob. There was a response from the crowd, angry protest that the Yankees were doing what they had done before, blind destruction thrown into the town. She heard the impact, saw a brief burst of flames on a street close to where the ball had been. She looked again to the river, the firelight reflecting on the water, rippling eddies from the movement of the Yankee boats. Fog was spreading along the water, rising like a wall of reflected fire, the silhouettes of the boats blanketed, hidden. Voices around her rose, protesting the blindness, and she looked toward the town, no fog there, not unusual so high above the water. But the smell came, thick and pungent, brought by a sharp breeze. It was smoke.

Close beside her, a small man stopped, gestured with his cane, and shouted out, "They's hidin' from us! Bah! Go ahead with your tricks. We'll find ya!"

She wanted to ask, *Hiding*? But the man kept up the chatter.

"They's throwin' out smoke so's we won't see 'em. Mighty dang stupid. The gunners know the range. Too many of us. Give it to 'em, boys!"

She stared at the river, saw breaks in the smoke, glimpses of the boats again, still the single line, some coming closer, one turning sideways, as though out of control. She saw flames now, on the boat, and the old man said, "Got one! Sink that devil! Hee! Send her to the bottom!"

The cannon fire was increasing, a steady rhythm, the guns downriver opening up as well, shot and shell now launched in both directions. The sounds came in a chorus of thumps and distant thunder, more impacts in the town. She felt a twisting nervousness, stared hard at specks of fire from the boats, obscured then visible, the surface of the river glowing with the fires. There were cheers around her, and she saw a burst on the boat, another hit, the old man coming to life again.

"Good shootin', boys! Keep it up! Nowhere for those devils to hide!"

She moved closer to the man, but he ignored her, cheered again, spoke out loud, as though everyone would hear him.

"You see that? Took off her smokestack! I'll bet they hit the boiler next! Hooeee, you might see one of them dang things go up in one big show of hellfire!"

There was another burst of fire mid-river, and the old man's joy was infectious, more cheering for the raw destruction, the good work of the men who worked the guns. She had a sudden urge to go down there, to be closer to them, to watch the deadly work, different now, the targets genuine, the *enemy*, the guns doing what so many had hoped for. *Killing Yankees*.

———

Her name was Lucy Spence, and she had spent all of her nineteen years in Vicksburg. Her father had been a preacher, made his living mostly traveling the countryside, offering sermons to anyone willing to put a coin in a collection plate. For as long as Lucy could remember, her mother had been sickly, never traveling with her husband, and finally, keeping to the house, then her own room. With her father off for a week or more at a time, it was Lucy who had become the caretaker, the nurse. She had no formal training for that, or for anything else, and so the chores of a household had been learned by necessity. There had never been the luxury of slaves, not even a maid to care for Lucy as a baby. She had clung most strongly to the reunions, when her father would return home, joy and hugs and laughter. But as Lucy grew, and her mother lost strength, the joy faded. With Lucy more able to care for her mother, her father's journeys lasted even longer. When the war began, he seemed to welcome the necessity of traveling, often for many weeks, and though he spoke of hardship, the people growing poor, she knew from the look in his eye that he looked forward to those days when the journeys began, when he no longer had to watch the skeletal frailness of what had become of his wife. And so it was no surprise that two days after Lucy turned eighteen, her mother died, with no one but her daughter to hear the last struggling breath.

Her father came home a few weeks after, had visited the grave briefly, tears and several days of sad silence. But then he was gone again. Now, more than a year later, there had been no word at all, and Lucy had steeled herself against all of that, did not press the army or the officials in Jackson, did not really want to know where he had gone. If he had ever been a husband, he had rarely been a father. And most certainly, he was not one now.

With the war growing closer to this part of Mississippi, the army came in greater numbers, outposts and defensive works spreading around the town. Lucy had been wary of soldiers, had heard too much talk of barbarism, that the army brought unruly men fueled by liquor and lust. She kept away from the camps, from the defensive works, avoided the men who paraded through the town in small groups. But soon the fear faded, none of the gossip coming to pass, no violation of some young innocent. Even the liquor seemed to affect the civilians more than it did the soldiers, and soon it was clear that the officers, those primly uniformed men on horseback, actually controlled these men. It was not a rabble. It was an army.

Comfortable now with the presence of the soldiers, Lucy kept mostly to herself, minding the family's home, sometimes helped by friendly neighbors. They were older women mostly, curious about this single girl who seemed to manage quite well. Their respect increased, though the help still came, lessons on cooking, on preserving meats, even a vegetable garden she tended herself. With her father absent for more than a year, talk of her disadvantages as an *orphan* simply drifted away. Not even the gossips taunted her, those who thrived mostly on vicious speculation. She was now an adult, in her own home, with every confidence that she could handle a household. To the neighbors, her greatest requirement was, of course, a husband. It was Lucy herself who realized with perfect logic that the opportunity had come to her along with this army. If it could be an officer, well, more the better.

Until now, the artillery duels had been mostly brief affairs, mere target practice. Throughout the chilly winter and into spring, the townspeople had often drifted down among the gun emplacements to watch the drills, the preparation. The artillery officers had encouraged that, their men showing off their accuracy, seeking targets on the far side of the river. Some had been offered by Yankees, men or wagons rising high up on some levee, inviting a response from the Confederate cannoneers. She had heard the talk, that it was something of sport, to both sides surely, and rarely did any harm result. But along with that playfulness, the talk had grown that the Yankees across the river were many, and now they were in motion, great columns marching south. Few of the officers would speak openly of that, and if the commanders had any real information about what the enemy was doing, they kept that to themselves, and so the soldiers spread rumors of their own. The boasting had been endless, the Yankees marching away altogether, those men across the river making their escape all the way to New Orleans. The civilians had come to believe what the soldiers insisted was true, that Vicksburg was a fortress, impregnable, that the bluffs that rose so high above the river could never be conquered. The presence of the massive cannon had only increased that confidence, and

Lucy had toured through the artillery camps, awed by the sheer immensity of the great black barrels. The artillerymen were awed right back, pausing to watch any young woman strolling through their camps.

She kept her gaze on the river, could see more of the Yankee boats coming downstream from the far bend, outlined still by the great fires. The cheers were constant, louder when the impact on the boats could be seen, the destruction seeming to impact every boat that passed. Beside her, the old man spoke again, his cane pointing high in the air.

"Damn fools! Sendin' them boats down one at a time! Dang shootin' gallery! Oh . . . well lookee there. They's comin' closer! And listen to them hound dogs! They know what's happenin'. Even they hate the Yankees! They're cheering us on, sure as can be!"

The howling came all through the town, the dogs reacting to the sounds with as much enthusiasm as the people on Sky Parlor Hill. It was a strange sound, a chorus of howls, low-pitched and high, and Lucy sensed more than some echo of their master's devotion to the cause. They're afraid, she thought. They hear the screams of the shells, and don't know what it is. Maybe it hurts their ears. Glad I don't have one. If he was that afraid, I wouldn't know what to do. Like having a frightened child. I don't envy the mothers.

She tried to see the Federal gunboats that were easing closer to the near bank, but the lay of the land and the rows of buildings below the hill hid them from view. She caught a glimpse of one slipping into the firelight, the reflection revealing the immense ironclad.

She moved closer to the old man and shouted above the din, "Are they coming? Will they land?"

"Missy, I served in the navy for thirty-odd years, learned somethin' about artillery. Hard to shoot pointing down. Some damn Yankee captain figured that out, too. Got hisself all shot to pieces, and so figured out that movin' closer to this side might protect him. Not gonna work. though. They ain't figuring on landing, no sir. There's a pot full of sharpshooters down low on the river, and if'n they don't kill every dang one of 'em, they'll be haulin' up prisoners!"

She coughed, fought through the smell of the smoke, looked at the old man, tried to see his face in the glow of fire light, familiar, a man some said was *addled*. But his words held authority, and she kept close to him, with an instinct that he really did know what was happening. He pointed the cane, kept up his monologue, didn't seem to care now if anyone heard him at all.

"Yankee navy's done for. Only thing that gave 'em hope. This is desperation, pure and simple! They's making a run for it, headin' to Orleens. I heerd word that a bunch of them Yankees upriver are already marchin' back to Memphis. Them scoundrels can do whatever they want back east, Virginee and all, but out here . . . they got no hope. No hope a'tall."

His speech was becoming redundant, a hint of boastfulness that began to sound more like exaggeration than fact. *Addled*. She focused more now on the sights, the stink of smoke, more explosions on the river, the parade of boats still ongoing, endless. The big guns farther downriver began firing, one more part of the great Confederate gauntlet, and she understood now what the army had done, that no matter how many boats came past, the army's guns were certainly too many, that Vicksburg was protected, invulnerable, just as the officers had claimed.

She felt stiffness in her legs, her eyes fogging, the sleepiness coming now, a long night made longer by the steady roar. There was nowhere to sit, the dress too clumsy, but the sleepiness was growing, the sights and sounds from the river blending together in a dreamy haze. She turned, moved past the glow on a hundred faces, and went back toward the winding pathway that led below. She thought of her young lieutenant and wondered where he was, if he was a part of this spectacle, the marvelous destruction of those who dared to disrespect the town, the army, the Cause. I'll see him again, she thought. I'll ask him all about guns and boats. She eased carefully down the path, smiled in the darkness, yes, you will be proud of that, will try to impress me with all that you know, will show off in front of your men. And I will blush and hide my smile, and enjoy every moment.

Behind her, up on the hill, people cheered again, the battle ongoing, the civilians knowing that no matter what the Yankees might believe about power, no matter the planning of their generals, the bravery of their sailors, tonight the vast fleet that dared trespass on this mighty river would be utterly destroyed.

Jeff Shaara is the *New York Times* bestselling author of *A Blaze of Glory*, *The Final Storm*, *No Less Than Victory*, *The Steel Wave*, *The Rising Tide*, *To the Last Man*, *The Glorious Cause*, *Rise to Rebellion*, and *Gone for Soldiers*, as well as *Gods and Generals* and *The Last Full Measure*—two novels that complete the Civil War trilogy that began with his father's Pulitzer Prize–winning classic, *The Killer Angels*. Jeff was born into a family of Italian immigrants in New Brunswick, New Jersey. He grew up in Tallahassee, Florida, and graduated from Florida State University. He lives in Tallahassee.

JeffShaara.com

Jeff Shaara is available for select readings and lectures. To inquire about a possible appearance, please contact the Random House Speakers Bureau at 212-572-2013 or rhspeakers@randomhouse.com.

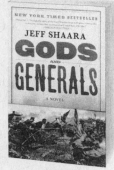